# *The*
# CHRONICLES of IONA:
# ISLAND-PILGRIM

# *The* CHRONICLES of IONA: ISLAND-PILGRIM

by

Paula de Fougerolles

ISBN-10: 0692122869
ISBN-13: 9780692122860

Library of Congress Control Number: 2018906902
Careswell Press, Hawley, MA

Careswell Press
61 Pudding Hollow Road
Hawley, MA 01339

Cover Art: *Hiberniae Britannicae Insulae, Nova Descriptio,* from the atlas *Theatrum Orbis Terrarum* (c. 1573) by Abraham Ortelius. Property of the author.

Also by Paula de Fougerolles

*The Chronicles of Iona:*

For Tony,
my love and companion

Many credit the foundation of the nation of Scotland to the efforts of two men, an Irish saint, Columba, and a Scottish warlord, Áedán mac nGabráin.

This is their story.

There was a man of venerable life and blessed memory, the father and founder of monasteries, whose name was the same as the prophet Jonah's. For though the sound is different in three different languages, in Hebrew *Jona*, in Greek *Peristera*, in Latin *Columba*, the meaning is the same, 'dove'. So great a name cannot have been given to the man of God but by divine providence ... The reader should also be reminded of this, that many things worth recording about the man of blessed memory are left out here for the sake of brevity, and only a few things out of many are written down so as not to try the patience of those who will read them.

Adomnán of Iona, Vita Columbae (c. 690)

A son of the clan of the Shadow
will take the kingdom of Alba by force of strength,
a man who will feed ravens, who will conquer in battle:
*Ferbasach* will be his name.
Alas for the Picts to whom he will go eastward,
the distressed traveler, the red flame that awakens war.
With grey men, the rider of the swift horse
will cast the Picts into insignificance
and will seek Hibernia in one day.
After the slaughter of Picts,
after the harassing of Foreigners,
many years in the sovereignty of Alba.
He will not be king
at the time of his death, on a Thursday, in Cendtire.

The Prophecy of Berchan (1165 × 1169)

# · WITH THANKS ·

This third volume in the series has been a while in the making, due in large part to moving the family to three different homes in two different countries over the course of four years, a once-in-a-lifetime but nonetheless time-consuming adventure. The writing of it has kept me sane, grounded, and happy. The book would not be here now without the support, inspiration, and expertise of the following fine people. Without them, the work would be less worthwhile and far less fun. Thank you: Antonin de Fougerolles, for everything. Mila de Fougerolles and Simon de Fougerolles, for everything else. Joyce Charland, as always. My beloved shadow, Cookie. Dorothy Charland. Joanne Gannon. Elsie MacDonald. Camille White. Lida de Fougerolles. Robert de Fougerolles. Marie Nemçova Banerjee and Ron D. K. Banerjee, whose own work has inspired me these many years. Joseph Nemec II. Judy Nemec. My dear companions and fellow travelers Kristina Lumsden, Cora Skidmore, Tad Gallion, Melanie Anderson, Michelle Muhlbaum, Muriel Barnes, Kate Simonutti, Ermanno Simonutti, Simon Young, Tom Polapink, and Allison Lockwood, who have each helped to move this book along in invaluable and much appreciated ways. I am grateful for you all every day. For championing the series' links to Scottish and Irish communities in New England, I must thank Randy Labbe of the Saltwater Celtic Music Festival; Larry Bethune of Berkeley College's Fusion Magazine; Art McCabe of the City of Lawrence; Jason Waddleton of The Haven Scottish Pub; Katie Baxter; The Irish Ancestral Research Association (TIARA) and The New England Historic Genealogical Society (NEHGS). In Northern Ireland, Máirtín Ó Muilleoir of Belfast Media Group and the Golden Bridges Conference, Caroline Nolan of BBC Radio Ulster, and Susan Whiorskey of the Donegal Diaspora Project have been invaluable in getting the word out about the series' roots in the history of the North of Ireland, for which I owe them an enormous debt of gratitude. In Donegal, I would like to thank Eileen

Burgess and Donna Quinn of Donegal County Council Public Library Service for spearheading the inspirational <u>One Book One Community</u> transnational reading project with Libraries Northern Ireland; the historian Helen Meehan for her unparalleled knowledge of Donegal history and our memorable visit to Diseart; Martin Egan of the <u>Columba Heritage Center</u> for his personal tour of the Columban sites of Gartan Lough, Laec na Cuamha, Templedouglas, and Kilmacrenan; and the Donegal County Councilors Dessie Larkin and Micheal Heaney for their unceasing efforts on behalf of the people of Donegal. In Poland, my thanks to Jacek Gaworek, Agnieszka Ploch, and Katarzyna Dałkowska of <u>Duc In Altum</u> for introducing <u>Exile</u> to a Polish audience. In Scotland: my thanks to Anne Smart and the Kilmartin House Museum; Peter Macdonald of the Iona Community; and a special thank you to Sandy Campbell of <u>Venture West</u> for his expert help getting me to the more remote island sites which appear in this series. And latterly, much love to the good people of Tayvallich which I am delighted to now also be able to call home. Lastly, as the years travel on, so do titans in my field whom I am blessed to have called mentors: Gwyn Thomas, Christina Ward, Charis Conn, Donnchadh Ó Corráin, and Jonathan Riley-Smith. Safe travels home, my friends.

Please see the appendices for a chronological guide, a glossary and pronunciation guide, and historical notes.

.

# · CONTENTS ·

Part Three:

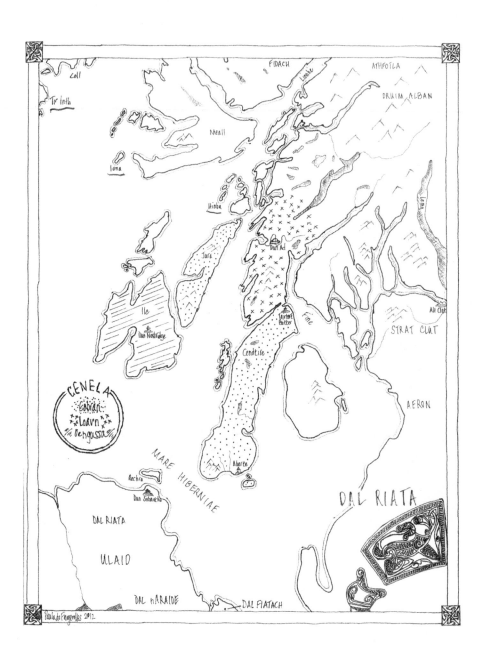

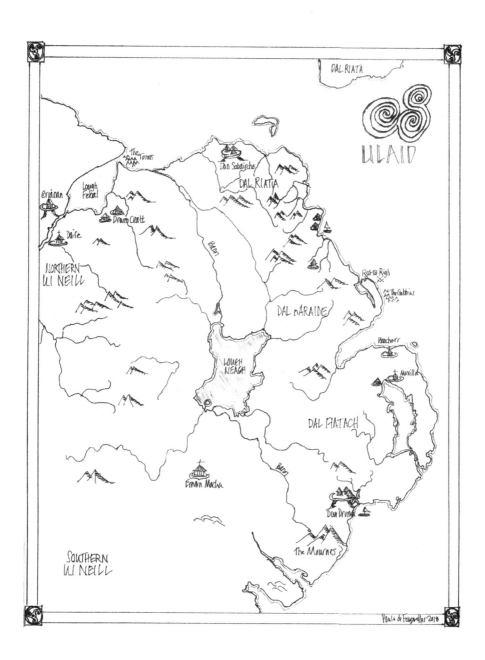

Paula de Fougerolles

# · CAST OF CHARACTERS ·

## IONA

COLUMBA or COLUM CILLE, abbot, "prince of the blood" of the Ui Neill in Hibernia, cousin to Hibernia's current high-king Aed mac Ainmerech: exiled to Dal Riata in 563.

BAITHENE, his cousin and right-hand man.

DIARMAIT, a young man, his servant.

## DAL RIATA

### THE CENEL GABRAN

AEDAN MAC GABRAN: king (*ri*) of the Cenel Gabran, overking (*ruiri*) of Dal Riata.

AMA, Lady of Rheged: his consort.

ARTUR, Aedan and Ama's son.

AFRELLA, Lady of Guined, Queen (*rigain*) of Dal Riata: his chief-wife.

FINN, Aedan and Afrella's son.

BRAN, Aedan and Afrella's son.

EOGAN MAC GABRAN, Aedan's brother, former king of the Cenel Gabran: now a novice-monk on Iona.

GABRAN, Aedan and Eogan's father: killed in battle in 558 by Bridei son of Maelchon, overking (*mormaer*) of the Caledonian Picts.

SILLAN, an old warrior in Aedan's warband.

FRAICH, a young warrior in Aedan's warband.

LUAN, Lady of Berneich, Aedan's British mother.

FAILEND, Eogan's Hibernian mother: killed by Conall mac Comgall in 574.

## THE CENEL LOARN

CONALL MAC COMGALL, Aedan's cousin, former king (*ri*) of the Cenel Loarn and overking (*ruiri*) of Dal Riata: killed in battle by Aedan in 574.

EITHNE, his wife: Aedan's first love.

DUNCHAD, Aedan and Eithne's natural son, raised as Conall's heir: killed in battle by Conall in 574.

IAN MAC CONALL, natural son of Conall, tormentor of Dovey and his family.

LAM DESS MAC CONALL, Ian's brother.

DOVEY, a farmer, persecuted by Lam Dess and Ian mac Conall, befriended by Columba.

DOVEY'S WIFE.

LIGU CENNCALAD, Dovey's infant son.

## THE CENEL OENGUSSA

FERADACH, king (*ri*) of the Cenel Oengussa.

FORINDAN, Feradach's father, former king of the Cenel Oengussa: executed by Aedan on Conall's orders in 567.

# ALBA or PICTLAND

## THE CALEDONII

BRIDEI son of MAELCHON, overking (*mormaer*) of the federation of Caledonian Picts.

DOMELCH, his daughter: Aedan's first wife.

GARTNAIT, Aedan and Domelch's son: Bridei's heir.

DRUST, Domelch's brother: Aedan's former brother-in-law.

UURGUOST, Drust's second-in-command.

BROICHAN, Bridei's chief-mage.

BRED, a Caledonian boy: raised from the dead by Columba in 565.

## THE MIATHI

GALAM CENNELATH, overking (*mormaer*) of the federation of Miathian Picts.

## THE INSI ORC or THE ISLES OF PIGS

UURAD, king (*regulus*) of the Orkneys.

TARAN, his son, a mage: Domelch's consort.

# THE BRITISH KINGDOMS OF THE OLD NORTH

## RHEGED

URIEN, overking of Rheged: Ama's step-brother.

OWAIN, his son and heir.

## STRAT CLUT

TUDWAL, overking of Strat Clut.

RHYDDERCH, his son and heir.

## THE GODODDIN

MORCANT, overking of the Britons of Gododdin: Aedan's hated foster-brother.

TENEU, Morcant's sister: Aedan's foster-sister and childhood friend.

KENTIGERN, Teneu's son by incestuous rape by Morcant: a Christian priest in Strat Clut, Columba's friend.

## GUINED

RHUN, overking of Guined.

BELI, his son.

## ELMET

GWALLAWG, overking of Elmet.

# HIBERNIA

## THE NORTHERN UI NEILL

AINMIRE MAC SETNA, former overking (*ri ruirech*) of the Northern Ui Neill and high-king (*ard-ri*) of Hibernia, Columba's cousin: now dead.

AED MAC AINMIRE, his son, overking of the Northern Ui Neill and high-king.

## THE SOUTHERN UI NEILL

DERMOT MAC CERBALL, former overking (*ri ruirech*) of the Southern Ui Neill and high-king (*ard-ri*) of Hibernia: enemy of Columba, assassinated by his foster-son Black Hugh.

# ULAID

## THE DAL FIATACH

BAETAN MAC CAIRELL, king (*ri*) of the Dal Fiatach and overking (*ruiri*) of Ulaid.

DEMMAN MAC CAIRELL, former overking: killed by his brother Baetan.

FINNIAN, abbot of Movilla: Columba's childhood teacher.

## THE DAL nARAIDE

BLACK HUGH, once child-king (*rí*) of the Dal nAraide: exiled for assassinating the high-king, his foster-father Dermot mac Cerball.

FINDCHAN, his friend: a Christian priest.

COVNA LURGAN, Lady of the Dal nAriade, Black Hugh's cousin: sold into slavery by Black Hugh, rescued from the Pictish mage Broichan by Columba and Aedan; now handmaiden to Afrella, queen of Dal Riata.

FIACHNA LURGAN, Prince of the Dal nAraide, Covna's brother, Black Hugh's cousin: heir-apparent (*tanaise*) to the Dal nAraide.

COMGALL, abbot of Banchorr: Columba's childhood friend and schoolmate.

## THE DAL RIATA

STONE, Lord of the Foxes.

TWO, Lord of the Hares.

LASSAR, Lady of the Eagles, steward of Dal Riata in Hibernia.

*A youth shall be born out of the north*

*With the rising of the nations;*

*Ireland shall be made fruitful by the great flame,*

*And Alba, friendly to him.*

Mochta of Lugbad

Prophecy told to Columba's mother at his birth on 7 December 521

# · SHADOWS ·

Oh! Dear God!
There! There! The boys!
The boys will die!

Not much time now. No time to race to them through the crush, to intercede, to step between them and those slashing swords. To save them.

Except … they are no longer boys. They are not as they are now. They are men. Valiant, vibrant men, in the prime of their lives; vital and strong. Look at them on their bright steeds! At the fore of the vanguard, laughing! Just as their father Aedan had taught them. Just as Aedan had done.

Aedan, Columba's friend, his soul's companion. His  *anam cara.* None more dear.

These boys? These men! They are invincible! They will live long lives. No spear can reach them, no arrow; certainly not those horrible, relentless, hacking blades. They are safe from harm. Free from pain.

Aren't they?

No. Blood is dripping from their beautiful faces. They are ripped from their horses. Their enemies have them now. They loom over them, taunting and laughing as they torment them.

He is too far away to save them. He will not be able to reach them in time.

He knows what is coming. So do they. There is anguish in their eyes as they look for one another; one brother reaching for the other.

Oh! No! No! No!

There go their heads.  *DREAM*

It is too much. Columba forces open his eyes.

A scream is choking him. He tries to push it out, but his throat is shut tight with terror. He gasps in little panicked pants of air as he looks around wildly. Where in the name of God is he?

Some of his fear abates as he realizes that he knows this place—*Deo Gratias*! He is in his little sleeping hut. On Iona. Iona. Yes, here is proof: here is the smooth grey sea-stone he uses as a pillow because the cold surface pressed against the back of his neck helps him sleep; here is his serviceable blanket; all around him is the tightly interlocking masonry of the curving walls of his cell, damp now with morning mist, sea breezes whistling in through the cracks. He remembers when they built this place: after the *magna domus*, the needs of his men for a communal dwelling coming before his own comfort, but before his *scriptorium*, his men declaring his health more valuable than his beloved books, though he disagrees. The fact that the morning light is not yet leaking around the doorframe lends some welcome credence to the thought that what he experienced was merely a nightmare.

Until he sees movement in the shadows.

He looks again in horror. The half-light, there in the dim recess of the cell, is shimmering. Sheets of light and of dark are flickering, shifting discordantly in a jolting kind of jig.

He knows what this means: he may feel that he is awake, but he is still between worlds, caught between sleep and true wakefulness. His terror rushes back. If possible, he is more horrified than before.

The sheeting of the half-light means that the terrible vision was not a dream. It was a communication, a message. He was *seeing through.*

With a cold shiver of dread he struggles to rise, but he is pinned to his bed, sweating and trembling, unable to move in the grip of some heavy, unnatural paralysis. He fights it until he again has some weak control of his limbs. With supreme effort, he breaks the monstrous bond and jerks himself upright.

The small victory of the additional height does not dispel his dread. In the curve of his hut the shadows are still shivering, almost alive. The sheets of penumbral light shudder and lurch.

It is a dance, and not a merry one. The wraiths seem to mock him with what they know. What they wish *him* to know.

He will not have it! He calls forth some of his usual bravado. What are they to him? What has he to fear? He, Colum Cille? He is a person who lives on the edge of the veil, gazing out into the darkness. He has encountered these kinds of otherworldly apparitions many times before, has dwelt with them in amity or has vanquished them as needed. There is divine fire in his heart. He is a warrior for the light.

Besides, these are his customary domains. This is Iona! His Iona. His home. He brought her to where she is now. If she has a master, and he is not sure that she does, then surely he is it. How dare they disturb him here?

He will banish them.

He grabs for the well-worn cross of wood around his neck, thrusts it out in a fist he is alarmed to see is still shaking, and begins to croak the *Pater Noster*, the holy Our Father. He takes immediate comfort from the rite. This prayer of prayers always comes easily, always manages to exorcize the darkness, in whatever form it has thought to come to him.

*Pater Noster, qui es in caelis,*
*Sanctificetur nomen tuum.*

*Our Father who is in heaven,*
*hallowed be your name.*

Oh, yes. This prayer has power. He can feel it begin to course through his blood, wind up his spine, surge into the crown of his head. With growing confidence, his voice gaining strength, he continues to intone this most holy of protective spells.

*Your kingdom come,*
*your will be done, on earth as it is in heaven.*
*Give us this day our daily bread,*
*and forgive us our debts,*
*as we also have forgiven our debtors.*
*And lead us not into temptation, but deliver us …*
*Deliver us …*
*Deliver us …*

Unbelievably, he falters. He. Falters. And on the *libera nos*! The *libera nos*!

He clears his throat, straightens his spine. Threatening the shadows with his outstretched cross, he marshals all his will, all his power, and tries again:

*Libera nos …*
*Libera nos …*

Astounded, he realizes that he has cannot remember the rest of the prayer. He cannot find the words for what comes next, as if he never knew them.

No—that's not quite right. Rather, as if something is squeezing shut his throat, preventing those most important next becharmed words to be canted into the light.

Dear God! He will not allow this! He will not!

The boys are precious. Aedan loves them. He loves them. They are the sons Columba will never have.

Again, his innate stubbornness rears up. If the prayer will not work—because his own weakened body cannot call it forth—then he will reason through the madness. He will employ the great acuity of his senses, the towering intellect for which he is famed.

He reasons: this nightmare is a creature of his fears, conjured up by the violence of his affection for the friends, the family he has unexpectedly found in his exile, here in Dal Riata. It has to be.

If not that, then by his shame at what he did before.

He himself has brought this atrocious phantasm out of the unmade void and into the bright world of men. He is its creator.

So this vision is not true, he tells himself: it is _not_ a message from his Lord. It has nothing whatsoever to do with what his Lord revealed to him in the spring, before he consented to ordain Aedan as king.

It is not premonition. In no way is it prophecy.

He will not permit it.

Suddenly desperate to be free of his cell, to flee the mocking shadows he has been unable to banish, Columba throws off the blanket tangling around his legs. But those normally sturdy limbs will not obey him, buckling under him as he tries to stand. Instead, he lurches for the door, throwing it open to thrust his sweaty face out into the brisk morning air. It is fresh and salty and there are drops of rain and sea-reek in it. Braced in the doorway, he welcomes the wind and the rain with upturned face. Shaking his head to clear it, he trains his eyes on the beloved, familiar sights of his island-monastery home, hoping they will anchor him here, pull him back from that other, wretched place of pain.

But there is a strangeness to the air, even outside his hut. It too is shimmering, shadows clinging stubbornly in a way that is not a precipitate of sea-mist and morning.

He curses foully and casts his eyes in another direction. Any other direction.

The shadows follow.

Again, he looks away.

But they keep up.

It takes a long time for his world to return, to settle back firmly into its accustomed forms. It helps when his brothers begin to emerge from their own cells into the early morning light, their sleepy voices calling out to one another companionably. He takes immeasurable comfort from their dear faces.

Columba huddles in the doorway, on the threshold, shivering, until this mortal realm clicks back into place. Eventually he can rise and begin his day. He can wash his face with clear cold water from the stone trough set by his door, refreshed for him each morning by his men. He can don his sandals; make his way to the chapel for the hour of *prime*. He can lose himself in the lilting, measured, joyful songs they sing at that hour to greet the day, to welcome their Lord back into the light.

He can reassure himself: *it was not a communication. It was not a vision. There is nothing to fear. It will not come to pass.*

He can ignore the fact that he has never known his Lord to lie.

Paula de Fougerolles

# · PART ONE ·

*Bronze hanging-bowl escutcheon (Historisk Museum, Bergen, from about 675)*

# · 1 ·

# CRECH RIG

*Dal Riata:*
*Beltane, 574*

His people had a saying: *heaven lay beyond the ninth wave of the sea.* Out there, on the horizon, where matter has no meaning, nor even time. Over that threshold, through that watery door. And he often thought there might be some truth to this which he would one day discover for himself—but only after his life was wrested from him and he punched through the veil between the worlds and at last stared his gods in the face; on his own terms and with a death he himself had finally permitted.

However, today Aedan mac Gabran, newly acclaimed king of the Scots of Dal Riata, had to fully disagree. Today, this fine last day of April of the year 574, heaven lay not beyond any wave on the horizon, not the ninth or the tenth or even the eleventh, but here before him, in Dal Riata; here in the land of his people.

Below him, in a break in the mountains' fold, lay the wide, flat, fertile Valley of the Kings. It spread out before him like a blanket, its gentle terraces green and welcoming and hummocky, the sun riding overhead in an azure sky. Through the heart of the glen a river, the river Ad, snaked back and forth as it made its way to the sea, a cool blue tempt on the near horizon, there not too far to the west.

His eyes followed that river until they found, nestled in one of its bright bends, a precipitous hill rising up cleanly from the marshland around it. At the foot of that hill were homesteads, those who needed protection, those who did not have strong forts of their own. More homesteads and outbuildings were dotted here and there across the marshy glen, extending up the valley behind him, while others crowded the three distinct precincts that rose up the rock itself: the artisans', the nobles', the king's own.

His eyes took this all in, traveled some more, came back, held and could not look away: for this was Dun Ad, the chief seat of the kingdom of Dal Riata; that storied inland-island, that formidable citadel, at the top of which, sitting above it all like a crown, was the Great Hall.

The king's Great Hall.

Once his father's. Then lost for a time. But now his.

His!

It could scarce be believed. A year ago Aedan would have deemed it all impossible. Yet there it was.

This was his home.

Or, as he should say: his home once more.

He loved this place. He loved Dun Ad. He loved how behind him the thickly-wooded hills grew to mountains which, stepping up once more, opened to white-headed peaks so forbidding that you crossed them only in the greatest need and at your peril. He loved those high, cold towers of stone. They kept his people safe: safe from the Britons, safe from the Picts. He loved all the little islets and skerries and sandbanks that crowded the mouth of the harbor, for they obscured the sea-approaches to his kingdom. He loved the subtle colors of the land and of the sea, so many hues of brown and green and blue and grey and russet that he hadn't names for them all. How, in addition to the great fort of Dun Ad there below him, the valley was strewn with the tumbled-down remains of the dwelling places of all the people that had lived here before, so many and so varied and so aged that it made him think with wonder that the tales told around the fire of the gods and goddesses of old must be true. And how it was all so changeable! Never dull. Every day the land showed a different face: cloaked in mist, ethereal; or wet and moody, altering itself by the hour; or, more rarely, bright and blindingly clear and hot, as it was today. There was no part of the valley of Dun Ad, or of the kingdom of Dal Riata as a whole, that did not both delight him and arouse in him a fierce, protective kind of loyalty and affection.

This was heaven. This land. These people. The Scots. His heaven. For, against all odds and every reason that he could think of, they had acclaimed him their king; he who had only ever been a second son of a slain king, an unwilling warrior, an exile.

He who had had nothing, been nothing, had been given everything.

Now, for as long as he managed to keep his head attached to his shoulders, the Scots of Dal Riata were his and he was theirs. He would protect them, keep them safe; ensure not only that they survive but that they prosper. Indeed, while kingship was a task he had never sought, now that it was at hand Aedan could not be more full of love for it than if his love lay before him, her arms open, her ready smile welcoming him home.

Which he very much hoped she soon would be. It had been a long month, this month of his *crech rig*, his king's circuit, visiting all his people, all three kindreds, to prove to them that he was strong, and that he deserved their loyalty and their render and their fighting men, to fill out his new warband. Since it was a tour Aedan had never imagined he would take, he supposed it had gone as well as could be expected. He had given the people what they wanted, had performed the necessary rituals: two more king-makings in fact, to shore up the one already performed at Dun Ad. One on an outcrop near Aberte, his father's old fort which clung to the rock at Cendtire's end, in the footprint carved in the rock there, the one that pointed back across the water towards Ulaid, their ancestral homeland in Hibernia. That ancient rite had made him *ri*, the king of his own kindred, the Cenel Gabran.

The other king-making had been performed on a similar rock carving, this time near the royal stronghold of Dun Nosbridge on the island of Ile. That had made him *ruiri*, the over-king of the Cenel Oengussa.

That left only the Cenel Loarn. Since that kindred had been so recently at war with his own—so recently at war with everyone, in fact—there was little he could do but move amongst their strongly fortified hilltop *duns*, farmstead to farmstead, cajoling them, intimidating them, doing his best to persuade them of the rightness of his rule. He didn't yet know if it had worked. He wouldn't know that for a while. Their king, Conall, Aedan's own cousin, was dead. Whether or not they had liked Conall while he was alive was no longer the point—it was Aedan who had killed him.

Still, the Cenel Loarn owed him tribute, as they would any new overlord. It was Aedan's to take, so he took it. That tribute now made its way to Dun Ad for the festival of Beltane, the second greatest of the four quarter-festivals. But the carts and wagon trains were still a half-day behind, toiling towards the citadel on Dal Riata's rudimentary track ways.

Which was a mercy. It left him just enough time for something that was in no way kingly. What he wanted was on Dun Mor, that modest stronghold not a third-of-a-league southeast of Dun Ad. There it was, rising on its little hillock; seemingly insignificant, dwarfed by the larger hillfort, yet precious to him.

Flanked by his retinue, some newly recruited, others hand-picked from amongst his very first men and promoted now with him to high lords, Aedan forded the river Ad, crossed between the two ancient standing stones that guarded that part of the valley, and came to the rise. At the base of the hill, he dismounted, bidding his retinue stay. He also bade stay his overly affectionate, very large wolf-hound, Ceo, his companion these many years. She licked his hand, then sped off to investigate the terraces, slipping through the high grass like the mist for which she was named.

Aedan climbed the path to the summit, the sun hot on his leather breastplate, his helmetless head, his spirits rising. At the top, he didn't bother to announce himself but pushed open the gate of the *dun* and entered.

The farmstead was a simple place. Stone walls, twelve-feet thick and seven-feet high, enclosed an oval-shaped dirt courtyard. At the far end of the courtyard, a thatched roundhouse hugged the wall. Chickens scolded him from underfoot; the housedogs ran to snuff at his hands. The servants, Colgu and Mugain, were grinding grain in the afternoon sun, the kernels spewing from the querns as they were crushed. He had startled them, they scrambled to their feet before their king but, with a finger to his lips and a smile, he silenced them. Crossing the courtyard and ducking his head under the low lintel of the door, he entered the house.

"Yes?" she said. "What is it?"

It was dark in the windowless dwelling and he couldn't see her. Then his eyes adjusted to the dim. Ama was half-turned to him, busy with some work on the table before her. Laying out wool for a tunic, perhaps, for their son Artur, though why she continued to bother he never knew: she was easily the worst seamstress he had ever encountered, a fact to which she herself would cheerfully admit.

*She thinks this is what women must do—and perhaps they must. But she was also born to rule.*

In two strides he had her. Ignoring her squeal since it could not be protest, he lifted her to set her before him on the table. She was smiling hugely, her beautiful brown eyes bright. Her long legs came astride his hips; she was already fisting his tunic to pull him in for a kiss.

He kissed her thoroughly. Then, running his hands up her thighs, his mouth never leaving hers, swallowing her delighted laughter, he tugged at her tunic until it caught around her waist, freed himself from his trews, and took her.

It was vital. Hot. Full of love. Just like her, just like his people. Just like the threshold. Just like the day.


She was cradling his head on her breast as they sprawled on the table. Her fingers were entwined in his long hair, brushing it back from his temple. Her tunic scratched his cheek. For a moment he let himself simply enjoy the rise and fall of her breath, her scent, the heat coming off her. She was humming, which made him smile.

"You're back," she said.

"As you can see," he said with a laugh.

He turned his face to kiss her breastbone, the closest he could get to her heart. "I've missed you."

"Is that so? I wasn't sure."

He snorted with laughter. "I'm sorry. This is still all so new—to be able to be with you. To just be with you. Whenever, wherever I like." He smiled, shrugged, the motion lost in the tangle of their clothing. "That was for me."

"That was *good*." Letting go his hair, Ama drew her arms over her head and stretched lazily. Under his chin, her ribcage expanded. In reflex, her thighs locked more tightly about his waist, which was wonderful.

He had to see her face. He levered himself up on his elbows to get a good look at her. Her cheeks were flushed, the corners of her generous mouth tipped up in an indulgent smile, her earth-brown eyes so full of love it was as if a physical thing pulsed between them. Many would say that it was not a beautiful face—not, say, like Eithne's—but the life which shone from it, the wit, the amusement, as if she saw clearly things that others only half-glimpsed, drew him in like the moths that danced around the summer fires, their wings singeing in the flames.

She was smiling at him now. Brushing away her thick brown hair, he took her beloved face in his hands and kissed her.

Then he pushed himself off her. Disappointed, her mouth

turned down in a pout, which made him laugh: he never felt more alive than when he was with her, She tried to pull him back to her, but he brushed her off and, planting a hand on her chest, pushed her back down.

Intrigued rather than insulted, she watched him while he shimmied up her tunic until it gathered above her breasts.

One hand sought, found a breast. The other fitted itself to the long muscle of her inner thigh, pushing gently until she was open to him.

She sucked in breath and smiled. Her arms fell out to either side, palm-up on the table.

As he brought down his eager mouth, he said, "This is for you".

There is a massive boulder just before the gates of that hilltop farmstead, left by the gods when they made that hill, a plaything picked up, tossed hand to hand, held up to the midday sun, studied, perhaps admired, but then discarded; an afterthought left behind as they strode further down the glen to the loch-mouth where, squatting, they pissed out the sea. They were sitting on that giant boulder, she and Aedan, he at rest with hands clasped on bent knee; she behind, her arms and legs wrapped around his waist. The leather of his breastplate, worn smooth by years of near-constant use, was warm under her chin. The tips of her fingers traced the image embossed on its front, a symbol she had no need to see to know: a sea-eagle, wings spread fully before the down-thrust, talons stretched for the kill-strike—the be-magicked totem of Aedan's people, the Cenel Gabran.

She loved the smell of that breastplate: the suns it had seen, the mists and the rain, how the burnished leather remembered every exertion of the body it protected, every martial encounter, every fight Aedan had won in lands she had never seen. The scent of that second skin was him, more than any other.

"You've been well?" he asked her. "Safe?"

"Yes. She's not sent anyone to kill me. Yet."

Her eyes strayed across the valley, to the citadel of Dun Ad, where there was great activity. It had been that way for the better part of the month; had begun, in fact, the moment Aedan had left with his retinue. Scots moved about the levels of the fort, scurrying about the terraces, very busy in preparation for the Beltane feast, where they would both try to impress their new, un-tried king, and take stock of him. Even at this distance, the energy of the place pulsed.

Just now, Dun Ad's massive main gate was opening. Wind took Aedan's long, sleek black hair and whipped it about, obscuring her view; then, the wind shifted, and she could see again: a mass of riders spilling out. They scanned the hills, then turned and made straight for them over the plain between the two hillforts.

She tensed: but soon two little figures separated themselves from the pack, galloping at break-neck speed, quickly outdistancing the others. She had no need to point them out to Aedan for he was already leaning forward, pulling away from her, eager to see them again after so long on the road.

Soon they could make out details. The boy rider in the lead was Aedan's son Finn, his bright-white hair a flash of light easy to follow against the dun-colored turf, as if a ray of sun were illuminating the crown of his head. Behind him was his twin, black-haired Bran; a shadow where his brother was light. Headlong the boys sped across the plain, trading happy glances, their cloaks billowing, their laughing shouts carrying on the wind.

"Ah, would you look at them!" she said.

She could tell he was smiling.

"And none the worse, I think, for discovering that Artur, our Artur, is also their brother," she added. Not their cousin, as they had been raised to believe, but their brother in truth. "How did Artur do?"

"He handled himself well. Very well."

"He's down with the men?"

"Aye. At first I thought he would dash up here to see you. But then he remembered his new place … "

"As one of the king's own."

He ducked his head. It didn't yet sit well, the kingly mantle. He had been alone, on his own, for so long.

"The men are new companions for him," he said. "And he intends to learn what it takes to be a warrior—even if it means postponing a longed-for reunion with his mother. He's a young man now."

What it takes to be a warrior. Unwittingly, her gaze strayed up the glen, towards the stone cairn where Aedan's first-born son, Dunchad, lay buried alongside the man he had both slain and been slain by—the man he had known until late in his life as his father: Conall. The late king. Aedan's hated cousin. They had buried Dunchad there in the field of the cairns of the kings.

By the tensing of the muscles in Aedan's back, he had followed her gaze, had read her thoughts, was also turning to the past. How long did one grieve a lost child?

Not hard to say: until death wipes memory clean, starts it anew.

She still found it strange. Not two months ago Aedan had been a man of little standing, of almost no force in the world. Now, he was not just a *ri*, but a *ruiri*: not just a king of one people, but an over-king of three—an entire realm. One could hardly make up a more fantastic tale. Yet it was one she'd gladly pay a bard to tell—though she no longer needed to. They already were.

And, in this tale, what was she?

She laughed. For her, it was a question of what she was not. She was no longer the wife of Aedan's brother Eogan. She was no longer *rigain* of their people, the Cenel Gabran, Eogan being no longer *ri*, but a novice monk, of all things!

Which left her ...

She shrugged. The truth was, she hardly knew what she was. There was no word for it, certainly no legal standing. Indeed, if she cared overmuch to give it definition, there was only one thing she was. Or, rather, three. Three in one. She was her own, of course. She was Artur's mother. And she was Aedan's.

But this last in a new way. A radical way. A way which unnerved others. Everything had shifted, all known relationships. The world was changing, the pieces moving across the great board; were still on their slow march, being repositioned by the high hands of the gods; had not yet come to rest in their new squares. Would not finally come to rest in their new affiliations of power until three days from now, at the end of the Beltane feast.

Then they would see which squares they all now occupied; and who was to either side of them, who in front and who behind. Also, if the square in which she would stand was better defined, less tenuous and threatening, than the one she shared with Aedan now.

She was thinking about these things, tracking the boys' joyful ride across the plain, when there came an enormous rumbling on the wind, like a vast ocean-wave breaking on the shore. Looking up the glen, she could just begin to make out what must have been apparent to the boys from the vantage of Dun Ad's greater summit; indeed what must have propelled them to their ponies, sped them on their errand to their father. From the higher ground to the north, a huge herd of cattle was washing into the valley. Tough little black-haired kine—milk cows, bulls, heifers, yearlings, and calves—were spilling out of the mountain pass, with ever more sweeping down after them, guided carefully by their drovers, some on ponies, others on foot. And following them all down the crooked pass to the valley floor, on horseback and by chariot and cart and wagon and foot, came the lords of the men of Dal Riata, and their women and their servants and their children.

There seemed to be no end to them. The din they made was tremendous.

The tribute, Aedan's tribute, had arrived.

Ama let out a low, appreciate whistle. "The *crech rig* did go well."

Aedan shrugged.

"So the *cenela* will submit."

"The loyalty of any man can be bought at a price, or so I have found. You only need discover it."

12

"True. But it will help that they acclaimed you."

"They did. We'll see what that counts for, if anything. I am not such a fool as to believe that I can keep their loyalty without proper—and recurrent—inducement." He nodded at the approaching sea of cattle.

"The Cenel Loarn."

"Aye. They are wary, just as we expected. But also resentful, since they are leaderless—and I am the one to have made them so."

"Aedan, don't jest!"

"I don't."

"They acclaimed you!"

"They did."

"Well they can't very well change their minds now."

"They can."

He paused, shrugged again. "But I should like to see them try."

She felt rather than saw his grin.

"But it's not just the Cenel Loarn," he said. "The Cenel Oengussa are chary as well."

"But they are your staunchest allies."

"Well, Feradach has had some time to think on it. In his new memory, the king-making was a lot closer than it was. More men wanted him. In fact, an equal number of men acclaimed him as chose me."

"That's not true!" Like Trump!

"Aye. So?"

"It should matter."

"It doesn't. In Feradach's sleep, his supporters accrue, night after night after night. Next week no doubt his numbers will have grown so that—yes, my love, you have guessed it!—I stole the throne. You would weep to see it as he does now! The sword-clash on shields, the rightness of his name being shouted to the gods from the Plateau of the Kings. Everything amplified, everything as large as he can make it: his men's love for him, my treachery, his own magnificence—especially if, earlier, there had been a drink in his hand, as there usually is. Then he will look out over his men and see reflected in their eyes his own sense of betrayal; he will see thwarted hopes and assume they are for him, rather than for their own suffering and hardship—how they should have liked him to be *ruiri*, not me. How badly he has been wronged! How they wanted that honor for him! To be raised even higher above them! His elevation, above all things, as high as is humanly possible over their own sorry selves!"

What a tale! Ama let out an exasperated sigh, but then thought the better of it. Though grandiose to the extreme, none of this was terribly unexpected. "What of their desires?" she asked. "The men's. Are they for him or for you?"

"It's hard to tell. Or, I should say, time will tell. I suppose it is not yet safe for them to come down on a side. Or, they wait to see which side will be the more lucrative for them."

"Aedan! So mercenary?"

"'So'? Always. In the meantime, I am reminded that Feradach did lose his father recently. Again, by my hand … "

"Aedan … "

"Yes. By Conall's command. But nevertheless: by my hand. That would make any man struggle with his reason, and with his affection for me, as I myself know. Perhaps we should give him time too."

"Time will not make right his recollection, my love, nor make him love you more. And you are far too understanding of his lot. While he of yours? Not at all. Who here hasn't lost? Conall's war— Conall's wars—treated none of us well. No one knew what would come of them, for good or for ill. And yet … here we are."

His shoulder shifted. He looked at her. His gaze was cloudy at first, then he seemed to see her and not the fog of memories crowding his mind. The transformation was breathtaking. He wasn't there with her, and then he was: his black eyes aflame, his fine face alive with light, his smile wide and wicked and full of joy.

He kissed her, quick and hard. "Ah, my love! Nothing truer! And thank the gods for it! For now that I am *ruiri*, I shall keep the peace. No more wars. No more raiding. No more bloodshed." Warming to the idea, he grinned. "Only eating and drinking and fooling around and rutting. That's all we'll do. Day and night. That's it. In fact, let us make ourselves known for it. The Scots of Dal Riata! Such an ample, carefree, happy lot!"

The thought settled in, took hold. He turned, said gravely to no one in particular: "By the gods, I shall make it happen. I shall keep the peace. By sword-point if I have to".

Below them, the cattle were being driven towards the ford of the river. The boys bolted through the standing stones that marked that ford, ahead of the great bovine wave. At the foot of the hill, they disappeared from view. But when shortly later they came up the path on their ponies, it was three who came, not two.

In the lead was ten-year-old Artur, his pony skidding to a halt with a snort. The young man's black eyes, the fine structure of his face, his full mouth and black hair named him clearly for who he was: son of Aedan.

"Mother!" he said. More soberly: "Father".

"Father!" shouted Bran. Four years younger than Artur, he was already nearly as tall as his older half-brother. "Can you see? The tribute arrives!"

Aedan came to his feet, suppressing a grin. "Where?" he asked.

Ama loved him for it. He would not ruin this moment for his sons even though anyone with eyes to see could discern for themselves that the meadows below abounded with the beasts.

Finn rolled his eyes. "Father! Would you *look* at them all! Have you ever seen so *many*?" His clear grey eyes, a gift from his mother Afrella (though no one knew to whom he owed the bright white cap of his hair), were wide with wonder. "And all for you!"

Aedan did smile then, a flash of a grin that caused her stomach to turn over with love and sharp desire, just as it always did. "If only they were all mine!" he laughed. "For today, at least, I suppose they are."

He gazed out upon the tribute below, amazement on his dark features. After days on the hoof, the cattle had come to a halt at last, lolling and bellowing their discomfort and displeasure. The rumble they made was astonishing; through the stones underfoot Ama could feel it reverberating up into her bones. So many! She felt a thrill on Aedan's behalf.

"Enjoy them, boys," Aedan said, a hand on the shoulders of the younger boys, a proud look for the older. "At least for tonight. Tonight they're all ours. But tomorrow?" He sighed dramatically. "Tomorrow we weep, for tomorrow I must give them all away again."

With that, he moved to the path which would take him away from her again, asking her as he went, "Are you sure I can't persuade you to come?"

"Yes. Tonight is for her."

She had resolved to remain firm on the matter, but some insecurity and longing must have shown on her face for, with one long stride, he was back, bending his head for a quick kiss and a squeeze of her hand. He turned, thought better of it, stopped; and came back to kiss her once more, this time thoroughly.

"Come along, boys," he said as he left. "Time to determine who gets what."

He strode down the path, cheerful boys on clattering ponies either side. At the base of the hill, he would reclaim his own horse and whistle for his hound Ceo, his retinue swinging around to flank him again.

Indeed, there they were now, come back into view, striking out across the plain.

They had not yet reached the safety of the citadel when, from the harbor, the blast-horns blared. One. Two. Three long, terrible, ear-splitting shrieks.

Enemies approached.

Aedan shouted commands. His men drew into a tight circle around the twins, Artur remaining to the outside, while Aedan looked for the source of the danger. He had it quickly: logboats bearing down on them on the river, oars thrashing, shooting the boats forward, sunlight blinding on swords and shields and spears.

Another clipped command and his men drew their own swords, kicked their horses to gallop, and charged for the riverbank to intercept the vessels before they reached the landing place below Dun Ad's gate. As his men saw for themselves what was rapidly becoming clear to him, they cried out: these were Picts—their greatest enemy, who had killed his father, who had slain a great many of their people. There was no mistaking it. In garb and mien not so very different from the Scots, the war-party which bore down on them was nonetheless so foreign as to have escaped from the shuttered realms of the *sidhe*-folk, for every inch of their visible skin was covered with wild blue tattoos. It was an ornamentation that Aedan knew from experience extended even to their hidden skin, to their secret selves, so that the body of a Pict wielded a fierce and formidable magic.

Skin too blue in the sunlight, spears thrust to the fore like the bristles of an onrushing boar, the Picts came on. Five boats: sixty warriors. And Aedan with only his house-guard; only twenty-eight.

He drew his spear, readied his aim.

But then …

"Hold!" he cried.

A grin burst from him. He knew these Picts, at least the two huge warriors at the front of the lead boat. That was Drust's sharp-toothed grimace, as were the sensational sunsets tattooed onto the cheeks. They were as much him as his name. Aedan himself had given Drust the wretched scar that marred what was otherwise a splendidly-pure, ferocious visage. With Drust was Uurgost, his second-in-command, also heavily armed, and an unknown holy man, a mage of the Picts, with unusually striped hair.

More wondrous to tell: conveyed within the tight ranks of the warband behind the three was a small party of Pictish nobles. A compact, dark woman glared out, found him on the bank. Her body was held ramrod straight, her cunning face a mixture of fury and joy. With her was a boy with long black hair, creamy skin not yet fully flushed with tattoos, and an open, curious expression which held none of the woman's anger but a good deal of her longing.

Aedan's heart leapt.

"Father, is that them?" Escaping the safety of the retinue, Bran and Finn had charged alongside, small swords defiantly drawn.

So fierce was his joy that it took him a moment to find his voice.

"Aye! The ugly one is your uncle. The lady behind him is Domelch, my wife. And that boy? That lad? That's Gartnait. That's your brother."

# · 2 ·
# ARTMUIRCOL

*Artmuircol, Dal Riata*

W*ill there ever be an end to want?*
The man's face was a mask of destitution: skin pitted and grey; hair stringy, lifeless; teeth rotting or gone. Threadbare clothes hung from his meager frame, his fingers were as thin as sticks, the nails yellow, broken. And yet the man, called Little Dove, or Dovey, shared with them the hospitality of his home, a cave scratched out of the hummocks of the hillside, with no hesitation that Columba could see. The hide covering the hovel's low door had been drawn back to let in the early spring sun, weak but warming. A wicker cradle had been set in the little path of light. The babe in it, Dovey's son, batted his hands before his face, his eyes screwing in frustration as his thumb failed yet again to find his mouth.

Columba sat on his heels before the fire, which had been lit on this bright, cold April morning in the cooking pit outside the shelter, for the cave itself was too small a space for a fire within. Dovey's wife ladled peaty water into a rusty cauldron suspended over the spitting flames. That thick water, and the two shriveled roots and the onion that had preceded it into the pot, would break their fast.

Columba traded looks with his companions. His servant Diarmait, now a young man of seventeen, was captivated by the gurgling child. Eogan was scowling, but at what, Columba could not tell: his friend's regal face revealed nothing beyond a dissatisfaction he did little to conceal. This year was a test for him. Columba had known, had loved, him as his king. Now Eogan was a novice monk under Columba's care. He had chosen the Life willingly. Whether or not he would prosper in it had yet to be ascertained.

Both men understood Columba's unspoken suggestion: that they partake of the meal so as not to insult their hosts, but that they do so sparingly.

"The last time that bastard showed up," Dovey was saying, "I had taken the cattle up the glen, which is why we still have them." He pointed to the slope above the hovel where a handful of cows scratched for grass in the ankle-deep mud. They were so scrawny their ribs racked their skin. "He didn't get them—or her or the babe."

Dovey laid a protective hand on his wife's thin shoulder. "He didn't get any of us because we weren't here to be gotten. I was with the poor, wee creatures up the glen, as I said and … speaking of the beasts, you'll bless them for me before you go, won't you, my lord? My lord *Abba*? So that they'll increase?"

At Columba's nod, Dovey beamed in triumph. "Ah! Of course you will!" he said. "They said that about you, my lord: that you were like that. Kind. Generous. Even to the likes of me. The likes of us. Yes they did!"

Dovey shared a hopeful look with his wife. "In fact, if you could manage, my lord, it's not five of the wee beasts we'd like, but one-hundred-and-five! I know it's a lot to ask—one-hundred-and-five!—but with a herd like that we would never want again. Never. You could make that happen my lord, couldn't you? Arrange it—with Him as is above? He wouldn't take offense, would He? A man can't be faulted for asking, can he?"

With a shake of the head from Columba, Dovey beamed again. "Good! Good!" he said. "Anyway, as I was saying, when he came my wife here was gathering kelp down by the shore, with the babe in its basket, so was not here, thank the gods ... Thank the *God*, that is, I do mean, my lord ... "

Dovey shot Eogan a flustered glace, worried he might have offended his former king. "My *lords*, I am sure ... "

Columba nodded in a reassuring but noncommittal fashion, and rubbed his hands before the fire, without much hope of chasing the chill from his bones. They had passed the night wrapped in their cloaks huddled against their *curragh* which had been set on its side to break the sea-winds that blew constantly from the west, their faces to the bleak stars, shivering, for Dovey's hovel could barely accommodate his own small family. All this time later, Columba still had the cold bite of the sea in his limbs.

Face now to the sun, Columba longed for a roaring blaze to speed the dissipation of his chill, but would not ask the woman to stoke the fire. Of the fifty or sixty cartloads of turf needed to keep just one small fire going for a year for just one small family— good, rich, dense, old turf—this family had but a handful. Rather, in desperation, they dug the poor soil from under the hooves of their cows.

In part, this was the fault of the land in which they now found themselves: Artmuircol, a rough tongue of moorland thrusting belligerently out into the sea of the Hebrides some ways to the north of Iona. Heather-clad, bare and wild, this peninsula takes the full brunt of the gales that come in off the west, and lochs and coves bite deeply into its mountainous fringes. Its sandy beaches are cold and white, and from its uplands, frigid burns cut sharp courses to the sea. The sea rules it: it is bounded by the sea and, at the time that Columba found himself there and for a long time afterwards, the sea was the only way in.

There is no doubt that Artmuircol is a land apart, wild and rough, which makes it beautiful. But it is a place where lowly men like Dovey had almost nothing, and were left either to cut turf where they could from the depleted earth, which spoiled the grazing for their cattle, or to burn desiccated cow-dung, which could more profitably be used to enrich the fields.

Perhaps this was why Eogan scowled: no one should live like this, so close to ruin. But who could help? Not them: not at that moment. So Columba balled his frozen hands into the folds of his cloak cast his thoughts elsewhere.

Homeward.

Homeward to Iona.

Iona! At the thought of her, the blood in his veins pumped as if singing, and a ready smile came to his lips. He had never expected to feel such a thing as love for his island of Iona, yet love her he certainly did. He had never expected to take to her at all, coming as he had an exile to this strange, dangerous land, he who had once been an intimate of God and the cousin of kings. And she, nothing.

Or so he had thought.

Because Iona had proved herself to be a place of very old magic, perhaps the oldest. Not so long ago the haunt of *magi*, only with his coming chased away by the new divine, Columba had found that heaven is near to you there, the Otherworld peeking through as flickers of a greater intensity out of the corners of one's eyes. On Iona the divine brushes right up against your skin. You tremble there, as if in expectation. It's as if the air itself is dancing, is full of joy. A porous place, things leak through.

Even portents that are unwanted.

He and his men were thriving there. Which is why it was with some reluctance he had left Iona a month back, taking a number of his brothers with him. Eogan had told him of a place in Artmuircol north of where they now were, at the mouth of a river called the Sale where it empties into a tidy little sea-loch. Nominally Dal Riatan, that region dangerously abutted the territory of the Picts, but it was worth the risk to journey there, Eogan said, because it was clothed in broad-leaved pine and oak woods and Iona had very little timber of her own. Wait until Columba saw it!

And indeed it was extraordinary. Columba had never seen the

like, many of the old groves where he grew up in Hibernia having already been felled, and when they got there he took it all in joyously. The forest was alive in a way that astounded all the senses. Mosses and lichens and liverworts seemed to cover everything. All the branches and trunks, the stumps, the fallen logs and boulders were garbed in infinite shades of wet green. His eyes absorbed the variety of colors without being able to adequately differentiate them; he found something to love in each smooth, supple, verdant lump. Underfoot, the forest floor was like a vivified carpet, giving beneath his step only to spring back with a touching little sigh. And the air! The air was heavy and wet with trees coming to leaf. He could almost feel them unfurling. Every happy inhalation brought the tang of pine into his mouth where he could savor it on his tongue. When he closed his eyes, he could just about hear the trees breathe.

Everything in those groves was so hugely alive; and he so small. The trunks of the pine trees were so wide it took two of them, hands linked, to encircle them. Overhead, the trees' cones were bursting, sending winged seeds into the air. When they peeled off the pine trees' dark bark-plates, they glowed in the sunlight, warm and ruddy. It made him expect heat—but when he put his hand to the heartwood, it was cool to the touch.

And all this splendor was warded by the oaks, the ancient guardians of the greenwood. The *druidi* used to worship in oak groves—*nemeton* like these were their sanctuaries—and, of all trees, Columba loved oaks the best too. It recalled to his nostalgic heart his beloved Daire, his first monastic foundation, back home in Hibernia. They had cut down part of the druids' *nemeton* to build it, right alongside the old sacred precinct on the island in the embrace of the river Febal, as blessed a place as there ever was, he himself carefully choosing which of the ancient oaks to fell, leaving the hoariest to continue to flourish as was only right.

He was still in awe of that greenwood, these many days later. It had felt like the work of giants, the Old Ones' secret playground. Compared to where Columba now found himself, here with Dovey and his family, the vast pine and oak woods on the Pictish frontier

23

had been a place of beauty and abundance. Those groves were a gift.

Naturally, his mind had turned to how to use them.

Columba had known, and so had Eogan: ships' planks and masts, especially the pines which grow so tall and true and, being full of resin, are slow to take on water and to decay. A longship was what Iona needed next, to ferry them to and from the island of Hinba, their first foundation here in Dal Riata and where in due course Columba wanted to establish a community of penitents, if all continued to proceed as it should; and to the citadel of Dun Ad; and to the land of the Britons and the Picts again as needed; as well as to Hibernia—though, this last, not for him since it was a place as an exile he could no longer go.

For, as surprising as it was, Iona's influence was growing in tandem with her fame, their work broadening to welcome in new peoples from many new places. Their numbers were increasing steadily, more brothers arriving every year to learn the ways of their community. So, in addition to a much-needed longship, they also needed to enlarge the *magna domus*, where the men ate, worked, and sometimes slept. For such a purpose, pine is also ideal. And Iona's lovely little chapel also needed repair—but for that they would use only the even-grained, honey-colored, strong wood of the oak, the king of trees.

There are other uses too, of course, for all parts of a tree— medicines, book inks, tonics, tinctures, aromatics—so they were careful to preserve and transport every bit of what they harvested. When everything had been made ready, they brought down a few of the oaks that grew just above the river and, stripping them down to the roundwood, rolled them down the bank and into the water where they made a tremendous splash. There they were corralled into large rafts and tied to their convoy of *curraghs* to be towed out to sea. It was strenuous work and exceedingly hazardous—if mishandled, the enormous logs could break limbs, crush skulls and bones—so they proceeded carefully, carefully, carefully, their exertions eased by songs and prayers sung in time with the natural rhythm of their labour.

At last, at the mouth of the river, *curraghs* at the ready, they had waited for a favorable wind to put to sea. And indeed, time was passing, they should be off home again.

Yet, as much as he longed for Iona, Columba found himself in little hurry to leave that place. The verdant oak groves were beautiful, without doubt, but even more wonderful was what the place was calling forth in him, an emotion he had not felt in so many years that it took him some time to give name to it: contentment, ease. The feeling of being safe enough to let yourself rest.

He had been on the move for so long. There had been much work to do; much danger, turmoil and pain. But now Aedan was *ruiri*. That meant everything. As Aedan's friend, indeed as his premier counselor, Columba enjoyed his protection. The need to watch constantly over his shoulder for the next mortal challenge had been diminished. While there was still much to do to consolidate Aedan's reign, to help the Dal Riatans, to protect and nurture his brothers on Iona, it now felt right simply to relax, to take stock, to explore this unknown, delightful corner of his new world.

This was not a moment to wish away.

And providence seemed to agree, for when they turned to the sea that day they found it becalmed, the water in the little bay as smooth as glass. There was hardly any wind. It was best to wait for it, he told the others. Given the load they had to tow, they would get nowhere with the oars.

Besides, he had discovered that the sprightly river Sale hid another treasure.

It was fistful of salmon.

He chuckled to think of it now. At sight of the thick, muscular bodies twisting in the green-hued water, he had cried out with glee. "Praise be to God there is no wind, lads! Look at all these great big leapers! Break out the nets, boys! Break out the nets and let us fish!"

Eogan had taken up the challenge gladly. "Nets?" he said, a competitive gleam in his eye. "What's next: spears? Traps? Leave those to the others, my friend. It is the rod that is the tool of princes, the proper instrument for the likes of you and me. Unless such a contest frightens you?"

Clapping Eogan on the back, Columba had laughed. "Big talk, my friend! Big talk! Have at it!"

Each took to their own method. Casting their nets across the wide river-mouth, their companions caught five fish with hardly any effort, the river rewarding their honest industry. Sun on their upturned faces, the brothers joyfully ate.

The rodded princes, however, went without, the morning growing longer, their contest a draw, they landing nothing but empty hooks, short tempers and frustration.

Until it was time to depart. Then, just as they were about to cast off, a large shadow passed darkly by under the surface of the water. Their hooks hit the water as one.

It was Columba who brought it up—a magnificent salmon, big and brawny and old and smart, which Columba marveled at it even as he struggled to bring it in. It fought so bravely that Columba considered releasing it, but Eogan was observing Columba's success with an envious scowl, so he did not. Eventually, after much effort, the brothers encouraging, cheering, ribbing, the fish lay on the riverbank, gasping, its eye gaping as Columba gave it thanks for its life and clubbed it to death.

Columba could not help but gloat. "Did you see how it leapt onto my hook?" he said to Eogan. "Now that's providence for you! And such a kingly creature it could be The Salmon of Knowledge itself!"

While the brothers laughed, calling it a miracle, poor Eogan turned away with a curse of defeat.


Eogan was still sour when the wind had begun to turn, sending them hurrying to their *curraghs*. Out from the mouth of the River Sale the little convoy of twelve boats rowed, the monks pulling hard on the oars. At first their passage was smooth and Columba was looking forward to an uneventful journey across the open ocean, but then a contrary wind sprang up as if out of nowhere, as it often does in that part of the world, blowing head on against them from the west, and a heavy black cloud swept in overhead. As the sky let loose, they put into the lee of the nearest isle, a place called Airthrago, to wait out the squall in the sheltered water along its foreshore.

Rain pelting his head, his back bent to the tumult, Eogan's mood had not improved. "Where's your vaunted luck now, *Abba*?" he grumbled. "Where's the providence you like to gloat is yours? Can you not call up a more favorable wind? Tell me: what good is the gift of miracle if you cannot call it up on command?"

Columba was chuckling when something over Eogan's shoulder caught his attention, causing him to laugh out loud. "Hoist the yards cross-wise, lads!" he said, barely able to contain his glee. "Spread the sails! Draw those sheets taut!"

The brothers sped to comply. And just in time, for a wind which had begun to blow violently from the northeast seized their sails, and from a standstill they were effortlessly off.

"No!" cried Eogan. "It cannot be!"

"And yet there it is!" said Columba with utter delight.

Homewards they sailed, with Eogan sullen and silent and the rest of their pleased companions proclaiming the change of wind a manifestation of both Columba's power of miracle and his prophetic foreknowledge. Indeed, they were later to tell stories about it that people repeat to this day.

And Columba, who had merely read the movement of the air in the vast, emotive firmament? He grinned all the way.


All that day along to the east the rough headlands of Artmuircol had loomed, worrying Eogan, who warned of dangers lurking in the dark fortresses that clung to the cliff sides there so ominously. "We must be on guard here," he said. "We must keep watch. This place is crawling with bandits. And the Cenel Loarn."

Yet Eogan had said that Artmuircol's cliffs gave way to the south to another great belt of oak woods, further inland along a loch that could provide safe anchorage for many boats. Those ancient oak woods, Eogan said, were something Columba should also surely see, especially now when the early–spring hyacinths would be covering the forest floor in a wondrous haze of blue. So, with a shout and a wave, Columba had sent the convoy on home. Given the fair following breeze, and barring any mishap, the monks should reach the safety of Iona by nightfall of that same day.

With Eogan and Diarmait, Columba sailed southeast into the sound between Artmuircol and the island of Meall until they reached a bay called the Camas, and there they had put to shore. In the fields that backed onto that bay, below the dark and steepening slopes of a ben, beside a standing stone encrusted with lichen which in the dim light took on a symbolic cast, they had found the mean homestead of Dovey and his family who had received them as honored guests. There they had spent the night, more vigilant in those rough lands than they had been while harvesting timber or pulling up salmon on the border of the territory of the Picts.

Now, in the cold light of day, Columba could see grit suspended in the dark brown liquid Dovey's wife was ladling into the cauldron in a vain attempt to extend their meal.

"For your son's baptism," Columba said to pair, "fresh water is best. A spring. A well. From where do you draw your water?"

Dovey spat through the gaps in his teeth. "Fresh water? A well? For the likes of us? Bah! It's true, there is a lovely burn farther up, just there … " A broad thumb, flattened by hard labour, pointed to the mountain along one side. There a stream cascaded, a bright white slash on the slope. "But we are forbidden to take from it. It is clear and sweet: *it is for the lords*, for Lam Dess and his ilk. Us? That's ours." The pool towards which his thumb swung was sludgy, the place where the burn flattened to marsh before it seeped into the sea.

Anxious eyes flashed up. "Will it do? Will your God refuse? We don't wish to offend Him."

"Let me see what I can do."

Columba collected his staff and, summoning Diarmait and Eogan, took to the track that led up the hillside on the opposite side

28

of the bay, not towards the lords' burn, but into the wilds.

"Diarmait," he said, "give them all the provisions we can spare. Then catch up."

"Of course, but they won't accept them, *Abba*, I don't think. They mean to feast *us*, since you'll be blessing their son, with the baptism."

"Then tell them … tell them that it's our custom. That it is the way of the Christians. That since our Lord fed the multitudes, we must do our best when we can, so as to do as Christ did."

Columba warmed to the idea. "In fact, my fish? That big beauty that came up last? Yes, I know. You had hoped to smoke it. I'm sorry. There will be others. It will make a worthy feast for the baptism of this child."

Columba did not miss the look that flashed across Eogan's face—not triumph so much as approval. Good, Columba thought. He sees. Eogan had been a worthy king. He would make a formidable monk, should he last out the year of his intiation—and become yet another weapon in his brother Aedan's expanding arsenal.

With Eogan alongside, Columba began his search. Up the path they trudged until they came close to the top of the hill. At the limits of the land farmed by Dovey, Columba turned off the path towards a steep bank where ferns swayed and dense green moss furred the protruding stone.

When he heard a faint, vaguely cheerful, tinkling sound on the wind, he stopped and set his ear to the bank. He sniffed the air. He pressed down hard on the spongy turf. It gave a little under his hand. But then that hand encountered something unyielding; not natural, but made by man.

*What devilry is this?*

With hands and staff and Eogan helping, he tore at the turf. Underneath, just as he had begun to suspect, he found roughly-hewn planks set into the bank. They had been newly put in place. Grass had only recently begun to overgrow the edges.

He pried off the planks and turned aside some rock. Immediately, water began to bubble from the bank. Pooling some in his hands, he brought it to his nose and sniffed. The scent was tangy, clean. He tasted it. It was lovely: pure and sweet.

It was a spring, an old spring, a long-standing water source, its liquid clear as a shallow loch on a sun-filled day. While not copious, it was certainly enough for Dovey and his family.

He looked at the bleak land about him. In this place, hardship was the only promise. Yet the land itself was not the greatest of Dovey's enemies.

Mortal devilry was. Men's malice. For the little spring had been intentionally hidden.

With the spring his font, Columba baptized the child, sprinkling its head with water, bathing its soul with the gleaming liquid, the infant squirming in his hands.

"What destiny do you see for him, my lord *Abba*?" Dovey asked, taking back the baby to bestow a gentle kiss on its forehead. "You can see it. I know you can. It was told to me that you have *the sight*, and now I see for myself that it is true! Why, without knowing you yet for a full turning of the day, you have filled our cauldron with plenty! With a bonnie great fish, the grandest my eyes ever saw! The king of the red leapers! And here you have coaxed water from stone! This little spring! I know you can *see*! So, tell me! Tell me! Tell me about my son Ligu!"

It was true: sometimes the second sight came to him. But sometimes it did not. Lately he hadn't actively sought it out, afraid he might be forced to relive the premonition of Aedan's sons befouled. But here, Dovey was so shyly hopeful. A fierce desire had come into his wife's eyes.

They had so little. Could he help?

He would try. He nodded and looked inward.

Very quickly, behind the noise which was the chatter of his own ceaseless thoughts, he was filled with a quiet sense of peace and plenty, as if this boy's life would be long, uneventful, and generally happy. In a world where one's fate was often met early and cruelly, such a life for the child would be a rare blessing.

"This boy ... Ligu, you are calling him?"

"Aye! Ligu Cenncalad, my lord *Abba*."

"Cenncalad. *Hard head?*"

"Aye! He will need a hard head to prosper in this life, my lord *Abba*!"

Columba laughed. "And so he shall! You have named him aptly. For your little Ligu will live a long life."

"Ah!" Dovey beamed. His wife's hand flew to her mouth.

"He will live a long life. Into extreme old age."

"Extreme old age? Could it be true?"

"Aye! And ... "

"And, my lord *Abba*? And?"

Columba saw in his mind that Ligu would be a comely young man, his hard head sporting a cord of thick light hair braided long down the middle of his back. He would be so uncommonly well-formed that he would be favored by the women of this region, a shining beauty to delight the eyes, offsetting some of the bleakness of their days. For, as he often thought, that is the purpose of anything we find beautiful: to remind us that in this mortal realm of challenge and pain we sojourn only briefly, and then we are off home again. Yes: in Columba's mind was a tangle of bare limbs. On a mat, in a hut. A brazier burning. Soft voices, content, but rising. Absently counting those limbs, Columba realized with a snort that there were a few of them, more than eight.

Comely Ligu would bring joy to this region many times over.

With a rueful chuckle, Columba turned his thought away, gave Ligu privacy, telling the father, "He will ... *enjoy* this long life of his and bring pleasure to many".

*He will be a slave to the desires of the flesh, more like it. And why not? Indeed, with so little else to look forward to, why not?*

"Ah! My son! My son! I will tell him of you, my lord *Abba*. I will tell him to aspire to become a great man like you, to become your God's man; you with your miracles of power and prophecy!"

Columba doubted it, but then ... upon his mind's eye a flash of grey, the swish of a modest robe, aged, gnarled hands clasped in prayer. Death; then a simple cross incised in stone atop a grave.

*Yes. Perhaps!*

What a marvel: this life, he thought. How consistently astonishing.


Up on the hillside, beside the font, they began their baptismal feast. But no sooner had they begun to rejoice than there came the awful low of cows in terror; deep, wrenching bellows of bovine distress from the direction of Dovey's homestead down by the beach.

They raced down to see raiders at the homestead. They were making off with Dovey's cattle, driving them up the gangplank of a boat that had been drawn close to shore. The poor beasts were terrified. Only the flats of swords hard across their rumps could encourage them to board.

A wiry man emerged from Dovey's hovel. His mop of auburn hair merged with a long, unkempt beard, his vociferous curses ringing up to them on the wind.

Dovey let out a wail. "That's him! The one I told you about! That's Ian mac Conall! Ian of the Cenel Loarn! Him as tried to steal us!"

Eogan let out his own furious bark. "Did you say mac *Conall?* Of the Cenel *Loarn?*"

Eogan took off, reaching for his sword as he ran—a sword that, as a monk, he was no longer permitted to carry. He skidded to a halt in front of the bandit, shock on his face as his hand came up empty. Ian mac Conall fell back, surprised by the unforeseen attack and the unexpected size of the monk who offered it.

But when he saw Eogan's befuddlement, he chortled, then lunged.

"Watch out!" Columba screamed.

The band of raiders in the boat were wading back through the surf to come to the aid of their leader. But Eogan's training had taken over; his earthly training. Eogan had been a novice monk for only a few short months, not nearly long enough to begin to transform the truth of what he had been: a warrior, a king of men, a leader of his people. A man accustomed to meting out justice, to taking life.

Without taking his eyes off his opponent, Eogan crouched, searched the sand with a hand, came up with a piece of driftwood that had a sizeable knot at one end. He brandished his newfound club and grinned.

With his free hand he waved Ian closer. "Come on, then," he said. "Let's see what you've got."

"Eogan!" Columba shouted. "Wait!"

The brigand's hairy head swiveled. "*Eogan?*"

Diarmait and Dovey had come skidding up. Keeping them behind him, Columba got as close to Ian's sword as he dared. They had only minutes before Ian's band of men reached them. "Ian!" he commanded. "Give back the cattle and we will let you go!"

Ian roared with laughter. "Ha! You will 'let me go'?"

He lunged at Columba but did not get far, Eogan's club knocking his strike aside. Ian fell back with a grunt, but managed to hold on to his sword. Up close, Columba could see that the blade was not one of which anyone might boast: heavily nicked, it had been dented and repaired many times.

Behind them, Ian's men gained the beach and were sprinting as hard as they could through the heavy sand, knees pumping to chests. Ian shouted, waved half of his men to his side, the other half around to outflank the monks.

"Ian! Do as I say!" Columba cried. "What's a leaky cauldron? A handful of cows more skin than bone?"

"Do as *you* say? Ha! Who are *you*? It's *my* cauldron, now. *My* cows. Skinny's as good as fat, where they're going. The cauldron doesn't care."

Ian lunged again. This time, Eogan's makeshift club found Ian's shoulder, the blow dead-on. There was a sickening *crunch* and the scrabbly little sword went flying.

"You!" Ian snarled, cradling his useless arm. "I am going to hurt you! You're no man! You gave up being king! And for what? To become his bum-boy? Ha! Then I know just what to do with you, when we're done with this. What you'd like."

They were quickly being encircled. There was a scream in the distance: those raiders not closing in on them were chasing down Dovey's wife and son.

Dovey shouted in fear, grabbed up Ian's sword from the sand, and took off after his family.

"Ian!" Columba said. "Don't be a fool! If you know who *he* is, then you know who his *brother* is. I'd take care there, son. I'd take very good care. If you hurt us, any of us,"—the sweep of Columba's staff included all of them, even those disappearing down the beach—"he will find you. You will be made to pay."

"His brother? What about *my* brother? My brother is the lord of this place! My brother, Lam Dess. I obey no man but him. And he says that I can make free with his clients. Especially that miserable little man." A snarl at the retreating figure. "He has escaped me twice, but not again. Today, his cattle. Tomorrow, his wife."

A greasy grin thinned his lips. "In a year or so, when he is old enough to take all of me, his son."

Ian's men guffawed.

Columba had had enough. He drew himself up. He thrust his staff towards the heavens, his other hand pointing unequivocally at Ian. "You mock me? You mock him? Then I curse you!" he shouted. "I curse you! May all my Lord's might fall upon you—you and your men!"

Ian's eyes widened and against his will he took a step back. A superstitious hush fell upon his men. They began to mutter amongst themselves and to shift nervously from foot to foot. Did this holy man have the power to maledict? Would they risk it?

Columba did not know if his threat would be enough until, with a convulsive twitch, Ian waved his men off. With a sharp whistle, he called back those pursuing Dovey's family.

He glared at Columba, and said with a bravado that did not quite obscure the wary look in his eyes, "Curse me all you like, but

I am keeping the cows. And when I'm done with this lot, I'll be coming for you, make no mistake. I know where to find you, you and all your boys! You think Iona's magic will protect you? It won't. Nothing can. Nobody can".

With alacrity, the gangplank was raised and the raiders pushed off, the stricken cattle bellowing in terror as the boat was rowed away on the rollicking waves.

Columba followed them, wading out until the water rolled coldly against his thighs. He raised his hands to heaven. Watching the boat retreat westwards, he did not know whether to rain out a litany of maledictions on the raiding party, on all their offspring, their lives and their memories, or to pray. The bitter words that spilled out of his mouth were a little of both.

Out on the northern horizon thunderheads formed, came to life. Darkening, they gathered mass and force; rose. An angry wind began to needle the waves.

Columba stood in the surf, torn between compassion for them all and a seething impotence, waves breaking about his legs and receding, breaking and receding, Ian's taunts ringing in his ears until, with a hand on his shoulder, kind but firm, Eogan drew him back to shore.


A great wind squalled in fits and bursts all night violently. It howled against the hovel, gusting rain through the fur flap of the door. Inside, Columba and his companions huddled, knees up-drawn. In the face of such a storm, they had been permitted into Dovey's home begrudgingly, but no one slept. The babe whimpered in fear at the relentless racket; Dovey's wife rocked the child and wept, the folds of her cloak failing to muffle her sobs. Save to call them in, Dovey had not spoken to any of them, his face turned darkly to the damp wall. Whether the poor man was filled with humiliation and shame at his own terminal weakness, or anger at Columba for failing to stop the raiders from making off with the last of his herd, Columba did not know.

Eogan and Diarmait had done their best to comfort them all, but Columba would not be appeased. Inwardly, he too raged. Part of him, a small but still strong part, fumed at his exile from Hibernia and the contempt which wretched scoundrels like Ian were now allowed to heap on him, he who so greatly outranked all but a handful of men then alive. He couldn't silence this terrible passion and in fact didn't try to: he was a man like any other. Another part of him railed against his own foolish actions, deeds that had doomed him to exile from his homeland in the first place. He had brought this fate upon himself: no lie. Mostly he raged at the relentless need and the want which would turn a man like Ian against his own people, condemning a family like Dovey's to fear, destitution and, now, certain slavery.

Unless a means could be found to put an end to it.


His dreams were fitful, confused and dark. He wielded a dagger; and then he didn't. Its blue blade was slick with thin, red blood; then it was clean again. A dead boy came back to life at his prayer; but instead of thanks, profane curses were shrieked at him from a mouth rimmed with rotting teeth, and there were eyes as black as death.

Behind that boy, other children, on a windy hill, whimpering.

Bad dreams, hard dreams, and then a hand on his shoulder shaking him awake, "*Abba*, come! Come and see! There's been a wreck!".

Columba's first thought was: *Good. Ian and his men have received their just due.* His second: *I hope the poor beasts have managed to survive.* Other uncharitable thoughts followed as, under clearing skies, he ran with the others down to the beach. On it, amidst the far-flung debris of what had once been a ship, a man sprawled, facedown, arms outstretched.

Seeing him, Columba was filled with a sudden, horrible dread. Ian's boat was not the only one to have been out upon the open ocean that day. Was this one of Columba's own men?

Eogan turned the body. Sodden, it squelched in the tide-wash. He cleared seaweed, sand, and strands of reddish hair from the grey face.

Columba's loyal heart swore. *Deo Gratias*! It was not one of his own.

But neither was it the bandit Ian.

Eogan looked up, confused. "Do you know this man?"

Columba bent to study him, then pulled back in surprise. The hair had been shaved from ear to ear, right over the top of the head. The stranger's forehead and a good part of his fore-skull were bare. The skin there glinted with bits of broken shell.

This was a monk. Not one of Columba's, but nevertheless a monk. And indeed, in case he needed it further confirmed, the man wore both a monk's habit and a Christian cross on a fine gold chain.

An unknown monk here? One who was not one of Columba's men? Given the prevailing winds and currents, there was only one other place from which this man could have come.

Hibernia.

Eogan bent his ear to the man's mouth. "Lucky bastard! Would you believe it? He's alive!"

"*Abba! Abba!*" cried Diarmait who had been searching the shore behind them. "Here's another one!"

Columba ran to the second prostrate form but drew back with even more surprise than at the first.

It was another monk, but this time he knew the sea-stricken man cradled in his young servant's arms. He knew him—but from a very long time ago: a time which Columba did his level best to forget but which only the previous evening had soured his dreams.

The man was opening enormous, bulbous eyes of so deep brown a color that they were almost black, now red-rimmed and veined from his time in the sea. Slowly, those eyes focused and color began to return to his face. It was a well-made face, muscular and broad, with black, arching brows and full lips. It was sensual, the face of a man who had no trouble taking enjoyment from the world.

Nevertheless, it was not a face Columba had any wish to see.

He felt his known world turn, spin. What had been safe and secure, shatter.

Columba would have fled—his pride be damned!—but the man's hand shot out, capturing his cloak in a vice-like grip. Columba tried to pry off his cold fingers, but they held on like the death that should have taken him.

The man tried to speak, coughed out water; tried again. "Colum! Brother Colum!"

He fixed Columba with a stare that made Columba shiver. "Sanctuary!" he croaked. "Sanctuary!"

Iona. As abbot of Iona, Columba was compelled to give sanctuary to any who sought it, be he king, exile, or criminal. It was monastic law; sacrosanct, inviolable. This man gasping in the sand at his feet, this Black Hugh, once king of the Dal n'Araide in Hibernia, was all three.

"Sanctuary?" Columba cried. "No! No! Never."

## · 3 ·

# GARTNAIT son of DOMELCH

L ike ghosts, they would come at him unawares. With Domelch, it was strange recollections that haunted him, the oddest memories. A cautious laugh through the partition of his bedchamber would suddenly become his fierce former wife's, not the servant girl's to whom it rightly belonged. He could never catch sight of small daggers but that she also sprang to mind. Even as innocuous a thing as a sea eagle, the noble totem of his beloved kindred, was now inextricably linked with the creamy skin of her inner thigh.

She had had the last tattoo inked there on purpose: he could not now think of himself without thinking of her.

*Witch*, he would remember laughing.

And Gartnait? For Aedan, the memories of the son he had been forced to leave behind in Caledonia were even more visceral, almost impossible to bear: his remembrances less specific in their detail but more cruel in their toll. When Bran and Finn were born and he became a father again, it was like a torture. Their precious tiny hands and feet. Little toes spreading, fingers flexing. Their impossibly-smooth skin. How they gurgled as they followed his movements with learning gazes. How their hairless, unblemished heads fit in the palms of his hands. How anyone could snap them in two.

It got worse as Bran and Finn grew. They'd be running or shouting or wrestling, they'd turn in the courtyard and for a moment it was Gartnait's face he'd see, superimposed on one of theirs like a vying spirit; usually Bran's since he was dark in demeanor like Gartnait, but sometimes Finn's, who shared Gartnait's vivid spark of life. To see three where there were only two was like grieving the death of someone still alive.

With all his heart Aedan had hoped to see his Pictish wife and child again before he died. But the chances had been slim. Few kings, either here in Dal Riata or anywhere, survived more than a few years into their reigns. He did not know of a single *ruiri* who had died peacefully in his bed.

That was the way of things, and Aedan was a pragmatic man.

Which is not to say the ghosts did not creep in.


And which is why he stood there dumb with joy. Here she was: small and dark and spare, as free-spirited and imperious as the day he had first met her, hurtling through the underbrush of wild Glen Mor, in flight and in the guise of a slave. But Domelch, daughter of Bridei, king of the Caledonian Picts, had never been anyone's slave, and the look she bestowed on the Scots who had assembled in the Great Hall to gawk had all the hauteur one might expect of the daughter of so great a lord.

The mood was as tightly-wound as Aedan had ever felt it, like the strings of an unseasoned harp about to played for the first time—and more than likely, broken. They had a brand new king, untested. And that king had just allowed—indeed welcomed!—Picts into his hall! Picts! A thing no other king of Dal Riata had ever done. Quite likely a thing no other king of Dal Riata had ever even imagined.

He would have laughed had the situation been less absurd—or of someone else's making.

The Pictish house-guard felt this too and had taken up a defensive position around Domelch and Gartnait. The Picts had been stripped of their arms at the door, as was custom—all save Drust, who had coolly refused. He stood calmly, with a seeming disinterest, but Aedan knew from deep experience that his brother-in-law could spring into lethal action from a dead stop. The unknown mage, whom Aedan could now see had a most remarkable streak of white hair at his temple, was trying to keep Domelch safely behind him, with no luck. Domelch stood her ground, glowering at them all. It was so like her that Aedan felt like grinning.

Aedan looked for his other sons, found Artur and Bran and Finn halfway between the Scots and the Picts, unsure where to place themselves now that their father had the right to stand before them all. He would have welcomed them up but the mood was too chancy. The boys were gaping at their newfound half-brother with as much ill-concealed suspicion as astonishment. Gartnait, meanwhile, had eyes only for Aedan.

Aedan looked around for someone to take control of the situation before heated tempers flared into bloodshed—Eogan maybe?—but realized with a shaky chuckle that that someone would have to be him. They had acclaimed him king for just this sort of occurrence, to foresee a solution where others couldn't.

And, thankfully, he did know what to do. There was only a handful of men and women in this hall who knew the customs of both peoples here, as well as both their tongues. He was one of them.

The question was: could he get them to speak to one another?

"My people!" he began.

They quieted down, ready to be persuaded, to be turned, to be led; a hopeful start.

He got no further. At just that moment, Afrella, his British chief-wife whom he had not seen in nigh on a month, came barreling into the hall, her skirts in her fists and fury on her normally timid face. With her was her handmaiden Covna, the comely Hibernian girl Aedan and Columba had rescued from the randy old Pictish mage

Broichan.

The women had taken time to dress Afrella in her best attire, to render her as beautiful as they could: this was her first occasion as *rìgain* of the company. It quickly became apparent that they had tried too hard. Afrella wore a creamy-white shift overlaid by a tunic the color of daffodil flowers. It was the right choice, given the nature of the festival Beltane, which was a way to welcome in the spring, but the light-green cloak clasped at her neck was too heavy and the pin holding it in place was both overlarge and too ornate, as were her other jewels. Long, snaky earrings caught in the bunched sides of her hood, and chunky armlets rode her slim forearms hard.

All in all, too fussy, too belaboured. Also surely stifling, in this rare April heat. He felt for her: her frantic show of finery overwhelmed her petite frame and nondescript face. It spoke of anxiety, not power.

It was all made worse by her high temper. She pushed her way to his side and rounded on the assembly. Just in time, Aedan grabbed her by the wrist. She was about to overbalance the very little control he actually had here. She glared at him, ready to shout, but he held on, loosening his hold a bit but conveying with a firm shake of his head that he needed her help, not her ire. Their sons were there, right in the middle of that volatile mix. Couldn't she see?

To her credit, she could. She bit back what she had been about to say.

Turning his hand to hold hers rather than restrain it, he faced the crowd and took a deep breath. "My friends! My people! All our *cenela*! Every one of you! Welcome to my hall!"

There were uneasy stirrings at his words but as yet no outright opposition. He would have taken that as a minor victory except that he knew the reason: now that he had welcomed them formally, they could all eat and drink to their hearts' content for the next three nights and three days, the duration of the Beltane feast—and all at his expense. (The problem of how he was to afford it all having been left for another day … )

He plowed ahead. "Also welcome are these Caledonii, who are

my friends … "

Now murmurs began to bubble up.

He ignored them; pressed on. "Who are, indeed, my family."

That disturbed them. He raised a hand, was amazed to achieve a modicum of calm through the rumbles of unease.

"This is Domelch, daughter of Bridei, king of the Caledonii. My wife."

There were roars, looks of derision leveled at Domelch. Afrella tried to yank her hand from his, but he grimly held on.

"This is Gartnait. Our son."

That brought down the rafters. A shudder ran all the way through Afrella. The Pictish house-guard bristled; Drust's grip tightened on his sword.

Aedan raised his voice, used the tone of command that on the battlefield would bring near-instantaneous compliance. Because otherwise people would die. "It is Beltane at which we have come together! Remember that! Beltane! Remember that, on such a festival, while under my hospitality and in my hall"—he punctuated his ownership of these things with a glare—"there is a prohibition on many things: on abduction, on theft, on the levying of debts. But most especially on violent behavior! Of any kind! I forbid it! Our god Belenos forbids it!"

Afrella's hand shook with outrage in his. He looked at her, comprehended; added, "The Christ does also".

The crowd had calmed down somewhat but not nearly enough. Luckily, if the threat of the displeasure of two gods could not sway them, he knew something that would.

"My people! These honored guests?" He was shouting now. "They are under my protection. They are under the protection of me, your over-king. Do you hear? Every man, every woman, that boy. Every Pict here. They belong to *me*."

He repeated this in Caledonian, for good measure.

At last, a wary silence descended. As it should. Not for nothing was it said that the honor-price of a king was too high to be claimed against. If anyone here were to be foolish enough to harm anyone he had just put under his personal protection in any way, they would have to pay Aedan his own honor-price, the honor-price of a *ruiri*—a sum he knew not even one of them could afford, since he couldn't either.

*And then they'd pay with their life.*

Aedan nearly laughed. Domelch was about to strike him—here, before the whole company. The delicate muscle under her right eye jumped, as sure a sign as any of the violence of her emotion. As overjoyed as he was to see her—her rich raven hair, braided tightly about her head for travel, the blue swirls inked onto her cheeks, the fierce intelligence of her alert face being in every way as he remembered them—he could not ignore the fury that was etched onto every inch of her slight frame.

There was no doubt: she was about to strike him. And, under other circumstances, he would consider letting her. But he was *ruiri* now, and all this was unfolding as a spectacle the likes of which his people had never seen. And of course Domelch was realizing this too. She was a Pictish princess through and through, the daughter of a great king. She knew better than to shame him in front of anybody Aedan had later to lead, for the sake of their son Gartnait, if not Aedan himself.

Unless of course she no longer cared for him. Unless he was unforgiven.

With bated breath he waited to see what she would do, until by force of will she softened the fierceness from her face. Her dark eyes remained steely, but the corner of her mouth tipped up into the semblance of a smile.

He bent his head and kissed her mouth in welcome. Though this was a formal gesture meant for the benefit of the rapt crowd, he gentled his own mouth, hoping she might intuit his true regard.

He risked a few moments of private speech, quietly using the Caledonian he had perfected while a hostage of her father. "Domelch! It gladdens my heart to see you at last!"

"Does it?"

"I have missed you."

Though her face remained regally still, her eyes lit up with surprise. Her head tilted infinitesimally. "You lie," she said.

He was sputtering out a denial when she stopped him. "It hardly matters," she said. "Had you returned, you would never have been allowed to cross my threshold."

Now she was the one lying. He could tell because she wasn't looking at him, but at some indeterminate point over his shoulder. He didn't contradict her, however: she despised any show of weakness, most especially her own.

Aedan was acutely aware of all the eyes watching their reunion with a morbid fascination. The crowd was beginning to grow uneasy again. Afrella was bristling. Her handmaiden Covna had stepped forward belligerently in mute protection of her mistress. But he had one more thing to ask Domelch before releasing her—something he very desperately needed to know. "Did having him, did having Gartnait with you … "

His eyes sought out their son, a watchful, self-possessed figure who seemed much older than his nine years. "Did it give you comfort?"

When she gave a curt nod of her black-braided head, relief flooded through him.

Domelch stepped back, setting her shoulders as she let her gaze wander imperiously over the room before coming to rest on Afrella.

A cruel smile crept up Domelch's mouth. "Is that her? The one who has your heart?"

Aedan winced. Domelch had switched to Scottish. And was speaking loudly. Very loudly.

Afrella gasped, then glared at Aedan, waiting for his defense.

"This is Afrella, Lady of Guined, my chief-wife," Aedan replied with as much dignity for Afrella as he could muster. "Rigain, the queen of Dal Riata."

"Ah!"

Domelch turned her back to Afrella. "She is *not* the one who

45

has your heart," she said to Aedan. "Good. I expect better of you."

She had switched back to Caledonian. Some mercy on her part? "Domelch … "

"Please! Do not tell me that she is a *good woman*. Many women are good women. That one is without fire—which she would withhold from you in any case, had she had any. I suspect you have wronged her. Badly."

He winced again.

"Am I wrong? No. I am not wrong on either count. She is beneath you."

A wicked cock of her head, a long glance at the vee of his trousers; a coy smile. "Or perhaps she is not beneath you, and that is why she is without fire?"

With another toss of her head, Domelch dismissed Afrella, and Aedan's union with her.

"Come now," she said to him. "Come and meet your son."


Gartnait had put on his princely self. He was the heir-apparent of the Caledonii, in audience with the over-king of Dal Riata.

A man who also happened to be his father.

In the quiet of the antechamber to which they had repaired alone, he studied the tall man before him. Black eyes and brows, shoulder-length black hair, a straight nose. A strong face in which Gartnait recognized many of his own consolidating features. Intelligent. Kingly. He might even say kind. His father wore all the accouterments one expects of a king but, strangely, without the ostentation. Leather breastplate, obviously well-used; finely-decorated, but not new (so it will move seamlessly with him when he fights, Gartnait realized, like an additional layer of skin). Long, elegant but deadly-looking great sword; a two-hander, heavy (it takes real strength to yield such a man-killer, or so Uncle said). Short sword at the belt for good measure, and no doubt another one hidden in his boot. A dark-colored cloak and tunic, trews and boots, all of which looked as if they had been on his father for days. (Ah! The

stains of travel, from days on the hoof and nights by the fire! Their
traveling party had surprised him and he had not had time to change
his clothes as a king ought to when welcoming very honored guests.)

It added up to an arresting figure: a man who did not need to
seek to impress, the man in the room you would instinctively turn
to were the door being hacked open by brigands. Or by … Picts. It
was how Gartnait supposed a king should look. How he hoped he
would look, when he became king.

His father was staring back, his gaze so intense Gartnait had
to fight the urge to squirm. Instead, he reminded himself to focus
on how his father's appraisal was making him feel. His mother had
taught him to do this: to look deeply when taking the measure of a
person, to look deeply not so much at the mask being presented to
him by the other, for that can deceive, but within himself. To focus
not on what the eyes saw, but on what the body felt, for between
the body's response and the knowing soul there can never be falsity.

Remarkably, under his father's penetrating gaze, Gartnait did
not feel himself judged. Part of this was that he had no fear that his
father would find him wanting. Gartnait wanted for nothing. There
was nothing lacking in either his abilities or his character. He had
been raised since his infancy to be a leader of men, all faults quickly
unearthed and expunged. Mother expected the best of him and the
best was what he gave.

But more so it seemed to him that his father did not expect to
find him wanting, that he knew he would find something in him
worth his admiration even though, for all intents and purposes, they
had only just met.

*That's what she has always said. There is something extraordinary about
my father. Something that makes people come to love him—even our people, who
intended to boil him in the Cauldron of Rebirth as sacrifice.*

*She said:* it is because he loves them first.

As if his father had read his thoughts, he reached out to touch
Gartnait's face. His hand hung between them for a moment, then
dropped.

*Good! I am not a child to be caressed! I shall be king of the Caledonii!*

But his father was looking at him so sadly. "Gartnait," he finally said, in a fluid and lilting Caledonian which retained only a trace of accent. "I am sorry that I couldn't—that I didn't—come for you." Yes

This statement astounded Gartnait. It was not how he expected his father to begin. And Gartnait did not know what to say next because what he was feeling quite fiercely was: *I didn't need you! I didn't miss you! I didn't want you!*

His anger frightened him. He hadn't known that some part of him was furious at this man. He said, "It's alright. Mother explained".

His father's eyebrow shot up, and then the corner of his mouth. "I bet she did."

Unwillingly, Gartnait felt laughter bubble up in his chest. However, he didn't yet feel like being friendly towards his father, so he did not let it out. "Other boys had fathers," he said. "I shall be *king*." This wasn't the truest expression of his feelings just then, but he said it anyway.

His father flinched. Then he nodded sharply. His hand came up again to touch his face, but stopped.

"Is it enough?" his father asked.

There were tears in his eyes.

Tears! For some reason it felt suddenly to Gartnait that the earthen floor underfoot, the floor of his father's Great Hall, was collapsing from under him.

*He longed for us?* It had never occurred to him.

Gartnait's thoughts came rapidly then, a volley of fire-arrows across the sky, some hitting their mark, some missing widely, some glancing off and skittering away. *Is it enough? Is it enough that he wanted me with him? Is it?*

*He asks this as if he had had a choice.*

*There was no choice. Was there? Mother said there was no choice. Grandfather said. My people …*

*This man is a king? The over-king of Dal Riata? He looks so fragile at this moment, as if he might break. As if I could break him.*

*If this were a battlefield and he were my enemy, I would. This is the point at which I would take him. He has made himself vulnerable to me.*

48

*Where was he all this time? All this time I didn't know that I wanted him. I didn't know until now.*

There was a long moment of awkward silence. Gartnait had no idea what to say next. Finally, his father asked, "Did you get the things I sent you?"

The short blade. The round shield. The bow and arrows and spear. Weapons. *Scottish* weapons.

"Yes."

"Have you trained with them?"

"Yes."

"Good."

"I can kill Scots now."

His father winced. "Actually, I was hoping they would make it more difficult for Scots to kill *you.*"

*Oh.*

A long breath from his father. "But you've outgrown them, clearly."

Not quite a nod.

"I'll get you more. Larger gear. For a young man. We'll visit the smithy tomorrow."

Gartnait found this almost impossible to understand. "Why would you, if I am the Great Slayer, the *Ferbasach?*"

His father startled. Then his eyes narrowed and his lips thinned.

His father was displeased. Yes. This was the crux of the problem for Gartnait. This was why he had consented to come with Mother and their people on this mission; also why he had asked to speak with Father alone, a request that Mother had honored without liking it in the least.

"You want me to not be the Great Slayer of the Scots? To not kill them?" he asked his father. "Is that it? Are your people worth *redeeming?* This is the word Mother and Uncle use. Grandfather? He uses different words. But Mother and Uncle? They love you. They want you and your people *redeemed.* So, should you be? Or should you be culled? Exterminated? Driven from Alba, never to return? Grandfather goes back and forth on it. But he is getting old. I think

49

he too comes to want peace."

He had surprised his father with his speech. Gartnait continued, squaring his shoulders in the way Mother would do when she intended to have her way. "Since I will one day not only be king of the Caledonii, but the *Ferbasach* of the prophecy, I have come to see for myself whether or not this is something for which I should also wish."

There. He had said it. It was out in the open at last. But how would his father respond?

He watched closely for his father's reaction, surprised that he also suddenly craved his father's good opinion. Where had that come from?

But it was more than that. What he had just revealed to the man before him he had not yet admitted even to his mother. This was the first time he had spoken the words aloud. Were these worthy thoughts, he wondered, thoughts he should keep hold of and let grow?

For they were novel thoughts. Dangerous thoughts. Liberating. His mother and uncle wanted peace with the Scots, cohabitation. His grandfather, as well as grandfather's foster-father the mage Broichan and most of their people, wanted the Scots dead. And both sides looked to him to make their desires so.

But he had decided to throw off the role of the unquestioning heir to the Caledonian throne. He would no longer be that biddable puppet-prince. He would make up his own mind.

*And if you do not like it, father of mine, then tell me now. Reveal your true self to me now.*

He held his breath as he waited for his father to speak. Which side would his father advise that he take? Which desires of his father would he be required to make so? Perhaps his father's own side?

"Gartnait. Son. Let no one thrust upon you a prophecy which is not to your liking—ever."

*What?*

Gartnait's head spun and he faltered for a response. "But I *am* the *Ferbasach*."

50

"Are you?"

"Yes."

Of course he was. Wasn't he?

"I'm not sure," his father said after some hesitation. "I'm honestly not sure. You know, they thought it was me. Your grandfather certainly thought so, or did, until you came along."

"But, Father, you know what it says. It says …

A son of the clan of the Shadow
will take the kingdom of Alba by force of strength.
a man who will feed ravens, who will conquer in battle:
*Ferbasach* will be his name …

After the slaughter of Picts,
after the harassing of Foreigners,
many years in the sovereignty of Alba.

Gartnait shrugged. "You are the *Shadowed One*. That much has been made clear. And I am your son."

"Yes. That is what it says. But is that what it means? I don't know. It's a foul logic. I can tell you I want nothing to do with it."

"You don't?"

Who wouldn't want power? Glory? Renown?

"I don't, son. Honestly, I don't. Chasing down glory gets in the way of other things, or so I have found. Like love. But that's not really the point. This is about you. Do you want it to be you? Because, the thing is, I don't think that damned prophecy need be fulfilled by either of us. It needn't be fulfilled at all."

This was entirely new. Ignore the prophecy? Could that be done?

Gartnait had never known a day without it. He was the *Ferbasach*. He was the Great Slayer. No other but him.

He would probe further. He had lived with this understanding of himself for far too long to let it go without question. "It is me," he said. "Everyone says it is. Mother. Grandfather. Uncle. The mages. They all want it for me. Why don't you?"

His father's hand shot out, gripped his shoulder so hard it nearly hurt. His voice cracked like a whip: "I wouldn't wish that burden on anyone, especially you".

Gartnait jumped. His head reeled. It had never been even remotely suggested to him that he had a choice in the matter. It was simply who he was.

His thoughts scattered again, came to rest on the sensation of his father's hand on his shoulder, now warm and steadying. It felt good there.

"Father," he said. "I tell you, many of our people do not want peace with the Scots. No, I under-represent there, so as to be kind to you. *Most* of our people fear and hate you. And why should they not? Nobody invited you to our Caledonia. But you came, and you took, and you take. You take our lands. You enslave us. You with your strange new god! And you are not going home again. But some of our people do want peace, like Mother and Uncle and Taran, Mother's friend … "

"Her friend? Do you mean the mage? The one with the strangely-striped hair?"

"Yes. That one. Taran. Taran preaches peace. He does not like to make war, which is not very Pictish. They hate him for it, and also because he's a pompous ass. They want him dead in fact, but he's been our royal hostage for years now so no one's been able to get to him. But lately they've been trying harder. Not two weeks ago, at The Craig, someone tried to assassinate him again."

"With no luck?"

"No. Mother got her knife in first. She usually does. So he has journeyed here with us, to get as far away from The Craig as possible."

Then an idea came so suddenly to Gartnait that he took it for inspiration, the voice of the gods which all his life he been trained to listen for and to heed, if he could. "You know, Father, he'd be safe here, in exile with you."

This took his father completely by surprise. "Is this something your mother wants?"

52

"I don't think it has occurred to her. But he would be safe, here with you, wouldn't he?"

His father was silent for a time. Finally, he said, "Your people did not harm me, when I lived amongst them".

"True. But you were married to Mother then. And no one crosses Mother."

His father burst out laughing, his grin blinding.

Something hot flashed in Gartnait's chest. Surprisingly, it felt like admiration. The start of affection. It felt good, and he smiled.

"Will you come, Father," he said, "and meet Taran, and tell me if you can give him sanctuary?"

# · 4 ·
# AFRELLA

"Get rid of them! At once!"

Aedan had expected Afrella's displeasure of course, and had brought her to their sleeping quarters so as to receive the full brunt of it in private, but this was different. His chief-wife was not the sort to allow herself to confront anyone outright. She had never dared: she had been taught to bide. Rather than to attack full on, she jabbed from the side or from behind; usually after the fact and cryptically.

But now she was spitting with anger. Her teeth were bared and wisps of hair had escaped from their tight braids to fly about her face. Aedan had never seen her so passionate, so embittered, so unhinged.

It was remarkable. Beautiful, even.

"You," Aedan said to the hovering handmaiden, Covna. "Out." Oddly, the girl looked as if she might disobey him but then she came to her senses.

"Send them away?" he asked Afrella once Covna had left. "You would ask that of me? You would have me deny my own son?"

Afrella's face contorted with resentment. "Another son! Yet another son of whom I knew nothing! Dunchad! Artur! And now this one from this ... this *Pictess*! How many more have you? How many more sudden sons will you have me endure?"

Endure? That rankled; he could not lie. Yet he tried not to find too much fault with her feeling. He too marveled at the convoluted paths his life had taken. His was not a straightforward destiny, and it required a great deal of forbearance and understanding on the part of any woman who would be his wife. However, he could find desperate fault with her logic, and her memory. She had known about Gartnait before their marriage. Gartnait's existence had been no secret—indeed the making of a son had been the point of Aedan and Domelch's union. The Caledonii had known. Aedan's whole kindred had known; all the Scots. By the gods, even the Britons had heard of Gartnait! Afrella knew this better than anyone.

He tried to find communion with her. "I am sorry it has happened this way," he said. He wanted to add, *sorry that you were demeaned before our people today*, but he did not wish to further wound her pride.

She was not appeased. "Sorry for the way it has happened! Not that it has happened!"

"Afrella! All this took place long before you and I met."

Her mouth grew tight. "You should never have been there! Why were you there? What man, what Scot, lays with the enemy? The *pagan* enemy?" She shuddered. "With that ... that pagan whore of the Picts?"

"That's convenient," he said, with much more heat than before. "It was because I had 'lain with that pagan whore of the Picts' that your father, the mighty king of the Britons of Guined, forced you on ... "

*Forced you on me.*

"Engineered our marriage," he amended quickly.

But not quickly enough. Horrified comprehension flooded her face.

He tried to find a sense of shame for the thought, but couldn't.

However unpalatable, it was the truth. And it was self-serving of her not to admit it.

Be that as it may, he had no wish to hurt her. "Afrella," he said, "you know this. Your father wanted an alliance with the Picts. He wanted something no other British king had. Why else would he have married you to me? You are a lady of Guined! You are very high in the world. And I am … I was nothing. I was possibly useful, and I was … novel. And the cause of that novelty waits for me now in the hall. I will not send them away."

He had been waiting years to be with his first family again. Years. It took little imagination to see the miracle in the reunion, no largeness to feel wonder and gratitude on his behalf.

But Afrella was not the sort to look beyond herself to celebrate another's joy. This saddened but did not surprise him: she had never been large of heart. UNLIKE JIVI!

He was turning to leave her. Again.

Afrella could not bear it. She screamed out in rage. Lunging at Aedan, she grabbed his cloak and pulled back on it hard. He tried to shrug her off, but she dug in her heels and grimly held on.

They had been wed over seven years now and she felt no closer to him, no more loved or wanted or needed by him, than she had on their wedding night. Even after serving him and his strange kin loyally, after taking the blows of his neglect and disinterest without complaint, time and again. After giving him two fine flourishing sons.

It was the sight of the Pictess that had set her off, his tender reunion with the woman who had given him the son with whom he had learned those paternal skills with which he now so effortlessly bound all his sons to him with love.

A love she stood firmly outside of.

"What is it?" Aedan snarled.

His tone startled her. She had been willing to be contrite, to make amends. Her earlier demand had been something of a test. If only he would move towards her, she might find her balance again. But there was disgust in his eyes.

"What is it? What is it? I am your legitimate wife! Your only legitimate wife! I am the *rígain* of Dal Riata! Yet I am no more to you than one of your spoils!"

The strength of her pain was too much. She fell to her knees and clawed at her clothes—her gorgeous, queenly clothes which he had not even acknowledged!—her cloak pin ripping off to spin into the reeds on the floor where it glinted forlornly in the candlelight. She pulled and tore at all the layers binding her until she reached her skin, her breasts spilling free of her tunic—breasts she so desperately wished for him to desire but which he failed even to see.

"Shall I render tribute to you now?" she cried. "Shall I render tribute to you with my mouth, my lord?" She grabbed for the tie to his breeches.

He slapped her hands away, yanked her to her feet. "Afrella!"

"We are no more than spoils to you!"

"Who is? What are you talking about?"

"We are! All your women!"

"All my women? I have only … "

He stopped himself.

*Ah. Damn it! That was the heart of it.*

*He had only one. And it was not her.*

He was keeping her from tipping backwards by the deathlike hold he had on her wrists, his fury-filled face inches from her own. The beautiful curve of his lips, so close, arrested her for a moment. Dear God, how she wished he would bring that mouth to hers and kiss her with even a tenth of the passion he had shown the strange Pictess this evening. If he could only do that, she might be whole again.

Or at least patched up enough to go on a while longer.

But he wouldn't, she knew. If possible, he had withdrawn even farther into himself.

"I am the daughter of the king of Guined!" she cried. "And I am the *rígain* of Dal Riata!" She pulled a hand free, jabbed at her bare

58

chest, her finger slamming into her breastbone with a dull insistent thud. "Me! Me! And I want her gone!"

"Who? Domelch?"

"Yes, her! But the other one too! That British bitch! I want her gone!"

He went completely still. His face shuttered close. The air between them chilled.

"Afrella. Don't."

"Why ever not? Ama is no lady of Rheged, but a whore!"

"Afrella … " His tone was careful, but she could hear the icy warning. She had gone too far.

But not nearly far enough to begin to feel better. "What is she then? She is unmarried! At your bidding, she lays with you! She is a whore!"

Yet even as she screamed these things, she knew his response: only the law sees Ama that way. Only the law, and Afrella's own Christian God.

Not him though. He sees her as his true wife. His true wife whom he would take in a heart's beat … save for an unwanted responsibility to me.

In her calmer moments, Afrella knew this. But generosity of spirit was so far beyond her at that moment that all she could do was rage and hope he could find it in his own heart to be generous enough for the both of them.

And damn him, he did. Which is why, in spite of it all, she still loved him so.

He released her. She rocked back on her heels and would have fallen but for his steadying hand on her elbow.

"Please," he said. "I don't wish to see you hurt."

"See me hurt?" Her own laugh was too shrill in her ears. It sounded as if it had come from someone else.

"Don't ask what you would ask of me."

"Why ever not?"

"On this you will lose."

Damn him! He said this as gently as he could.

And that was the truth of it, what she could not change no matter how she railed.

He does not want me. It is her that he wants.

It was in the way he looked at Ama. When he looked at her he seemed to come alive.

And it wasn't just Ama. It was Eithne too. He had loved her once. And the Pictess. There was love there as well.

Aedan had loved each of them in his own way.

*But not me. He has never loved me.*

There was a deep and terrible ache in her gut. It felt like fire and loss. She could have wept.

But she was done with weeping. What had weeping ever accomplished? Nothing. Nothing. It did not draw him in to care for and protect her, as it might another man. Rather, it repelled him.

So be it. She would give him the emotion to which he did seem to respond.

She drew herself up. Arms rigid at her sides, not caring that her clothes still hung awry leaving her breasts exposed to him, she commanded, "Give her up!"

She knew what his answer would be. Of course she knew. Nevertheless, she needed to say it. And she needed to hear his answer.

And, generous in all things, he gave her what she needed.

"Never," he said.


Covna had swept her up in her arms. The handmaiden was trying to rock her, but Afrella felt stiff, unyielding. She was not weeping.

"Ah, my poor lady! My poor dove," Covna crooned. "*Woe is to the one who must wait for love to come out of longing!*"

Afrella hardly heard. Something vital had shifted between her and her husband just now. She could feel it.

*Is it me,* she wondered suddenly? *He has not altered in his desires, his demeanor towards me; but we are not as we once were. I can feel it. So it must be me.*

I *have shifted.*

I *did that. It was not done to me. Rather, it was something* I *did.*

She searched her heart for the familiar feeling of sadness and longing that had so darkly cloaked her days since meeting him, but could not find it. She had cast it off.

Curious. Very curious. Why, in at last repudiating the man she loved so desperately, did she finally feel her own power?

Afrella thought about that as Covna rocked her and crooned; observed with a growing interest as an insidious little voice inserted itself into her clearing thoughts, weaving itself into the plaintive sound of the handmaiden's lament, murmuring, suggesting, rumbling, hissing, inciting: *now that I have power, what shall I do with it?*


If they did not come soon they would miss the lighting of the Beltane fires. Aedan felt a flash of worry: had some mishap befallen his friends?

He needed them here. Now.

He had desired solitude, some time to think. Afrella's boundless displeasure in their marriage always unsettled him. Her unabating grief left him feeling somehow unclean. Ignoble.

But tonight there had been a darker emotion tucked into the tail of it, uglier and much more worrisome. In the midst of her outburst, there in their bedchamber as he had watched her rage, trying impotently to find communion with her, it had suddenly occurred to him that this evening was the first time she had ever seen a Pict alive.

And they had repelled her.

Repelled her!

These people! These people, his family, in whom he could see only beauty and worth.

It was a hard truth, and it had stolen away his breath.

But there was worse.

His next revelation?

If she felt this way—and believed herself justified in feeling so—then so might everyone else.

*So might everyone else.*

All this time later, his head was still reeling. His heart still hurt. So, preferring to be alone, he had left the Great Hall as soon as he was able, Ceo bounding ahead, in order to find some respite from the crush. But his retinue had followed him, Sillan and Fraich and the others. More than a little inebriated, they were joking and jesting, their bawdy banter entirely disrupting the inner quietude he was craving.

Aedan let out a heartfelt sigh. It was their job to follow and protect him now wherever he went. He was king.

Nevertheless, he needed clear air and space. He would try to give them the slip. So, up he went, up past the guesthouse where they had lodged the Picts, until he had climbed the hillock that rose up at the far end of the top of the rock, opposite the Great Hall. Nearly as high that peak, there was nothing built on this one, it being too narrow to support more than one or two people standing. And indeed his men left him to it, either because in their current state they weren't up for the climb, or more likely because from that point there was nowhere he could go but down again, right past where they lay sprawled drunkenly on the ground. Besides, loyal Ceo was with him, should he need protection. They'd pick up their duties again on his way back down.

From the vantage point of that little peak, you can see all the way across the great moor to the harbor. So he and Ceo, who had sat herself at his side thoughtfully, gazing where he did, his hand at rest upon her massive head, looked. It was quiet and bright. A fine night for travel. Safe. Clear. Settled. The moon was rising fat and heavy over the water, warm creamy moonlight glinting on the waves so clearly it was like a road leading travellers out to sea. Tomorrow the harbor would begin to fill up with ships carrying the big men from all the neighboring kingdoms, those with whom, as king, Aedan must now treat. Tonight, however, there was only one particular little hide-covered *curragh* he wished to see coming down that sea-road, the one with the cross of the Christians sewn defiantly onto its sail.

But, as yet, nothing; so, to calm his thoughts, he rubbed his dog's ears and trained his eyes instead upon the emerging stars.

He always found reassurance in the constancy of the stars. Whatever the madness that was presently occurring down below, they continued to wheel overhead; a bigger wheel turning over the smaller one, the one upon which he dwelt.

It was always beautiful, when one looked up. Tonight, especially so. The sky was clear of clouds, the heavens strung with countless bright pricks of light that under one's questing gaze knit themselves together into forms, tremendously vast and readable.

They made stories; tonight, seemingly just for him. For instance, there was the Northern Crown, its four bright stars a radiant diadem. His?

Yes. And wasn't that a lovely accident? But, lest he get too comfortable, he reminded himself that his was just the latest crown. There had been countless others before his and there would be countless others after.

And there, the herdsman. Hard to miss, with his hunting dogs alongside. ("See? There you are, my love," he said to Ceo, pointing them out with a pat to her head.) Tonight he liked to think they were his herds, to serve that crown.

And of course, there was the maiden. *His* maiden. The latest to be adored by the man who wore the starry crown before the cosmic wheel turned again.

He chuckled. (Ceo glanced up: did he need her? He put a hand to her head: no.) How slyly appropriate. Didn't the gods like a good laugh!

A laugh he hoped was not at his expense.

He lowered his gaze to the horizon. There to the east were the towering peaks of Druim Alban. Quiet there: stars bursting above the bens.

Ahead: on the little hill of Dun Mor, where Ama was, light shining from her dwelling, the faintest flicker; a fire being tended, perhaps by her hand.

She was so close! But not right by his side, where he wanted her

63

to be.

He sighed, then chided himself. His heart was ever greedy, wanting more—he, who had been given so much!

Below, the valley at the foot of the fort was strung with its own net of lights, innumerable campfires mirroring the brilliant canopy overhead. A low thrum of merriment rose from the makeshift dwellings sparkling on the plain. As if in perfect agreement with the choice of him as king, everything had come together, on time, and with a noticeable exuberance. The lords were assembling. The cattle had been gathered. Today had been warm. Tomorrow, probably warmer. Even the hawthorn had begun to blossom in the hills, always an auspicious sign if it happened before Beltane.

His people would say that the Goddess was pleased—or that Columba's God was. Aedan smiled ruefully. He hoped that both were, and that they would bless the Beltane games, and all that would come after. The time of the greater sun beckoned, *an ghrian mor*, and the gateways between the worlds were opening. All had been made ready. The festival could commence. Tomorrow night they would light the new fire, the following day begin the games.

But not, he hoped, without his friends.

Sweeping his gaze around the valley one last time, his sacred charge, he repeated the prayer he had been trying to perfect these past two, challenging months: *It is time to come into my strength, to make manifest my desires. It is time to take the path of strength.*

*Please gods! Help me figure out what that is!*

Turning to go down to the guesthouse, his gaze was drawn back to the bright, flickering plain below, mesmerized. He looked up at the stars, down again.

It really was rather like a world with two heavens, one above, one below, and he balancing precariously on the shifting pivot in between, trying his very best not to fall off.

"Tell me," Aedan said to Domelch a little while later. "If I befriend your mage Taran, if I take him under my protection, then whom will

I make my enemy?"

"What do your eyes tell you?"

He found the mage Taran glowering at them, pacing, and studied him closely; saw the telltale signs easily enough: the fine clothes and plentiful, rather muscular silver jewelry; the imperious tilt of the head; the censorious frown between the brows; the way of looking at everyone else as if you expected them to heed. Those things spoke of authority, of high caste.

But what spoke loudest to Aedan was the man's remarkable parti-colored hair. It was altogether dark save for a vivid streak of pure white that rose up from his brow to sweep back over the crown of his head like the froth of a wave.

It was a rare mark, and it pulled Aedan back to The Fortress of the Bulls, on Caledonia's northern coast. To the sacred Well of the Bulls and its brutish, elemental, stone god. To that profane sacrifice he and Columba had been forced to witness, the royal hostage whom King Bridei of the Caledonii, Domelch's father, had killed in three ways: by drowning, beheading, and immolating. The sacred three-fold death.

That unfortunate man also had had remarkable, parti-colored hair. In his mind's eye, Aedan could still see the damning white streak floating on the water like a scream as the man went under with a cry of terror which no one but Columba had dared to try to aid.

That sacrificed man had been the brother of Uurad, the *regulus* of the northern isles of the Innsi Orc, an under-king whom Bridei was certain had betrayed him.

"Taran is the son of Uurad," Aedan said.

"Not the nephew?" Domelch asked. "Not the brother?"

"No. Not high enough. Knowing your father, after Uurad's betrayal no hostage but the man's son would satisfy."

Aedan was rewarded with Domelch's proud smile. She had always enjoyed testing him. She especially liked it when he passed one of her tests.

"So, Taran was sent to replace his uncle at your court as your father's royal hostage?"

"Yes. That was how Taran and I met."

She wouldn't look at Aedan when she said it. How unlike her! Gartnait had intimated that she cared for this Taran. Could it be true?

"So if I keep Taran," he asked, "would I make an enemy of Uurad … or of your father?"

The corner of her little mouth quirked up and her dark eyes danced.

"Or of both?" he amended.

She laughed. "Of both, certainly! If you take in Taran, Father will not like it. Not one bit. Nevertheless, I think Gartnait is right on this. My clever child! Father will be terribly angry though. Make no mistake."

"This is something you would risk?"

"It is not safe for Taran at court. If Taran dies whilst Father's hostage by any other hand than Father's own, it will mean war with Uurad. That is something we should all seek to avoid—even at the price of Father's fury."

She shot the mage a glance. It lingered longer than Aedan expected. "Also, hidden here," she said, "Taran might be safe."

*Curious.*

"Then there is Uurad," she said. "You will make no friend of Uurad if he discovers that it is you who has his son! He has already lost his brother to Father's wrath—that man you saw sacrificed in the Well of the Bulls. Uurad will not risk losing his son the same way. He has only the one son so Taran is precious to him. Once he knows Taran has escaped Father's court, Uurad will search for him high and low and try to reclaim him. What father would not?"

Everything Domelch was saying rang true. Aedan had never known Domelch's logic to falter, and it was faultless now. Except for one thing. "Once Taran is here, how do I know that he won't flee *me*? Were I he, I would. The first chance I got."

She laughed. "You would! You would indeed! As would I! In fact, as I have done. But I will talk to him. Make him swear an oath. Aedan—he is an honorable man. A peaceable man. A *good* man.

That is a rare thing."

"If he is so good, why the target on his back? Who is after him?"

She grimaced. "Some of my own people, I'm afraid. Good men are not always well liked. Others find their standards ... inconvenient. They don't wish to also be held to them."

There was truth in that. "Anyone else?" If he were to do this, he would need to know in which direction to keep watch for his enemies.

There was that scowl, that look of pure hatred which Domelch reserved for only one man.

"Galam Cennalath," Aedan answered for her. The over-king, the *mormaer*, of the other confederation of Picts, the Miathi. Just like Bridei, Galam Cennalath claimed supremacy over all the Picts, both his own Miathi and Bridei's Caledonii. Since Galam overruled four of the seven Pictish provinces, one more than Bridei, it was Galam's claim that Aedan had to credit.

"How many of these assassins have you stopped with your own knife?"

She smiled dangerously, her dark eyes glittering. "They no longer try while I'm around."

Yes. Well done.

"What is it about the islands of the Innsi Orc?" he asked. "Men? Metal? Grain?" The Innsi Orc had to be very important indeed to have secured the interest of not one but both Pictish over-kings.

"Men, of course. But, yes, you are right. It is primarily the grain. You wouldn't think so with the islands lying so very far to the north, but the land is flat, fertile. Bountiful. Much wealth is derived from the Isles of the Little Pigs."

Aedan nodded, taking it in. These were things that he, as king, now needed to know. In his travels through Caledonia as Bridei's hostage, he had never been allowed to get anywhere near the Innsi Orc. Now he knew why.

And then the true cunning of Gartnait's plan blossomed in Aedan's mind, as well as all the implications, the good and the bad. He could see it all unfolding: *holding Innsi Orc, overruling Uurad, siphoning off his grain, his men, is the thing keeping Bridei strong—perhaps the only thing keeping Bridei strong. It is what keeps his rival Galam in check. The Innsi Orc are the key.*

And the royal hostage Taran was the key to holding the Innsi Orc. On two accounts. If Taran died at Bridei's hand for some transgression, perceived or real, on his father Uurad's part, then Uurad would retaliate in one of two ways: he would do nothing; or he would protest.

Uurad would, however, be unlikely to openly revolt. After all, it would have been his betrayal that had caused his son to be sacrificed. Just as his brother had been. The matter would become a legal one, to be resolved before the mages. And then no doubt another royal hostage would be hauled off in chains to placate Bridei.

All that changed, however, if it was at Galam Cennalath's hand that Taran died. If that were to happen, if a Miathian assassin were able to sneak in, then all bets would be off. Uurad would openly attack Bridei for failing to protect his son's life—a retaliation that Bridei would wholeheartedly deserve. That was the price you paid for holding royal hostages at your court: you protected them, you educated them, you treated them as your own. You let them marry your daughters, if it came to that, or your sons. You might even come to love them.

Inwardly, Aedan laughed: who knew this better than he?

If Bridei failed to protect Taran, there would be war. A just war, as far as that was concerned. And into this war between Caledonia and the Innsi Orc, Galam Cennalath would happily step, offering his support to Uurad. Against such a combined force, Bridei would lose. He would lose the Innsi Orc, and the Miathi would take over the Caledonii once and for all.

Galam Cennalath would win. He would win everything.

And the mage Taran was the key.

The cascade of possibilities flowed forth in Aedan's mind, a likely sequence of events, a certain future, clear where to others it might be murky. Aedan had been trained since his boyhood to think

68

about war and he was very good at it; certainly the best he knew, besides his own brother Eogan, and Columba.

That his son Gartnait should also have worked this out for himself made Aedan suddenly and immensely proud.

With that in mind, Aedan forced himself to consider the problem not as Domelch's former husband but as the king of his people. A voice cautioned: *Isn't war between the two confederations of Picts something you should want? Shouldn't you want the Picts to suffer at one another's hands?*

*If they look only at one another, neither will look at you.*

"If you take Taran into your safekeeping, Galam Cennalath will come looking for him," Domelch warned. "He will come looking here. You should know that. That's what I would do."

Ah! Could he do it, Aedan wondered? Bring down upon Dal Riata the roving eye, the wrath, of the over-kings of the Caledonii and the Miathi, as well as the ruler of the Innsi Orc?

Such a chancy undertaking! Three irate kings.

*Surely that is something I should avoid.*

He said, "It is a cunning plan: to hide Taran with me—a man who is friend to none of them. You have taught Gartnait well".

She smiled a warm, intimate smile. "He is a worthy pupil, being also *your* son."

Their son. The most important piece of this puzzle.

"Taran must not die," Aedan said.

"No. He must not."

"Domelch ... you trust me with this?"

"I do."

"Why?"

She gave him a long look full of an old sadness and a longing. "You too are an honorable man. A peaceable man. That is very beautiful. And very rare."

It rose up again between them. The heat and the love.

"Aedan. You asked whom you would anger were you to do this. Now you know. It is not just my Father, and Uurad of the Innsi Orc. It is Galam Cennalath. You will be making an enemy of all three of them."

She shot another glance at Taran, said, "But you would be making an ally, a friend, of *me*".

*She does love him. How extraordinary.*

For that reason alone, he would do it.

But Domelch was not finished.

"And of our son. You will be making a friend of our son."

She took his hand. Her expression had cleared of everything except hope for the future. "There has been such enmity between our peoples, such fear and pain," she said. "And yet, you and I found a way to be at peace with one another. To love one another."

There was no hesitation on his part. "Aye, we did."

"Gartnait will soon rule. *Our son* will soon rule. We owe him the same peace—or at least a chance for peace. Do we not?"

# · 5 ·

# BELTANE

*First Night*

At last! Rowed with a steady purpose by its two cloaked oarsmen, the boat punted upriver from the harbor just in time. At the signal from the watchtowers, Aedan sprinted down the terraces and through the main gate to the dock below the hillfort to haul his brother into a heartfelt embrace.

"By the gods you had me worried! What happened to you? Why the hell are you so late?"

Eogan pulled back, eyebrow raised. "Such a welcome! Shall we leave again?"

"No, no!" Aedan studied his brother—the simple monkish attire; his long black warrior's hair cropped short, a prelude to the tonsure he would receive should he progress successfully to monastic orders; the noticeable contentment around the dark eyes which had for so long been pinched with unspoken pain.

He ruffled Eogan's hair; pulled a face. "At last—I am the more handsome!"

Eogan laughed. "Never! Even when it is entirely gone."

"What say you, old friend?" Aedan asked Columba.

"I agree."

"See?" Aedan said. "He agrees."

"Yes," Columba said. "I agree that *I* am the most attractive of this sorry lot."

They grinned at one another, slapped one another joyfully on the back. "Ah, it's good to see you!" Aedan said. "You must tell me everything! I want to know exactly what's been going on. You've got stories for me, I can tell! Good ones! We'll see if they're anywhere near as good as mine, because truth be told I may win this time! You will never guess who's here!"

"The Caledonii?" Eogan asked.

"What? Yes! Yes! But how can you know? Have your new monkish ways given you *the sight*?"

"They have, I am sure. But, lest you think me more discerning than usual: it's hard to miss their warship in the harbor."

Aedan laughed, then sobered. "I had feared … "

Eogan laid a gentle hand on Aedan's arm. "Of course they would come, Brother, once they heard. This is *you* we are talking about, after all. And I am happy for you—and eager to meet them at last. Nevertheless, I must say … what would Father have said? Picts *inside* our Dun Ad? And you, its defender, not only still alive but feasting them … and the Lord knows what else?"

Since this proclamation was uttered with his brother's customary sardonic grin, Aedan returned it with a similar lightness of heart. "Aye! Aye!"

"Aye … *what*? What else? Are you so happy to see that wife of yours again at last that you are in need of confession, Brother?"

Aedan slapped away his brother's hand, laughing. "Listen," he said to Columba. "There's the new-fire. Will you light it?"

Columba drew back. "Are your people ready for that?"

Aedan smiled ruefully. "A Christian priest to perform the sacred Beltane rite? They're as ready as they'll ever be—"

"—which is to say not at all," Eogan said.

"Precisely. So there's nothing for it but to get on with it. So, come up! Come up! Let's get it done."

For the first time, Aedan saw tension cross his brother's face, a covert look up at the king's bright hall on the height.

Aedan hesitated, stopped short of rendering physical comfort; said, "She's not here, Brother".

Eogan cast him a haunted look.

"She's at Dun Mor. She's safe."

Eogan gazed towards the little fortified dun on the horizon. He sighed, gave a stiff but relieved nod, and up they all went.

"This is my chief-priest, Colm Cille," Aedan exclaimed from the Plateau of the Kings to his assembled people, "who fetched his learning from Hibernia."

"As your Belenos is a God of Light, a Good God," Columba said, "so is my Christ. Yet it is my Christ who reigns supreme because he is not one aspect of God, but all aspects. Not just light, but dark as well. All things. It is he whom I will beseech to bless and strengthen the new-fire. It is he who will provide for and protect our herds as we take them to the high summer pastures, who will later bring meat and milk to our tables. All of creation rests in him. With him, we are safe. With him, we are loved."

There was a horn blast, then all the myriad sources of light on Dun Ad were extinguished. All the cooking fires, all the torches, all the candles, all the lamps. It was disconcerting to see the teeming hillfort so suddenly devoid of light, the only illumination coming from the now-full moon casting a path of white light on the sea, and rippling on the gentle river, and shining on the night pools in the marsh.

A hush fell over the hill. All eyes looked upwards.

Bodhrans began to beat, drums pounding out a primal rhythm. The insistent thrum would encourage the gates to the Otherworld to open so that the anointed ones, those who are holy, which had until recently been only the *druidi* but was also now priests like Columba,

73

could travel to the inner realms and converse there with the gods. Spells were incanted, both under breath in the old forms, and out loud in the new, and suddenly on the uppermost level of the fort, on the Plateau of the Kings, an enormous bonfire burst into flame: the divine spark called forth from no other source but the vigorous friction of dry wood, as had been humankind's very first made-flame. There on the summit the bonfire took hold greedily, surging forth to lick at the underbelly of the stars.

Then the fire was brought down from the Plateau, down the winding terraces of Dun Ad, on a torch held high by a white-robed Columba with Eogan alongside, all the way out of the massive main gates and then down, down, down, to cross the long plain to the standing stones of Dunamuck; a stately, measured, hopeful procession of a single flame. At either standing stone an enormous heap of wood had been piled and these Columba ignited while he sang out prayers. When the flames had grown higher than a man, encouraged by wild, loud, ebullient chanting by the people, the animal pens were opened and the cattle were driven out. With people lining the way, many deep and singing, there was only one path for the terrified beasts to take, and that was straight to the fires.

There the bellowing, stampeding, frightened cattle were herded between the flames.

They did this to stop plague and other diseases that might have fastened onto the hides of the cattle while they were closed-in over the winter. The fire would burn it right off them. And to prevent the little folk from drawing off the cows' milk when they now went to pasture. The sheep and the goats were also driven through until all the animals were thoroughly cleansed.

When all the precious livestock had been driven between the sacred fires, everyone carried home a glowing stick of tinder with which to rekindle their own hearths. And this they did one-by-one, moving slowly upwards until strings of lights netted the hill and all of Dun Ad was ablaze again with the new flame.

74

"What are our chances?' Columba asked Eogan as the people dispersed.

"That Aedan will let you baptize him?"

"Yes."

"None."

Columba grumbled. "He should convert. It would send the proper message to his people."

"They know his message to them."

Looking at his brother work his way towards them through the crowd, Eogan could see it. Aedan was a man in his prime. Not so young that mere impulse might sway him. Not so old as to refuse to take chances. There was a seasoned vitality to him; a wisdom he carried on his shoulders like his new kingly robes. He was a man who had weathered many storms, to whom others looked instinctively to steer their course. He had conquered turbulent seas and knew the way: the uncharted trackways across the waves.

He is a new start, Eogan thought. He himself is that message, the symbol of the hope of their deliverance.

And he could chart that course because of the light made by the new star in the heavens—the one presently standing beside him grumbling.

"Am I not prize enough?" Eogan joked to Columba just to rile him, because he found it amusing. "You have already got yourself a king."

That earned him a quick, hard, affectionate smile. But the inner gaze was still far away.

"Don't let greed for new Christian souls get the better of you, my friend," Eogan said. "Remember his promise to you: he will protect you, and bring you new lands and new people if he can—though what they decide to do with you is up to them: he won't force them. That's quite a lot. That's more than you'd get from most. Surely that's enough?"

Eyes on her target, Eithne hurried to catch him as he was going up to the Great Hall. She would get him to listen. If there was one thing she could count on, it was Aedan's loyalty to his kin, even those who had betrayed him, as she had.

"My lord," Eithne began, catching his sleeve to stop him in his tracks.

He turned. Recognition flared in his eyes "*My lord?*" he asked with a smile that was welcoming but reserved. "That's new."

"Aedan." She changed her grip from his sleeve to his hand. Surprisingly, he let her take it.

How to begin? How to get him to see?

"Do you remember … " she began, but just as quickly faltered. She berated herself. Where was her usual courage?

Sadly, she knew the answer: gone with her son to the grave. She had not been herself for many months.

This was what she needed him to see, since her survival depended upon it. And indeed, he was looking at her kindly enough, but was holding himself very still as if he expected to be hurt by her.

She tried not to be offended by that. Indeed, it was not so very unexpected. She had wounded him. A lot. And badly. At the same time, she needed him to remember that it was she who had taught him that the making of love could be pleasurable. Despite the lessons she was given of it as a child.

That thought often amazed her: how remarkable it was that she had been able to later find joy in an act that had hurt.

"Do you remember how it was between us?" she asked.

He hesitated, then said, "I do".

Who could not? How wonderful it had been to be joined, the two of them. Their untried bodies, hard and soft at the same time. The heat of the barn. Their eager mouths. How very young they had been. That she could not get enough of him, so gentle, so loving, so beautiful. The way his skin had leapt to her touch. And everything leisurely and sweet and shy, as if they had all the time in the world before them, which of course they had not.

"I remember too," she said. "All the time. It has never left me, even after you went away."

A chill came between them. He withdrew his hand. "Eithne," he said. "Please. Remember the other part too. Remember it rightly. I did not 'go away'. *You* left *me*."

She could not contradict him. It was both true, and changed nothing. In fact, if she had to make the choice again, she would do the same, even knowing what it had cost her. How could she not? As much as she had loved Aedan, Conall had been king. He was her way up and out.

But all this was old ground, well-trodden. She needed him to see the new, the one before them now.

And perhaps he did see it, because he was saying, more gently then she deserved, "It's not that I don't understand. I do. I understood then. But what is this about now?"

Here it was at last. She screwed up her courage, said, "Now, you give that to *her*".

He studied her briefly, coldly. Said, "Yes. And?"

She shrugged. She was so sad that it took effort to speak. "And he's dead," she said. "They're all dead."

A sharp stab of sorrow crossed his face. Their son Dunchad.

He grabbed her hand again, gripped it hard.

Her chance was now. He was feeling compassion for her, rather than anger or bitterness. "Would you ..." she asked. "Do you think you could you take me in?"

There was surprise in his dark eyes. "As ... what?" he asked carefully.

"I could make you love me again," she said.

"Eithne ... " he said, his expression pained. He was trying very hard not to hurt her.

Too late.

The crushing sorrow came flooding back, the grief she had tried to hold at bay with this one last gambit.

"Eithne ... "

"No. Don't," she said, giving in at last to the darkness that had been stalking her since Dunchad's death. "I can see that you would not wish it back. Because of her."

"Because of many things. But yes, because of her."

She looked down and away. "Then what is to become of me I do not know. How am I to get on? They are all dead. All dead. And I belong to no one." *Important for a woman then*

Over the course of that day, the aching sadness of that meeting was to haunt him, not to be lifted again until the morning when the hubbub of the gathering woke him with a pulse of energy in the air.

He was soon fizzing with it. He couldn't have brooded longer if he wanted to: it was Beltane, the first day of May, and the start of three days of feasting and games. Aedan pushed aside the rowan twigs that had been set at the doors to all the dwellings to counter the mischief of the fairy folk to find that everything had been festooned with garlands of green leaves and bright, fragrant hawthorn blooms. The young maidens were on their way out, skipping lightly down the terraces to wash their faces in the dew at dawn, the dew which was neither rain nor sea-water, nor river nor well-water, but took up the blessed space in between those things, that shimmering state of flux. Would they meet their love this year they wondered, giggling? Would their fresh youthful beauty, the allure of the bud of the rose, bring them a true heart? *A Threshold*

The young ones on their way down, the others coming up in crowds to the Plateau of the Kings to hail the sunrise, to fetch in the month of May; to see the sun welcome in the coming summer.

All these things they do at Beltane's dawn because it is a door.

As soon as the sun began its dance with a stab of light over sacred Druim Alban, the cooling bannocks were brought out from under cloaks. On his flat oatcake, and the ones he handed to Aedan and Eogan, Columba had inscribed the cross of the Christians. Some of the people had followed suit. Others promised their bannock to Belenos and for that they used the Sun God's spiral. Then they threw bits of their cake over their shoulders as an offering to the eagles and the foxes and the wolves and any who would harm the herds. The rest of the bannocks they rolled down the hills. If the cakes broke, or did not roll far, or landed with the marked side up, misfortune was foretold. If not, then fortune would be good.

With prayers for his family and his people, Aedan tossed his bits of cake, then bent and gently rolled the better part of his bannock down Dun Ad's steepest slope, wondering what it would divine when it came to rest at the bottom of the hill.

It was his hill after all: would the cake dare to prophesy any kind of doom on a day such as this? *yes it would !*

It was a wonderful day, a carefree, happy day. The horse races on the plain: hoofs pounding, turf clods flying, bets lost and won. Rousing games of the beloved ball game *baire*: sticks clashing, the young men, bare-chested, glorious, and grunting, striving to score, to win themselves a wife from the adoring crowd. The contests of strength, of horsemanship, of wrestling, of archery, of fighting, of draughts. The trading, the bartering, the measuring of cloth for trueness against the marks on the standing stones of Dunamuck where they hold the tryst. Everyone in high, fine moods; everyone drunk on the bright promise of Aedan's new reign; and even the gods delighted, both the old and the new, which you could tell by the dizzying height of the uncloaked sun and the heat in the shimmer over the green and bursting plain.

Aedan presiding, moving here and there, greeting all, welcoming all. And his family and friends, even the Picts, all around, all well.

It was a wonderful day, a rare day at Dun Ad, until the ships came in.

Then, business.

Envoys came from all the kings, bearing regal gifts for the storied new *ruiri* of Dal Riata.

From the British kingdom of Guined, Afrella's homeland away down south, there came a self-important man who brought Aedan many donatives that were received with gratitude.

Not so the news that man would bring back to the ears of the great king Beli: proof of his daughter Afrella's repudiation and disgrace. ?

From the British kingdom of the Gododdin, away to the east, an offer to foster one of Aedan's sons, an offer chillingly rebuffed; then reasonable terms, since their two kingdoms flanked the dreaded Miathi, keeping them in check; and finally the gift of Draig, the great warhorse of the Visigoths, captive of the Gododdin these many years.

"What a glorious gift!" many said, marveling at the ferocious beast.

But Aedan laughed, knowing not to thank his foster-brother, Morcant, Lord of the Gododdin. "Indeed he is. He is a true killer of men, as Morcant well knows."

The envoy startled to find such keen understanding in the man he had been told was no more than a brute, for it was true: his master Morcant bore no love for his erstwhile foster-brother, Aedan, and the stallion was less a gift than a hoped-for curse.

The envoy, wondering at this enmity, was moved to compassion for the strange Scot: he, too, had cause to dislike his fierce, cold master.

"In truth, my lord," he said to Aedan once the snorting, prancing stallion had been brought to bear, "I am glad to be rid of him. What a beast! What a handful he has been, on the track ways here to you from Din Eidyn! He took a finger off one of the lads, bit it clear off at the joint! He was ruing the whip that day, Draig was, having given us cause time and again to bring it down across his stubborn rump, but how else to get him to heed? How else? Does he deserve kindness? I don't know. He never had it in the stables at Din Eidyn. He received none on the road. If he does, perhaps he will find it here, for they say that you are the only one who has ever been able to ride him."

"Aye," Aedan said, putting a tender hand on the forehead of the animal and rubbing it, to the marvel of all who watched. "Aye. We have both known the whip, Draig and I. And have both had cause to bite."

Aedan tugged gently on the reins; the warm stables waited. There the stallion's wounds could be cared for.

Draig nickered, ducked his head, and followed.


From the British kingdom of Strat Clut, an envoy whose meager gifts came cloaked in a demand for Aedan's submission, which Aedan refused to give. King Tudwal's betrayal before that last decisive battle, the battle of Telocho, when the world turned on its head to spit out Aedan as king, was still fresh, still raw. Tudwal had betrayed Aedan then; Aedan would not submit to him now.

In addition, there was troubling news: Tudwal had driven the young priest Kentigern from his kingdom. "It was Tudwal's wish," the envoy said. "And so he exiled him."

"To where has he gone?" Columba asked, worried for his old friend.

"Away south. But to where, I do not know."


And from Rheged, no royal envoy, but bright-haired Urien himself.

"Where is she? Where is Ama?" the king demanded.

"Your sister is safe."

"She had better be. But she is also not here. I will not treat with you until she is brought out from wherever you have hidden her away."

So Ama was brought down from Dun Mor to the Beltane festivities at Dun Ad which, while it addressed Urien's first concern, did not alleviate his others. "Why haven't you taken her to wife? You make a whore of her! She, who was *rígain*! What if there are children? By all account the two of you rut like animals. We hear of it in Rheged!"

"You hear of it?' Aedan asked. "Or hear it?"

Ama snorted with laughter. She took her stepbrother by the hand the way she used to when he was young. "Brother," she said. "You cannot make me marry, and I will not. Please, be at peace. The unity of our souls is not easily severed. It is a truer partnership than either of my marriages. For me, that is enough."

She sighed. "And as for children, I am no longer young. I am unlikely to bear any more, though I should dearly like to."

"If she does," Aedan said, "they are mine as well and, by the gods, I would welcome and claim them."

"You shall have to," Urien muttered. "Because I should not like for there to be enmity between us. In addition to your submission, brother-mine, I need your help."


"The Saxon threat," Urien said, brotherly drink now in hand. "The rumor for which we derided poor Gwallawg of Elmet all those years ago; that we dismissed as unthinkable? Well, we have had occasion to rethink it."

"How so?"

"Last winter we came across a band of Saxons hiding in the wastes along the old Roman Wall. Normally we cut down Saxon dogs, no thought. And with pleasure. But my son—my marvelous Owain—found pity in his heart for them and stayed my hand. They were not just fighting men, but their families. They had so little, almost nothing, and would not have lasted the winter without help of some sort or another. I am amazed to admit it, but we have taken them in. Saxons! Of all things! The men fight for us now and, as they grow accustomed to our ways and trust that they are safe with us, and to know a broken-down version of our tongue so that we might begin to converse, if not freely then at least with some small hope of understanding, they begin to reveal worrisome tidings. Trouble between their two kingdoms, between Bernicia and Deira—"

"Battles?"

"Yes. For supremacy. What else? Our men, our adopted Saxons, had served Theodoric of the royal house of Bernicia. Yes—I know.

82

You bear that house no love. Neither do I. But my men? Those sorry Saxons? I have come to trust them—even, I admit, to respect them. They swore me their allegiance and they keep to it. They have wanted a true lord, is all. They tell of suffering too horrible to relate, of needless cruelty inflicted by one Saxon upon another—of terrible deeds levied by the house of Deira, of Aelle, its king, upon the house of Bernicia which had laid it low; of bloody revenges and ruthless savagery. You know the story. It is not so very different from our own, now and again. A king rules. He is envied. His enemy takes aim. That aim is good. The king goes down. His enemy takes over. That man rules. He is envied. He makes enemies. Those enemies take aim … And so on and on."

Urien laughed bitterly. "You and I must watch our own backs, my friend! So that that story does not also become our own!"

"What help do you seek?"

"I am re-garrisoning some of the forts along the Wall—not all, of course, but those that are principal to our defense from attack from the east: Coria and my own Caer Ligualid. Also Trusty's Hill, to which I have a mind to move my court. Know that these preparations are not done against you, but against the Saxons. But it is help for my son that I seek. Owain and his men raid the Bernicians, raid the Deirans. They raid the Eastlands. It is our hope that we might wreak havoc amongst the Saxons, cause their heads to ache and their bowels to burst; to destabilize them—if not drive them out, outright. I ask for the safe passage of my son's warbands through your lands if their need ever pushes them this far north; that you give them sanctuary and protection if they ask for it. More: that if you can ever come to their aid, you will. If not for me and our bonds of friendship, then for the love you bear my sister."

A memory flashed in Aedan's mind: blond-haired, bright young Owain in command of the only British ships to honor their oaths and come to Aedan's aid at Telocho.

"I will help Owain happily," Aedan said. "Whenever and wherever he needs it."

Urien nodded his thanks, then sighed. "I knew you would help if you could—unlike Morcant of Gododdin, that crafty bastard, who is another matter … "

Urien shifted, his face brightening. "Another matter, for another day. Enough of statecraft! How I long for another drink! And a good song."

He turned to his waiting retinue. "Taliesin? Come! Aedan, do you remember the poet Taliesin?"

The young man he called forward with a happy wave had a shining countenance and very clever eyes. "Yes? Of course you do! Who could forget? Well, I have him now! I have wooed him from Cynan Garwyn of Powys to my court with the anticipation of fine gifts—as he tells me after the high inspiration has drained from him and he is in a sweat and bother: 'My lord! I have just given you a poem that is worthy of a horse!' And I laugh and laugh at his wit!"

"Before you have given him a horse? Or after?"

"Oh, I laugh before, after … and during! He is not just my best poet—he is the best of the Britons'! And it is Rheged he has chosen to lavish with his high talents! I would not trade him for ten Hibernian bards—famous though they are."

"Numerous though they are."

"Indeed! So numerous that no one can afford to house and feed them. I hear they roam the countryside in large packs, like wolves, casting satires on and maledicting with glee any who refuse them food and drink, or who throw them out before they are well and truly ready to go." Urien shuddered. "It's extortion, it what it is. Who needs that?"

"Not I. And so is he your gift to me? Your best, cheap, honest poet Taliesin? Today is the day for people to give me things."

"Ha! You wish! Never! We cannot do without him and his fine, fine words! How would we pass our evenings? He creates our memories! He fashions our reputations! It is through his lauding of us that we shall be remembered! In fact, that we come to know ourselves. Do you know what he has christened me? *Fflamddwyn!* 'Flame-bearer'! By which I think he means my sword. My metal one, not the other! Ha! It is superb!"

"Yes. That's a good one."

"And my son Owain?"

"Tell me."

"*Dwyrein ffossawt*! 'Scourge of the Eastlands'! My son! My wonderful son! A moniker for the ages! One I dare say shall never be forgotten! And do you know—and this is God's luck itself—today is Taliesin's birthday! Is it not, Taliesin? Today, the first day of May! Well, not the day of his birth, exactly, at least not the first one, for reasons you shall soon hear, but the day he was found by Elphin in the salmon weir."

"What? Found in a salmon weir? How so?"

"How so? Well, let me tell you! It is such a story that I shall see if I can do it justice. Our Taliesin here was once called Gwion and as a boy he served the lady Ceriddwen who above all things desired knowledge. So she prepared a potion with much trouble and effort, luring the Salmon of Knowledge himself from the river which flowed around her island-home into a silver net and killing him and tearing at his flesh to make a magical brew which would endow her with the limitless insight and knowledge he possessed—in fact, inspiration itself. It was an exceedingly potent concoction which needed to be stirred unceasingly every day for one whole year, and not tasted all that while, not even one drop, and so she set little Gwion before the cauldron with the task of the stirring. Being only a boy and a good and faithful one at that, he did as he was told, stirring and stirring day after day and never tasting even one drop of that marvelous elixir for nigh on a year, no matter his own hunger and how good it smelled. Until, until, the very last day, when quite unexpectedly the Cauldron of Inspiration at last boiled over; but not entirely, only three drops of it, three small drops which oozed up and over the cauldron's lip to scald his little thumb as he sat there dutifully stirring, his thumb which he then stuck immediately into his mouth, as anyone would do, to soothe the terrible burn of the boiling brew. And lo! All the knowledge for which his lady Ceriddwen had so desperately labored passed instantly and irretrievably to him. And he knew. He knew *everything*. Right then and there. Everything there was to know in the world, he then knew. Which of course enraged his lady Ceriddwen, why would it not!, and she moved to murder him on the spot. So he fled, turning himself in his panic into a grain of wheat, the powerful new magic he had ingested, however inadvertently, allowing him effortlessly to transform himself into any form he wished; and as a grain of wheat he hid in terror for his life amongst the dirt on the ground. And Ceriddwen, seeing this, hoping to regain the knowledge lost to her by ingesting *him*, turned herself into a hen and pecked and pecked and pecked at the ground until she had gobbled him up."

Urien sucked in air and, seeing his audience spellbound, continued with relish. "Alas for the lady Ceriddwen," he said "this did not transfer Gwion's knowledge unto her, but only succeeded in getting her with child, a pregnancy she abhorred, abhorring him as she did (she was a *goddess*, the lady Ceriddwen, as you will by now have guessed; and didn't she have better things to do with her time than care for a babe who had stolen away her power, even a babe such as Gwion) so, to be rid of him—only after, it must be said in her defense, growing him up fully in her belly and expelling him at last … "

"After nine months as a woman? Or days as a hen?" interjected Aedan, he thought rather cleverly. In the background, watching shrewdly, Taliesin, the subject of the marvelous tale, chuckled.

Urien cocked his head in thought, then shrugged, saying, "I haven't a clue. But, look, the point is that she needn't have bothered to birth him at all, being as he stole from her in such a crass and appalling manner, and so if you'll stop interrupting me with questions, because we come to the heart of the story now, I will tell you that as soon as she had him out of her she stuffed him into a leather bag and cast him full-long into the river that flowed around her home quite fiercely, she living on an island as we have said, a river that does not stop its delirious tumultuous rush until it joins the sea."

"No!"

"Yes! But rather than drown (as would have any other babe) the

boy, little Gwion, was fished out of the water, still bound up in his
leather bag, by a man called Elphin, a lord actually ... "

"Of course ... " said Aedan.

"... who had taken it upon himself to fish for salmon—yes,
salmon!—at that very weir that very morning for no reason that
he could later credit other than divine inspiration, given the way
things were to work out; Elphin who, expecting a fish, hopefully
one of great size—even, were he lucky, the Salmon of Knowledge
himself!—instead to his astonishment drew forth an utterly soaked
but otherwise quite resplendent tooled leather bag and, from it, a
babe, a beautiful babe, wriggling; and, loving him instantly as his
own mother did not, she being a goddess and busy with other
things as we have said, took him in and raised him as his own. And
called him "Taliesin", *radiant brow*, for the knowledge which sits so
shiningly upon him. Taliesin! Yes, he! He, there! Can you believe?
The very one. What a tale! What a birth! Or, I should rightly say,
what a rebirth! What an extraordinary, improbable rebirth, as is
the way with those who are gifted by the gods. For he is gifted by
the gods, our Taliesin, make no mistake! Both before and after he
partook of the Salmon of Knowledge in his lady mother's Cauldron
of Inspiration. His was a life not to be cast away so blithely. No, it
was not. Not Taliesin's. For his gift, his great gift, as you will hear in
due course, aside from his knowledge of everything there is possibly
to know, is his wonderful, beautiful, breathtaking, radiant, most
glorious way with words."

"Ah! Ah!" Aedan said, sitting back and sighing. "Such a tale!
And such fine words are these, of yours! Who was it who told you
this remarkable tale? He himself?"

"Indeed yes!"

"Hmm," said Aedan, amused and gladdened by Urien's own joy.

While Urien praised Taliesin and saluted him effusively with his
sloshing tankard, the young poet had been quietly studying Aedan,
as if searching for the words with which he might christen him. "My
lord," Taliesin said with a nod to Aedan when at last he had been
given time to speak, "I myself had occasion earlier to see the gift the

Gododdin gave you—that Visigoth, that stallion, that great beast of the baleful eye! He repaid my admiration by nearly taking off my head! And so I say to you that I am exceedingly perplexed."

"How so?"

Taliesin dipped his head. "I shall try to enlighten you. I consented to come to this land of the Scots with my beloved lord here on the promise of gifts, for sure, but also of mysteries ... and of shadows."

"Mysteries? Shadows?"

"Yes. Everything here is upside down. Or, rather, inside out."

"Is it? How so?"

"Well, I have come to suspect that you Scots are shape-shifters."

"We are?"

"Yes. And here is why. You are in and out of boats, on and off land, up and down mountains, then back to the sea, all day long, day after day—and yet you, yourself, seem to me a man as any other."

"As any other?"

Taliesin laughed. "Yes. And no. I see that you have a woman. Yet that woman, who is not married to a king, is queen of the people—and the true queen, not. Also, you Scots worship the Old Gods, or so I am told—yet you name that priest of Christ there your chief holy-man and grace his upturned hand with the sacred new-fire."

Taliesin surveyed the company. "These are perverse customs," he said, "which ought to frighten one off, and yet you have the most extraordinary friends—for, in addition to envoys from all the British kingdoms near and far, aren't they Picts, here, in your hall, the Great Hall of the king of the Scots?"

The poet's all-seeing eyes came at last to rest upon Aedan again. "It is an uncertain magic you have here. Perhaps an inverted magic. Yet, a magic it is. And so I have cause to thank you, for I am a collector of stories, the more improbable the better: I am one who marvels at man! And here I hear tales the like of which I have never heard, witness wonders the like of which I have never seen. So much so that I do truly believe that here, in your Dal Riata, the world has been turned on its head for, thinking again of the Gododdin and their gift to you, I ask: surely gifts are meant to improve one's life, not to take it? What a strange, enchanting land indeed!"

"And I its strange king," Aedan said.

Taliesin shrugged, his face alight with mischief, which caused Aedan to laugh.

"So what do you think of my horse?" Aedan asked him.

"Ah, that horse! That horse, my lord, is worthy of a poem."


Aedan took Ama's hand as she was leaving. "Ama, love. Stay with me. You're here now. However it came about, I am thankful for it. Stay."

She touched his face lovingly, lightly. "No. But I will stay with my brother—though perhaps not in the same guest house as the Picts?"

"We will meet again,
but not yet."

# · 6 ·

# LAM DESS son of CONALL

*Second Night*

That night they feasted. Aedan did his best to accommodate everyone. There wasn't much yet. Winter had only just turned. With industry, compliant weather, and luck, there would be much more come the harvest. But for now, at least there were meat stews thickened with what little remained of last year's oats and barley, and fish soups. There were bannocks baked golden on griddles over the fire. There was porridge sprinkled with preserved hazelnuts, dried raspberries and cherries, and with new herbs, sea salt, and honey. Knives speared their targets in the shallow wooden bowls arranged in such a way on the tables so that all could partake, fingers scraping up anything that remained.

A triangular harp was brought out, and a pair of triple pipes, some cymbals and drums. They sang. They danced. They emptied seemingly-bottomless beakers of ale and of mead. They might have looked for wine, but no merchant vessels had pulled to shore for nigh on a year. Aedan did not know if there was trouble in Gaul, or if Gaulish merchants had heard of the recent trouble in Dal Riata and wished to avoid it. He would have to gather intelligence, see what could be done about it: his people enjoyed their luxuries, few though they were. He wanted his people to have them.

His family were far more reserved, acutely aware of the current of tension that undercut the festivities. Afrella sat with him in a place of honor before the company, but coldly. Ama was with her people, the Rhegedians, in a way that was neither hidden nor overtly displayed, but some awkward place in between. Domelch remained amongst the coterie of watchful Picts—that is, she did until mid-way through the feast. Then she and Drust rose and came forward, laden with gifts.

The music and merriment skidded to a halt. The eyes which had been keeping covert watch on the Picts all evening now stared outright.

"Here," Domelch said in her lilting Scottish. "See? We are friends. We bring gifts from Father. A white fur from the mountain hare's winter coat. See here? It is run through with streaks of mauve, for even the hare knows that in its world of blinding snow it is the shadow which brings out the light. It is made for a queen, who should also know such things. We wish to give it to your wife."

She looked around in feigned confusion, eyes alighting on Ama, then on Afrella, then back again.

"To whom do we give it?"

Aedan loved Domelch, he truly did: but this was too much. "Domelch," he chided softly.

He made a show of accepting the hare coat with as much dignity as he could muster, then raised Afrella by the hand and draped it with ceremony across her slender shoulders. Doing so, he felt a surge of compassion for his chief-wife. Small in stature, the magnificent coat overwhelmed her, making her look like a child. He could not fail to humiliate her no matter how he tried!

"And these river pearls?" Domelch asked. A long strand of iridescent, irregularly shaped pearls dripped from her tidy fingers, catching the firelight to the gasps of the crowd.

As he moved to take them, Aedan thought, *these go to Ama.*

But Afrella's hand shot out, holding him back. Very bravely she marched right up to Drust. She had to crane her neck to stare down the massive Pict, but she did, and then she skewered Domelch with a look of utter contempt. She thrust her hand out defiantly.

Drust laughed, a booming sound. Domelch's eyebrow twitched, and Aedan watched with astounded approval as the glowing string of pearls was laid on Afrella's outstretched palm.

There were other gifts too, from both the Caledonians and the Britons, though not the finest and not many, Aedan not yet being the man to whom all other men must bow their heads; and these Aedan distributed amongst his retinue and the chief men of Dal Riata's other kindreds. Fraich was given a sword, Sillan a horse. Aedan's other men, gifts as befitted their status and their service, until all his people had been rewarded.

Yet there was one whose dissatisfaction rode him openly and hard. With a sneer, Feradach, the overlord of the Cenel Oengussa, held out the fine weave of cloth that had served as his gift. "Where is the favor in this?" he asked. "This is a trifle. A woman's reward. Though you were made king, others might have done better: *A king must be without miserliness.*"

Aedan forced down his ire. "You cite the laws—those laws which you imagine to be in your favor," he said to Feradach. "But there are others, Feradach, like: *All men must be without jealousy.*"

Aedan took back the cloth, ran his hand down the weave, admired it. "This is very fine. This is also what we have now and you are welcome to it—all of the Cenel Oengussa. In time, and with luck, there shall be more."

"My lord! Here's another one."

The new man was brought forward. "My lord!" the messenger

began. "Baetan mac Carell, king of the Dal Fiatach in Hibernia and *ri ruirech* of the province of Ulaid—your lord, your suzerain—sends greetings."

Aedan had been expecting this particular envoy. In a way, the meeting was pre-ordained. And he not surprised that the man had contrived to arrive just at the peak of the Beltane festivities: no better time to undermine Aedan. No better time to stir the pot.

So Aedan played it out. He hoped to draw the envoy into revealing more than he ought. Aedan also needed his own people to witness the encounter, for their lives too would be bound by its outcome.

If he were to sever this false relationship with the tyrant of Ulaid once and for all, as he intended, there would be consequences.

Aedan had his answer to hand: "Welcome to my hall! Please, join us! Be merry! You are welcome to what we have. But partake of your own accord, as your own man: Baetan is not my suzerain".

The messenger gave a false-grin, stiff and diplomatic. "He said that you would say that. They all say that. But more so would you say it, my lord said to me. So I am bid to remind you that your cousin, your former king, Conall mac Comgall—may he rest in peace!—submitted to him. So … "

The envoy shifted the travel sack he carried on his shoulder, held out a hand. Placating. Soothing. Stating the obvious. " … Baetan is suzerain of this Dal Riata."

"Please, have a drink," Aedan said. He motioned for a servant to bring two cups. "Let us toast this former cousin of mine. Who, as you so helpfully point out, is dead."

Aedan raised his cup to his lips. "Very dead," he said.

He took a mouthful. Swallowed. "As dead as you can get. May he rest in peace!"

Draining his cup, he set it down on the table with a *thunk*. "And since he is dead, also dead are any contracts he made with Baetan. That is the way of it, as your lord well knows. It is why your fellow envoys have also come here this Beltane—to begin relations anew."

Aedan pointed at himself. "New king. New treaties," he said.

"My good lord! It may be as you say. It may not. That is for you and my lord Baetan to decide when you meet."

"We are not meeting."

"Ah! Yes. He said that you would say that. Which is why I have come to ... *invite* ... you to Ros-na-Righ in two weeks' time to bring your hostages and give him your submission or ... "

A watchful stillness descended on the hall.

"Or? With what will he threaten me? Can he sail the seas in ships he no longer has?"

This was it: either Aedan had him here, or he did not. If Baetan had managed to rebuild his navy after Aedan had destroyed it, it was either by miracle or at someone else's expense, which Aedan thought unlikely. Without a navy, Baetan was powerless to harass Aedan and his people here. They were mere threats shouted from the far shore of the sea, carried on the wind, empty.

The envoy set down his cup. He swung around the bag he had been carrying. "Or the people of Dal Riata in Hibernia—your people there—will be put to fire and sword. My lord. If you doubt him, here is proof."

The envoy tossed the bag. It rolled once awkwardly, twice; then, knocking up against Aedan's boot, fell still. It had been left untied so that its contents could spill out at his feet.

There were two heads, hacked off at the neck. A man's. A woman's. Rot setting in.

Aedan choked back revulsion and pity. "I don't know these people," he said.

"Do you not? That's the old steward of Dun Sobairche. *Your* citadel of Dun Sobairche, back in Hibernia. The one who governed that half of the kingdom of Dal Riata in your name; the *rechtaire* left behind to clean up your mess when your people fled here. And that was his wife."

With his toe, the envoy prodded the heads until they faced each other, the woman's gaping mouth on the man's ruined chin, an eternal kiss.

"Your steward. His wife. Doing your work for you. And you

95

don't know their names?"

He shook his head. "My lord Baetan says that lest you think to ignore this, we have sent a similar message to the steward who took this one's place and governs at Dun Sobairche now. In that package I think Baetan sent the severed hands. I don't know. Possibly also the feet./Of the father, certainly his member. Of the mother, I think he sent the breasts that had done the suckling."/

"If you fail to come meet with Baetan and render your submission, your Dal Riata in Hibernia will suffer. And they will know who is to blame for it. Be sure of it."

The look the envoy gave him was not without sympathy. "You know my lord Baetan. You have made his acquaintance," he said. "You know that what I say is not false."


"But first, me," said a menacing voice.

Three men, unknown to Aedan, barged up from the back of the crowd. In a hall where the greater part of the company had reached a boisterous level of camaraderie which, while temporary, having been helped along by an unhealthy amount of drink, was not at that moment false, these three fairly screamed aggression, belligerence and, strangely, hatred.

Aedan snapped to attention while his men quickly surrounded them.

"And you are?" Aedan asked the one who seemed to lead them.

"You do not know me? You should. I am Lam Dess. From Eilean Righ."

Eilean Righ. *The Island of the King.* Aedan knew of no such place in Dal Riata; if there was such a place, it would be his now.

"What island? What king?" he asked.

"The king, my father. You should know him. You slew him."

Aedan had indeed killed many men. But thinking back on it furiously as he sized up the interlopers, he was quite certain he had not yet slain a king, rightful or not.

Except, that is, for his cousin Conall.

"Yes, you get there," said Lam Dess, his voice rising to a near bellow. "I am Lam Dess, son of *Conall*. Conall of the Cenel Loarn. Your cousin, your rightful over-king. The over-king of everyone here—until you butchered him like an animal at the gates of Tairbert."

Aedan knew of only one son of Conall, Dunchad, who of course had not been Conall's natural son after all, but Aedan's. If this man here were indeed Conall's son, then his father had never claimed him, at least at court.

Looking at him, Aedan saw an echo of that hated cousin. Wiry hair that was neither brown nor red, a beard braided into two, tubular seashells strung on the spiky ends. A robust, healthy form; strength in the shoulders, arms and legs. A look of meanness about the pale blue eyes, carried over into the lips.

This man could be Conall's son. And Aedan could begin to believe that the many rumors of Conall's wide-rangings, his unnatural freedom with the women of his kingroup before his slide towards madness, might be true.

Nevertheless, he said: "Prove it".

Lam Dess laughed harshly. "You would be such a king to ask for proof."

"I know of no Eilean Righ. No King's Island. Who named it? Conall?"

A proud nod.

"Give it whatever name you like, but it is not kingly for calling it so."

*A clumsy retort*, Aedan admonished himself, certain that his clever brother Eogan, watching shrewdly from the half-shadows, would have produced one far more cutting.

"What do you want?" he asked the man.

"You have assembled the men of your kingdom. I am such a man. To them you give your support. I claim it as well, *cousin*."

Lam Dess had a point, even if it was an unwanted one. Aedan ruled them all now, including any of the Cenel Loarn who might emerge from the dank holes of their *duns*. Perhaps especially them.

And where a king ruled he gave support. That was why he existed.

"What is it you want?" A cow, a jeweled brooch, a weapon, some cloth? What overt symbol of his alliance with the new king of Dal Riata did this man require?

"It is not a man who does not avenge his kin," Lam Dess said.

He swung about, looking for something, or someone, in the hall. He hissed when he found him.

Of all people, it was Columba.

"I want him. Murderer!"


"*What?*"

Columba did not know the ferociously aggrieved young man who was spitting in his face. "Of whom?" he asked him. "I don't know you."

"Of my brother. Ian!"

Comprehension dawned. "Ian … mac Conall?" The wretched bandit from Artmuircol who had run off with Dovey's sorry cattle?

"Yes. Ian was my brother."

"What do you mean *was*? He was regretfully still very much alive when last I saw him." Ian had sailed off before that wrathful storm, the reived cattle on deck bellowing their distress. "Why do you say murder?"

"You cursed him! He was dragged down to the deep!"

"Your brother is drowned?

"Yes! His ship wrecked upon the shore! I found him foully strewn among the bloating cattle! The death flies alighting on one, then the other! Eating out his eyes! His eyes! Crabs tearing at the soft flesh of his mouth!"

Lam Dess wailed his grief. "He did not deserve such an end! You cursed him!"

Columba had indeed cursed the bandit Ian—but only a little. However, how did Lam Dess know this? Had he been lurking on the headland, watching?

"If he drowned at sea, it was that terrible squall," Columba said

98

to him. "His was not the only boat to wreck that day."

That storm had also vomited up Columba's old enemies, the exiled king Black Hugh and his monk-companion Findchan, whom Columba had not seen since he had denied them sanctuary on that destroyed beach.

"A squall you raised with your foul curses!"

"I assure you: I did not only speak against your brother. I prayed for his sorry soul as well. It was the open sea that got him, the trackless ways between Meall and Coll. It has claimed many a person who deserved death much less than did your brother. If he is dead, I am sorry for it … "

*Am I? Not really.*

" … but it is by the hand of my God that he was drowned."

*And it is not to heaven that he has gone, evil, perfidious man!*

"It is by your hand! By the sorcery of your words! From up on the heights, I saw you knee-deep in the swell! The very air about you seethed with your foul curses—you set the air on fire! You summoned the sea god Manannan from the deep, raised the wind and the waves! Told Manannan just where to find him! Defenseless and petrified in his little boat! You did curse him, you wizard! And I will kill you for it!"

And with a dagger artfully produced from the folds of his cloak, Lam Dess lunged at Columba to get the deed done.


Columba sensed the attack before he saw it. The sudden spike of energy, the kind the skin feels before the eyes see.

Eogan had sensed it too. He threw himself in front of Columba, shielding Columba's body with his own.

But Columba didn't need much help. He had trained as a warrior as a boy, which was something one never forgot. He didn't need to use those skills often but when he did he employed them naturally and well.

Others joined in. The two hooded men who had come with Lam Dess threw themselves in, trying to flank Columba and hold him so that Lam Dess' dagger could gut him. Here, Eogan's clinical assistance was very welcome, and the former king held off one, then the other, which allowed Columba to concentrate on rebuffing Lam Dess—and then Aedan was there with his men, hauling the three heaving attackers off with shouted curses and threats; until a modicum of order was restored.

In the melee, hoods had been thrown off and anger-filled faces brought out into the light. Columba was horrified to see the enormous, black eyes of the hated monk-king Black Hugh glaring back at him; and behind him, panting with exertion, his friend the monk Findchan.

Despite Columba's best efforts to evade them, they had tracked him down again.


Before anything else could happen, there was a terrible shrieking from the crowd of enthralled onlookers. "*Fingal!* Murderer!"

It was Afrella's handmaiden Covna. The young woman had lunged at Black Hugh and was clawing madly at his face.

"What?" Black Hugh cried, using the advantage of his superior height to slap away her wild hands. "Who? Who? What king have I killed?"

For that is what a *fingal* is: a king-killer.

"My brother!"

Hearing this, Columba's mind raced, picking at the puzzle; coming up short. "What do you mean?" he demanded of the girl. "Who are you?" Who had she been in Hibernia, before her captivity amongst the Picts? Before he and Aedan had rescued her from the slave bed of her Caledonian master, Broichan the mage? "Who *were* you?"

She shook off the hands holding her back, launched herself at Black Hugh again with a fury that was astonishing, but was again restrained.

"Covna Lurgan!" she screamed. "I am Covna Lurgan!"

Black Hugh heaved in a stunned breath. So did his friend

Findchan.

So did Columba.

This was astonishing news.

In fact, calamitous.


"Aedan!" Columba said with some effort. "This is … This is … This is best dealt with in private."

Aedan could see that whatever the girl's disclosure actually meant, it seemed to have the most extraordinary effect on the three men. The two unknown monks, having given up all pretext of helping their friend Lam Dess disembowel Columba, had turned ashen; for his part, Columba looked positively devastated.

There was nothing Aedan should like so much as to have them all removed from the hall at once—in fact, if he were honest, to have them tossed straight into a leaky *curragh* on an outgoing riptide before a fresh winter gale with neither oars nor sail, and no clothing or food either, while he was at it—but moments earlier Columba had been accused of murder before the whole company. And now that Aedan was king, he was judge as well.

First order of business: this new cousin of his, the one he had had no idea he had.

"All of you! Silence! No! No! Not a bloody word until I say so! Right! You, first," Aedan said, rounding on the snarling Lam Dess, waving at his men to let him go.

Released, Lam Dess charged Columba (really, this young man was all bluster and no sense: did he really think to hurt any of Aedan's people here, now?), but in one long stride Aedan had him hauled up by the collar of his tunic. Being a good head taller than Lam Dess and twice as broad about the shoulders, he hoisted him up with no problem, his toes scraping for purchase. There he could see that Lam Dess' eyes were run through with red veins. He had been drinking, recently and hard, which would explain some of his fool-hardly bluster though not, Aedan suspected, all of it.

Aedan had no real wish to be gentle with his new cousin. He

preferred to make an example of him, to forestall any further threats from any other unclaimed offspring of Conall who might yet spring from the shadows. Certainly that would have been his father's careful counsel; it was what Conall would already have done.

But, by the gods, Aedan was sick to death of it all. Hadn't they just emerged from a war and many long years of hardship brought about by the enmity between their two kindreds? Did this young man really crave more?

He might but, up close, Aedan could also see that for all Lam Dess' princely posturing, the clothes he wore were as threadbare as they were old. The washed-out wool twisting in Aedan's fingers would have a hard time keeping a babe warm come winter. Aedan would rip holes in it if he pulled any harder.

Conall had certainly fathered the boy: father and son shared a certain canny look. But had he cared for him in any other way?

Another fatherless son.

"Enough!" Aedan said. "Enough! If you have a grievance against this man, speak it plainly."

He set Lam Dess back on his feet. But the young man only grunted and made for Columba again.

Aedan grabbed him back up. "That man is under my protection," he said. "He is under the protection of the *ruiri* of Dal Riata. *Me.*"

He rattled Lam Dess to underscore the point. "The person who causes him harm, or causes harm to any of his men, shall have to deal with me! Is that clear?"

Aedan punctuated his last point with three decisive shakes. He doubted it would do any permanent good: though Lam Dess no longer resisted physically, the fire of hatred flared even brighter in his bloodshot eyes.

*He will be trouble, this one,* Aedan could see. *This will not end well.*

There was little Aedan could do about that now, so he set the young man back on his feet and smoothed the tunic which had bunched around his neck.

"Let us start again, *cousin,*" Aedan said. "Let us be friends. I am the man to keep the peace. For the sake of a new Dal Riata."

"Then keep it!" Lam Dess shouted. "Make him pay for the murder of my brother!"

"Tell me: was your brother alive when he set off in his boat?"

"Yes."

"Then both you and Columba agree on this. Columba cannot have killed him. He did not die by Columba's hand."

"By his words! By his words!"

"Listen. I am sorry for your brother's death. I am. But I cannot adjudicate against a man's words."

"But ... he cursed him!"

"The sea took your brother, cousin. The sea. And I cannot bind the sea by judgment."

"But ... "

"Enough! I have ruled."

"Your ruling is not just!"

"It is. And if you were not grieving the loss of your brother, you would see so."

Lam Dess fumed. His cheeks stained red. He looked to his two monkish companions but no help was forthcoming from either them or the crowd.

But then a new thought occurred. "If you are just, as you claim," Lam Dess said, "then make him pay another way! Make him give back my clients! If you do this, then perhaps I will agree that you are just!"

"What clients?"

"From Artmuircol!" Lam Dess yelled. "That good-for-nothing man and his pitiful wife and his snotty child. Dovey! That swine Dovey and his family! Where are they?"

"Did you take these clients, Columba?"

Columba tried to hide a smile, but Aedan knew him well enough to catch it before his face was wiped clean again.

Columba answered the man, but it was with the tone Aedan had come to recognize meant the recipient was about to be brilliantly outmaneuvered—had already been bested, in fact. The voice of the jurist.

103

"Since your brother, their lord, is now dead—God rest his soul!" Columba said, "then Dovey and his family are free to choose a new lord."

Lam Dess didn't recognize the undertone, or didn't understand its meaning. Or didn't comprehend that he was pitting himself against the brightest mind of their age.

And would lose. Every time.

"You, a lord?" Lam Dess sneered.

"Iona. Iona is their new lord. They are now clients of Iona."

"Clients of an *island*? I have never heard such a stupid thing. Thief!"

"A free man is free to choose his master."

Lam Dess spluttered in disbelief. "What say you to this, *my king*?"

"Are they free clients?" Aedan asked Columba.

Columba nodded.

*Oh no, indeed,* Aedan thought. *There is no way this will end well.* Columba had just made himself a very chancy enemy: a man who would not be bound by law.

But then again, when didn't he?

Aedan sighed; turned resolutely to Lam Dess. "They are free to choose," he said. "And he is not a thief for offering them a better master than you."

"Now, the rest of you! Keep your traps shut and follow me!"

# · 7 ·
# THE BATTLE OF THE SEVEN KINGS

"Now," Aedan said. "Who the hell are you all?"

Columba swallowed a growing sense of panic. This was complicated. Though seemingly concerning distant affairs across the narrow sea in Hibernia, it had implications that hit very close to home. Too close.

He would try to explain—enough, but not all.

"If she is who she says she is," he began, indicating the still-fuming handmaiden Covna, "then her brother—this Fiachna Lurgan—was 'of the blood', a prince of the people of the Dal nAraide in Hibernia. Yes. The Dal nAriade. The neighbors of your Dal Riata there. And he was not just royal, but was *tanaise*, the heir-apparent of the kingdom. He should have ruled the Dal nAriade. Would have ruled ... "

Columba jabbed his chin at Black Hugh; how he hated the man. "But for him."

"And he is?"

"*I* am the king of the Dal nAraide!" Black Hugh shouted. "Not that boy. Me! I am the rightful king!"

Black Hugh strained against the hands holding him; got free. Went for the girl's slim white throat.

He got nowhere near her. Before Columba could intervene, Aedan had it in hand: "I don't care who you are. Don't touch her, if you wish to live".

"If you are the rightful king of the Dal nAraide as you claim," Aedan said, "then what are you doing here?"

Everyone shouted at once, desperate for Aedan to hear his side.

Aedan held up a hand. "You," he said to Columba. "Explain."

"There was a battle," Columba said.

"When?"

"Before I came here."

"Yes! Tell him of it, Colum!" Black Hugh roared. "Tell him of it!"

"Quiet!" Aedan said. "You will have your turn. What battle, Columba?"

They had called it the Battle of the Seven Kings, after it was done. Which said it all, if you thought about it. It had begun simply enough, not as a battle but as an assembly to decide who would next rule the Dal nAraide, the king having died. But how it had ended ...

Columba shuddered.

All the rival claimants of the Dal nAriade had come, all who craved the throne. Black Hugh's kin, Covna's kin, all the big lords had brought swords and men. In all, seven under-kings set out from their hearths that day, full of dreams. Seven heads of kindreds. Seven very needed men. With wives and children and kin to care for and support.

Seven under-kings rot there still.

A generation of the Dal nAraide gone. And for what? The answer never changed. Vanity. A lust for power. A generation of fatherless children left to the pleasures of other violent men, and why? Because seven shortsighted kings could not step aside to let any other rule, could not comprehend that life offers other, more subtle, more rewarding prizes for which one should also vie.

Columba would have laughed, had it not struck so horribly close to home.

"So who won?"

"I did!" Black Hugh said.

"My brother did—or should have!" Covna said.

"No one did, Aedan." Columba said. "No one did. Their kin—hers and his—all died that day. And these two here—these cousins—and her brother, were left, all but children."

"So no one ruled after?"

"No ... That is, I mean ... "

Black Hugh snorted with derision. "Ha! Yes! Do tell, Colum! Do tell! Who ruled? Who ruled after?"

Columba sighed. How to tell, and not to tell, at the same time? In the aftermath of the battle, confusion had prevailed. Opportunity the likes of which men rarely see. With so many of the Dal nAraide dead, the province of Ulaid of which Dal nAraide was the major part was ripe for the taking. A great, unholy prize.

Others stepped in, from outside. Picked sides.

Co-opted. Usurped.

Columba opted for the barest facts. "Dermot mac Cerball came to rule," he said.

"What do you mean?" Aedan asked. "The old high-king of Hibernia? Your enemy? The one who threw you out? He came to rule the Dal nAriade?"

"Yes."

"How so?"

"Yes! How so, Colum? How so?"

"There were two possible heirs to the throne. Both were children. Him. And the boy, her brother. Dermot stepped in—to help him."

Black Hugh gasped. "He *stepped in*! To *help* me! Oh, that's pretty! Rather, he *took me* ... "

"What do you mean, he 'took' you?"

"As his foster-son. Dermot took him as his foster-son. And put him on the throne of Dal nAraide in proxy. And then ... "

Covna, who had been following the heated exchange silently, began to sob.

"What happened?" Aedan asked the girl gently.

Through her tears, she snarled at her cousin Black Hugh. "He got rid of us! First thing! My brother and I."

Oh, it had been a bad business. Very bad.

"Had you no protectors of your own, in the way that he had Dermot?" Aedan asked the girl.

"We thought … That is, it was promised … But no. We had no one. If we had had, my brother would be king, and I would not have been … No one would have *dared* … "

She shuddered, glared at Black Hugh. "You stole us away. You killed my brother. Your very own cousin." She gulped down a sob. "And you sold me to them."

Aedan frowned, already knowing. "To whom?"

"The Picts."

A very bad business indeed.

"Right," Aedan said, rounding on Black Hugh. "You. Is it true? Did you kill her brother?"

Black Hugh's enormous dark eyes strayed to his friend Findchan. A cloud crossed his face.

Columba saw it; began to wonder.

"I took care of him," Black Hugh said.

"Monster! *Fingal!*" Covna cried. "Child-killer!"

"Child? He was my rival. What choice did I have?"

"He was a little boy! No older than … "

"He was a devious child," Black Hugh broke in. "Untrustworthy. Dangerous."

"Dangerous? He was two years old!"

"He was a rival. What choice did I have? I dealt with him." Again, that furtive look at Findchan. Then, "You protest! You complain! Yet I took pity on you! Other kings would have strangled you, or worse. Yet here you are! You live! You owe me gratitude."

Covna's eyes narrowed dangerously. "You sold me into slavery."

She turned to Aedan. "He took me to the beach market himself.

Sold me to the slaver who offered him the most in exchange: a sword from Gaul. A pathetic little rusty sword from Gaul."

She laughed without mirth. "It was on the boat over to Caledonia that I was first ... "

Black Hugh jumped. "First? First *what?*"

"I was five years old." Covna's voice was very pointed. "My family, my freedom, my innocence, for a throne for you to hold only as a puppet for your new master, and a sword that could kill no one."

Black Hugh's eyebrows shot up over the great orbs of his cold dark eyes. He smiled, slowly and lasciviously. "Indeed? Your innocence?" His gaze strayed to her breasts. "Hmm."

Covna launched herself at him. Columba was happy to see that Aedan let her land a few solid blows to her hated cousin's gloating face before pulling her off.

She shook off Aedan's hands, said to Black Hugh, "I shall make you pay. I shall see you dead. But before I kill you, you will suffer as I have. As my brother did".

Black Hugh's laugh was high and incredulous. "Would you now! What a fine boast! But do you think you can do worse to me than has already been done? I should like to see you try! I too have known hardship. Pain. No longer am I king! Now my enemies pursue me night and day. I have been in exile these ten years, with only my true companion Findchan here to comfort me. Ten years! It is high time that it stop. But only this man, my old ... *friend* ... Colum, is strong enough to protect me. Only he is high enough. It is only under his height that I might find shelter. And so—we are here for sanctuary."

"I have already told you no."

Black Hugh growled. "You owe me. You know that you do."

"For what do you owe him, Columba?" Aedan asked.

"I killed him!" Black Hugh said.

"You killed who?"

"He killed the high-king."

"He killed Dermot mac Cerball?" Aedan asked.

Columba nodded. "Yes. He killed the high-king. His foster-father."

"My *foster-father*! Ha! I repaid his 'love' for me the first chance I got, and with a great amount of pleasure, by separating his body from his head! And not only that, but I took his head to Cluain and his body to Connor so that he cannot rise with Christ at the end of days. Not that he would want to, horse-fucker, but still. I became *fingal* for you, Colum! King-killer. And for that I am exiled, and am hunted. I killed your enemy, and for that, at least, you owe me. It is a debt that I am here to see you repay."

It was all so dangerously close: this very bad business.

"Like me, Colum," Black Hugh said, "you are a man undone. You owe me sanctuary on Iona. It is a boon you cannot refuse."

"I have told you no."

Black Hugh's face flushed with fury. He shared a knowing look with Findchan, then said, "Your answer will be yes! And I will tell you why. Actually—I will tell *him* why".

He turned to address Aedan, his smile cunning. "Has he not told you? Has he not admitted? After the ... "

Columba rushed forward. "No!" he said. "No!"

A triumphant smile from Black Hugh. "Yes. It is as I thought. You are a coward, and if you wish me to keep your secrets, you know the price."


The three friends sat without ceremony before the fire, a jug of ale making its somber way between them, Aedan now and then throwing bits of straw onto the flames just to see them hiss and sputter, because this in some way mirrored his thoughts.

"That just got complicated," Eogan said.

"In what way, Brother," said Aedan, "was it not complicated before?"

"Indeed," Columba said. "Whenever was it simple? Nothing has been simple for a very long time."

"That's disingenuous, my dear master," Eogan said. "If you

want simplicity, stay out of things. Go back to your cell on Iona and shut the door. Trouble does seem to follow you around you know."

With a groan that was half amusement, half agreement, Aedan took a long swig of ale and wiped his mouth on his sleeve. "It's true," he said. "We've got a host of problems. But first things first. This Black Hugh of yours, Columba. What of him?"

Columba took the jug, drank, passed it to Eogan; rubbed his palm down his face wearily. "This Black Hugh? This Black Hugh! He may be tonsured, but this Black Hugh is a very bloody man. It seems that his time as Dermot's captive twisted him. Or perhaps he was born craven? I do not know. But it is clear that he is suffering from a void of spirit. He got rid of his rivals, his cousins, the children, when he could have protected them."

"He is not the first king to have resorted to such tactics," Eogan said.

"No," Columba said. "You are right of course. But in this case it did little good. His passions got the better of him. He killed that foster-father of his, High-King Dermot, the man who had put him on the throne, by a vile trickery. And while I am not sorry that Dermot is dead, the way he was slain was shocking, even by our standards."

"We have standards?" Eogan asked.

"Aye. We do. Or we should."

"What happened?"

"Dermot was on his circuit, making his way round his lands, eating and drinking his food-renders, as kings do. At one of his stops, a beautiful, young girl was offered to him. He should have declined of course, but he did not. His wife wasn't with him, so why not? It's one of the benefits of kingship. Besides, they had made sure to ply him beforehand with ale and fine clothes and bacon, so he was fine fit to continue his merry evening. But it was a ruse—too good to be true. While he lay with the girl, they locked the door and set fire to the house. Dermot sprang up, looking to escape—and there at the door was Black Hugh, saying, 'Come this way! Quick! Foster-father, this way! This way!' But instead of letting him out, at the last second Black Hugh blocked his passage with a spear. The high-king ran straight onto it, impaling himself like an old boar, and Black Hugh used it to push him back inside, locking him in. In a vain attempt to ride out the flames, Dermot submerged himself in a vat of ale, and drowned when the burning ridge beam of the house collapsed on his head."

"That's some death."

"Yes. Threefold, which is the way kings should go, in this case by impalement, drowning, and immolation. But it was a ludicrous way to die, if you think about it, for one so high, and was brought about by sex and wiles and outright cowardice. What's worse is that it had all been foretold—the druids had warned Dermot of the manner in which he would be slain, told him in fact to avoid beautiful girls and fine clothes and bacon when offered all in one go, especially if Black Hugh was about. That's pretty precise. And still Dermot could not avoid it."

"Well, that's prophecy for you."

"And ale."

"And bacon."

"And the girl?"

"Burned to death with him."

"Bastard."

"Indeed."

"And for this Black Hugh was exiled?" Aedan asked.

"Yes. For what he did to Dermot, his own people the Dal nAraide threw him out. The high-king dead by the wiles of his foster-son! Not openly, by his own hand, as a brave man might have done, but by trickery. That's *fingal* for you, without doubt. Killing a king in a dishonorable way. Warranted though the whole thing may have seemed to Black Hugh, it stretched the bounds of decency a bit too far."

"We have bounds of decency?" Eogan asked.

Columba arched him a disgusted look.

"Now, is this where Baetan comes in?"

"Yes. After Dermot was murdered—the high-king of Hibernia

dead!—it was chaos, as you can imagine. On all fronts. The small, the medium, and the large. The small: who to succeed Black Hugh as king of the Dal nAraide? The medium: who to take over the province of Ulaid and rule its three peoples, the Dal nAriade, the Dal Fiatach, and the Dal Riata? The large: who to succeed Dermot as high-king? While rivals vied on the grand scale for the high-kingship ... "

"Your own family included," Eogan said.

"His own family succeeding," Aedan corrected.

A blush from Columba that somehow did not convey pride. "Yes, my cousin Ainmire mac Setna succeeding, becoming high-king at last—a dream close to his heart from childhood."

"That part worked out well for you, *Abba*," Eogan observed dryly. "Your cousin on the high throne of Hibernia at last ... and you cast out of it altogether."

"Hmm."

"It got him here, so that's good," Aedan said. "But, tell me, what of the medium? The province of Ulaid? For that, I think, is what Baetan is about."

"Yes. The Dal Fiatach—Baetan's people—swept in to rule Ulaid at last, once and for all, and without opposition. They had been waiting a long time on the sidelines, the least numerous of Ulaid's three kindreds, overlooked, outnumbered, insecure, seething with secret resentments. And then! Seven kings dead! Seven! And an untried, foolish boy-king thrown out by his own people! With no one to rule it, Dal nAraide was at its most vulnerable. The mac Carells simply helped themselves to the spoils, stepping into the vacuum; Demman first and, after he killed him, his brother Baetan. Who wouldn't? And by controlling both their own Dal Fiatach and the Dal nAraide, they controlled the whole province of Ulaid at last—the needs of the Dal Riata, the third kindred there, *your* kindred, be damned."

The ale-jug came round again. With a sad shake of his head, Columba refused it. "Since his exile, Black Hugh has been wandering in the company of that monk Findchan, becoming a monk himself, bearing the trappings of the Life while observing very little of its substance, seeking sanctuary from any who could be forced to provide it. He is biding his time, is all. Trust me—he seeks to retake the throne of Dal nAraide. He wants it back, and will use the safety of sanctuary on Iona to begin to plot his return."

There was a thoughtful silence as the fire crackled and hissed.

Aedan sat up, stretched his shoulders, said with renewed purpose. "All right. I understand. That's Black Hugh and the Dal nAraide. Now to the problem of Baetan. I don't like Baetan threatening our Dal Riata here, or there."

"Ah! But isn't that the crux of it, Brother? Are they our people?" Eogan asked cautiously. "Is that other Dal Riata ours too? Now is the time to decide if it is not. You needn't claim it. No one would fault you for staying out of this. There is much to do here. And our claim on the other Dal Riata has been theoretical only these long years. Who amongst us has even been there, besides our Columba here, before he ever had cause to know us? Father hadn't. We haven't. You can let it go. You can concentrate your energies elsewhere. Here, if you want to. Look all around you! Look in every direction! Save west. Don't look west across the waves. If that Dal Riata is not ours, then you owe it nothing. And can ignore Baetan—unless he thinks to attack us here, though how he could I know not, without a fleet; in which case we fight back."

Aedan nodded, taking in his brother's counsel. Eogan was the sort of man who saw all sides, and no merit in holding any of those opinions back: a wonderful trait in a trusted brother. What he suggested warranted careful consideration.

The future hung balanced; here, now. And the choice of path was Aedan's alone.

*To say yes. To say no.*
*So many lives dependent on one word. One word of mine.*
A son of the clan of the Shadow will seek Hibernia in one day.
*Was that prophecy said of* me?

*Is* this *that day?*
*Regardless, do I make it happen? Take it on?*
*The distressed traveler.*
*The red flame that awakens war.*
The fiery sword.


Finally, Aedan knew his heart. "I claim it."

After a moment of his brother's silence, Aedan asked Eogan hesitantly: "Do you agree?"

"I do, Brother."

"So do I," said Columba. "It is how a great king would speak. And since that's decided, listen, because this is important for our purposes: Baetan and the Dal Fiatach rule Ulaid only because the other two, the Dal nAraide and your Dal Riata, are presently kingless. The Dal Fiatach have the run of the province all to themselves. However, their numbers are small. Baetan overrules precariously, and he knows it. It is why he shouts so loudly. And punishes those who have done him no wrong."

"It is too bad that the boy Fiachna Lurgan is lost. That would have been an opportunity," Eogan said.

"Yes! Yes! You read my very thoughts! I have been thinking: it is very curious that Black Hugh will not account for the boy's death. He says, 'I took care of him'. But what does that mean? Why not claim the boy's demise as his victory? He would, if he could. His reticence gives me hope. Black Hugh sold the sister Covna rather than kill her himself. That speaks of cowardice to me."

"Or a twisted sort of piety," Eogan pointed out. "Maybe he is more a monk than you would like to let on. Perhaps you should ascribe him more morals?"

"Perhaps. And perhaps the sun will rise over that way tomorrow. But, yes, I begin to suspect that the boy might also have been sold. And still lives. I don't know, the chances are slim—but the sister survived when others would not have. That is most astonishing! And to see the fire in her now, after all her tribulations! Perhaps the boy is of a similar stock. Perhaps—like you my friend—he is hard to kill."

There was another long thoughtful silence. Aedan drained the ale-jug dry; couldn't be bothered to get up and find a servant to bring another. In any case, he was already nodding. "There is a path open to us. A brilliant path."

"An unlikely path, Brother." Eogan said. "An impossible path."

"Ah! But if it works! We will at last have thrown off the shackles of those who seek to enslave us. If I could find Fiachna Lurgan! The Dal nAraide might rise up, on our side! We would be two against one. The Dal Riata and the Dal nAraide against the Dal Fiatach. Yes: this is the way forward. I should go to Hibernia and look for the boy."

"I think so too," Columba added.

The three friends looked long at one another, their minds rushing over the terrible logic of their plan; if their reasoning was faulty in any way; if any alternatives had been overlooked. None had, all three minds working shrewdly in concert.

But neither had they overlooked the risks.

"Leaving Dal Riata now, with Lam Dess unveiled … "

"Your reign so new … "

"And we may not find the boy," Eogan said.

"'We'?" Aedan asked. "I."

"He may not live! If he doesn't, or if we can't find him, Brother—you will have to submit to Baetan."

"Aye. I may have to regardless. I haven't much time."

"And Brother, I'm sorry to point this out but, if you fail in this, if you are forced to submit … "

All of Eogan's probing intellect fell away. Aedan could hear the worry, the compassion, in his voice.

"Have you given thought to whom you will hostage?" Eogan asked.

"He won't take you," Aedan responded gruffly. "Don't offer."

"No, he won't," said Columba. "You may have been a king, and are his brother, but Baetan is after a bigger prize."

There was a long fraught silence. Eogan sighed. "Then I am sorry, Brother. Please forgive me—but do you know which of your sons you would give to Baetan?"

Aedan glared at the floor, his fists clenched.

Abruptly, Aedan burst to his feet and began to pace. "I won't let it come to that. Columba—I could use your help. You know Ulaid: the land, its people. You know the men with whom I will have to deal, all the big men. Your cousin's son too! Aed mac Ainmirech, who is now high-king in his father's place. I need you to tell me all that you know. I'll be going in blind … "

"*We'll* be going in blind," Eogan said. "I am coming with you."

Aedan stopped his frenetic pacing. "No," he said, "you're not."

"Of course I am."

"No. You're not."

"I … "

"Eogan! What about that?" Aedan pointed at his brother's new tonsure.

"Oh, that's not a problem." Eogan patted his bare forehead. "He'll let me go, for this. Won't you, Columba?"

Columba drew in a quick breath, looked at the rafters.

"What … *No?*" Aedan asked.

"You won't let me go?" Eogan asked. "Not even for *this?*"

Columba grunted. "Of course you can go. It's not that. I can't very well stop you. You're not a child. But … but if you do go, Aedan has the right of it. Your probation will have to end."

"I do?" Aedan asked. "It does?"

"It will stop outright, Eogan," Columba said. His year of probation. His initiation. The months he'd spent on Iona preparing to become a monk. "When you get back, you'll have to start anew."

"From *scratch?*" Aedan asked.

"Aye. From scratch."

At Eogan's pained look, Columba shot out a hand. "It's not you! That's just how it's done."

"Don't give me that," Aedan said. "Surely you could make an exception for him. This is Eogan we're talking about."

"I can't. I won't."

"Why not? You're the abbot. You can do as you like."

"There are rules."

"Rules, my ass. Now you like rules?"

"Well. No. That is … "

"Don't give me that. Prove it." Aedan was losing his temper; didn't care.

"Not here. Not with this."

"*Hypocrite.*"

Eogan gasped. "Aedan!"

"My friend!" Columba said. "Please! Listen! It's not just the rules. Your brother will come back a different man, regardless of how you fare. He may not want the Life … and the Life may not want him."

"That's asinine and you know it. This is Eogan we're talking about. What could possibly go wrong?"

"I won't do it. I can't. Don't push it."

Columba turned to Eogan. "Eogan—please! Give this careful thought. I know there is much at stake here. I know the responsibility you feel for your brother, and for these people you so recently ruled as king. If you feel you must, of course I will let you go. But there is a price: you start again."

"*Abba* … "

"No! Not now. Think on it. Pray on it. Let us speak of it again tomorrow."

"You rule wrongly here, Columba," Aedan snarled. "Wrongly!"

"Please! Brother! Let it be!"

Aedan stared down Columba. A minute passed in frosty confrontation. Two.

Aedan had to breathe long and hard before he could speak again. "Tomorrow then. We will speak of it again tomorrow. First thing. In the meantime, you should pray too, Columba. Pray that your god softens your desiccated heart."

Another minute of icy silence.

The fire crackled. Columba moved.

"Let me be the one to help you." Columba said. "But not just with information. I'll come with you. I'll come with you to Hibernia."

# · 8 ·

# SEA ROADS

What had made him say it, Columba wondered wildly? To offer to go back to Hibernia when there was a death sentence on his head? The one place in the world he could not go?

He was not one to sit idly by a friend in need, he told himself. And Aedan did need his help, no matter his current surly mood.

True—but hardly the whole reason.

Baetan might have a part to play in the terrible premonitions he'd been having about Aedan's sons. The signs pointed that way. If so, Columba would stop him.

Again, true.

The most true, though?

The other reason. The appalling one he might admit to, if he were being honest with himself, and brave, at that moment.

Which he wasn't. So he let the thought pass unchallenged.

If Columba expected Aedan's gratitude, he did not receive it.

"That's very useful," Aedan said. "Thanks for that."

"Aedan!" Eogan gasped.

"But I could be a true help," Columba said to him. "It is as you say. I do know the land. I do know the big men."

"He does, Brother."

"Eogan. His offer is useless. He can't come. They'd kill him for it. He can't ever go back."

"I probably could," Columba said.

"How? Already in your coffin?"

"Aedan!"

"Listen: I could get in, help you, and get out quickly again with no one the wiser."

"You mean you lie about it."

Columba felt himself wince. "It would require a disguise, yes," he said. "A trick or two."

"You, travel *incognito*? I should like to see that. You might successfully hide your face, I grant you. But your pride? There's your true challenge, Columba."

"Aedan!" Eogan said.

"I don't like this, Brother. There's something he's not telling us."

"What do you mean?"

"Look at him! It's writ plain on his face."

"Is there, *Abba*?" Eogan asked. "Is there something you're not telling us?"

Aedan was studying him with piercing eyes, head tipped goadingly to the side. "It has something to do with this Black Hugh," he declared.

"Does it, *Abba*?"

"What hold has he over you?" Aedan demanded.

As much as he longed to say nothing more about it, Columba felt himself soften. These were his truest friends. He loved them. He was safe with them.

A long sigh escaped. "What hold? What hold! One I would not share, my friends, with you or anyone. One I would not share. Can you trust me on this?"

Aedan was shaking his head, unable to so quickly put aside his anger. "I don't know. Can I? Should I?"

"Aedan!" Eogan said.

Aedan stepped back. "Yes. All right. Yes, of course I trust you, Columba. Even when I don't comprehend you. Like now. But. But." His finger shot out to stab empathically at the air. "I am no longer just your friend. I must be friend to all. Will this … secret of yours—whatever it is—will it harm our people? Will it harm *him*?" A chin-thrust at Eogan.

Columba took a long, inward look. He considered. It was a fair question and it deserved a thoughtful answer.

"No," he said.

"Are you certain? You don't look certain."

"I don't think it will."

"That's not good enough. How can that possibly be good enough?"

Columba, who was feeling very overcome by it all, had no better response than to shrug.

Which of course did not soothe. "Are your people blameless in this affair with Black Hugh?" Aedan probed. "Tell me: are you blameless?"

That hit very close to the nerve Columba had been doing his level best to avoid. "Please, my friend!" he felt himself say. "Please! Let there be peace between us! I would never harm you! Any of you! If ever you need to know what happened, I promise: I will tell you. That is the best I can do here."

"That's precious. What prevents you? No—let me guess: your pride again, right?"

"Aedan!" Eogan cried.

Columba wrapped his arms around himself. His heart felt sad and tight.

They squared off again.

It might have gone on a very long while had Eogan not intervened. "Well, that's all very comforting," he said. "I, for one, am vastly relieved that the two of you will be joining forces again.

God help the Hibernians! Look how well it turned out for the Picts!"

Against his will, Aedan snorted. It just sort of burst from him. Hearing it, Columba felt a small smile crack open as well.

Dear, dear Eogan!

Eogan came up, clapped Columba on the back, then his brother; drew the three of them together. Shook them stoutly and affectionately.

"And, if you're going, I'm going," he said.

"But ..."

"No. That's the end of it. Where you two go, I go. You'd leave me behind? I'd be bored to death. I'd rather come along to mock."

Eogan smiled. "Now all we have to do is figure out how to get us there and back again, all in one piece."

The rest happened quickly; the course set.

To the envoy of the Dal Fiatach, Aedan said: "I will come to Ros-na-Righ. Fourteen days from now. Inform your lord Baetan".

Surprise flooded the stalwart envoy's face, but he nodded.

"You seem a right enough sort of man," Aedan said. "Can you return the steward's head to his body, and hers too, so that the family might bury them with honor? My abbot also worries: he tells me that without their heads, they cannot resurrect with their Christ. Would you deny them the end of days?"

The envoy shifted from foot to foot, his face coloring. "My lord, I would. That is, I would not deny them. But my lord Baetan ... "

"Then I will do it."

To his Pictish family: "I cannot keep your mage, Taran."

Gartnait startled. A look of betrayal flooded Domelch's eyes. Drust growled. For his part, the mage Taran nodded, as if his deep-seated but as yet unspoken suspicions about the perfidy of the Scots had just been confirmed.

Aedan held them off with a hand. "*At court.* I cannot keep

him—you, Taran—at court, here at Dun Ad. Whatever kind of man you may be—peaceable, good, honorable, as Domelch claims—you are Caledonii, and my people fear you. They have a right to fear you. I cannot subject them to that. And you will become a focus for any discontent while I am gone, mark my words. This you can already see. Knives will fly at you, here in the dark when I am not close enough to protect you, as I won't be now for a while. I am sure of it."

There were unwilling nods at his words.

"But I have made an oath," Aedan said. "And I will keep to my promise. I have an idea."


To Feradach, the recalcitrant lord of the Cenel Oengussa: "You ask for my favor. A way to earn gifts. Here is a way you can ensure it twice over. Will you shelter the Pictish mage at your citadel of Dun Nosebridge until I return? Will you care for him as one of your own?"

Feradach weighed the request. Finally: "That will bring your favor?"

"Aye."

"Bring him to me."


"Will you stay with him, with your mage Taran, here in Dal Riata?" Aedan asked Domelch. "We could shelter you too."

"No." There was no pleasure in her tone. "I go where our son goes. And our son must be with our people. We will leave when you do."

He hated to see her go. Felt he had not had enough of her yet, or of any of them.

"When you see your father, embrace him for me in fellowship," he said.

Drust snorted.

Aedan grinned. "Too soon? Too much? What will finally earn

me his affection?"

Aedan pretended to ponder the problem. Then he snapped his fingers, as if delighted by a sudden burst of inspiration.

"I know just the thing to finally fill his hard heart with love for me! As you leave us, at the harbor you will find another ship. Don't fire upon it! Don't sink it, or board it, or set it alight! For its cargo is precious: our Pictish slaves returning home with you, as I once promised. That will make the old bastard smile, don't you think?"

Drust gaped, then smacked Aedan on the back.

"Return the ship and crew safely to Dal Riata, will you?" Aedan asked. "Also, can I ask you? There is a young man here whose family is still missing after many years in captivity amongst your kind. Fraich is his name. He has searched all these years for sign or word of them, to no avail. The grief of their enslavement weighs heavily on him. Let him describe them to you, give you their names. If ever you discover them, will you purchase them for me, or release them, and send them home again?"


At the same time, elsewhere, Columba's work.

To Black Hugh, Columba said, "I will give you sanctuary".

Black Hugh cast him a wary, disbelieving look. "*What?*"

"You heard me."

"Him too? Findchan too?"

"Him too."

The two exiles shared broad, stunned smiles. "Ah, Iona!"

"No!" Columba's voice cracked. "Not on Iona. Make no mistake. Never on Iona."

"Then where? How?"

"Leave that to me," Columba said.

There was a place on which he had had his eye for some time, a fertile and low-lying island called Tir Iath, a half-day's sail to the west of Iona, almost at the world's edge. Though Baithene would give him hell for it, for any number of good and sound reasons, it was time to start the next phase of Iona's work. They would set up a daughter house on the island, a new monastery dependent on Iona—and stick Black Hugh and Findchan out there where they could harm only each other.

"I will give you sanctuary," Columba said, "in exchange for the safe return of the girl's brother, Fiachna Lurgan. I will give you sanctuary once you tell me what you did with him and where he is now."

Black Hugh's remarkable eyes narrowed. "I see. Of course. What a bargain you strike! What generosity of spirit! Such a holy man is our Colum! You say you give sanctuary! Yet you demand something of me in return. Can we then call it a gift?"

Columba said nothing, holding his breath. He could be so very wrong about this. If he was, then all these new plans they were spinning would be for naught.

"Sanctuary in return for the boy," Columba said. "That is my offer. And not the one without the other."

Black Hugh sighed, shared another of those long, knowing looks with Findchan; came to some inward decision, said: "Regardless of your uncertain charity, for my life, for his life, for sanctuary, I would do it. I would give you him".

"Do it."

"I will tell you what I know. For sanctuary. Agreed?"

"Agreed."

"He does live."

"Ah!"

"I can tell you where I left him."

"Good."

But then a cold, happy smirk inched up Black Hugh's face.

"But I have no idea where he is now."


Aedan found Eithne out walking, deep in thought. A lock of bright hair had separated itself from the mass of its sisters. Slanting in the wind across her face, it caught on her frown.

"I was thinking ... " she said before he could speak. "I had hoped that if you will not take me in, then your monk might do it. On his Iona. Do they take in women, do you know?"

"Oh, Eithne." He reached out, took the lock of hair in his fingers; smoothed it from her brow. Such a wondrous face, now so full of doubt and sorrow. "I don't know. But if they don't, he is such a man as would make it happen."

"I have this."

Eithne reached down inside her tunic and withdrew something on a cord of black silk. It was the gold cross Columba had given to her husband, King Conall, all those years ago. The one with which he had hoped to buy him off. The magnificent garnets with which it was inset caught the light.

"Columba valued it enough once to bribe Conall with it," she said, "so it must have worth. It might bribe him too."

"Eithne! I don't think they make you pay for it. And if they do, he wouldn't. Besides, you are worth much more than that bright cross."

Unconvinced, she gave him a little lop-sided grimace.

"If you feel that it will bring you peace," Aedan said, "then by all means ask him. But I have another idea. A favor to ask, really. I need your help."

In this way Eithne was taken into Aedan's household, not as his wife or concubine, but nevertheless as honored and protected kin; and installed again at Dun Ad as steward, to rule much as she once had, for Aedan in his absence; and to keep careful watch over her dead husband's dangerous, unclaimed children, Lam Dess and his ilk. And he left his beloved, aging, wolf-hound Ceo with her to help her with that task.

"Not Afrella as steward? Not your wife?"

"No."

For the first time in months, there was light in her eyes when he left her.

To his embittered wife Afrella: "Get Bran ready. You and he leave

for Guined with your brother's envoy and men. Go to your brother.
Bran will stay and be fostered with him. I want you out of here until
it is safe for you to return".

"What of Finn?"

"Finn goes to Britons too, but to Strat Clut."

"No!"

"Yes."

"You will separate them?"

"For now, yes."

She made to complain. He took her hand. "I don't like it either,
Afrella," he said. "But it is the safest arrangement—for all of you."

Afrella withdrew her hand with a snap. "And what of Covna?
Have you told her of your search for her brother? Is it fair to give
her hope?"

"Yes, I think so. It is never unkind to give hope."

Afrella laughed bitterly. "Is it not?"


To his son Artur: "You will go to Rheged with your uncle Urien. He
will take you into his house-guard. Serve him. When it is safe for you
to return, I will send for you".

His son's mouth crooked as he considered what it would mean
to serve in the famous warband of the Britons of Rheged. Then he
nodded.

"Be safe," Aedan said. "Be well. Learn from him, and from your
cousin Owain. I know you will make me proud."


To his sons, the twins Bran and Finn: "Boys. It is time to take your
leave of each other".

They tried to be brave, but their eyes filled with quick sharp
tears.


And the last, the hardest, since Aedan's hope of reunion with this
particular son was the most slim.

"Gartnait! Son. Please. A minute?"

129

"Father?"

Finally, Ama.

"Will you return home to Rheged with Artur?"

"I should like to, yes: I will not lie. It has been a long time since I was home. A long time. And to be without Artur … But I don't think it is something Artur should like. It would suggest to others that he still needs my protection, that he is not now his own man."

"Aye. And in any case, he is past the age where he will be told. That is, he could be told, but he might not heed."

"Indeed!" She gave a laugh that nevertheless sounded a little lost.

He understood. He too dreaded the separating of his sons, their dispersal into the world.

"Urien will look after him for us," Aedan said. "And Owain. Artur will be lucky to ride in the warbands of such men."

"You are right. Of course you are right."

Her eyes were full of worry and sorrow, but she set her shoulders, accepting it.

At last she smiled. "However … if you think to leave me here you are mistaken."

"My thoughts exactly! I thought for you to come with me to Hibernia. I do not wish to be parted from you ever again. But … "

"But?"

"Eogan comes with us as well."

She inhaled deeply, said after a time, "If he can bear it, I will come. If he cannot … "

"I will square it with him."

When she nodded, unconvinced, he drew her close and buried his face in the sweet-smelling hair at the nape of her neck, an old song of love whispering through his thoughts:

*To separate us two is to*
*Separate the children of one home,*
*It is to separate body from soul*

Paula de Fougerolles

# · PART TWO ·

*The Arrival of Fergus Mor mac Erc, The Annals of Tigernach*
*(The Bodleian Library, University of Oxford, MS Rawlinson B.488, fol.7r, 14ᵗʰ century)*

# · 9 ·

# BANCHORR

*Hibernia*
*Three days later*

The old man perched at his writing desk in the dark *scriptorium*, the light low, the nightly devotions over, his brothers abed. They had partaken of their evening meal, their one meal of the day. Sated on the bread and herbs and water, his mind was alert. His aging body stiff after a day of instruction, he intertwined his thin fingers and bent them back one by one, enjoying the relief brought on by the resultant cracks. Stretching his arms overhead, he breathed in deeply, felt the vital humors run up his spine and then down again. Ready, he settled onto his stool.

Now: to write.

With no one to watch or critique him (for an abbot was as much a model of the devotional life as he was a leader), Comgall let his excitement rise. He felt giddy, almost like a schoolboy again, and would have danced with glee, had his body allowed. After nearly a year of painstaking labor, his great work, his *Regula monachorum*, a set of rules that over many long years he had devised for the men living in his monastery here at Banchorr, was nearly completed. This was his life's work, something he hoped to bequeath to the world when he was finally asked to quit it; his ideals, his wisdom, his experience, distilled into one instructional text. When to eat, and what. When and what to pray. The penances prescribed for each kind of sin. How to organize the day to optimize the hours, every minute allotted a task or a prayer. In short, how to achieve the best chance of coming close to God. For wasn't that the point of being alive?

He knew of many monasteries that had faltered in the years following the great Patrick, houses that were now havens for depravity, vice, and sin. But by God, his Banchorr would not be one of them!

They needed his *Regula*, and soon. Unfortunately, with all his duties as abbot he rarely found time for it. Nevertheless, he would not entrust it to another: his students were not yet capable of the technical craftsmanship, the artistry, it deserved. Nor perhaps were they ready for the level of commitment the *Regula* would require of them, once it was firmly implemented. Some would be weeded out. He regretted the necessity of this, but was certain of his course. There were other monastic houses to which they could go, some that had not yet fallen. He expected much of the men who would choose to remain here to undergo the new disciplines. They would need to be strong, able to withstand much hardship, without complaint. Nothing less than excellence would do. Banchorr would not be for the training of weak men, those who sit meekly with their faces to the wall, their backs to the door. Rather it would produce elite scholars, rugged soldiers—*miles Christi*, Soldiers for Christ.

Aye. Aye. Only the best.

Were any of his men currently ready? He was certain of only one, perhaps two: his prized students Columbanus—such an intellect, that one! Yet such a brawler!—and of course Cellach. Both fine men. Men to move mountains with their shoulders and their words, to bring the word of God into the wilds and survive.

So close! So close!

So, although everything ached, his back, his shoulders, his neck, his eyes, he drew the candles closer, cracked his spine one more time, dipped his quill in ink, and set to work.

Ten minutes crept by. Twenty, before he finally gave in and set his quill back down again with a huff. He could not settle. For some reason he could not put his finger on, the quiet bliss that usually accompanied the exacting nature of his work, the contentment of writing he so craved, was eluding him this evening. He could not sit still. A restlessness was upon him. A churning in his stomach, as if a need to act. A sense that the shifting flames of the candles cast light differently than they normally did and were warning him.

He'd run through it all: was anything amiss? Did anything require his attention? Had he forgotten something? His nimble mind clicked through its habitual concerns, his monkish habit of order and extreme attentiveness helping him to tick off his enormous list of daily affairs quite rapidly, one after the other: the men, the novices, the livestock, the crops, the food stores, the buildings, the fields, the lay community, his correspondence, his sins, others' sins, both those executed and those anticipated; his grasping overlord Baetan.

Everything was accounted for. All was in order.

Time to get back to the task at hand.

Except for that damned prickling at the back of his neck.

Just then, there was movement by the door. He started, thought he saw something which surely could not be there: men in the dark shift of the shadows.

He blinked, cleared the film from his rheumy eyes.

No good: three hooded figures crept into the candles' uncertain light.

Comgall jumped up as the cowled forms, who were dressed in attire exotic to him, and armed, threw off their hoods. There was a large man, and a larger man. The two looked to be brothers. They shielded a third man behind them.

Comgall was about to shout for help when he abruptly checked himself. For all their unexpectedness, their stealth, and their size, they did not seem disposed to accost him. Given the enormous sword the big one carried, he'd already be dead if they did. Rather, there was an air of supplication about the whole thing, a question hanging in the air. Almost a greeting.

The third man, the shielded man, stepped into the light.

Comgall's heart leapt. Was it? Was it? Could it be?

"Colum?" he whispered.

Columba smiled.

"*Deo gratias!*" Comgall cried. "Oh! Oh! I never thought to see you again my whole life! My whole life!"

Comgall ran to Columba, bumping up against his writing desk in his haste to greet his old friend. Quills flew willy-nilly and the ink swelled up in its well, threatening to overspill. The candles teetered dangerously, righting themselves at the last second, sparing his precious manuscript.

Comgall grabbed Columba, shook him, wrapped him in an embrace, shook him again, then stepped back to study him, grinning.

"Oh dear God, it is good to see you!"

A second more of searching the face smiling at him—yes, this was his beloved boyhood companion. One of his dearest friends in all the world.

Then Comgall reared back and punched Columba so hard in the jaw he sent his old friend sprawling.

"What the hell was that for?" Columba cried from the floor.

"*What was that for?*" Comgall spluttered. "*What was that for?* Dear God!"

Comgall's hands flew to his head, gripped his weak fringe of hair with enough force to yank it out. "Too many reasons to tell! Shall we count them, for Christ's sake? How about for a battle you had no business being in? What the hell were you thinking? I know he was your cousin, but Sweet Jesus! Learn to say 'no' once in a while! How about for provoking Dermot and getting yourself exiled? To Dal Riata, of all places! Jesus, Mary and Joseph! If you had only

136

apologized! Showed a little contrition! How about for the worry you have caused me all these years, wondering if you still lived or if you had long ago been torn limb from limb by those Scottish savages you call friends ... "

Eogan growled a warning, and Comgall seemed to see him for the first time. Comprehension flooded his face, but not atonement.

"And what about Finnian?" Comgall continued. "What about him? To steal from him so! You left him in the lurch there, by God you did! He did not deserve that! Our old master! No, he did not! And then to hear of the Picts! The Picts! If half the tales be true ... "

Columba raised a hand, got to his feet; wriggled around his aching jaw until it clicked back into place. "So you did know I lived," he said.

"Aye, I did, you old bastard! But with no thanks to you! You could have sent word. Why haven't you written?"

There were a myriad of answers on Columba's tongue, all of them true, but none of them sufficient. Why hadn't he written? He wasn't quite sure. He felt a moment's shame, a hot flare in his chest. He had spent years of his young life with Comgall. Years. But while his destiny had taken a sharp turn towards the farfetched, Comgall's had not.

"I'm sorry," Columba said. "I've missed you. In my heart, I carried you with me all this time and we were never parted."

Comgall heaved a sigh. Some of his high mood drained from his face. "Right, well ... Right. And you, me. And you, me, my friend. And now you're here. You're here! That's something. Something quite wonderful! But why are you here? No, wait! Don't start yet! Let me call for some supper for you ... "

"No!"

Columba's curt refusal of Comgall's hospitality earned him speculative looks from his silent friends.

"What, too high and mighty these days for the good fare of Banchorr?" Comgall asked.

Columba could have laughed. The good fare of Banchorr? Bread and herbs and water, more like. And only bread and herbs and water. That was the *Rule* here. That was Comgall's way. Columba knew of no man more strict, holy or constant. His old friend Comgall was disciplined, ascetic, some might even say militant—an administrator with an unsparing hand. Everything Columba was not. And though Comgall had argued endlessly that a demanding *Rule* hardened the body to better fulfill their Lord's holy plan, Columba doubted that the seven companion monks who had starved to death out on Lough Eirne would agree, had they been able to be asked, which they were not. The one meal per day had served only Comgall well that dreadful winter. The rest slept there still.

It had always been a sore point between them. Columba had sometimes wondered if their differences over how to manage their men might have parted them in time, if his exile hadn't accomplished it first.

"If high and mighty gets me meat on my plate, then yes," Columba said. "But that's not what I meant. No one must know that we are here. Not your brothers. Not anyone. In stealth we have come, and in stealth we must leave again, or … "

"Or?"

Columba drew a finger across his throat. "Or there is the small matter of my head. If you still love me enough to agree that I should keep it?"


"Yes. I do see," Comgall said once the introductions had been made and Aedan's story told. "If you had the boy, that might do the trick. Have you consulted the others?"

"The others?" Aedan asked.

At the innocence of the question, the old abbot muttered crossly. "No. Of course you haven't. You think you must always go it alone! Pride makes few friends! And you! As proud as they come!"

Eogan laughed. "That's true enough. Though to be fair, in his case it has made him at least two."

"Right. Well. I will help you. Of course you knew that I would.

But there is only so much I can tell you. For the rest you will have to go to him."

"I had hoped to avoid that," Columba said.

"Of course you did," Comgall said. "But it's a little too late for that, wouldn't you say? If anyone knows the whereabouts of that boy, it'll be Master Finnian."


That start of that long overland walk to Movilla was conducted in a weighty silence. It was the dead of night, so they passed through the quietly undulating landscape like nocturnal creatures; a creak, a rustle, a sigh which might have been the wind in the trees and hedgerows; shadows moving through shadows.

Movilla. The great monastic-school where Columba had gone to study once he had advanced sufficiently with his letters, and where, in due course, he had attained the rank of deacon. He hadn't stayed long; had certainly never returned to it—which he realized with a sudden flash of self-awareness, following the old byways now, was something of a habit with him. His life had been a series of short stays, of abrupt and wrenching departures—of his own making. Where others, like Comgall trudging so stiffly beside him, remained gently with their kin, or in their communities, for all their lives, Columba would barge in, full of bluster and demands and promise, learn what he wished to learn, whether or not it was desired to be taught him, and then move on, often with little or not opportunity for farewells. Time and time again.

It had seemed right to him each time he did it. He was a traveler. A pilgrim. He ate up living, all that it offered him. He had gifts given to him by God, and he went where divine will directed him to go. Once his horizons were known, his new skills mastered, he would push past them. Move on.

Yet suddenly he felt a moment of doubt: had it been courage and destiny, as he had hoped?

Or cowardice?

Sneaking a glance at his old friend in the moonlight, he could not now say.

After a short while, Columba was moved to speak. He grabbed Comgall's sleeve. "I was afraid that they might come for you too," he said to him.

"What?"

"That you would be imperiled."

"I don't … "

He stopped Comgall in his tracks. "I was afraid that if they knew that you were still associating with me, they would come after you too. That's why I didn't write."

"Oh."

"That, and … " Columba took a deep breath. How to admit this? His militant old friend had such impossibly high standards, most of which Columba did wholeheartedly admire. "After what I did," he said, "I wasn't sure you wanted to hear from me ever again."

"Oh. Oh." Comgall's expression turned sad. Then his face split into a lopsided grin. "Well, you're an ass. I did! I did!"

He slapped Columba on the back. "How I have missed you! Now—tell me everything!"


"Yes, I see now," Comgall said as he studied the two furtive figures striding ahead down the moonlit path. Below them, the wide valley pitched down to the loch-head, boats creaking at anchor in the sweeping harbor there. Rising to the right and keeping close watch over it all was a sharp hill crowned with a fort. From within that fort, fires flickered, smoke rose, voices drifted down.

Ahead, the path split. "That way," Columba called softly to Aedan and Eogan. "And quickly! That's one of Baetan's citadels. Best not to be seen!"

Staying low behind the brush, they took the path which led up a slope to the left. Some ways ahead, lights glowed from within a banked and gated monastery, large by the standards of Iona; almost a small village.

"You are lucky in your friends," Comgall said as they skirted quietly along.

"Yes! I always have been. Luckier than I deserve, perhaps."

In the recesses of Comgall's hood there might have been a thin smile. "Perhaps."

"Where is it, you thief!" Finnian roared. "What have you done with it?"

With a word from Comgall to the sentry at the gate, they had been waived in, then led along the dark footpaths of the sleeping community to Movilla's Great House where they had been asked to wait.

Not long. Very quickly, Finnian had been brought to them.

Columba was startled to see his former master, an ancient, stooped shell of a man, collapsing in on himself, bleaching, shrinking, yet with eyes as bright as ever; was astounded to be welling up with affection for the old man, considering everything that had happened between them.

Comgall turned wide eyes to Columba. "Wait: you never gave it back?"

Finnian hobbled forward, his cane beating a furious rhythm on the floor. "You had no right!" he rasped. "You miserable upstart! Mister 'High-and-Mighty'! Mister 'Won't-be-Told'! Mister 'Prince of the Blood'! Bah! Always think you know better, don't you! You arrogant, pig-headed ... You are the most obnoxious student I've ever taught, to this day! To this day! I told you no, and I meant no! Where is it? Where is it? You liar! You sneak! You thief! I'll ... I'll ... By God I'll strike you down!"

Finnian hoisted his cane, swung it tremulously at Columba's head, the bluing skin of his fist, nearly translucent in the thin light, tight with an old rage.

"Don't you worry, old master," Comgall muttered. "I took care of that already."

Columba, accustomed to his old master's outbursts but much more adept now at standing up to them, held his ground, his chin coming up. "Threaten me all you like. It didn't work then. It won't work now. It wasn't yours to hoard."

"Hoard? What do you mean, hoard? It was mine! I carried that book all the way back from Rome myself—Holy Rome! The Chief of All Cities!"

"Yes, you did! And thanks be to God for it! And while we are all indeed grateful, a thousand times did we have to hear that story! A thousand times! How bandits did try to steal it away from you in the treacherous pass through the Alps, swarming you from the dark crevices as rats to a scrap of meat, but for your prayerful intervention! How after untold hardships from which you should surely have perished did you arrive safely in Gaul but, while boarding the ship which would bear you back to blessed Hibernia, the book did seem to leap out of its satchel and into the sea! But neither did it drown nor soak, but float! Thanks again to your prayerful intervention, to how our great God does love you! Finally, how your triumphant return here, to Dal Fiatach, was attended by every known miracle, and many others besides, you praying every step of the way!"

Columba hadn't meant to get carried away—but how quickly the old passions, the old grievances could come flooding back! "A thousand times have I heard that story," he said, "you pompous ass! But never have I heard the story that truly needed telling: and that is by what right you could deny such a sacred thing to others!"

Finnian's contrary face took on a petulant cast. "What say you? It wasn't denied anyone. Anyone could come here to see it, to study it."

"Yes. What you mean is anyone could come here, pay the fee to enroll in your school, and then study for a year in silence and obedience before being allowed to gaze softly upon the sacred book for the first time. Not to breathe on it, mind you! Only to gaze lovingly from a safe distance. Then, after another year—and yes! More fees!—to stroke the marvelous covering of the blessed book with the barest caress of a finger. After another, to lay open its first page, that same single forefinger trembling with want and desire to see more, to know more. But not until an additional year, and

142

more tests and more fees, to begin to read it! To finally read it! With you hovering over one's shoulder! Tut-tutting, counting down the seconds, snatching back the book! Tell me: how many of us ever managed to pass your tests? How many in the end ever got to see that precious book in its entirety?"

"Those were God's tests, not mine. Those who deserved to read it, read it."

"Deserved? It is a book of God's word: a new translation of the Psalms. Direct from Rome! It belonged to everyone. Everyone! You had no more right to be its gatekeeper than ... "

Columba had easily justified stealing in. He would not go so far as to steal the famous Psalter (that was an act beyond him at the time)—but he could make a copy of it. That he could do without compunction. Indeed, he felt compelled. There was a higher order, he had assured himself, a higher law: God's law. Finnian was a brilliant teacher, but not perhaps a brilliant man. A new translation of the Psalms! What sacred lore might the book be keeping? What new truths might it reveal? Were there new ways to understand God? To understand living?

"Of course I copied it, you sour old hierophant," Columba said. "First chance I got."

Oh, Columba had easily justified it at the time.

But now, after many years, Columba could be honest with himself: he had also delighted in disobeying his intransigent master. The thrill of it had been absolute, a heady rush.

And then to defy High-King Dermot, who had been called in to rule upon the dispute? To not give back the copy he had made, as ordered, but to steal it away and, in due time, bear it out of Hibernia altogether?

Intoxicating.

Finnian hissed. He lurched at Columba, but Columba easily held off his flailing hands. The cane went flying and he would have fallen, but Columba and Comgall were there to catch him.

"Dermot made his judgment!" Finnian cried, spittle flying from his lips. "*Le gach bó a lao agus le gach leabhar a leabhrán.* 'To every cow its calf and to every book its copy'. The copy you made does not belong to you!"

"Dermot—God rest his soul—was an ass."

"Stop it now, the both of you!" Comgall roared. "Master Finnian! Compose yourself! Columba! Do you really think it wise to taunt him, considering what it is you need?"

Finnian was panting. "What does he need? The answer is no!"

"Master!" Comgall implored. "Please. Listen. They search for Fiachna Lurgan. The-boy-who-would-be-king."

Finnian immediately stilled, his gleaming eyes flicking back and forth between the two men holding him upright, his two former students. "Is that so?"

"It is. If we can find him, our chance to bring down Baetan may have come at last."

"I should like that! Yes, of all things! But! But! Surely you knew? It was Baetan who took him."

"There was a light to that boy's countenance that brought affection out of one," Master Finnian was saying. "But not Baetan. When he heard that the boy was for sale, he bought him from Black Hugh straight away."

They had sat Finnian down on a stool. He leaned forward eagerly with the telling of his tale.

"Dear God how that boy had wept! It was as if he knew that he had just escaped the crow's talons for the hawk's, and the fear of it was on him! That was the last I saw of him. It is at Dun Druma that you should look."

"Dun Druma?" Aedan asked.

"Ah yes!" said Columba. "Of course! Clever bastard!"

The great fortress of Dun Druma. On a ridge by the sea at the far end of Baetan's territory—as far from the border with the Dal nAraide as one could get and still be in country under Baetan's dominion. Overlooking not one but two great bays, one within the other, so that Baetan might both hide the boy and retrieve him easily when he wished, to move him about at will.

"Yes—that is where I would have put him too."


"There, you ingrate," Finnian said. "I have helped you. Now give me back my copy or … "

"Or what?"

"Or … " Finnian threw up his hands. "Or, I don't know! You remain corrupted? You find no redemption for your sins? Your precious soul is never saved?"

Columba had no answer.

"No? Not even that can sway you? How far have you slid, my old friend, back into sin and transgression? Can you not admit even now that you are pig-headed and proud to a fault and just give it back? Or, if not admit it to me, then to our good Lord? Will you not heed? Will you not heed *anyone*?"

Columba studied his old master, finding it not difficult to recall the man's own intransigence, and obstinacy, and disdain. Columba decided that, if he did feel these things—shame, contrition—it was not to his old master that he would admit them.

Seeing no confession forthcoming, Finnian observed with a huff, "One would think that exile would change a man".

That made Columba burst out with laughter. He felt himself soften. Just a fraction. "You can have no idea!" he said.

"Then where is the copy you made of my book?"

"Ah! Well, that is a long story. One you would appreciate." Being the long-winded gasbag that you are.

"I'm not going anywhere," Finnian said. "Tell it. Where is it?"

Columba tried very hard not to gloat, but there was something rather delicious in what he had next to say: "Do you mean right now? At this very moment? I suspect it is in the pocket of the king of the Picts".

# · 10 ·

# DUN DRUMA

One minute the whistling guard was daydreaming about the steaming bowl of oats awaiting him on the hearth up at the great dun on the high ridge behind him, the fortress he protected by patrolling these vast sand hills at harbor-mouth. The next, he was being hauled head-over-heels to land arse-down in the freezing estuarine mud, the wind knocked from him, a hard hand clamped over his mouth and the tip of a dagger jabbing into his throat.

He struggled wildly in panic. Slavers? Raiders?

But then, "Where's the boy?" one of his attackers demanded in a rough whisper. "Give him to us and you will live."

The guard gave a jerky nod and the hand eased a little to let him talk. "The boy?" he asked. "What boy?"

His answer was a ruse of course. Of course he knew for whom these raiders searched: there had only ever been one boy; one special boy, by the way it had turned out. But he would be damned if he told them! He was the king's guard—he would break free and kill them.

But there were three of them, all large enough, and the most formidable of the three, the one with his hand clamped around his throat, had a strength he doubted he'd be able to overcome.

The guard looked for a different means of escape, but they had him in the hollow of the dunes where he would be discovered by no one not already looking for him. The wind was blowing such a fine fit off the bay that no one would hear him should he cry out. It was hopeless and he knew it, but nevertheless he threw himself backwards in the cold streaky mud, only to find himself backed up against the dune itself.

The raiders were not amused. To help jog his memory, the big one hauled him up and gave him a shake good enough to rattle his teeth.

"Do you mean the-boy-who-would-be-king?" the guard gasped out. "That boy? The boy who was put into the ground up there, into the pit beyond the fort?

It had been many years ago. The start of the rough times. Turmoil and fighting on all sides, all the time. To bring it up now, after all these years, would cause trouble. The kind of trouble that got one killed.

But to put a boy in the pit? The guard hadn't liked it at all. It shouldn't matter that they said the boy could be king and to fear him. He was no more than a child.

But what was he to do but guard? If he hadn't, he'd have joined the boy in that pit for sure, no question.

"Yes, that boy," one of them said. "Fiachna Lurgan of the Dal nAraide."

The man who had spoken was older, gruffer. Kinder? His words were easier to understand too, which was a curious thing.

"My friends come for me! Here they come!" the guard cried. "Run now! Run for your lives!"

"Nice try," said the third man. "But you're out here all on your own. Do you think we'd have taken you before we watched for a while? You took a crap back there over an hour ago—with no one to wipe your ass for you. If your friends weren't around then, they'll not be coming now—no matter that now you really have cause to shit yourself."

The guard's stomach turned over. That one was right, on every count: he'd void his bowels for sure now.

The big one shook him again. "Just tell us what we need to know."

"Ah. Ah." There might be a way out, he realized. But not by trickery. The guard supposed it made no difference, given what had happened. Indeed, if these raiders kept their word and let him go, he might never have to speak of this to anyone. He could be back with his porridge before long and none the wiser—especially his lord Baetan.

With some of his fear abated, he looked at all of them more closely than before. He did not recognize any of them. If they had come by ship, he had not seen it approach, which worried him. It was his job to guard the inner bay. It must be anchored out beyond the narrow channel, out in the great outer bay, beyond where even the guards in the fort above could see it. Otherwise he'd have heard a warning blast.

No matter that it wasn't his fault, that these raiders had enough sea-craft to safely navigate the bewildering tides and the ever-shifting sand bars that made the great bay so feared by mariners and so defendable, they would all be made to pay if Baetan got word of it! Especially him, to have allowed them to get this far.

Were they Dal nAraide, come looking for their boy-king?

No—they didn't speak like Dal nAraide. Strangely, they spoke like he did: or, as his grandfather had. Especially the older, kind one.

Curious.

All right. He had to talk, that was clear. And if he was going to talk, he'd talk to the kind one. Improve his chance to survive this.

Because the tale he had to tell could scarce be believed.

"Right. Well, if it is that boy you look for, that one, that Fiachna Lurgan, then you are too late. It is to Tír na N'Og that he is gone. And you cannot get him back."

"Do you mean that he is dead?" the kind one asked.

"He is neither living nor dead, but in Tír na N'Og, as I have

149

said. Manannan wanted him, so Manannan took him. From just down there."

He pointed back towards the narrow mouth of the inner bay, to the sand hills that rose up either side of the little channel, the tides roaring in through that tube, the tides seeping out again, the wind and the water carving out new tracks, different rivulets every day, the treacherous bars of sand shifting before your very eyes, never the same one day to the next.

That was from where they must have come at him, must have beached behind the shelving shoreline to sneak up on him while he relieved himself.

That would teach him to mix ale with oysters before a shift. He thought to give himself a treat, what with the boy gone and Baetan away. But damn it if it didn't make his bowels run.

"It was the day my lord Baetan came for him, to take him out of his captivity," he said.

The big hand on his throat gave an involuntary squeeze.

"Ah! You know my lord Baetan then?" he guessed. "I pity you. As you should pity me should he hear of this! Since you do know him, you may suspect what happened next. Such hope there was in that boy's eyes when the door to his pit swung open at last to my lord Baetan there, the keys to freedom dangling from his fingers! Such hope! But it was not to free him. No, it was not! Which you shall have guessed, seeing as you know him. No. My lord Baetan released the boy from his chains only to kill him."

The kind one gasped. The big hand on his throat let up a fraction before tightening again.

"My lord Baetan dragged him down to the channel-mouth just there, the boy so weak he could hardly walk. It had been so long since he had seen sunlight that tears streamed from his eyes! The wind was howling, the gulls were shrieking at the sight of him as if he would soon be breakfast, and he was as pale as a ghost, but still he turned his face to the sun. We all pitied him! Of course we did! He's not much older than my own lad; and we all hoped for the best for him. But what could we do but my lord's will? There at the waves' edge my lord Baetan screamed at him and, though I know not what he said, it can't have been good for the boy began to sob and to plead for his life. But my lord only laughed and thrust the boy's head under the water."

He shuddered at the memory. The boy had struggled weakly, but had quickly gone limp. But rather than finishing the job as a merciful lord might have done, Baetan hauled him out again. He rattled the boy until the boy breathed. All who watched hoped. But Baetan, hearing life in his lungs, only pushed him back under.

The boy would be drowned, of that the guard was certain, but not before he had been tormented.

Baetan did this over and over again, the boy's suffering giving him pleasure. All the while, however, behind them the white line of waves that had been building in the outer bay had been growing closer and closer together, one after the other. The guard could see them rise on the horizon to make their way to the narrowing channel, much as they had ever done. But their pace! Their pace was quickening! Onward they came, almost as if heading straight for the two figures, Baetan and the boy, oblivious at water's edge.

And then … and then! Two waves stacked together, the back one riding the fore.

"We all shouted," he told them. "We all warned! We did! But my lord Baetan was bent on killing the boy and would not heed! We saw it coming! No one could miss it! We saw the third wave come right up and ride the first two so that all three came on together with a tremendous roar!"

"The boy is drowned then," the third one said, and turned away.

"No! No! It was the third wave! The third wave in a row! The wave that marks the road of the *sidhe* folk—the sea-road the spirits travel! Rudhriaghe's wave, roaring, rending as it lashed, screaming into the bay!"

The peaceable brigand perked up, animated. He began to nod.

"Yes! You see!" The guard couldn't help himself. He ought not to be divulging quite so much to the strangers, but there seemed to be kindness in them—a kindness which his lord Baetan lacked.

And besides: it was a tale of wonder which he himself might scarce believe if he hadn't witnessed it with his own eyes, and he could not help but to share it.

To see a god so close!

"The third wave was fierce and high and strong and it snatched the boy from Baetan's grasp! The boy went under and we thought him drowned at last—but then didn't he rise up from the swell, the waves cloaking him like a glittering silver hood, the water sloughing off the filth of his captivity—washing him clean as a babe!"

A shiver ran through him as he recalled the sight. Standing there gob-smacked, he could see a water-horse in the froth and curve of the waves, straining against its reins, its glistening hooves pounding the mud as it pulled the chariot of the sea-god himself. For it was Manannan! Plain as day! And his mighty steed Enbarr! Enbarr of the Flowing Mane! Who can ride as well on top of the waves as on land! The boy flailed, then his hand found purchase—a bridle, it had looked to him. And he managed to get his fingers right around it; a good, tight grip. And where the boy had gotten the strength to do what he did next he do not know, or perhaps it was another wave which bore him up, but by the gods didn't he manage to haul himself into that chariot and with no time to spare too because his lord Baetan was already after him cursing and screaming—but too late! Too late!

What a sight it had been!

"It was Manannan," he told them, "and no other. And didn't he laugh! What a roar! Waves punishing rock! And turning his chariot back to the deep, he bore the boy away."

The big one let him go. "Are you saying the boy was rescued by a *god*? The sea-god himself?"

The guard got to his feet, nodding vigorously in his need to have them believe. "Yes! Yes! That wave! That monstrous wave! We all agreed: it was Manannan. For who else could have done it? Who else? My lord Baetan was not best pleased, I tell you! No he was not! To be so thwarted! He stomped and steamed and sent his own men after the boy by boat."

"When was this? Has he been found?"

"Not a week back. Why, could it have had something to do with you, I wonder? It is almost as if my lord Baetan knew that you … "

Now that was a thought worth considering. He cast wondering eyes upon his would-be captors. Who were they, to frighten his lord Baetan into action after so long in neglect of the boy?

He also realized suddenly that he did want the boy rescued. He wanted the boy saved from Baetan quite desperately. No one should put a boy in a pit and then try to drown him. Even the gods knew that—as they all now well knew.

In fact, there was no better way to catch a god's eye, to earn his wrath, or so he had been told. The young ones. The innocent ones. The gods kept them right close.

"No," the guard said. "They've not found him yet, my lord. Not yet. Not as I've heard. At least not on the water."

It seemed right to call the big one "my lord" and he did so now without reservation. He had kept his word. He was free. He lived.

"Do they still search?"

"Aye."

"Where?"

"You don't know? You're not from around here, then," he said. If the big one were, he'd know.

Under his concealing hood, the eyes of the gentle one were glittering. He knew.

"Who are you?" the guard asked him, intensely curious as to their identities and their purpose, now that he no longer feared for his life. "Could you be … "

But the kind one ducked his head and did not answer.

"Since it was Manannan took him," he informed the big one, "they search the banks of the River Bann, where it is birthed up in the hills, there. High, high up, where the mighty river emerges from deep in the cold heart of the mountain."

He pointed at the range of stark black peaks that stuck up over the tree line to the south, as if straight from the sea. Ragged cloud caught on the shoulders of the cones and was sucked down into the deep clefts between them, where it stirred and frothed like a cauldron on the boil.

The guard laughed uneasily. The Mountains of the Mournes; as dark as sin or death, and didn't he know it! Good luck to them if they went there!

"They follow the river down the mountains to the great loch. If the boy is not on the River Bann, then he is on the loch. And if he is not on the loch, then Manannan has taken him home."

How the guard hurried home, up and over the dunes to safety!

"Can we believe him?"

"I don't know," Columba said. "Does it matter?"

"How can it not matter?"

"Whatever the true agent of the boy's deliverance—sea-god, a rare wave, his imaginings—that man saw him survive," Columba said. "So did Baetan. If he sent boats and men, then Baetan too believes he escaped with his life. Therefore so should we. We would do well to search where Baetan searches. There must be a reason he searches the Bann."

"We're running out of time," Eogan said. "He has to be at Ros-na-Righ by week's end." An anxious tip of the head in Aedan's direction.

"We should split up," Columba said. "Let me go look for the boy."

"No. It's not safe for you," Aedan said. "That guard was on to you."

"Yes, I think he was. But I know this country. I know where to look. I know where to hide, should it come to that."

To hide. In a country he once helped to rule. The irony of it startled him.

"And I can't be you," Columba said. "You are the one who must meet with Baetan."

He had convinced them—Eogan, at least, was nodding.

"Will you go to the mountains?" Aedan asked. "To where this

river, this Bann, is born?"

"The Mournes? No. I should not go there unless I am forced to. Besides, it's too late, I think: surely they'll be gone from there by now? I'll go overland from here and pick up the Bann before it spills into the great loch at Bannfoot. There are paths there I can follow. Secret ways. If the boy is being brought down the Bann, he will have to come that way. Thence to the loch."

"I don't like it. This is Dal Fiatach territory. If you are caught … "

"Is there a better way? I don't see one. I'll be careful. Once at the loch, I'll search, make inquiries. If he has gone that way then surely he will have been seen—especially if Baetan's men follow. There I should be able to discover if I should turn back up the Bann, or go forward, through the loch and down to the coast to the north."

"I'll make the inquiries," Eogan said.

"Sorry?"

"You'll be in disguise, my friend, the better to protect your head. I am coming with you."

"Disguise? You have a plan?" There was a mischievous cast to Eogan's grim grin which gave Columba pause.

"I do."

"I'm not going to like this, am I?"

"Probably not, but it should work. And we'll be quick. How long to this Bannfoot?"

"If we hurry, two days' hard march from here."

"All right. Two days to the loch, a day or two at the loch to look, then two days' back to you, Brother. We'll meet you at Ros-na-Righ by week's end—with the boy in hand."

# · 11 ·

# PATRICK'S ROAD

They kept to the river valley, following the path that ran along the Bann as it wound its way northward, the forbidding mass of the Mourne mountains at their backs blocking out the rising sun and casting the early part of their way in shadow. Except for the anomaly of those mountains, the land they passed through was a gentle, fertile country—or should have been, had there been anybody about to till the rich soils. But the countryside was strangely deserted and those few they did see gave them a wide berth. They did not like strangers here.

In this way no one bothered the middle-aged monk and the old woman who attended him. They saw what they expected to see: a religious on some business of his monastery accompanied by his devoted, overworked servant, a woman so ordinary, so nondescript that no one could later describe accurately her if required to. That first day, they saw no sign of the boy or his captor.

By noon of the second day of their journey, when the country all around had become even lower, more grassy and wet, they at last reached the place in the Bann where the river swelled open so widely and for such a distance that it looked and behaved like a sea-loch, a proper inlet of the ocean, though it was not. And what a sight to see! Bulbous clouds and mist hung over the enormous expanse of shimmering water. Rafts of waterfowl wheeled overhead, swooping down to settle on the glassy surface; white swans glided silently in the shallows. It was a beautiful, eerie place, the water and the sky mingling so seamlessly that all was a single blinding sheet of silver.

Here at the loch's edge the mouth of the river was too deep to be forded by foot. A ferry could take them over, but they worried about the risk of discovery. After some deliberation—should they head downstream a ways to shallower ground and attempt to swim across? Was there a boat they might commandeer for a time?—they decided to take their chances and hail the ferryman who held forth at the jetty, a spritely soul of indeterminate age with corded muscles and an inscrutable face, the latest in a long line of men to carry all manner of cargo, human and not, across the river-mouth without question so long as the fee was paid first and handsomely.

The ferry itself was a rickety affair, a few planks bolted together to make a floating platform that cleared the water's surface by mere inches, large enough to accommodate a cart and horse and with handrails but no proper sides. Eogan stepped out onto it first, the ferry tilting drunkenly. In as dutiful as manner as he could, subservience not being in his nature, Columba followed, the folds of his headscarf knotted at his ducked chin, his stride shortened, his tunic altered to look like a woman's. He shouldered their bags on his bent back, stood where Eogan told him to stand, looked to Eogan's comfort, enduring his clipped commands as if they were an everyday nuisance, saying nothing, as a servant might. And so the ferryman saw only a monk of some importance and his lowly dependent, perhaps the elderly, destitute aunt he had taken in as charity, as he ought.

"Enjoying yourself?" Columba muttered to Eogan.

"You can have no idea!"

They greased the ferryman's palm with the leg of the hare they had trapped the previous evening and with a jerk they were off, the ferryman pulling hand-over-hand on a heavy rope strung across the river. Once started, the ferry glided smoothly enough. The ferryman did not speak and neither did they.

Once across, they pressed on, keeping to the path that skirted the loch in a westerly manner for another hour or so until they came to a track running north to south, worn bare by many feet and lying at odds with their own.

They took this new path northwards a short way until it abruptly dropped off at a secretive landing place right at the loch's edge, an ominous little dell hung over with ancient, gnarled trees and shrubs. Some distance offshore lay an island that was gently-domed and heavily forested. Of no great size, the island was nevertheless distinguished on the loch for having no neighbors nearby.

"Right," said Eogan looking around for some clue as to what they should do next and finding none. "Explain."

"Oh! May I speak now, Master?"

"Honestly, you amaze! What's this about, then? Why are we here?"

"Ask me nicely."

Eogan growled, which made Columba laugh. "Fine! Fine!" he chortled. "I will tell you and not make you beg. This? This is Patrick's Road."

"Patrick's Road? But this road goes no where."

"On the contrary. It takes us there." Columba pointed to the island.

"How?" Eogan asked. "By ferry?"

"There is no ferry. We don't need a ferry."

"I know you love your jokes, but enough is enough."

"Look again, my friend," Columba answered. "Use the eyes the good Lord gave you."

"Ass," Eogan muttered, but he did look, and he could see many things: the constant shush, shush, shush of the gleaming water pushed along by a gentle breeze lapping against the embankment. The loch so vast he could only just make out its other shores.

Sizeable birds soaring over the island ahead, of a kind he could not yet descry; other waterfowl on the water itself, honking, calling, gliding, diving, their bottoms upturned in the air as they fed on sweet sunken grasses; others in the trees here and there trilling and tittering happily: so many varieties he might not be able to name them all. The sun which was beginning to set over his shoulder tingeing the underside of the clouds an orange verging on pink. To the east, the sky darker, almost ominously so.

Eogan saw and felt many things, but he could not see the fabled path of which Columba spoke.

Columba pointed to the water at their feet. "Try it," he said.

"Try what?"

"Just walk."

Muttering, "Honestly, you are such an ass," Eogan nevertheless took a tentative step out upon the water. He flailed for a second, then landed clumsily on something which was not immediately visible—a causeway submerged a foot or two under the surface of the loch. Knee-deep in water, he probed with his toe. The hidden causeway extended the width of two men before falling off to the sides. More encouragingly, it extended out into the loch—but for what distance, Eogan could not tell. He supposed it would take them all the way to the island.

"That's extraordinary!" Eogan said. "To look at it, you'd not know it was there!"

"Yes! Isn't it marvelous! It's not always underwater. It depends on the time of year and the weather. If there has been drought, for instance, it slashes across the loch to the island clear as day."

"Is this really Patrick's Road?"

"Oh yes! They say he often came this way to rest out on the island. He loved watching the birds. The herons in particular. There's a sacred spring on the island, which the Old Ones guard. Many come to partake of its waters. Many are healed. I hope to speak with its keeper. She might know of the boy."

"How do you know of this place?"

"I came here once as a young man. A woman tended the holy

spring at that time, who was ancient even then to my young eyes. I wonder if she still lives? If so, you will have to question her, lest she recognize me. If we follow the secret road here, we should reach the island in a half-hour or so."

"So long?"

"Yes. It is further out than it looks. Such a large body of water plays tricks on the eyes."

They unlaced their boots and, tying them together, draped them around their necks. Then they pulled up their tunics and wrapped them around their waists. Ready, they waded out, their feet finding the submerged causeway as much by faith as by feeling.

They plodded ahead cautiously. Ahead, the island was coming more clearly into view. The grey herons glided over the tops of the lofty chestnut trees, their elongated necks tucked in, their tidy heads drawn back, their harpoon-like beaks jutting forth as their ponderous wings flapped, their thin legs trailing with an unexpected elegance behind. Though they soared and swooped, they made no sound.

The light was beginning to fade. Columba cast a worried look to the sky. Soon it would be dark. They sloshed forward, determined to reach the island before night fully fell, and had drifted into a lull, not speaking, when a large group of waterfowl that had been idling on the water some way off to their right took suddenly and raucously to the air. The birds wheeled overhead with bitter complaint.

"Something has disturbed them," Columba said. "Can you see what it is?"

They searched the loch but could see nothing except the rapidly setting sun staining the clouds a rather beautiful haze of pinks and oranges and reds.

The birds fell apart overhead and regrouped, chattering to one another nervously.

"What do they say?" Eogan asked.

"Something is coming."

The flock reeled and dove, screeching.

"It is something they fear. Look!"

To the east, from whence the birds had fled and not too far from where they stood on the causeway, the sky was filling up with an ominous, strangely-formed cloud, dark-bottomed and arching up, like an overturned cup. Under it, a light-colored disk was forming on the surface of the water.

Columba started. Looked again. The disk looked like an eye, glaring upwards. The water around this eye grew darker and more and more unsettled. They watched in horror as the outer, darker, ring of water began to churn. It churned faster and faster, the cloud above it turning blacker and blacker.

Suddenly the dark disk erupted, exploding upwards, water surging up all around its edge. The tower of water grew higher and higher until it had formed a funnel. It made a sound like a scream. The funnel wobbled, almost like a finger pointing accusingly at the angry cloud overhead, and looked as if it might collapse, but then it found its center again and surged higher.

*"What the hell is that?"*

Up and up the waterspout spiraled, a hundred feet or more, until it pierced the underbelly of the clouds, linking water and sky.

Then the whole churning, spiraling, hissing vortex began to move. It swung about and seemed to hesitate, but then it settled on its course—straight towards where they stood vulnerable and exposed on Patrick's secret road.

"Sweet Mother of God! Run!"


The roaring tower of water thundered. It roared and it sucked like a swarm of a million, million angry insects; all the world's wind at once. The air itself seemed to grow heavier. Their ears screamed from the pressure, the sharp popping in their heads an unbearable knife of pain.

Headlong they threw themselves towards the safety of the island.

Columba flung one foot in front of the other, Eogan a blur ahead. Water pelted his face, stung his eyes. The wind tore at his clothes, ripped off his headscarf, bore it away, snapping and twisting. Blinded by the spray thrown up by the towering spout of water, he could not see two feet in front of him, did not know if the causeway would stay true underfoot or if at any moment they would topple over the side.

"*Oh God! Oh God! Oh God!*" he panted in terror. If Eogan were doing the same, he could not hear it.

It bore down on them, on a path to intersect the causeway, as if it were hunting. Them, he wondered wildly? It did seem hell bent on them. The waterspout was so wide that they would not be able to put it behind them. Their only hope was to reach the island before the funnel reached them. But where was it? Through the wall of water he thought he could make out a general darkening ahead. The island? Columba sent up a prayer as he made for it, sent up another prayer that the causeway would hold true under their feet. To fall off in this maelstrom would be to perish. They would drown for certain.

At last! They were close! There! There! With only seconds before it swallowed them up, Columba shoved Eogan forward with all his might. Eogan might make it to safety! At the same time, Columba was himself lifted off his feet—by Eogan who had made a wild, desperate grab behind.

They landed facedown in a bed of reeds. Columba grabbed at the slim fronds, not caring that his hands were sliced open by their razor-sharp edges. He threw an arm over Eogan and held on, Eogan holding tight to him also.

The waterspout closed overhead, screaming.


It tore. It sucked, yanking their hair from their heads, pulling their lips from their teeth, their clothes from their backs, stealing the breath from their lungs, tearing at their skin as it railed and teemed.

They flattened themselves to the strongly-rooted reed bed and grimly held on, praying, praying, praying.

And encouragingly, at one point it did seem to abate, the world growing quieter, the onslaught lessening, but as Eogan loosened his grip on Columba, Columba shouted with all his might, "No! Not yet!" for it was only the still eye of the spout passing over them. And then came its other wall.

They entwined themselves deeper into the dense net of reeds and prayed every prayer of protection they knew. But the waterspout was immensely strong, and Columba felt his grip slipping. But just as he was about to be torn loose, it began to weaken. Little by little he could feel it losing its power until, with a defeated sigh that was almost human, it gave up and let go.

Columba risked a look to see the spout retreating both up and down at the same time, until with a snap it collapsed and was absorbed again either end to disappear into a suddenly subdued sky and a now-flat loch.

They scrambled to higher ground; caught their breaths; scraped hair and mud from their faces. Save for a certain buzzing sound still ringing in their ears, it was eerily quiet. Too quiet; curiously calm. There was no sign of the waterspout. Dark smudges appeared in the sky: birds returning grumpily. The surface of the water, recently so furious, was smoothing itself out, the trembling reeds settling. The sun was falling as it always does; the twilight was just a twilight—and they shook their heads with wonder.

"What the hell was that?" Eogan asked.

"Something I've never seen."

"It felt like the very wrath of God."

"It was someone's wrath, that's for certain—but not our Lord's, I don't think."

"Why not? How can you know?"

"I think our praying helped deplete it of power. And … "

"And?"

"It's like in Dal Riata. Here, here in Hibernia, everything—every mountain, every great tree, every notable rock, every body of water, be it river, spring, stream or, in our case, loch—everything has its god or its goddess. Its spirit. This one's … *anima* … "

"It's female?"

"Wouldn't you say?"

Eogan snorted shakily.

"It doesn't like us."

"*Like?*"

"Well, perhaps *want*. It doesn't want us," Columba said. "It is very curious, but I don't think we were meant to reach this island."

"Who was it is trying to scare off? You or me?"

It was Columba's turn to laugh. "Probably me."

"Why? What have you done?"

Columba hesitated, said, "Any number of things, I'm afraid".

"All right. Let us say that it was you. How did it know that you were you?"

"What do you mean?"

Eogan waved his hands up and down. "Look at you! You're a woman, for God's sake! Your skirts! In this case, a mess!" Eogan gave a wobbly chuckle in which Columba was glad to hear some of his customary sarcasm returned. "You look like a fishwife. Recently tumbled. In the bottom of her boat. By a man who is not her husband. In fact, isn't that a fish there, in the folds of your cloak?"

From the twisted recesses of his tangled clothing Columba withdrew a wriggling fish that, upon closer inspection, revealed itself to be a trout of a kind unique to the loch they found themselves in.

"Ah!" he exclaimed, holding the beautiful brown speckled fish up to what remained of the early evening's light. "Supper!"

They shared a relieved laugh. But Eogan was soon turning worried eyes back to the skies.

"But truly, Columba," he said, "do you know her? The goddess here? That is, do you know her name? Can you beseech her? Tell her that we mean no harm, that we come in peace?"

"I do. She is Banda. She is the river itself—both the upper and the lower Bann, and this swollen middle."

"If she is the anima of this place, why doesn't she know what we are about, that we come in love? Well, not love precisely—I am finding this a hard place, one I am not certain I can warm to—but that we come to avenge a girl's dishonor, and a boy's. She should know this. Can you not tell her this?"

"I don't think I am the one for it. You do it."

Eogan had questions in his eyes, but he did not probe further. He nodded, looked up at the dark and now cloudless sky, said: "Please. Lady Banda. We seek to help Covna, a girl who in her youth drank your waters. And Fiachna, her brother." He paused, considered. Said: "Please help us to help them. If we can, we will return them to you".

He looked to Columba. Columba nodded, shouldered his pack. "Well my friend, if it wasn't clear to us before, it is clear to us now that there are secrets here, on this island. Ones we may not be meant to find. Nevertheless, let us do our best to uncover them."

If she heard Eogan's plea, it was in the gentle question of the wind in the frill of the waves. If she answered, it was in the slow roll of unseen currents deep in the heart of the loch.

# · 12 ·
# THE ISLAND OF THE BLACKWATER

The path that led through the thick forest was well trodden and easy to follow: a white scar in the dark. The heave and thrum of insects that had resumed as the men entered the confines of the grove grew to a dull, oppressive roar, as if the forest itself was humming. Up ahead, light was glinting through the trees. They made their way towards it.

They emerged into a clearing at the island's center. A small fire was throwing up fitful flames, spitting smoke into the air. Behind the fire was a jumble of rock; behind the rocks, a yew tree, by its girth and height, ancient. Strips of cloth had been threaded throughout the tree's lowest branches. The brightly colored rags shivered in the flickering light of the fire.

It should have been a welcoming sight, but after their near miraculous escape on Patrick's Road, Columba was feeling jumpy, unsure. His body wanted to bolt from the place then and there, even though this was a grove that had always been holy. It should have been a natural sanctuary for someone like him. Why, then, did he feel so on edge?

Just then, there was a sudden movement. What they had taken to be a pile of stone was in fact an old woman, squatting on the far side of the fire. A faded grey shawl that might once have been striped covered the woman's head and was pulled low over her sharp eyes. She was hugging her knees to her chest, the bones of her attenuated arms bulging out clearly between the sinews, her fingers gnarled and bent willy-nilly. The rest of her was obscured by the folds of her threadbare cloak so that she seemed to be rooted to the ground. An old, burly, knob-headed cane lay at her feet.

She herself was very still, almost preternaturally so. It was the air around her that was moving. At first Columba could not tell if it was a trick of the light, or some magical emanation coming off her person. But then he looked more closely and saw that bats were swarming around her, darting and dipping so quickly that he could glean only vague impressions of their forms. It was almost as if they were trapping nuggets of thought in streams of energy he himself could not see swirling above her head.

Her glittering eyes stayed on them as they approached, she saying nothing until they stood before her. Then she spoke, a deep, raspy whisper: "She didn't clear you two out? Hmm".

She shifted. The bats scattered, then regrouped above her head. "Too bad," she said. "Too bad."

Eogan did a kind of bow, said, "My lady ... "

She snorted in laughter. "My lady? That's rich."

"I'm sorry?"

"You will be, I can assure you. But right now you need a healing."

"A healing?"

"Not you. That one." She laughed. "That old woman! That *lady*. She needs a healing! And I know what ails her!"

"What? What ails her?" Eogan asked.

Without really moving at all, she grabbed the cane that had been lying so innocuously at her feet and struck out at Columba with it. The attack was so sudden that he flinched, but she had only snagged the hem of his tunic.

But then she thrust the cane violently upwards, exposing him. She giggled into the folds of her scarf. "Her sex! That is what ails her!"

Columba cursed, shoved the cane aside and yanked his clothes back down.

"I see you!" she said, her shrewd eyes sweeping the rest of Columba's disguise in a way that left him feeling wholly exposed. "Yes. I see you, old *man*. I see truly where others see only the … "

Her eyes narrowed. "The *deception*." She drew out the word to its fullest accusation.

It was unnerving. She had thoroughly uncovered him, and he had yet to speak a word.

Columba thought about unburdening himself of the truth there and then, but something about her manner put him off. If he were to admit to everything, it would not be to her.

His chin came up. His shoulders went back. He would force the issue, if he had to. There was too much at stake here to be thwarted now. "We have come to consult the holy well," he said to her. "As far as I know, it has always been open to all."

This caused her to cackle again. "Do as you like," she said, shrugging. "You will, regardless. But remember what has not changed: you will get from it only what you give."

She pointed behind her with her cane. "You remember how it is done."

The entrance to the well was hidden in the jumble of rocks. Columba ducked his head under the low lintel and descended three shallow steps, walls hugging him tight to either side, to find himself in a dark, damp chamber. As his eyes adjusted to the dim light, he could see that things were as he remembered them. A small iron cup had been affixed to the wall by a chain. Further down at the edge of the well, there was a moss-grown stone slab. It was the well's *bullaun* stone. Shallow indentations had been worn into it by the knees of countless supplicant pilgrims, come to the well for healing.

He had been one of those pilgrims. His knees had rested there, back when he was a young man. He recalled it so clearly. There had been a serenity to the little chamber which had felt ancient to Columba who, though still young, had sought out as many such places of old magic as he could.

With the thrill of rediscovery he acknowledged the power of this place again.

That last time, the well had answered the question he had put to it in an immediate and irrefutable fashion. But he had been freer of both care and sin then. How would it answer him today, he wondered, if it did at all?

He knelt on the *ballaun* stone and looked down into the well. Water glinted back blackly, its surface disturbed only by what little light managed to leak through the gaps in the chamber's walls above.

He looked carefully for a while, alert for any sign whatsoever, any change in sight, sound, or smell, but nothing new came to him. His mind was still in a silent uproar of thought and worry, his shoulders too tense and tight.

He closed his eyes, breathed deeply, tried to rid himself of any tainting concern save the purity of his purpose, and that was to find the boy. Surely the holy water would respond to that, if nothing else.

Quashing his rising impatience, he waited a moment, then looked again.

This time, the thing that stood out to him about the well's appearance was not any dramatic change, as he had previously sought, but rather its ordinariness, the sheer evenness of the ripples of light and dark on the water's surface. There was as much light as there was dark, and no more of one than the other.

It was a small thing, one others might have missed, but not Columba: the water of this holy well was imbued with secret meaning, half of which was dark.

Blessings, yes, but also pain; and not the one without the other.

As the impact of this insight sunk into his receptive mind, he reared back. Small though the sign was, it was nevertheless a warning, as shrill and intractable as a shout. If he continued to seek guidance and counsel from this sacred gateway, he might receive that which he sought, but he might also be shown things he did not wish to see, be reminded of things he preferred to forget. Be asked for things he did not wish to give.

The finding of the boy would require a sacrifice.

Seized by a sudden fear, Columba heaved in breath. He lurched back on his heels. His heart was hammering. There was a terrible noise in his head, like someone shrieking.

He was not ready for what might be asked of him. He might never be ready.

He was losing control of his nerve. Of his confidence. Seeking some way to calm himself, he took charge of his wayward breath. He turned his eyes away from the holy well and trained them overhead, to what he could see of the heavens: not much, a truncated constellation of stars behind the roughly-hewn edge of the doorway above.

But what he saw was enough. He quieted the storm in his mind. He remembered who he was. He remembered his friends.

Yes. For Aedan, for Eogan; for his brothers on Iona; for Dal Riata, both halves of it—for Aedan's boys, and the lost boy he sought—he would give what was asked of him, if he could.

For his friends, he would try his best.

Composed, he rocked forward onto his knees again.

Now that he had accepted this holy well's terms, how to unlock it?

The keeper's gravelly voice drifted to him down the stone steps. "If you need to know a thing from this holy water, this is what you say," she said. And she taught him the prayer, which he then repeated.

When he peered down into the water a second time, something was glinting at the bottom of the well.

He hesitated.

"If it is speaking to you," came the woman's voice, "do as you are told."

Hiking up his sleeve, Columba fished around until his fist closed around the shining object. He pulled it out and looked at what was cradled in his palm. It was a cream-colored stone, polished to a high sheen. The stone was crisscrossed with streaks of yellow and red, as if someone had struck it so hard that it had cracked and bled.

He breathed a sigh of relief. He knew this type of stone. They were highly prized. His people, his former people the Cenel Conall who lived not far from here, would hunt for the best specimens to carve into gaming pieces, or baubles for bracelets and necklaces. They would keep them in pockets as talismans. Cast them into holy wells as offerings.

His palm tingled with a kind of recognition as he put the stone in his pocket.

He made his way back to Eogan. When he showed him what he had found, the old woman laughed. "Is that the only treasure you drew up?" she asked. "Because this well of mine hides other treasures. Many others."

She cocked her head, listening to something: perhaps one of the bats still swarming around her. "Oh yes, that's right. Thank you, dear one," she said, nodding. "I remember now. It will hide them *in time*. In time to come. It does not hide them yet."

Eogan took the stone from Columba, rubbed it dry on his sleeve to get a better look at it. "It looks rather like a skull, doesn't it?"

"Yes, I suppose it does."

"Are you certain it's a sign?" he asked. "It's such a small thing. A mundane, everyday kind of thing."

"It is a sign."

"Of what?"

"That we go north out of the loch," Columba said. "That we follow the river-road—the River Bann. Because these stones are found in one place only, on a beach in a twist of the Bann as it makes its way north to the sea. I know exactly where to go."

Columba, relieved to have been awarded such a happy outcome, turned to the woman and thanked her warmly. "Is there anything you need?" he asked her. "Anything we can get you before we go?"

"Hmm. I like that cloak of yours."

Columba looked down at his cloak, surprised. Hardly his finest, it was one he had chosen to best appear a humble old woman, a servant. Nevertheless, he unclasped it and gave it to her.

"Ah!" she said. "This is the cloak with which it is said you will cover the whole world with your light. I'll not be cold this winter."

They turned to go.

"Wait!" she cried. "It is bad luck to leave before making your own offering."

"How?"

Her cane lifted to point decisively over her shoulder at the great yew tree which draped itself over the well, at the strips of red cloth dangling from its lowest branches.

"To resist evil," she said, "red is best."

Columba tore a strip of cloth from the hem of his once-white but now filthy tunic. Eogan did the same. They went back down into the well chamber and, using the iron cup chained to the wall, ladled up water which they poured over their strips of cloth. Then, while praying, they drew the soaking wet cloths over their hands and faces.

When they were done, they tied their rags to the great tree, adding their supplications to all the ones that had come before.

"It's no good," the old woman *tssked* to her darting companions as the men strode away. "I told them, didn't I? They should have listened. No good shall come of it."

She laid her cane back at her feet. She drew her new cloak about her thin shoulders and settled in. To one looking, she would appear yet again to be no more than one of the jumbled rocks.

"The rags," said the rock, "need to be red."

"We go up the loch, to its most northerly point," Columba said, pointing, his mouth full of grilled trout. "There the river Bann begins again. It runs from there to the sea."

They were camped in a little clearing on the edge of the island. It was the hour before dawn. They had rested for a few hours, refreshed themselves, were finishing the trout they had cooked over their small fire to break their fast. The sky was quiet, with no sign of its former violence. Mist clung to the loch, the water glimmering. They had cast in a line to fish, the line swaying gently in the water. It was still, peaceful, beautiful.

"Will we be anywhere near our Dal Riata?" Eogan asked, his belly full, his spirits rejuvenated and optimistic.

"Yes. Next door to it. We will draw up in border country, between your people and mine."

"I am eager to see the place at last!"

Columba sucked fish juices from his fingers. "Oh, this is good!" he said. "I had forgotten just how good! They're only found here, these tasty wee beauties."

"Bless Banda, then, for having thought to plant one in your dress."

Just then, their attention was caught by movement out on the water. They tensed, but it was only a herd of deer crossing the straight from the mainland, their heads bobbing above the waterline, their breaths coming in little pants as they emerged from the mist. A magnificent buck led the way, parting the green reeds of the shallows.

"Oh, would you look at that!" Columba whispered, full of awe.

They were watching reverently, staying as quiet as they could so as not to startle the herd, when suddenly the buck reared back with a piercing bellow. From its thick russet neck, the shaft of an arrow protruded at a grotesque angle.

The arrow had come not from the far shore across the straight, but from the tree line behind them.

As the buck struggled to shore and collapsed onto its forelegs, grunting in pain, its terrified companions lurching, scrabbling for footing in the shallows and bolting for the safety of the trees, Columba and Eogan dove for cover.

Too late.

"If you move," said a hard voice in Columba's ear, "you are next."

# · 13 ·
# ROS-NA-RIGH

"This is not good," Aedan finally admitted to her. "Not good at all. Where are they?"

They were scouting out the big bowl-shaped bay where Aedan was to meet Baetan mac Carell later that morning, hoping for some sign of Columba and Eogan. A biting wind was hurtling down from the encircling headlands, causing them to huddle in the lee of an enormous erratic boulder, the height of a man and twice his width, which squatted on the hillside like a stunted primordial watchman, its blunted face, its heavy brow and jaw jutting out over the bay. Despite the stone's monumental size, it had the amazing property of rocking slightly when knocked against as if alone of its lapidary kind it was responsive and plodding incrementally towards vegetal life.

Below, the stone-grey sea threw itself against the muddy shingle of the shore. Aedan's warship was anchored restively, its oars poised for flight. Aedan, pacing anxiously, had his eyes trained uneasily on the seaways to the north, a series of towering headlands which stepped up the coast as far as the eye could see, for this was dangerous country, a borderland between warring peoples—a place where kings met, a *ros-na-righ*.

From the vantage point of the sentinel stone, Aedan could just make out bits of the three pieces of the province of Ulaid. South of the bay lay Dal Fiatach, Baetan's kingdom. To the west was Dal nAraide, whose lost boy-king they so desperately sought. To the north was Dal Riata, Aedan's ancestral homeland, its high, rugged protuberances, rippling ominously up the coastline, peopled by men and women who had no idea he was their lord—their own, long-lost lord, returned.

Ama nearly laughed: Aedan had yet to meet a single one of them. Yet here he was, about to negotiate for their survival.

She would have found it all darkly amusing but for the sense of deep unease which had settled in her stomach. So much could go wrong with this audience between these two old enemies today, and very little right.

Still, she refused to give voice to her apprehensions. Aedan needed her strength, not her misgivings. "It may be a good sign," she said to him.

He smiled darkly, grateful for her encouragement and yet thoroughly unconvinced by it. Taking her hand gently to thread his fingers through hers, he said, "No, love. It's not. If they found the boy, they will have returned, just as we agreed. If they have not found him, they will also have returned. They have neither found him nor not found him—and something else has occurred entirely".

Something unexpected. Something unpleasant.

She squeezed his hand. She would not give in to her fears: not until she was forced to. Columba and Eogan were well suited to the task; if anyone could do it, they could. "They must need more time," she said. "We will give it to them and not worry. They are canny, resourceful and, most importantly," she brought their clasped hands to her chest, "*lucky*. Especially Columba."

He nodded, but said, "This is not going to work without that boy".

"No. Not the way you had planned, in any case."

"Without the boy, I've got two choices," he said.

Yes. It was either diplomacy. Or show of force.

This understanding passed between them on a long, wordless look. As did the knowledge that diplomacy was too troublesome an art for a man like Baetan, a man who saw only his own side.

She pushed away from the sheltering rock. "With Baetan it must be show of force," she said.

For a moment, the world spun. She gasped. But it was only the great sentinel stone under which they sheltered shivering under her hand.

Aedan motioned for his men. He had positioned them on the ridge, on guard for Baetan's forces, but now moved them to even higher ground, bows at the ready. Then with a shout and a wave, he signaled to those left onboard to take the ship to safer anchorage in a little inlet they had spied on the other side, the sea-side, of the promontory, to trap Baetan's ship when it arrived in the bay.

Then, jumpy, moody, troubled, they waited.

The morning crept by. The tide turned and was sucked back out to sea. The sun clawed to its full height overhead and began to collapse again. The wind got no warmer, no less biting, scraping the water into white-capped waves. All the while, Ama's anxiety grew; sent her pacing too.

"I don't like this," Aedan said. "This is not like Baetan."

Finally, as day gave in to evening and the tide turned again, a dark mass suddenly rose up on the high, rolling, open sea, bearing down on the bay from the north. It did not diminish, as a sudden squall might, but grew steadily larger. When they could make out sails slipping under the waves then rising over them again, she instinctively began to count: one, two, three—four warships breaching the fateful curving bay of Ros-na-Righ and sealing it shut.

Her fear won out.

"Diplomacy," she whispered.

They could make a break for it over the ridge and meet up with their warship anchored ocean-side. They could turn tail, melt into the hillside. One could argue that nothing would suffer for it but his reputation amongst a people who did not even know he existed.

But putrid heads rotted in bags. And the lives of his people, even those he did not yet know, depended on what he did next.

And, much closer to his heart: the safety of Columba and Eogan, wherever they might be.

There was no choice to be made. He had no idea how Baetan had rebuilt his fleet so quickly or, more likely, from whom he had stolen these new ships, but there was no question but that Aedan had been outplayed.

"Will he kill you?" Ama asked as he made to go down.

Hearing the fear in her voice, he pulled her hood protectively over her head, tucked in her hair.

"Not with our arrows trained on him," he said, more hopeful than certain. "He's after something else today."

Or so Aedan was gambling.

Aedan met Baetan on the beach. He was as Aedan remembered him. Pale-blond hair. Ice-blue eyes. Cold lips that smiled only to convey superiority: the maw of an animal that opens only to bite.

Against the slate-grey sky, his enemy seemed to shine with a chilly light.

True to form, Baetan did not mince words. "I see no cattle, no tribute, as you were ordered," he said.

"I will not submit. Why bring chattel?"

Baetan inclined his pale head, his eyes cruel and knowing. "You think you are clever, but you are not. Your cunning is of a dull, blunt kind. Primitive. Dare I say stupid?"

Baetan waved a hand in the general direction of Aedan's men arrayed on the ridge, bows to the ready. "I'd very much like to end this here and now," he said, "but I cannot."

"You cannot? Then why are we here?"

"Because we must be. Because I need one more thing. And only you can give it to me."

"What thing?"

Baetan's hands swept in a wide arc north to south. "Overlordship of the province of Ulaid," he said. "Overlordship of all of this."

"What has that to do with me?"

"Right now? Everything. No! Before you speak again ignorantly, shut up and listen. Because it is clear to me that you do not know. There are things about Ulaid that I gather your father never told you—things that perhaps your craven father never knew. Ways we do things here. Proper ways. Old ways. For one, that the overking of Ulaid—that is, me—must exact hostages from as far north as Dun Sobairche. It is _geis_ to me not to." _Taboo_

The ancient stronghold of Dun Sobairche. The chief citadel of Aedan's people here, the Dal Riata of Hibernia, which lay somewhere up amidst all those forbidding headlands.

_Geis._ Aedan hadn't heard the word often, it wasn't one they used now in Dal Riata, but he knew what it meant. It meant taboo. Forbidden. Baetan was speaking of the ancient laws of kingship, the _gessa,_ of which Aedan's father had indeed often spoken. Ways a king must act so that the gods, the goddesses, and the people are pleased, and ways he must not.

"Dun Sobairche," Baetan said. "I require hostages from there. From its lord."

Ah, yes: this particular ancient _geis._ A time-honored way to ensure leverage over your rivals.

"I had them from the last lord of Dun Sobairche, from the steward there. But then you got him killed. So now I am at a loss. Luckily, this can be solved quite tidily, here today. For want of another, better lord, those hostages will have to come from you."

"Ah!" Aedan hid a bitter smile. Baetan thought him lack-witted, but he was not. Thank the gods Aedan had acted when he had. "I am terribly sorry," he said. "But I cannot help you there."

Aedan swept his own arms out: no sons alongside him. "Sadly, I have no more sons to give—they have all been given to lords greater than you."

"Yes," Baetan said. "I figured as much. It is what a simple man would do. I might have done the same, were I you. But I am not."

179

Again, that cold, dismissive appraisal. "I have been fishing," Baetan said.

Fishing?

Baeten snapped his fingers. Aedan watched with surprise as two figures were offloaded from the nearest of the anchored warships and hauled through the surf to shore.

Despite his fear, Aedan felt a moment's hope: could it be Columba and Eogan?

But then, no. The figures were smaller, slighter.

They were brought roughly to the beach, forced to their knees in the cold, hard, pebbles, their hoods yanked off.

His stomach plummeted. Dear God!

It wasn't the monk and his brother.

It was his wife Afrella and his son Bran.

*How in the world?* They were meant to be safely on their way to Guined! The ship transporting them there had set sail a day before Aedan's. It had all been carefully arranged. Or so he had thought ...

His eyes shot to the bay, took in details he had not seen before. Not all of the ships in the anchored warfleet were Dal Fiatach. Yes: one was from Guined. The one hidden artfully at the back. It must have been taken at sea while on its way home, and its crew now dead, or enslaved, and its tremendous prizes commandeered.

Aedan's wife and son.

How in the world had Baetan known?

"Look what I caught!" Baetan crowed. He yanked back Bran's head with one hand, grabbed Afrella's trembling chin with the other. "I caught one! A son! Oh, and look! Here's a wife! And not just any wife! The chief one!"

Bran was trying to speak behind his gag, his eyes huge and frightened. Baetan back-handed him with a neatly closed fist. Bran's head whipped around and he would have fallen but for the biting grip of the two warriors who kept him on his knees, blood seeping from his lip where Baetan's ringed fingers had split it.

Afrella cried out. Fury scalded Aedan's throat. Baetan's pale-yellow head cocked in a chilly approximation of sympathy. He did not smile. "You see, I am bound to do this, to take them whether I like it or not. That is, I *do* like it. Especially since it is you I take from. But I am also bound. The *gessa*, my *gessa*, require it. *He is not a king who does not have hostages in fetters.* And, as we know, the greater the king, the more numerous the hostages—and the tighter the fetters."

Baetan did smile then. But it was a cold thing.

"Come," Baetan said, taking Aedan by the arm. "Let us walk for a while, and talk. For now I think you have things you might say to me?"

"To be honest," Baetan said as they strolled along the beach, for all the world two old friends with amusing news to share. "I don't like you, Mac Gabran. I never have. I am certain I never shall. You and your brutish prophecy!"

The wind raked their faces, whipped their cloaks. Big-bodied gulls swooped down to investigate, their raucous laughter abrading Aedan's nerves, but he bided his time, listening, pretending to attend; his mind a whirl. They needed to leave this beach now, and all together. Baetan might speak of rules and prohibitions and ancient, ritualistic *gessa*, to pretend to abide by them, but Aedan knew that this was in large part a pretext. Baetan would bend them where he could, re-interpret them: adhere only to those that served his purpose.

If Aedan's family were to be loaded back onto Baetan's ships, Aedan would never see them again.

"Well, I also have a prophecy," Baetan said. "Did you know? I do. It is the custom of great men to have such things—or to have them made for them. After the fact, of course, and with all the unflattering bits taken out. For such is one made great. Not by what one has done, but by what others believe one has done."

Baetan's tone was scornful. Interestingly, he also seemed to be mocking himself. "And as good as your prophecy is," Baetan said, "mine is better. Ready? Mine goes:"

*The pale-yellow shouter will be sovereign of all Hibernia.*

181

*He will be king of Alba in the east.*

Baetan pointed at his face, said without irony this time, "I am, obviously, the pale-yellow shouter. Never was I happier with my looks—a source of derision since my youth! How they taunted me! But, in addition to kingship and tribute and power, which every man wants and I already have ... "

*By him every tribe will be drained.*

"Drained! That's very good. Very evocative. Wouldn't you agree? Certain images spring instantly to mind. Like: blood from a hog, hung and butchered. Or seed from a man's unwilling member. Who mocks whom now? I was born to rule Ulaid, that much is clear. That much is already done. But it seems that all of Hibernia will also be mine. That the high-kingship is my right, once I take care of a few things on my list. The scope of it is astounding!"

Baetan's words were speeding by in a buzz, Aedan's mind elsewhere. He was frantic: *how do I overcome Baetan's forces? How do I rescue my family? How escape?*

"But I must be honest," Baetan said. "Before hearing this prophecy I had never thought to rule *Alba*." He chuckled derisively. "Why would one? There has been little to take from it, until now. But now, having heard that my dominion of it is practically guaranteed (it is a *prophecy* after all), I think: why not?"

Aedan barely heard. *Could my one ship take his four? Swing back around the headland and come in from behind? With fire, possibly ... but I'd lose the ship for sure. And my men.*

"That's it," Baetan said. "That's what I needed you to know. Why I brought you here. I'm ready for your submission now."

*Which I would give in a heartbeat—but for Bran and Afrella. They won't survive.*

*No. No. No. Not that way.*

*Another?*

"You speak of *gessa*," Aedan bit out. "Well, then, let us adhere to them. Let us adhere to them all."

He pointed down at his feet, at the dirty pebbles and mud that made up the beach. "This is borderland," he said. "Neither yours, nor mine."

"'Mine'?" Baetan mocked. "You presume mightily. You've not been here even a full turning of a day."

Aedan plowed ahead. "As such, you have no house under whose roof I might make my submission."

"Ah! You have entered into the spirit of things! This will amuse! But every time you think to outwit me, I am there before you. It is true, I have no house but … I do have a tent. A sumptuous tent, as it happens; which will more than suffice."

Baetan snapped his fingers, sending his men scurrying to do his bidding. In no time at all, a makeshift tent was erected on the beach. With neither side-flaps nor furnishings of any kind, it was hardly a dwelling at all. Nevertheless, it had a roof under which the gessa said Baetan could offer his hospitality and enact his rule.

There was no way out of at least this part of it.

Fuming with fury and worry, Aedan entered the tent, knelt on the freezing shingle, and gave his submission.

Baetan clapped his hands when it was done. "Wonderful! What a day! But not as fine as those to come. So much to anticipate with pleasure! I have your wife, your son. They shall prove amusing. But by the time I am done with you, I will also have your ships, your rents, your men—"

He chuckled, enjoying the images of horror and pain he was creating for Aedan. "And—yes, why not? We both know it—your life."

Baetan snapped his fingers again. Again, his men jumped to obey, grabbing Aedan by the arms to drag him out of the tent.

Aedan scrambled for concessions. Any concession. "You will care for my family as your own now," he said. "Honor demands it. The *gessa* demand it."

"I'm sorry? What did you say?"

"You will care for my family … "

Baetan cupped an ear. "I'm sorry. I couldn't quite hear you. You said, *something, something.* And then perhaps you said, 'My lord?'"

Aedan gritted his teeth, ground out, "You will care for my family, *my lord.*"

Baetan shrugged. "Unless you give me cause."

"Give me your word."

"I will do my best to restrain myself—as long as you do the same. Yet, I find this revealing: you unman yourself to beg terms for your family, yet you make no request for the safety of the good people of Dal Riata on whose behalf you claim to have come here. Hmm. Does this mean I am now free to reive them at will? Wonderful. That will be fun. As I do, I will be sure to let them know that their great good king is to thank for it. That he may posture and preen about his 'goodness' but, at the end of the day, he is the same as any man."

Aedan was brought face-to-face with his family. Bran's eyes were wet with tears he was manfully trying not to shed. At sight of his father, he struggled against his bonds and cried out, his words muffled by the gag stuffed in his mouth.

Afrella was staring at him with a shocked, frigid sort of anger and disbelief.

It was now, or never. Either Columba and Eogan came storming over the ridge with the boy-king—and the might of the Dal nAraide—behind them, like a charge of heroes of old, or ...

Or nothing.

One eye on the ridgeline in the hopes of sudden deliverance, Aedan said, "I will speak with them before you go!"

Baetan leaned in, cupping his ear again.

"I will speak with them before you go, *my lord.*"

Baetan smiled. "No."

Baetan strode off, but then turned, triumph in his pale eyes. "Stop that. Stop looking for rescue. It's pathetic. They're not coming. The boy is long dead. And they themselves have suffered a similar mishap, a *mortal* mishap—whilst *fishing* of all things!"

And he threw in the sodden pebbles at Aedan's feet a pile of bloody and stained clothing, clothing which Aedan had last seen on the back of his brother Eogan.


Ama hunkered down in her heavy cloak, doing her best to stay unnoticed. They had been rounded up, were being escorted by armed guard back to their ship over the point. Sillan had grabbed her, pulled her into the middle of the men, where she now hid in plain sight. Were Baetan to look her way, Ama hoped he would see what she wanted him to see: a smallish guardsman; perhaps, by the way he cowered, one on his very first mission and no threat at all.

Ahead of them, Aedan, also under guard, was keeping track of her. She could tell by the stiffness in his neck and shoulders, by the way he was not looking in her direction.

She shuffled along, head down, face hooded, with one hand firmly on her short sword, the other on the lethal little Pictish dagger Aedan had given her all those years ago. It had been a mistake to stay on the hillside with the archers. She should have gone to higher ground and found somewhere to hide. There, she might have been more useful to them all. Here, there was little she could do. But who could have known the encounter would end so disastrously?

She must not be caught out. She must not let herself be taken. Baetan with two prizes was unbearable. Baetan with three? Unstoppable.

Aedan would give in for sure then, just to save them. And then they would all be lost.

In a strained and volatile silence they trudged to the place where the track began to wind back up and over the hillside. There, Baetan's party hived off, making for their ships in the bay.

Seeing his father hauled away was too much for Bran. He began to struggle in earnest, digging in his heels and thrashing about in an attempt to break free of those holding him. His guards simply sniggered and jerked him back into line. When he continued to resist, one of his captors, a square, brutish man with a destroyed left eye, backhanded him across the face with a clear delight. Bran went limp, blood spurting from a broken nose.

Afrella snarled and leapt to her son. The sudden burst of action from the slight woman took everyone by surprise. She was able to wrest herself free. She made a grab for a sword, got one.

"No!" Aedan cried out. "Afrella, don't!"

Afrella either didn't hear him, or didn't care. In any case, Ama suspected Afrella was past the point of obeying Aedan in any way, especially now.

Ama might not either, given the circumstances. If that were her son Artur.

Afrella flew at the guards, screaming. Unfortunately, the sword she had managed to get hold of was a warrior's, large and unwieldy, especially with her wrists bound, and it teetered drunkenly, the weight of it causing it to topple almost comically onto the unsuspecting cheek of the guard who had struck her son. Yet, it drew blood; just a drop, but enough to surprise everyone into a sort of stupefied inaction.

Head down, Ama began to work her way to Afrella.

The half-blind guard gaped as he pushed the tip of the sword away from his face. It took no effort at all to do that. He put disbelieving fingers to his cheek, pulled them back, stared at the blood, then turned murderous eyes on the woman who had put it there.

Baetan showed no sign of intervening, the fraught silence being filled only with Aedan's panicked pleas for his wife's life.

But who, really, in this situation would heed him?

Not the guard. His one eye grew huge and he roared like an animal at the small woman's temerity. Rearing back, he struck Afrella so hard that she flew backwards in the air, the useless sword flying.

Aedan's men tried to soften her fall. She landed at Ama's feet.

Afrella looked up, the wind knocked out of her, stunned.

But not too insensible so as to fail to recognize the heavily-hooded figure staring back down at her. There was a moment of amazed recognition.

Hands were already reaching for Afrella, to make her face more retribution. Or worse.

Ama tightened her grip on her weapons. Afrella saw this: recognized the flash of metal in the deep folds of Ama's sheltering cloak.

To be certain, Ama gave the barest dip of her chin, hoping that Afrella would understand: Ama would do her best to protect her.

Had she understood? It was difficult to tell. Afrella still looked dazed as Baetan's men hauled her to her feet. She swayed for a moment, looked to where Aedan was frantically fighting against his captors, then to where her son, knocked dumb by the guard's blow, bled.

Baetan's men cleared a path and then Baetan was there. He towered over Afrella, his eyes unforgiving.

"Don't touch her!" Aedan was yelling. "Baetan! Have mercy!"

Baetan laughed. "Shut him up," he ordered. With sharp blows to Aedan's face, the guards did.

Uncertainty washed over Ama. What could she do against so many men?

Against so many? Not much. Hardly anything.

But against one?

Against one. Yes. Maybe.

But did she dare?

Baetan was close, a foot or two away, his attention fixed on Afrella. If Ama was going to do it, it had to be now.

She inched towards Baetan. All eyes were locked on the pair; sick with the titillation of more violence, how he would hurt Afrella. Probably slowly and theatrically, since that was his way, but also because to see it done it would wound Aedan the most.

Ama palmed the dagger. That would strike upwards; the killing strike, if she were lucky. Baetan's chest was protected by the thick interlocking links of his chain-mail breastplate, but his side, there under his arm, was not. That was bare of protection. That was where to strike him. She would stab him there. Puncture his lung. And if she twisted the blade as it went in, thrust it upwards, she could do worse. Far worse.

With her sword she would also slash away; if her dagger missed, her sword would not. She'd go for his throat. Slice it open.

In and up with the one; across with the other.

She inched closer, sweat breaking out on her chest and brow, breath and fear thundering in her ears.

Locked in their confrontation, Afrella had squared her shoulders to stare Baetan down, keeping his attention away from Ama, allowing her to get closer.

Aedan was seeing all of this and understanding, because he cried out, trying to buy her time, "My lord! My lord Baetan!"

Baetan ignored him, keeping a withering eye on Afrella. "Well done," he said to her. "Truly! Well done! I hadn't expected that of you. I hadn't expected much of you at all, to be honest."

He reached out, caressed her cheek where the guard had struck her. "I must say, I like what I see."

Without warning, his ardent hand turned vicious, grabbing her face, squeezing it hard to haul her to the tips of her toes. "But if you try that again, I will kill you."

Ama was close. Nearly there.

Afrella shook her chin free. "You won't," she said, her voice more clear and strong than Ama would have thought possible, given everything. "Nor will you hurt my son."

Baetan laughed. He sounded both delighted and intrigued. "I won't? Why not?"

Ama was near enough now. Her hands were shaking so hard she thought she might be sick.

She had never killed before.

But this was a man who had to die.

Aedan was yelling, "Baetan! My lord Baetan! Not her, me! Me!"

Ama had never heard him more frantic. The guards silenced him with a blow to the face.

It was now or never. Swallowing her fear, she sprang.

The blades, her aim—mercifully on target.

But before they could strike, Ama's hands were knocked off course and the hood was yanked from her head.

By Afrella.

"Because I am a lady of Guined, *my lord*," Afrella said to Baetan. "And I bring you a gift." *Bastard !*

Everyone began to yell: Baetan surprised but exultant; Afrella rebellious and triumphant; Ama spitting with fury as Baetan's men stripped her of her weapons, hands using the opportunity to grab where they shouldn't; Aedan's men stirring, the energy surging; Aedan himself about to let loose—the consequences be damned—because they were all of them doomed if they were boarded onto those ships.

Since he and his men were being taken up the path to the rocking stone and, from there, over the ridge to his ship, he had only seconds to do what had to be done. Yet it had to be timed exactly right. If they moved too soon, they'd be overpowered. Too late, and he'd never see any of his family again.

The ground was getting higher: good. Baetan's men, more numerous than his and certain of their advantage now, were beginning to relax their guard, he could feel it—for who would be foolish enough to fight back with even more of his family within killing reach of Baetan's swords? Indeed, the two men shoving him gleefully forward had their eyes trained on Baetan's party making for the ships, rather than the deadly enemy between them.

It had to be now.

Aedan whistled sharply. Three pointed notes, which meant: "Separate! Attack!"

His guards jumped in shock and Aedan burst free, springing to the right, higher up the hillside, drawing them with him, away from his own men just behind. He didn't need to look to see that his men were also darting and dropping either to the sides or behind, forcing their own guards to stay abreast—increasing the area in which they could fight, increasing their own odds of surviving this.

By the sudden shouting, Aedan suspected that his family down on the beach had also heard and were obeying. They had all trained for this, and for much worse. In their case, his whistled command had meant: "Drop! Scatter!"

Aedan took down the guard on his right first. Then his left. As he sprinted up the hillside a few more steps, he spun, reaching for his bow; had it strung even before he had fully sighted the men on the beach. The arrow released, screeching, until it didn't anymore, stopping in the throat of Bran's guard, Bran dropping to the sand and scuttling rapidly backwards like a crab, back towards his father.

Not far from Bran, Ama was clawing at the face of the man restraining her. He howled, losing his grip on her arm. She reared back and shattered his nose with her elbow, his hands flying to his face even as her knee came up violently, crushing his groin, once, then again, causing him to collapse in agony, which was where Aedan's next arrow found and kept him.

Then Afrella. His wife was alone. Not guarded. Not fighting. Not escaping, her gaze trained on the hillside, to where he was, watching him.

Aedan held his arrow.

Baetan was howling in fury, screaming commands. But Aedan's men were making quick work of Baetan's men up here, on the trail. The men down on the beach, meanwhile, were struggling to regroup.

So, Aedan let arrows fly. As his men freed themselves, they did the same.

And he was thinking that they might prevail after all, a thought which momentarily amazed him, when suddenly both the trail and the beach were lit with a vast swarm of arrows. They came out of nowhere to fall all around him like rain. He ducked under his shield. Looked around in confusion.

The arrows had not come from Baetan's men—the beach was also under attack—but from somewhere else.

They had come from behind Aedan. From the dark headland behind them all.

Everyone faltered, broke apart. Another vicious volley. Arrows singing. There was screaming. Men fell from Aedan's warband, from Baetan's.

And then another rapid volley of arrows, but this time from a different source, from higher up the headland, the one on the far side of the bay.

And these were lit with fire.

The new arrows arced for Baetan's ships. They pinged off hard wooden hulls. Another volley. These caught in the sweet, giving fabric of the sails which burst into flame.

At the same time, there was a ferocious roar, a pounding on shields, blood-thirsty chanting, war-trumpets blaring, and not one, but two unknown warbands crested the overhanging headlands, one to each side.

More men than either Aedan's and Baetan's rapidly-diminishing forces.

More men than their forces combined.

They had been ambushed, all of them.

# · 14 ·

# THE SCOTTI

Monks! They had been captured by monks!
Columba could scarce believe it. Of all things! But there was
the proof: the long hair of the men rowing them back down the
loch so relentlessly had been pulled into messy plaits, their dirty
foreheads bare and slick with sweat.

To have been captured by their own kind was bad enough. What
was worse was that Columba thought he knew why.

There hadn't been any conversation, no way to sway them. Their
captors hadn't answered any of their shouted questions, had silenced
any further imprecations by gagging them. They had cackled as they
bound their hands and trundled them into separate logboats to take
them out again upon the vast loch, Eogan in the lead boat, Columba
aft, the big buck the monks had felled slung precariously over its
bow.

There, in delirious jibes traded back and forth between the two
boats, it slowly became clear.

"They're not from around here, I'll tell you that!" crowed one monk to another.

Eogan's frantic explanation, muffled by his gag, was ignored.

"No, they are not, Praise God! They're ours to sell, then! He'll have to pay them for us, and not just take! And they're worth a fair bit, I wager! Look at this one! Young and strong. He'll prove a far fairer haul than a basket of filthy eels, I'll tell you that! And the old slag in the back? Not near as much. But still, some. Not a bad day's work. Ha ha!"

The monks had been out trapping the eels with which this loch abounded; had chanced upon the herd of deer while it was swimming and at its most vulnerable—and, in what appeared to be a moment of sheer, absurd, blind luck, them as well.

And now, it was as if Columba were an afterthought—the sorry old servant he was still pretending to be meriting little of their attention.

His disguise held.

It was Eogan they wanted most. Indeed they had stripped him of his cloak, bloodying his nose quite foully when he had resisted, then had bundled it off with a runner, sent to where and to whom Columba did not know, unless it was to someone who might buy him. The monk had headed east.

Now they were being taken along the western shoreline of the loch with a mercenary glee, back in the direction from which they had come, their passage aided by how extraordinarily calm the weather was that morning. The silvery surface of the water, at that moment as smooth as a glass beaker, was marred only by the oars that were dipping in and out so intently.

But the sky was lowering, the clouds beginning to show signs of uncertainty, much like Columba himself. Should he reveal himself? Should he let them know they had netted a far more meaningful prize than Eogan?

Perhaps, but …

To what end? And when?

With every beat of the oars, the approaching shoreline was growing steadily larger, more distinct.

Until, it wasn't. One minute it was there, the low lick of land a dark grey smear; the next, it was obscured by a mist which had descended quite rapidly to render the world suddenly featureless. Where there had been the sky, the water, now there was only a silvery, formless ubiquity that muffled sound as it closed in wetly against their skin, bringing with it an eerie, unsettling stillness.

"Eogan!" Columba called out around his gag.

A ghostly reply came back straightaway from somewhere to the right and to the front of him.

"Shut your face, the both of you!"

"Get ready!" risked Columba.

His chance came almost immediately. With the onset of the mist, the dangerous shore so close and no more clear line of sight, the lead boat had pulled up in the water, afraid to shoal or dash itself against a sudden rock. Columba's had not. Following on as closely as they were, they plowed into the other boat broadside, the fearful faces of the occupants looming suddenly, startling white in the gloom, their eyes and mouths dark rictuses opened wide in terror as the boat tipped.

All of the boat's occupants were thrown into the water with a chaotic splash. They cried out, their shouts swallowed up as they went under.

Eogan popped back up quickly; Columba was deeply relieved to see his gagged mouth breaking the surface. Eogan sucked in air through his nose, his bound arms pumping in a frenzied attempt to keep his face above water. In his boat, Columba's guards sprang up to search desperately for their own companions who were struggling in the water loudly but just out of sight in the mist.

There was shouting, mayhem, and the panicked, uncoordinated movements of the monks, hindered by the large carcass of the buck strung across the bow, caused Columba's boat to teeter dangerously from side to side.

It was now, or possibly never. Columba went with the sway of the boat, slipping himself gently over the side and into the frigid water of the loch.

When the boat righted itself, he was no longer in it.


With his hands bound, it was devilishly hard to keep his face from going under. Columba rolled himself onto his back, kicking hard to maneuver himself around to where he had last seen Eogan. He bumped into someone—not Eogan; one of the monks. He kicked again, more viciously than before, heard a satisfying *oomph*! and the gurgle of someone submerging and, using the opportunity to yank off his gag, propelled himself away. He kept kicking until he had angled himself around to the outside of the two monks in the water, in the hope that Eogan had also thought to use this moment to try to get away.

It was impossible to see more than darks forms in the thick mist. The white disc of a face here, clumps of wet hair plastered across a slash of a mouth. The back of a head there. Lots of yelling and jerky splashing. A looming black mass: the other logboat, the one from which he had just escaped, the two monks peering over the side, fishing about with their oars. Their comrades grabbing hold, being hauled through the water to the boat where they could grip the side, staying afloat until they could be towed ashore.

But where was Eogan?

He risked giving away his position. "Eogan! Eogan!" he called.

A muffled cry: "*Abba*!"

Deo Gratias! Eogan was not drowned!

Eogan was somewhere between him and the logboat. Yes! There he was, thrashing his uncoordinated way to where Columba treaded water.

Just then, Columba backed into something. The logboat that had been emptied in the crash. He made a grab for it. Missed. It scooted away. He tried again. Got a hold this time. Gripped it with an insane determination, calling out to Eogan to guide him towards him. "Eogan! This way!"

He saw Eogan nod grimly, then Eogan rolled onto his back and gave a mighty kick, creating a wake all his own, the water swelling up around his shoulders.

But right behind him, the other boat suddenly parting the mist, dragging the two other monks, a monk leaning dangerously out over the carcass on the bow, an oar in his hand like a club as he hunted Eogan down.

"Eogan!" Columba cried. "Watch out!"

Eogan kicked hard to get away, but it was too late. The monk took a big swing with the oar and cracked Eogan viciously across the skull. The sound echoed, huge and gross, in the blanket of mist.

"Eogan!"

Eogan went under. Columba hurled himself back towards him. After an interminable moment, Eogan popped back up.

Facedown.

Columba kicked jerkily to try to reach Eogan, but the monks got to him first. They leaned out, grabbed hold of Eogan's collar.

Columba's last sight of Eogan was his rounded form, facedown and bobbing in the water as he was tied to the boat, blood streaming from his dear head, a flower of red in grey.


Aedan ducked and spun as he called for his men through the pelt of arrows. They came to him and, as a cohort, shields overhead, they sprinted for the beach.

"Baetan! Together!" Aedan was yelling as he ran. Together, he and Baetan could defeat whomever was attacking them from the headlands, both of the two new bands of marauders.

It was the smart thing to do: perhaps the only way to get out of this alive. It was also what one's overlord did. This was why you made your oath, why you submitted to a man who had proven himself to be more powerful than you. There was no right or wrong to consider, no weighing of the odds or of one's personal gain.

He took your side in a conflict, as you did his. That way, more lived. With luck, you.

Baetan did hear him because he stopped: his sword a still point in the blurry chaos of his harried men.

Just then the falling rain of arrows petered out, the awful heavy thudding in their shields overhead ceasing. The first wave of the ambush was over.

Aedan skidded to a halt, his heels gouging the dirt. He lowered his shield, risked a look back up the slopes. Yes. Bows were being re-strung. The two warbands were moving into the second phase of their attack. They would now charge at them down the hillsides in two groups, the one from the near headland, the other from the far.

What Aedan saw also convinced him of other things. Despite the suddenness of their attack and their numbers, they were not warbands. Not really. There were fighting men there to be sure, but there were also women, and boys not much older than Aedan's own, and girls. A makeshift force, haphazard, trained to work together where victory might be bought with numbers, but physically weaker if tested.

They were the *Scotti*. They had to be. The infamous brigands of Dal Riata.

His people.

Despite his astonishment, Aedan felt a moment's hope. Their attackers had had the advantage of surprise, but that was over. Although badly battered, all of Aedan's men were on their feet, with none left behind. None were dead. Which was some kind of miracle.

They could turn this. Just now. If Baetan took on one party and Aedan the other, they could prevail. But it had to be before the two parties joined up.

Aedan called out to his old adversary, pointing at the band closest to Baetan charging down the hillside. "There!"

Through his protective ring of men, Aedan saw Baetan square his shoulders, lower his sword. Nod.

He smiled at Aedan. He turned to his men.

"To the ships!" Baetan cried.

Rage and the bitter fury of Baetan's betrayal pulled Aedan up short.

Sillan's eyes were on him. The older warrior's exhausted face was smeared with blood, but his gaze was sharp and piercing. What to do? The men needed to know.

For Aedan, there was only one true course of action left, and he knew it.

But not for his men.

"Make for the ship!" Aedan said.

"Not without you."

Down below, Baetan's party was sloshing through the surf, bolting for those ships not yet aflame. Ama, Bran, and Afrella were in there somewhere, being shielded from any new arrow-fall.

"I'm not going," Aedan said. "They need time to escape."

Sillan wiped blood from his brow, nodded back grimly. "We know."

Assent passed through the men silently. Shields back up, swords high, hearts in their throats and defiant, they bellowed their war cry as they charged back up the way they had come.

Aedan swung and hacked, he pivoted, cursing; he pummeled, shoved, kicked and punched. He did everything he could think of to draw attention away from Baetan so that his family might get away.

But now, also—how to keep his men alive?

They cleaved their way through the band of fighters attacking them, blood spraying, grunts, gasps, cries, their attackers fighting back scrappily, as a pack. But it was too late. With Baetan's party escaping, leaving only one enemy now to subdue, the second warband joined the first, swarming Aedan's men from behind.

And then it was a fight to the death: straining, heaving, his men fighting as one, beautifully, as he had trained them to do, but also with desperation and blood, so much blood, as the two bands of brigands fought their way towards each other with Aedan and his men in the unsustainable middle.

Until, out of the corner of Aedan's eye, what was left of Baetan's ships stealing away out of the bay.

"Stop!" Aedan cried. "Stop! I submit! I am their lord and I submit!"

His men drew up, shocked at his uncharacteristic capitulation. He threw down his sword, threw up his empty hands. Their attackers pulled up.

A big man rushed him. Aedan's helmet was ripped off from behind, and then there was a terrible blow to the back of his head, a sticky wet stream gushing down this scalp, and searing, eye-watering pain.

Another blow. More astonishing pain. And he fell hard, his head slamming into the ground, to darkness.

# · PART THREE ·

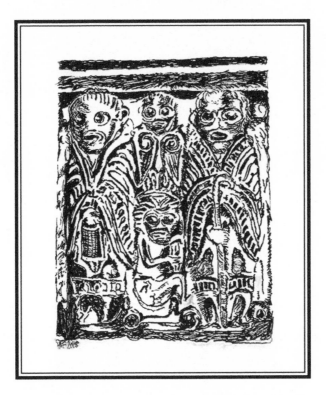

*Panel from the book shrine of St Mael Ruain's Gospel ("Stowe Missal")*
*(National Museum of Ireland, no. 1883, 614a; panel from 1025-1052)*

# · 15 ·

# THE BANN

For a long moment, Columba refuses to open his eyes. He will hold back yesterday's horror with a steely determination; refuse to admit it.

It will not be true, if he does not welcome it in.

Which it knows. It knows.

So it finds a hole, creeps through, and soon enough, soon enough, is flashing itself with a gaudy grin before his mind's eye.

With his hands bound, Columba had not been able to get himself into the boat he had managed to catch hold of. Instead he had had to use it as a kind of raft, holding onto it while he kicked his way away from the hunting monks, hopefully in the direction of shore, swallowing his sobs.

Behind him, the desperate sounds of their frenetic search rang out over the water. He kicked for all he was worth. Because of the mist, he had no idea where north was, where south; where he was in relation to the island of the holy well. For all he knew, he might be heading out farther out into the loch.

Slowly, the angry shouts of his pursuers faded away. He was desperately cold, his fingers like ice but, after what felt like an age, his toes encountered resistance—the sloping bank of the shore. He followed it upwards. The logboat groaned and came to a shuddering halt upon the bank, and Columba crawled his way up to the beach. There he lay for a minute, gasping, tears streaming. Then he rolled over, found a sharp-edged rock and clawed his hands free of the rope, not caring that he cut his fingers open as he did so.

He made his way back to the water's edge, scanned the loch. Saw nothing but mist. Heard only the water against the shore.

It was so quiet, so still, so formless, it was as if he was the one who had died.

He could do nothing while the mist held. Nevertheless, he stayed on the beach in heartbroken agony until he could no longer control his shivering. He was convulsing with cold. He dragged the boat into the underbrush and overturned it, hiding it as well as he could, then slipped underneath.

There he had huddled while night fell, listening for sounds of pursuit, for any sign of his friend. Eventually he prayed himself into an exhausted stupor that had none of the beauty of sleep.

Now it was dawn. The mist had lifted. Casting off the shelter of his boat, he hurried down to the water's edge. Although he now understood where he was—somewhere on the western shore of the loch, since the sun was rising in front of him—he could see nothing else of use: no sign of the monks; no sign of Eogan.

A terrible indecision overtook him. Uncertainty. He did not want to abandon his friend. Yet what were the chances that Eogan still lived? Small. Too, too small to be of any hope. There was that crack of the oar on his skull, that spray of blood in the water, bones certainly crushed. Eogan abruptly still. How he sank, then popped to the surface and bobbed there, without sign of life, to be towed like cargo. Like the other dead prize across the boat's bow.

Eogan was unlikely to be alive. Even if he did live, how in the world would Columba find him?

And even now, Aedan could be upon the beach at Ros-na-Righ—waiting for his friends who would not show. Waiting for a boy that could turn the tide.

Columba's heart, tight with despair, screamed for one course of action: that he go back, search for Eogan; at the very least, recover his body for proper burial. That he not abandon his friend.

His head counseled the other: Aedan also needed him. Aedan, who was almost certainly still alive. Who should also not be abandoned. Upon whom the hopes of all of Dal Riata rested.

Columba cursed the tears that continued to flow, berating himself for his weakness, hating the course of action he knew he had to take.

Eventually, he did what he had to do. Through a blur of tears, Columba tore a strip of fabric from the hem of his tunic. He arranged it into a crude sort of arrow, a sign that Eogan should go north, if he found it.

If he lived.


Keeping the morning's sun on his right-hand side, he shunted his way up the loch in his borrowed boat. A look around had shown him that he had fetched up some ways to the north of that cursed holy island, further up the great loch than he had dared to hope. He pushed himself hard, resting only to catch his breath, and by late afternoon had reached the mouth of a great river which had to be the upper reaches of the Bann. Here the river was wide as it carved out a path through the low country rising left and right, heading north.

He turned his boat in, let the flow of the river carry him inland, away from wherever Eogan now lay, only deploying the oars to keep the boat off rocks which lurked beneath the river's surface. Soon, the gloam began to descend, throwing the trees and the brush of the riverbanks into shadow, and then the river bulged out again into another loch, smaller than the last, but still sizeable.

He beached the boat on the western shoreline and stumbled out.

This was the damned place he sought: here where there were plenty of the smooth, yellow- and red-veined stones cursedly underfoot. He picked one up. Yes, it was twin to the one he carried in his pocket. But how would it help? It was just a stone, as were all the others strewn so uselessly about.

Maybe there was something to be learned from the beach itself? He searched anxiously for a time for any sort of portent. But there was no sign of the boy. No sign of any other living thing for that matter. There, on the edge of the beach, was a burned-out fire pit and evidence of quarrying and collecting, but there were no houses, no animal pens; evidence of human use but not habitation.

All right: no boy here. What about the stones themselves? How to distinguish between them? What had he been sent here to find?

With increasing desperation, he searched and searched, but found nothing as the light faded.

Despondent, he threw himself down with a curse. Tears he could not seem to check streamed down his cheeks to join the rivulets of water flowing amongst the rocks underneath him. What had he expected? That the boy would be waiting for him here, good as gold, like in the stories of old? That the god who inhabited this place— that damned Lord Manannan—would jump out from behind the headland just there to point Columba in the direction he needed to go?

That his own god would walk across the water, now, just when he needed it most, bringing counsel, comfort, deliverance?

This was no fable. Far from it.

They had lost Eogan, for what?

The whole enterprise was damned.

Perhaps he was the one who was damned.

He had returned to Hibernia, had set foot again on the soil of his beloved homeland even though it had been forbidden to him after his exile, on penalty of death.

He had hoped to hide his passage. To come in, to help Aedan, then to leave Hibernia again with no one the wiser.

What had he expected? Fanfare? War-horns welcoming? A feast?

No. No one was happy about it. Neither god nor goddess, woman or man.

And for his hubris those dearest to Columba were being made to pay.


Columba is in the loch, his mouth just clearing the frigid waterline. It laps the underside of his lip. He keeps his mouth closed—not tightly, but just so that the seam is not breached—and breathes steadily through his nose, feeling the air expand and contract in his chest, his arms threading the water, his legs scissoring; and he looks around in wonder.

He is some ways out into the loch. It is daybreak. The morning sun mounts the low hills behind him, flooding the gossamer mist which is draping the loch a serene color pink. He thinks perhaps he should be concerned, but for some reason he is not at all alarmed. He might be dreaming again. There is an element of the unnatural about what is unfolding. Except that the water is freezing and it is wet, and his muscles are working with the effort to keep him afloat. His lungs sieve breath and, as he exhales, his breath ruffles the water around his nose. The loch hums with the quiet activity of earliest morning: birds are chirping, frogs croak, water laps the shore ahead.

It does feel real.

For a while he is content simply to watch the play of liquid and light, for it is all very beautiful. He enjoys the sensation of being suspended between worlds. The colors. Their intensity—everything just slightly brighter than it ought to be, as if burnished to a high sheen, like just after it has rained. The sounds: crisp, clean. Very clear. Hanging in the air for an age. The scents: pure. Nothing dead or dying. Everything sweet, light. The way it is making him feel:

weightless. Suspended. Expectant.

His tranquility is a welcome relief after the tumult of his heart, broken open by the loss of his friend.

But soon there is movement behind him, coming closer. Ripples on the water, little waves lapping against his back. He doesn't turn. He doesn't feel he needs to. Instead, when whatever it is that is approaching comes up right behind him, he lifts his arms clear of the water.

And under each arm slips a swan. Large. Majestic. Pure, pure white.

Two of them, one to either side. Muscular necks, corded like rope. Slick feathers downing sinuous, elegant, supple throats. Broad, strong bodies. The inquisitive tilt of the heads, the black face-masks, the bright orange beaks.

How strange! And yet ... how right.

The swans are swimming to the beach. Arms draped about their necks, he lets them tow him along. Silently, their strong webbed feet paddling but their torsos preternaturally still, they glide towards the shore with him effortlessly in-between.

Mist parts. It is a magical passage.

As soon he can feel the ground rising beneath his feet, he begins to run, his legs pumping in tandem with theirs until his knees emerge from the water, then his feet.

With him now running in earnest, they take flight, lifting him from the loch. Powerful wings beating, they bear him up from the water. He rises with them into the air.

He looks down as they gain height.

How strange: there is a man sitting on the beach. Cross-legged. Hands palm-up on his thighs.

As they pass overhead, Columba's boots will just clear the mass of unruly hair that swims about his face.

The man's left hand shoots up. Catches hold of Columba's ankle just as he is about to alight into the sky with the swans.

Columba loses hold of his white companions. He slips. Down he falls.

To land squarely on his feet in front of the seated man, the yellow stones of the beach growling under his weight.

He looks at the man. The man looks at him.

"Who are you?" Columba asks.

There is a deep, assessing appraisal, but the man does not say.

"Tell me your name," Columba says.

Hair swimming about his face like water snakes, the man remains silent.

The hair on the back of Columba's neck stirs. The very top of his scalp twitches violently, as if suddenly ignited, a spiraling flame that spins and flares with a cold, scorching fire.

These are his cues. It confirms what Columba already suspects: the thing before him, though in the guise and shape of a man, is not in fact human.

It will have to be compelled.

So Columba asks a third time, the sacred third time, an order which all beings must obey, those dark and those light: "By the power of my Christ, I demand that you reveal your true name".

The being laughs. He is delighted. "You know my name. You searched for me, so I have come. To bring you what you seek."

"You are the Lord Manannan?"

The man's jaw drops open. Larger and larger his mouth grows—impossibly immense—until it can encompass all the world's oceans at once. Columba leans closer, gazes deep within, sees the ocean's abyss and all the life within it. A sound rolls out of the sloshing crevice: the roar of the seas. It reeks of brine and wind and rot; a roiling cauldron of death and of life.

The giant jaw slowly closes, water slipping out, the maw of a leviathan closing about a krill-clump it has chased up and up and up from the dark ocean depths to catch just at the edge of the light.

"Tell me," Manannan says. "I wish to know. Be true, if you can—if you dare. You have divined my name. I am as you say. It is I who tames the seas. No fish spawn save for me. Man rides me at my pleasure. Tides turn only at my whim. I am life. But your god. Your ... *Christ* ... "

The name comes out like a ship driven onto rocks by a gale. "Of what is your Christ the victor?" Manannan asks. "He gave himself to his enemies to die at their hands, strung up upon a tree which was also dead."

If this is a riddle, Columba knows the answer: "My Christ is the victor of the war over sin and death".

Manannan lets out a laugh like the tallest wave Columba will ever see, dredged up from far, far offshore to break far, far inland, full of power and fury and disdain. "Sin?" the god says. "You mortals and your sin! No sin. Only living. Living."

"And dying. Living and dying. It is the latter which my Christ conquered."

Again, that scornful laugh. "Dying? No dying. Only leaving, then returning again. Leaving, then returning."

The great god shrugs. "Death is rest. The sleep between livings. There is nothing to conquer. Nothing to suffer. Nothing to mourn."

"Perhaps for you, for you are immortal born. For us? Pain. Sin. Death. Grief. Thus, our Christ. His death, for us. It is because we die in him that we may live again in eternal life, as do you. Through him, we too become a part of god."

A slow, otherworldly smile, his vast, terrible voice the rumble and sigh of the sea. "Ah! Riddles. Yes. Yes. Good. Good."

Columba can barely endure Manannan's company a moment longer. It is taking enormous strength just to remain in the presence of this awesome, ageless god. "I have answered your question as best I can," Columba dares to ask, while he still can. "I have solved your riddle. Now tell me: what of mine? What of the boy?"

"Ah! The boy. The boy. The boy they brought to me bound with spells. One riddle for another. Look. Look now and you will see."

And Manannan's hand reaches out, his immense palm covering all the world from Columba's sight.

And just like that, Columba is hovering over an enormous cliff face, as if the eye of a gannet on the wing. Below, far, far, below, there is a great swell around the headland.

Columba knows this place. How treacherous it is for anyone out upon the water here.

How forbidden it is to him, being so close to his old home.

He cries out, full of fear. "I'll not be going down into that!"

From Manannan, that big, pitiless laugh. "No? It is you who brought this great turbulence upon us."

Columba understands. In the churning water, he sees wars. Blood. Invasions. Conquests. Enslavements. Heads cleaved. Hearts shattered. Turbulence and division and strife.

Loss. Loss. Loss.

The twist of time.

"And because it is so," the god says, "it is you who must now calm the waves. And you do it with a sacrifice."


Columba awakens with a start, on the beach, blood-yellow stones all around.

Despite the god's dire warnings, he is strangely refreshed. In fact, he feels invigorated.

He puts aside his grief as he stands.

He knows not only where he has to go, but what he must do next.

# · 16 ·

# STONE

It is the deep moaning that brings him up. It thrums through his bones, filling his ears and his throat, as much a sensation as a sound.

Someone is in agony. He can hardly bear it. It makes him squirm, want to spew up what little there is in his stomach. Such distress; pain from deep, deep within.

If he could, he would go to them, take them in his arms, rock them, comfort them. Help them heal. Aedan's instinct!

Ah! In a flash, he understands.

It will not work.

The wretched sound is coming from him. The anguish is his.

It is too much.

Aedan gives in and sinks back under.

*Get up! Get up! Fight!*
*You're not safe here! You're not safe! They'll kill you!*

*They'll kill the men!*

*They'll kill THEM!*

In his mind's eye, flashes of the faces of his family.

Aedan bursts awake. The pain, which had been so mercifully distant, comes screeching back, slamming into him hard. It is coming from his head. A bad blow. He will be lucky if his skull hasn't been split open. His scalp certainly has been. He retches, but gags on the bile he brings up. Belatedly he realizes that a dirty rag has been stuffed into his mouth. He will choke to death on his own vomit if he is not careful.

This sobers him, helps him collect himself enough to focus, to get control of his terror. Biting back the pain, he inhales deeply again and again, rhythmically through his nose, forcing himself to swallow his bile back down.

He tries to move. Can't. His arms have been bound behind his back, his legs tied at the ankle. He is lying sprawled on his side. On the ground somewhere. Outside.

Wary of discovery, he tries to take stock of where he is through slitted eyes.

First thing: it is nighttime. There is a fire. There in the corner.

No, not the corner. There is no corner. Everything is too green. Too round. He blinks his eyes until his vision clears a bit. He can see that he is in a forest clearing. There are high wooded hills to either side. There is a stony stream down at the bottom of the dell. He can hear it clattering. There is a rough stockade on the height above them, though no rustling or reek from within it: so, empty of any livestock. Smoke from the fire streaks the trees dirtily grey, blackens the sky.

There are men and women around the fire. The ones who attacked them.

Where are his own men? He searches frantically; sees them trussed up some distance from where he is. There is movement here and there: some, at least, are alive.

Time to act. He struggles against his bonds, trying to free himself, the pain in his head nearly overwhelming his ability to move.

But someone sees him. Someone hears.

Someone chortles, a greasy, mean sound, and then Aedan is kicked, the boot finding the precise spot where Aedan's scalp has already been split open.

And Aedan is lost again to the darkness.


*Aedan!*

Someone is whispering his name, calling to him where he is hiding in the shadows.

At first, he shies away, fearing he will be hurt again. He doesn't want to rise to it, to awaken. It is better to stay where he is, in the soft grey void. Here, it does not hurt. Here, he can sleep. Forget.

Aedan!

Ah! Unlike the brute who kicked him, there is a kindness to this voice! It offers comfort.

*Aedan!*

He knows this voice! The sweet timbre of it, its depth, its authority. It makes him think of fires in the hearth, of warm blankets pulled tight to the chin, a full belly, a tender hand after the terror of nightmare. It is as familiar to him as his own childhood.

His own childhood …

It is his father! His father is calling to him! His father is calling his name!

His heart bursts with grief and longing.

No need to grieve though—in fact, why has he ever grieved? How needless! His father is right here, kneeling beside him.

Oh, happy, blessed, longed-for day!

Tears start to stream down his face. Oh, to throw his arms around his father! To welcome him home!

Wait till Eogan sees him! And Mother! They will have such joy at their beloved one's return, after so long away.

Where has his father been? Where has he been all this time?

His father is reaching for him, a hand stretched out to cup his head, as he would when he was a boy. *Good relationship with Dad.*

215

He tries to sit up, to meet his father's touch.

But no matter how he tries, he cannot rise. His legs will not obey. Neither will his arms. He tries again, thinks for a moment that he has gotten his leaden limbs to where he wants them to be. But they have not moved at all. They are right where they were.

Odd, that.

Never mind. His father is here. It is all right. His father will look after things as he once did, so that Aedan no longer has to. And indeed, he is overcome by exhaustion. He is so weary. To be left in peace, to fall asleep again in the arms of the darkness which had been so undemanding, so accepting, so kind.

Yes. That's what he'll do. He'll greet his father, welcome him home, laugh, share a loving word; start the feast. Then he'll slip away, take his leave; rest. No one will fault him for it. Just a little more effort at communion and civility, then blessed, easy oblivion. His father will understand, forgive. He is here to take over! To take charge again. He is home now! They are all home, all together again, safe around the roaring hearth, their laughter effortless and familiar and easy.

There is nothing more to fear.

Indeed, his father is bending down. His face is very close. His dark hair swings low, his brown eyes tender and full of love.

And worry. His father's brow is creased.

Something is disturbing him! Something is amiss!

What? What is it?

Aedan will discover it! He will fix it, for his father.

His father leans closer.

*Son*!

Aedan feels the stir of breath across his face. It is sweet and cold, like the snowdrops that burst through the hoar frost in newest spring, the ones that vanquish winter, herald the light.

Cold? It is *cold*?

*Son!*

*Son! Go back!*

*WAKE UP!*

216

Aedan came to with a jolt, the pain from his torn scalp slamming back with such force that it took his breath away.

He was still on his side, trussed up like a hog. This time, his captors had taken care to blindfold him.

His father was gone, as if he had never been.

He ignored the flare of grief. Tucked it well away, in the place he usually kept it. He had no time for it right now. As far as he could tell, he had not been moved. By the light he could see flickering around the edges of the strip of cloth over his eyes, he guessed that they were still in that godforsaken clearing, and it was still nighttime. But of the same day? Hard to say.

The brigands who had taken them were still arrayed around the fire. There was a heated argument underway.

This time, Aedan played dead. His fingers worked clumsily on the ties that bound his wrists as he listened in.


"He's somebody, make no mistake. I say we bring him to her. She'll like it. It might work."

"No!"

"But it could be the thing! It could get him back!"

There was a plaintive quality to the voice that was doing the pleading, Aedan thought. This was a man who had cause to fear.

"I said no or didn't you hear? Doesn't matter what we bring her: it won't be enough. She doesn't play fair. *Bitch*. He's how she keeps you doing her things for her. Get used to it."

The second voice was gravelly, like a sudden rockslide. If Aedan had to guess, he'd say that this was the one in charge; and, by the way the lord's words were met with a torrent of grumbles, that he spoke for a majority of his companions.

"You!" Stony-voice growled. "Get your ass over here!"

There was a stir of activity as someone obeyed.

Aedan had been correct: Stone *was* the boss.

217

There was the sound of someone shuffling forward none too eagerly, then almost immediately the sharp slap of skin against skin (a hand across a face?) followed by a cry of shock and pain, swallowed—the yelp of someone who had been taught the futility of complaint.

Most of the crowd laughed, but some gasped.

Dissent?

"You had one job to do!" Stone said. "One! And you buggered it up as usual. How'd it get away? Now *that* would have been a prize!"

"I don't know. I don't know how they got away. We had that ship trapped, to be sure. But they were more skilled than we expected. Good sailors. Seamen. We chased them all the way down past the Gobbins ... "

There were gasps of unwilling admiration. "They got past the Gobbins?" asked the first voice, the subservient one, whom Aedan had begun to think of as Number Two, the second in command.

"Aye, my lord! Wherever they're from, they know the sea. They're on their way home now, my lord, and that's that. That's done. They're gone. There's nothing for it."

"I know you did your best," said Two. "Don't fret."

"He'll fret if it happens again," warned Stone.

There was a fraught silence punctuated only by the shuffles of the reprimanded man making his way back to the side of the fire furthest from Stone.

Then the rasp of someone clearing his throat, followed by a spew of spit. It was Stone. "What about Baetan?" he asked.

"My lord Baetan doesn't want them," said Two. "He sailed away first thing! That was strange, that. Unlordly. There's a story there to be sure, and not one that's good for us to be having any part in."

An uneasy silence descended again, the proceedings at an impasse, until a new voice piped up, a woman's voice. "What they'd be worth, on the market?" the woman ventured.

This excited her companions who barked and brayed, "Aye! Aye! What they'd be worth?"

"A lot," Stone said. "A lot, no question."

There was more excited chattering, but then the rabble abruptly ceased. Aedan could picture Stone holding up a quelling hand. "Big brutes, all of them," Stone said. "Healthy. And whole. At the moment, anyway."

Some cruel guffaws.

"But who's going to take them there, to market? Sell them?" asked Two. "Who's going to do it? Not me! Not us."

Aedan seized on this: there *was* dissent. These were at least two groups here, which made sense since it was two war bands that had attacked them back on the beach, but they were in an unhappy and an uneven alliance. Stone led one group, probably the larger. Two the other.

"Too risky," continued Two, which Aedan thought rather brave, considering the obvious temper on Stone. "Whoever he is," Two said, "he's too hot to handle."

"Who is he, though?" the woman asked. "He's somebody to be sure, but who?"

"Not one of us, or we'd know it."

"Right."

"Not Dal Fiatach, to be sure."

"No. No." There was some spitting. A lot of grumbling and cursing.

"He's not Dal nAraide."

"No."

"Not Ui Neill."

"No!"

"From the south?"

"I don't think so. I heard them yelling as we took them. They speak like us, more or less."

There were murmurs of unease, uncertainty. Then, "Do you think he could be … ?"

"Enough!" Stone yelled. "It doesn't matter who he is! Makes no difference!"

"But if it's … " said Two.

"I say we finish them off like we should have done first thing!"

yelled Stone.

There was the sound of a large person surging to his feet, accompanied by the rasp of iron from scabbard. "And I get his sword!"

Everyone sprang up.

"If you get his sword, I get his shield!"

"Wait! Wait!" someone whined. "What about me?"

"And me?"

"Yeah! What about the rest of us?"

"Aye! Everyone gets something, from him and from the rest of them!" Stone bellowed. "Everyone gets their fair share!"

Then Stone came barreling across the clearing towards Aedan.

The knots binding Aedan's hands were nowhere near loose enough for him to defend himself. He tensed himself for the blow.

"If she finds out, she won't like it," said Two calmly from the background.

Stone pulled up short.

"Plus, I would guess that's what Baetan wants," Two added. "Them dead, and us the ones to do it."

Two's mildly-spoken, well-timed observation seemed to decide it, because there were no more sounds of advance from the gravel-voiced boss-man. The rest of them fell unhappily silent once again.

There was a long, ominous pause. Then the woman spoke again: "Why not sell them, get them off our hands, make sure she gets her share?"

"All right," said Stone. "To market then. We all take them. We all take the risk. Then we split it, fair and square."

"With some to her."

"With some to her."

Decided at last, the crowd broke into raucous, greedy cheers.

# · 17 ·

# THE BEACHMARKET

There was a rhythmic scraping sound: a scratchy thrust forward, a clean sweep back; full of foreboding and menace. It raised the hair on the back of Aedan's neck and readily helped him to speed up his already frantic attempts to free himself.

"Are you ready?" Stone asked someone.

"Aye. Just about sharp enough," came the reply.

The grinding intensified. So did Aedan's efforts on his bindings. It was a knife being sharpened on a whetstone.

"Start with the big one," Stone said. "Him. The rest will come along easier once his tongue's out."

"Will do. Can you hold him down for me?"

"Aye."

"I wouldn't," Two said. "Not their tongues."

"Bloody hell! Why not?"

"Well, for one," Two said, "there's no time! We've got to get them down to market and sold before she finds out! Because she will find out, make no mistake. It's only a matter of when. If we are going to do this, we have to do it quick-like; quick as fleas to a fine fat dog. Like, right now. Tomorrow, at the latest. That's not enough time to cut them and let them heal."

Stone grunted in thought.

"If they bleed out," Two added, "what are they worth? Nothing. Then she'll really be in a boil."

Stone growled begrudgingly.

Aedan could not have been more thankful to be yanked to his feet. His hands were briefly freed, only to be pulled around in front of him where they were attached to a stout iron chain—a slave chain. He could hear his men being thrown into line behind him, the chain connecting them clanking unsteadily with their rising misery.

When the camp was made ready, they set off down a rough path. They walked downhill for a short distance, the gurgling river on their right-hand side, their captors saying little as the light gathered around them and the bird chatter which had filled the glen faded. By the rising of the sun on his face, Aedan knew they were heading east and indeed there was a general sense of the dense green canopy overhead receding, a lessening of the heavy, almost oppressive scent of loam, the occasional waft of a fresh breeze which smelled sweetly of the sea.

Then rather quickly they were out upon a headland. The sea was now a low constant *shush* on his right-hand side, the formerly welcome breeze now an unremitting cold slap against his weary face.

At mid-day, after a short rest upon what felt to him to be a beachhead where some preparatory work was undertaken by their captors, the nature of which Aedan could not descry, they forded a shallow river, then turned inland again. The ground began to rise. Blood continued to drip down his neck from his split scalp and at times he thought he might lose consciousness from loss of blood and the pain, but he kept himself trudging forward, one foot in front of the other, up and up the glen which was opening narrowly from the ocean.

They walked until just before nightfall. He was stumbling often now, his feet finding every boulder on the path, and was kept upright almost solely by the encouragement of the slave chain.

At last, they came to a halt. Nearby there was a waterfall of some considerable size: its normally happy roar unmistakable to a man who had spent his childhood in the mountains; though not cheering him as it had then. Up they climbed until they came to what Aedan presumed to be a gate manned by guards, for there was a terse challenge from above them, his captors' reassuring replies, more shouted discussion back and forth, not fearful or belligerent but formulaic—a warband being questioned upon its return home with booty. A minute's wait, then the creak of a big wooden gate opening and they were brought into a mountain citadel.

"Light the beacons!" Stone shouted as soon as they were inside. "And be quick about it! Let's see who's out there!"

Aedan was thrown against a wall of the fort. No sooner was he down than his head was grabbed and his blindfold, which had also been serving to bind his bloody scalp, was yanked off. His head was shoved between his knees and held there while water was splashed over his wound. He grunted with the excruciating pain. Then his wound was redressed, and his eyes were covered again.

Then it was the turn of his gag to be torn off. His mouth was pried open and water poured in. At first he choked, and was rewarded with a fist to the back of his head.

When his mouth was yanked opened a second time, he forced himself to submit, to swallow. He drank greedily. Then he just as pridelessly accepted the jagged strip of dried meat that was shoved between his teeth, gulping it down before rooting around his tented legs for any bits that might have fallen out. As his gag was retied tighter than before, the guard handled him brutally for the entertainment of his mates, a torment which Aedan hardly registered.

Then there was nothing more Aedan could do but wait. The beacon had been lit, for one purpose only.

He worked a little longer on the bindings at his wrists and ankles, his eyes and mouth, loosening them as much as he could. Then he forced himself to sleep.

*Da! Da!*

His son's terrified screams woke Aedan from his nightmare with a shout. Rancid sweat was streaming from his brow, his gulped breath, restricted by his gag, making his head spin.

With his shoulder, he pressed against the blindfold so that it would soak up the tears pooling in his eyes. He took in a deep breath. He couldn't afford the luxury of panic lest it cripple him.

Instead, he packed his fury and his dreadful fear into a cold, coiled thing and let it lay in wait in the pit of his stomach for the right time to strike.

In the morning, they came for him again. A hood was thrown on him and he and his men were rounded up. Down they were forced to march, down the winding glen, back to the beachhead. There was an air of expectancy and excitement. When they came to remove the slave chain and to bind him again with rope, he tripped himself, on purpose, so that he fell very badly, the shingle of the foreshore scraping his face. With a curse, he was hauled to his feet again and roughened up for their trouble.

He didn't care. In fact, he rejoiced. They had made a careless error there, one which Aedan wouldn't have made were the situation reversed and he the captor. When his hood and blindfold had been jarred loose by his fall, however briefly, the whole vista of the beach market had been suddenly and shockingly exposed to his rather expert perusal.

Those precious few seconds gave him all he needed to know. He now knew not only the size and weaponry of his main captors Stone and Two, but how many people they had with them, what kind of threat they were likely to pose, and where they were in relation to his men. Also, more importantly, he knew how those men fared.

They had just handed a desperate, very skilled man the means to his survival, and possibly his escape.

They were lined up, Aedan first. He was paraded about a bit, then brought to a halt where he was pinched and prodded by a silent buyer who circled him, assessing.

"Why the hood?" said the buyer after a time of thought.

Aedan's ears pricked up. He knew that accent. Pictish.

And not just Pictish. *Caledonian.*

"Is he leprous or something? Has he got pox? Show me."

"No. He's good," Stone said. "He's strong. Healthy. Just look at him."

"Not good enough. Show me."

With a grumble, Stone ripped off Aedan's hood. There was a curse as the merchant got a look at the wound to Aedan's scalp. "Ah! Thieves! He's been damaged!"

"He's still good. He's still strong."

"The blindfold. Take it off."

"But … "

"Got to see: is the wound deep? Is it putrid? You selling a slave who's half-way to his grave?"

"What do you take me for? He's good. It's just a flesh wound. He'll live."

"Take if off now or the deal's off."

Stone reluctantly removed Aedan's blindfold, his string of invectives burning Aedan's ears, and Aedan came face-to-face with the Caledonian merchant who thought to purchase him.

The merchant stared. Aedan glared back. The man was indeed Caledonian: the blue tattoos all over his face a startling contrast to the paler faces of the Scotti who were grouped anxiously behind him watching the transaction unfold with zeal and dread.

The merchant's eyes grew round. His head whipped around as he searched for Stone. "Are you trying to trick me? Get me killed?"

"What do you mean?"

"Not him. I'll not take him."

"Why not?"

"Not him." The merchant backed away, hands up.

"What's wrong with him?" Stone demanded.

"You don't know?" The Pict barked a nervous laugh.

"Now wait here … "

"No. That's me, gone. Next time you light those beacons, make sure you've got something you can sell."

"What about the rest of them then?"

"For the life of me, I'll not take any of them."

The merchant beat a hasty retreat. "And if you know what's best for you, you'd get as far away from him as you can. *Now.*"

Stone ran after the man, cajoling, pleading with him, but the Pict was faster.

The camp erupted in outrage and shock.

In the mayhem that followed, they forgot to put Aedan's blindfold back on.

Stone came roaring back into the clearing, sword out, hurtling torrents of abuse. "Right! Right!"

But Aedan's fingers had finally accomplished their task, the hastily-fastened knots binding him having been picked apart, the ropes falling away, and as Stone stormed over to him, brandishing his sword, Aedan tore the gag from his mouth.

In seconds, he had Stone's sword in one hand and Stone's thick neck in the other.

"Don't!" Aedan said to the Scotti who were rushing to help their captured comrade. "Don't! My men! Untie them now, and he lives!"

The Scotti hesitated, traded speculative looks, so Aedan drew blood.

Stone cried out. "Do as he says!"

"You!" Aedan said to one of the younger brigands, a ragged girl of about twelve. "You, there! Yes, you! You do it!"

With a nod from Stone, the girl did.

"Now, their weapons."

She re-armed Aedan's men one-by-one.

"Now," Aedan said. "We talk."

The brigand whom Aedan thought of as Two approached cautiously, hands out. "All right then. No need for more bloodshed. All right. Who are you? Tell us, then. You're somebody."

"I am the means to an end. *Your* end. And certainly worth more to all of you alive than dead."

"Yes. Yes. I can see that. But! Who are you? That bastard Baetan left you to die. The Picts won't have you to poke you. You're somebody. Who?"

"That's my business. But since you ask: I am the man that will defeat Baetan."

Two put on a skeptical look, tried, "Like you did before? When he took your wives? Your boy?"

Two was either more courageous than wise, or he didn't much value the life of his fellow brigand twitching under Aedan's sword. Aedan suspected the latter. So did Stone, because he gave a violent shudder.

Aedan's men did not like this either. "How dare you speak to him like that!" Friach cried. "He's … !"

"Fraich, no." Aedan said.

"But … "

"No."

"Who *are* you?"

"Listen," Aedan said. "I could kill him. Right now." Aedan jabbed the sword into Stone's stubbly throat.

He sized up Two. "Or I could fight you."

Aedan shrugged. "I could fight the both of you. All of you. Whomever you like. And it's true: it would be the spectacle of an afternoon and, after two days of what passes for your hospitality, rather fun for me. Or … "

"Or?"

"The fort where we spent the night? The cow pen?" Aedan lifted his chin in the general direction of the empty stockade up the glen behind them. "We could help you fill it."

There was a tense, surprised silence.

"What do you mean?"

"You are ... *adventurers*. So are we."

Two said, "Why?" at the same time that someone else said, "Baetan won't like this"; and another asked, "How full?"

"No, he won't," Aedan said. "Baetan won't like it at all. Which is precisely why we should do it."

There was a lot of muttering. Aedan needed more to sway them. "Look," he said. "You need cattle, don't you? As ransom. To get ... "

Aedan took a wild guess. If he got this wrong ...

He addressed Two. "To get ... your *son* back. From her. The lady."

Shock flooded Two's eyes.

Aedan had hit the mark.

"We are very good at what we do," Aedan added.

Two risked a derisive laugh, pointed at Aedan's wounded head. "Is that so?" But it lacked conviction.

"Try us. Make peace with us, and we'll do it together."

Two thought about this for a moment. Stone, who was pressed up hard against Aedan's cheek, gave a jerky nod.

"How?" Two asked.

"Point us in the direction you want us to go. Preferably in the direction of the Dal Fiatach."

A truce of sorts reached, Aedan released Stone who backed away, hands massaging his throat. He was breathing heavily and his beefy face was mottled with rage.

"Now," Aedan said. "Tell me ... "

Aedan got no further. Stone roared and, head down, charged him.

"Don't!" Aedan advised as he stepped neatly to the side.

Stone rounded, shook his head, bellowed, and his compatriots cheering, charged again.

This time, as Aedan danced away, the edge of Stone's very sharp sword which was still in Aedan's hand sliced open Stone's throat as he barreled by.

Stone groaned, hands to throat, his dying momentum hurtling him into the arms of those nearest. But he was a big man and, unable to be held by them, he toppled over, dead. The cheering ceased as quickly as it had begun.

Blood dripped from the blade in Aedan's hand. "Right," he said. "Anyone else? Now's the time. Have at it. No? Good. Because I, for one, am rather hoping to move on from this. My men too, I wager. Are we agreed?"

He took their awed silence as assent.

"Good. Now you—Two. Or should I call you Number One? We talk."


Not much later, around the fire, Sillan came, hunkered down next to Aedan. The old warrior was stiff with worry and dissent. But first he checked Aedan's wound. "Ah, laddie. That's a bad one."

His fingers pressed down hard on Aedan's scalp and, while Aedan cursed, he smoothed out the ripples to seal it shut, then bound it tight.

"But you'll live, laddie," he said, pounding Aedan on the back. "You'll live. When do you not?"

Then, "Listen, lad. I don't mean to question you, but can you say? The men need to know: why not just have a go at these thieves and be done with it? Wouldn't take half an hour now, with the big one out of the way. We could be done here and off after Baetan in the morning. We get your people, we find our ship, and then ... " He pointed out to sea. "Home."

"Yes," Aedan said. "The thought did cross my mind."

Sillan harrumphed.

"But it's not as simple as all that. Baetan is well away by now. He's no fool. We won't be catching him up that easily. We must come at this another way."

Aedan took a moment to study the ill-tempered Scotti ranged

warily around the fire.

"Look at them, Sillan. They're mostly young ones."

"But … "

"*My* young ones, though they don't know it yet."

"Thieves, more like. Ravagers."

"Well, yes. But what do you suggest we do, Sillan? Kill them all?"

A curt grunt.

"No." Aedan got to his feet. "Besides, as far as I can tell, they're taking us where we need to go."

"Where's that?"

Baetan had spoken of his *gessa*. That the overking of Ulaid must take hostages from as far north as Dun Sobairche.

Change of course.

"North."

# · 18 ·

# THE NINE GLENS

The next stop for Aedan's new ill-formed warband was a harbor
a short distance up the coast where rush-filled fields gave way
to moorland above. Many little burns found their way down the
slopes to the bay and the land along the shore was open and fertile.
Beyond, rising quite quickly from shore, were high mountains that
scowled down upon them, their dark peaks wreathed in mist and
rain.

The villagers came at them with flint axes, but they were no
match for the long swords of Aedan's men, or the mercenary zeal
of the many eager brigands who brought up the rear. To round up
their cattle was the work of an hour.

This allowed the opportunistic Scotti other sport. A woman
screamed.

"No," Aedan said.

"But … "

"No."

"But … "

"I say no. What say you, Two?"

In awe of how efficiently and bloodlessly their customary business had been dispatched under the leadership of the strangers, Two had no trouble siding with Aedan. "Let it be as we agreed," Two said. "Half their cattle, none of their chattel."

"But ... "

Aedan stepped in close. "Listen to your lord. Do as he says. If not, the man with the greedy hand speaks with me."

Further on now. Farther up the coast.

At a small but well-defended fort that sprang up as if straight from the rocky shoreline, Aedan shook off the chill and got to work. More cows were taken, more people were brought under his dominion, though they might not yet have comprehended that with the arrival of that particular raiding party at that particular fort that particular morning, their world would be altered for ever.

It was a change they would be made to understand, over time.

Word spread: beacons were lit on the hillsides to warn. It made no difference. The next fort up the coast, an incredible citadel on a promontory which backed on to cliffs with sweeping views of the sea, fell without a fight, Aedan and his men being welcomed in by a terrified strongman bearing gifts to appease them.

That night by the fire, Aedan allowed himself a moment's reverie. In his hands was the ruined cloak Baetan had discarded so dismissively at his feet. He ran his fingers over it; held it up to his nose. Breathed deeply.

His heart sank. Eogan's scent was heavy on it: that mix of sea salt and candle wax and ink and cow dung that Aedan had started to associate with his king-turned-monk brother. There was also an awful lot of blood. There had been a fight—by the looks of it, a mortal one.

Baetan had not been bluffing. This was indeed Eogan's.

Tears pooled in Aedan's eyes. Grief tore at him. He had not yet been able to reconcile it: how had Eogan and Columba been surprised and killed?

So much life yet to live, lost now on a task that had taken them far, far from home. *Aedan's* task.

For that matter, how had Afrella and Bran been taken captive? They had been safely boarded on the ship to Guined. He had kept watch as they sailed determinedly southwards. He had watched all the ships depart, all the ships that were bearing his sons away. Only then had he come west, across the sea.

What had happened there? Where were the men of Guined?

It had all spectacularly unraveled, and at great cost.

Where did their bodies now lie?

Their bodies …

*Their bodies …*

Aedan gasped, sprang to his feet, seeing something that his grief had kept hidden from him, until now.

If Baetan had really killed Eogan and Columba, why hadn't Aedan already been presented their heads on spikes?

That's what Baetan would do, if he could.

Then another thought struck.

Aedan nearly wept. This time with relief.

*There is nothing of Columba's here. Nothing.*

Whatever had befallen the two …

Aedan took a deep, cleansing breath. He forced his mind to clear, wiped it of all that he had been encouraged to believe. Instead, he pinned it only on what he himself had seen.

And that was two things. Two things only: his family, forced onto Baetan's ships. And Eogan's bloody cloak.

Aedan's heart became hard, invulnerable.

He knew what he needed to do.

He would stay this course.

And plot another one.

Their newly acquired cattle lowed restlessly in their borrowed stockade. Two sidled up to Aedan, saying almost companionably, "You spoke rightly. You do have a talent for this".

Aedan motioned for him to sit, to eat and drink.

"And yet ... " Two said.

"And yet?"

"You harm no one."

Aedan raised an eyebrow. He was thinking of Stone's slit throat, how the big man had toppled almost comically into the arms of his people, irretrievably dead.

"Well, almost no one," Two said. "But I won't count him. It is good that that one is gone."

Aedan passed Two the ale skin. Two took it, drank. Said, "He was a hard man, without heart. And while I understand that we must be strong in these times ... To be heartless too? That is a sad thing, to be sure. A bad thing, in anyone. To live without any kind of love".

Two looked up, braved Aedan's steady gaze. "And then you came," he said. "So I said to myself, why ... *Two* ... this is something new here. Change is afoot. As much as you'd like us to believe it, you are not some wandering thief, as I am. You are a lord of war. So Two, I said, why not take a chance on this man from over the water? That's right, isn't it? You're from over the water?"

Aedan did not answer.

"Not yet then? Not ready? All right. Anyway, I said to myself, Two, if this ... *adventuring* doesn't work, we can always kill him later."

Aedan snorted. "Is that so?"

"Yes. But now I begin to suspect that this adventuring could work. You make this all easy, where before it was hard. Where other big men bark hard orders, and hurt those who do not, or cannot comply, you—calm, wily, effective—you make things happen. That in itself ... Plus, I suspect ... "

"Plus what?"

Two leaned in close. "Hmm. Hmm. Not yet, maybe. Not yet. All right, then, *plus* ... I have come to warn you. They open the gates to you now, but don't be fooled. They'll close them, in the end. With you and your men trapped inside, and … "

Two slid a finger across his throat.

"They?" Aedan asked.

"The seven."

"The seven who?"

"The seven other lords."

"I'm not following."

"Nine glens. Nine lords. Well, eight lords, really. Plus the lady, who rules us all. So, nine. Here … Let me show you."

With his finger, Two leaned forward to scratch a rough map of the terrain thereabouts in the red-tinged dirt between his boots. When he was finished, it looked as if he had drawn a hand with thick, blunt fingers clawing at the ocean. Except that the hand had too many digits. Aedan had seen something like it before, from the beach at Ros-na-Righ. What Two had drawn was a flatter version of the series of great promontories that Aedan had seen stepping up the coast.

Two had drawn a map of Hibernian Dal Riata.

At that moment, Two was drawing his attention to where the webbing would be, were these truly fingers. "Glens, yes?" Two said. "Where the rivers run down from the mountains to the sea. Where the people live. Each of these glens is the center of a lordship; its heart, if you like. Each glen, a people. Nine all together. One, two, three, four, five, six, seven, eight, nine. Nine peoples. You see, yes? Here, at the bottom, where we took you after we took you, are the Hares. The Hares are my people."

With a fierce pride, Two tapped the most southerly of the glens of his makeshift map before moving up the coast to the next. "The land we have been moving through since then are the Foxes. They were *his*, so I don't mind overmuch that we are taking what they have. To be true—I like it. A lot."

Stone.

"But we're coming to a kind of border now," he said.

"A border with whom? Dal Riata?"

"Hmm. Yes. You do know. The Hares and the Foxes, my people

and his people, we're neither really here or there. Neither really Dal Riata nor Dal nAraide. We go back and forth as we see fit. Now, just around the next headland, the one we're coming to now, is Dal Riata proper. Which is why I am telling you this. I thought, being who I think you are, you might ... Well, in any case, Dal Riata is next. Dal Riata—all the other seven, from the Badgers, next, all the way up around the coast."

His finger found the glens, one after the other, leaving a red smear in the soil as it swung upwards. "The Badgers, the Sea Otters, the Salmon, the Hawks, the Wolves, the Seals. And at the top, lording it over the Sea of Moyle, the Eagles."

"Where is the lady who has your son?"

Two's finger pounded, obliterating the Eagles. "The filthy, filthy eyrie of Dun Sobairche."

Aedan's ears pricked. "Tell me about her, this Lady of the Eagles."

"She's a newly-come lord, not long on the job. Didn't want it. Had to take it, because my lord Baetan ... No other choice ... But still ... "

Two heaved a sigh of deep frustration and hatred as he came to his point a last. "Can you kill her for me?" he asked.

"You cannot do it yourself?"

Two ducked his head.

Aedan felt a moment's compassion. "I tell you what: I'll kill her if I must. But, first things first: let us start by taking it back."

"Taking what back?"

Aedan drew a circle around the grasping red hand of the nine glens. "All of it."

Two whistled. "You mean business."

"I'm not here for the view."

Two rocked back on his heels, thoughts passing rapidly through his mind, many of them writ also on his face: Incredulity. Temptation. Hope.

"Are you with me on this?" Aedan asked.

"My heart longs to say yes. What heart wouldn't? Such ease in improving, after so many years of loss and toil and hardship. In fact, if you pass me the ale skin again—ah! Many thanks!—my heart will ignore its misgivings and leap easily to your side. I am a hare after all. And what hare doesn't desire dominion?"

He drank. Wiped his mouth.

"But while the head remains clear,"—Two rapped on his skull with his knuckles—"it cautions me. Why do you do this? Why are you here? Why do you ... *help*?"

"We are here about a very ... particular business," Aedan said.

Two nodded. "Your family. The ones taken by Baetan at the beach of Ros-na-Righ."

Though Aedan answered Two with a scowl, Two's new-felt intimacy emboldened him to speak over it. "You were correct, more or less," Two said. "It is not my son the lady has, but my brother. He is a young lad. He was not made for the axe, much less the sword. He has more of the poet in him. His sword is his tongue. Plus, he sees ... *things*," Two said proudly. "Visions. That is his value."

"A value which also makes him vulnerable," Aedan said.

"Yes. You comprehend. I thought you might," Two said. "I have feared for my brother since she took him. But now, with you ... for the first time, I also have hope to get him back."

"There is your reason, then, if you must have one," Aedan said. "You want your family. I want mine."

Two lurched forward. "And more besides, I think," he said, his eyes bright. "You want more besides. You *are* he, aren't you?"

The fire crackled loudly in Aedan's noncommittal silence.

"What is *your* name, Two?"

Two grinned. Didn't tell him.

Aedan laughed. "All right, *Two*. Is it agreed then," Aedan said. "Let us be true allies, not just companions of convenience. I will help you take back your brother. You will lead me to where I want to go."

Two nodded solemnly.

"But," Aedan said, "if you betray me, I will kill you."

Two nodded again, said, "And if you betray *me* ... "

Aedan took back the ale skin. "You can try to kill me."


Quickly now. Quickly.

Not allowing himself to dwell on thoughts of his family, or of Columba and Eogan, Aedan pushed on, reiving, raiding, their herd increasing, until they came to a drove road over an otherwise sheer headland. They led the cattle over the narrow, rough track that threaded through the wooded slopes just above the coast, the cliffs falling straight to rocks and the pounding sea below. From that height, through a sudden gap in the tree line, the seascape opened to the east. In clear light, such as there was at that moment, he could see a lump of blue-green landfall not five leagues across the water, so close he could almost reach out and grab it.

Aedan realized with a start that it was Cendtire. The Cendtire of his childhood, rising up. There were other lumps of land, too, which Aedan thought he could put name to: the British kingdoms of Strat Clut, of Rheged. The Isle of Mann.

It was remarkable, how close home was, revealed on a clear day. How the ocean between them was something they shared, which linked rather than divided them.

Or should link—were there love between them rather than enmity.

Aedan laughed. All those times he and his father and brother had looked with a sort of ill-formed longing across the watery divide towards their ancestral homeland of Dal Riata, it was to these savage glens they had so lovingly gazed.

To this dark country, given over to these raiders, these reivers, these thieves.

He laughed again. Because all these things he had also himself become.

Two had halted a few yards ahead. Aedan joined him.

"Why do we stop?" Aedan asked.

Then he saw. Towering up at the edge of the cliff in front of them was a huge lonely pillar of white limestone, easily twenty feet high. The cliffs here, he had noticed, were riddled with caves and outcrops and strange formations, but this one before them now was somehow different. He backed up, looked again, certain that his eyes were deceiving him. They were not. The pillar, a natural pinnacle of limestone and not manipulated or shaped in any way that he could see, looked for all the world like a statuesque woman, shapely, imperious, vaguely luminescent, holding sway over her watery dominion—a realm that stretched all the way to Caledonia.

She was a sea-mark, helping mariners to shore. An ancient one. She was a goddess.

Aedan could not shake the thrill that ran through him.

"Good," said Two. "You see her. That bodes well. The White Lady marks the boundary. Now we must take care."

A little farther ahead and they were around the headland and looking down upon a vast bay. Not one but two rivers had ground out paths to the sea, slicing glens from a range of mighty mountains. Though the bay was majestic, grand, deep, and wide, it was not at all welcoming—on the overhanging precipices of rock were forts, fortlets, and raths, belching out the smoke of peat fires even though it was summer; keeping watch, constantly on guard.

One was not encouraged to enter these glens. The mountains ran down all the way to intersect the sea's edge, closing off each glen to movement north or south; impenetrable barriers. Once you were in, there was no way out again but by sea.

"That's Dal Riata proper," Two said. "That's where it begins."

How Aedan longed to go down! To explore, to investigate, to get to know his ancient homeland.

"What's that way?" Aedan looked left, up the first glen, into the mist-enshrouded mountains.

"If we go up, if we go over, we come to a sort of no-man's land. Not Dal Riata. Not Dal nAriade. Probably Dal Fiatach now. Or Ui Neill."

Two spat in disgust. "The Ui Neill. They push in. They drive us all to the very edge of the sea."

"Are there cattle to be had there?"

"Oh, aye!"

"Does that way also lead to your Lady of the Eagles?"

"Aye."

"Lead on."

# · 19 ·
# THE TONNS

It was a thing of beauty.

Through the waves Columba could see the gold of the little boat ripple. Oars were set in their locks, nine sticks flattened into paddles, another one to steer. A fragile mast where a sail was once sheeted. Simple benches bolted across the hold to seat phantom sailors who no longer rowed the ship.

He reached down and, hand wrapping around the miniature ship, pulled it up through the layers of water into the light, water sloshing out of the immaculate little vessel.

He knew what it was. It was a votive offering made to the sea-god Manannan, for where Columba was then is that god's home. That prominent, sweeping sand bank where, waves crashing, grand Loch Febal greets the sea, is the place where that god was born. People go there and throw things in the water while they make their wishes and pray their prayers. Heal my son, they say, who has taken sickly and is close to death, and here is a gold neck-ring for your consideration, my lord Manannan. Do you like the swirls? Your ever-shifting face is there, emerging cleverly from the spirals. See?

Or, why have I no children? My heart desires young ones above all things. Send me ones that look like the figures I have had carved here, sweet and strong. Speed their passage to me, my lord Manannan. Release them from the Otherworld, so that they might walk with me for a while amongst the flowers in the hedgerows under the sun. Open the doors to the light.

Or, make him love me. Please. Please. Please. Why does he not love me? Turn his eyes kindly to my countenance. Within this gleaming gold disc that I am giving you let him see the face of his beloved: let him see *me*.

Or, darker desires. Like, my wife complains day and night that there is no food for the little ones. That I drink their food. Feed them with this bowl that I throw in. For if they cry again I will have to shut them up. And they will have you to blame for it.

Or, I covet my neighbor's bull. It is a wondrous bull, black as night and mean as sin. With a pulsing, thick member that hangs to the ground, one that looks like this. Let my neighbor not have that bull. Snap its leg in the hare hole so that he must bludgeon it to death himself with his own club.

Or, kill the ones who have hurt my daughter. Hurt them as they have hurt her. In exactly that way. And for exactly that long.

No. Longer.

And here is the golden dagger with which to do it.

The votive boat gleaming in Columba's hands was a fragile thing. Beautifully wrought. A master goldsmith had made it, and no other. How long had it lain there, rolling about in the estuarine tides, he wondered? What desire had it been meant to achieve? What journey, pilgrimage, or raid, bless? Whose heart, heal?

And why had he been led here to it now? What import did it have for the finding of the boy?

Shedding his useless disguise, he had followed the river north in his logboat. It had taken him to the sea. He had let himself drift out upon the open water for a little while, the tides taking him where they liked, until he had fetched up here, on the sand banks at the mouth of vast loch Febal which he knew so very well, since his own first, now forbidden monastery of Daire lay on an island not far inshore.

He admired the boat some more, ran his hands over the impossibly smooth, glowing hull. The sheets of metal were so fine he could have bent them with his fingers if he had wanted to. Crumple the whole thing into a ball and stow it away in his pocket to melt it down later to fashion into something new, or sell it. But he wouldn't. It was too rare, too precious a thing. Besides, it had been wrapped around with charms and spells for a god that was not his. Each lost sailor it once held was a wish given to the waves. Who knew for how long it had lain forgotten in the sand?

He lowered the boat and let water flood the hold so that it sank gently to the sandy bottom of the loch more or less upright, as if it were sailing.

Perhaps it was the fire that Columba had set upon the beach that lured in the boat. The actual boat. The fact that he stood his ground and did not run away, as if in expectation, which drew in the landing party. That he did not resist which encouraged them not to bind him in chains but to take him aboard, a guest.

They were a rowdy bunch, a troublesome tribe. Drunk. Boastful. Garrulous in their cups. They over-spoke one other, bantering back and forth, their words flowing so quickly that they wove Columba into a sort of spell. By nature, he loved all kinds of word play and light laughter, but soon his head was spinning in his effort to keep up.

As far as he could tell, he had found himself on a ship full of bards making their way to a hastily-convoked assembly called by the high-king. Aed mac Ainmerech was meeting others, they said. The lords hereabouts. The kings and kinglets. Well, they might not be that high up, the bards said, but he could make time to meet with them too. Assemblies were not to be held without their kind present, for how were the common folk to know the truth of what transpired between those who ruled them, between kings, if their kind, the bards, were not there to report it? That was their job.

Besides, they too had grievances, they said. The bards did, which ought to be heard. The people no longer uphold the law, they said. They no longer quarter the bards as they come through the villages, or feed them as they ought; they refuse them hospitality. Doors were shut in the companies' faces.

What of their livelihoods? How were they to feed their own retainers, their camp followers, their fans? How provide their people shelter? As the bards moved through the countryside telling their stories, both the fine ones and the not so fine, on whose soft pillows would they, and the thirty or forty servants who accompanied them to attend to their needs, lay their heads at night?

They were *Aes Dana*! Not of the common people, but a special class. They could not be refused.

They would petition the high-king that he force the people to adhere to the law, would make known their grievances, lobby for their rights. If the high-king did not uphold the law, they would curse him. If he refused to venerate the power in their good words, they would give him bad ones. They would rain maledictions down upon his head, tell unflattering stories about him, until his people began to hate and to fear him.

They would make three blisters appear on his face with their satire. Make him come out all over with boils and sores and blindness until he was blighted.

And then where goes his rule? Right out the smoke hole, thank you very much!

As the night wore on, Columba listened to their conversations, to their complaints, until he had heard enough to understand who they were and where they were going. "You will dare curse Aed mac Ainmerech if he does not do as you demand?" he asked at last.

This aggrieved them. "Of course we will curse him! It is in our power to do so! It is our ancient right. No man stands above his reputation. Most especially not a king, whose notoriety is his power. Who does he think he is? His good name is entirely under our control. We can lift him up, if we like. Or we can tear him down and ruin him utterly."

"He is mighty, this man you intend to maledict," Columba pointed out in what he hoped would be taken as a helpful manner. "And dangerous. It might not end as you wish. I can speak with him on your behalf. Take me with you. I will go where you are going."

Amused disbelief ran through the company like water sloshing about the deck of the ship. "Why would he listen to you? He is the high-king. What are you?"

Columba said it: "He will not fail to trade words with a kinsman".

A hush descended on the bards so swiftly it was as if all the candles had been blown out in one go. Suddenly there were no more words. Instead, there were glances down at hands and fingers which begin to fly through the air, making elaborate, silent signs.

The bards were using their secret language. It was a language you could write out on parchment or vellum if you liked, or carve against the edge of a stick or a stone. But its real utility lay in its ability to be tapped out with the fingers of the one hand against those of the other—a language to be seen only by others in the know, and not to be heard by all.

A language which they, being either drunk or arrogant or both, thought he could not read. But of course he could read it. When he had lived here, there was no one in Hibernia with more knowledge than he, or more learning. So, covertly, Columba read what they were saying to each other, feigning ignorance.

*I told you it was he! None other!*

*Can you believe! What luck!*

*It was not luck. It was I. My doing.*

*How so? Dallan Forgall, you are a colossal braggart. Worse than most. You fancy yourself Chief Bard, Head of Song—but you are no more than a buffoon.*

*I am the best poet here. And don't you all know it.*

*Bah!*

*You know what we must do.*

*We will ransom him to the high-king. His life in exchange for the prosecution of our suit.*

*He has forfeited his life in any case! What impelled him back here? His life is ours to take. There will be reward in it, beyond measure! Enough to fill our bellies till winter, in any case. And to keep the rest happy.*

*Exile! Excommunicate!*

When they addressed Columba again, their eyes were gleaming. "You will speak to the high-king," they said. "You will plead."

And they covered his eyes with a blindfold, bound him with chains, and threw him into the hold.

# · 20 ·

# DUN SOBAIRCHE

On a craggy rock stack on the edge of a cliff on the Sea of Moyle there is a towering citadel. It rises straight from the waves and is higher than a hill. The sea thunders either side of the fortress, roiling and frothing and roaring, doing its best to clamber up and get inside. When the tide is high, the citadel stands alone on its stack in the waves. When the tide recedes, stony beaches appear at the shoreline way down below, and dark caves reveal themselves like maws, gnawed from the cliffs.

The citadel doesn't bother itself with the sea, or what may lurk there. It turns its back to the Moyle with a breathtaking insouciance, knowing it cannot be breached. When storms tear at it, furious at its indifference, or pirates sail by, all it does is laugh.

Venerable Dun Sobairche. Ancient Dun Sobairche.

Its eyes are trained on a greater prize, one that lies not out to sea but rather far, far inland.

It looks to Hibernia's sacred center. To Temair, where the high-king rules.

Hibernia has five fifths. Five ancient provinces. And so the high-king has five roads to reach them, radiating out from where he sits. Each of his roads pierces a province, runs right through it, and ends at the ocean at the far end, for such is his dominion.

If you take the road that heads north from Temair, it ends at Dun Sobairche, right at that citadel's main gate. That is where you will fetch up. The great hero of old, canny Cu Chulainn, trod upon that road, having outrageous adventures. Humble Patrick too often set out upon it, when he went collecting souls. In fact, it is at the citadel of Dun Sobairche that Patrick reached down into the grave and drew forth from his dead mother's cold clutches the sainted child Olcan, alive; Olcan who was later to set down the holy stones of Armoy for the worship of the Christ.

It is also there that the kings and queens of Dal Riata of Hibernia are acclaimed, in the royal precinct at the end of the high-king's road, at the foot of the fort. On the primordial stone which crowns the sacred high serpentine mound there.

And if you go further up, through the gates, into the fort, to the highest precinct at the back, to the very edge of the cliff, beyond which you cannot go without hurtling into the sea, you will find a sacred spring bubbling up. That is why they built a citadel here in the first place, to guard that spring. It is why Dun Sobairche laughs at its own immense importance. The water in that spring had a sanctity before the idea of a Christ was even conceived in the teeming heart of the divine.

That's why they all come to Dun Sobairche, the kings, the queens, the heroes, the heroines, the saints, Aedan and his motley crew. Because, before any of them, before any of it, here gods abided.

"That's it?"

"Aye."

Aedan whistled. "That's something."

Finding the high-king's road, straight and true and oddly

deserted, they had followed it north, through peat land and high moors, raiding where they might, until, almost at day's end, three days after they had set out from the coast, they crested a impressive rise to find Dun Sobairche lording on an isolated rock stack at the end of a natural hollow, almost an amphitheater of green grassy hummocks and peculiarly-shaped outcrops of stone. The road rose up, giving them a level view of the citadel's walls with long vistas of the sea behind and the vast sky, and then plunged down again, forcing them to cross the exposed hollow and come to the great gate from below.

There was the only one way in. Which meant, when in, there was only one way out. Even Aedan, who had seen more kings' halls than most, had to admit that it was all rather extraordinary.

"Isn't it, though!" Two said. "We go down, then up again; up, up the slope to the main gate—all the while under their very eyes."

Such a mighty place. Aedan was certain the citadel would not go down without a fight—a fight that, given his present, reduced, circumstances, he would have a hard time winning.

And yet, something was amiss. Surely the Lady of the Eagles had heard of their raiding in the countryside. They traveled now with a growing herd of cattle, not easily overlooked, and their numbers had swelled with recruits, mostly young men and women enthralled with the adventure this exciting new lord afforded. Yet they had not been challenged, or stopped upon the road, or otherwise prevented from making it here in any way.

Even if knowledge of their presence had somehow escaped her, they must certainly have been spied now, peering as they were up at the gate en masse, armed, and lit up by a sun setting athwart their faces.

It was all very strange.

"What do we do?" asked one of the Scotti. In the short time since they had captured Aedan and his men, they had grown accustomed to his leadership. No one now thought to question it.

"Well, at this point we … "

"I say we call 'em out, give them a good bashing!" someone

proposed.

"Actually I was thinking we would … "

"Starve 'em out! Wait until they have to open the gate and ambush them!"

"What we need are allies so … "

"Allies? But you said … "

"We burn 'em out! Excellent plan!"

Aedan held up a hand. "Sound strategies, all—at some other time," Aedan said. "But here, now? No, no, and no."

Truly, there was something odd about the whole thing. Something he could not yet put his finger on.

"We could go about this in the usual way, by bullying our way in," Aedan said. "But I think not. What's needed here is something far less … *expected*."

"What?"

He cast his eyes upon the fort's imposing rise. His mens' followed.

"We knock upon on the door."


Shouldering their weapons, shields overhead in case arrows were to be fired down, they dashed up the steep path that led from the hollow to the gate, prepared for any challenge. There was none. They drew swords, again without opposition. As they approached the gate, which had been adorned with the likenesses of the gods and goddesses of old but was now worn and faded by the abuse of the wind and the rain and the sea, it drew open without their even having to knock.

"Careful, now," Aedan advised. "This is probably a trap."

And they were in.

After the countless, breathless stories his father had told him as a child of the wonders of The Great Hall of Dun Sobairche, the chief-seat of the kings of Dal Riata of Hibernia, the ancient heart of Ulaid, their ancestral homeland and his birthright, it was fair to say that Aedan had certain expectations. The sight that greeted him upon bursting through the gate did not match any of them. It wasn't the citadel's size or its situation. Both were spectacular and could not be faulted. The fort was certainly large enough. Once past the guardhouse, the hill split open to two levels, one ahead, towards the sea; the other, back around the front, to the landward side of the rock stack. The sea-side of the rock was where the people lived and indeed there were plenty of huts and sheds and lean-tos up on that height. But they seemed strangely desolate; devoid of life. The king's precinct too, to the front, was marvelously situated. It was where he would have built the Great Hall, had it been his to build. Only one hazardous approach up a short, steep rise, easily defended with as few as five men; a plummeting death from all sides, then the nose of the Great Hall pointing back like an eagle's beak towards land, towards the high-king's road.

Ideal, really, in every way.

It wasn't any of these things. Rather, it was the air of the place, which was rather careworn and cowering. The fact that Aedan and his company had strolled in without challenge. Where were the fighting men? The fighting women? Here there were only old men and boys, and old women and girls, who peered out in fear at Aedan and his warband.

And still … there was something else, something more which Aedan could not quite put his finger on. Something he could not yet place.

There was no time to investigate further, for they were led to the gates of the royal citadel on its height.

A woman met them on the ascent. She was young, not yet thirty, and regally attired. She was accompanied by a handful of retainers, all much older and more frail than she. She had the translucent skin and red-flamed hair that one often sees in the isles, and her mouth was a red scar on her tired but defiant face. In her hands was a great sword, its point in the dirt at her feet.

"You are the Lady of the Eagles?" Aedan asked her.

"Yes," she said. "I am Lassar. What do you want? Why have you come?"

How to start? "We mean you no harm … " Aedan said.

A disbelieving laugh burst from her lips. "The man who can do no harm is the man in his grave."

Aedan cocked his head in acknowledgment of the truth of her words.

"Besides," she said. "You are armed to the teeth."

"Yes, well, we'd like a place by the fire," he said.

"Tonight?"

"Yes."

"And tomorrow?"

Aedan shrugged.

The world-weary laugh came again. It was sad to hear in one so young. "All right," she said. "Tonight, a place by the fire. Because, really: as you can see,"—her sword swept about in a pitiful arc— "how could we stop you? And tomorrow, when you begin to harm, you will see that the fire is all you shall get from us. Because even if I were inclined to host you as an honored guest in my Great Hall, as the great lady I once was, I can offer you nothing—for nothing is all we have."

"Do not trouble yourself on that account, my lady," Aedan said. "For as I am sure you have heard, we have brought our own."


"My lady. Tell me: where are your people? What evil has befallen this place?"

He could account for her father, the former steward of Dun Sobairche, and her mother, whose heads rotted in their bag. But where were the others?

"Our people are gone."

"Gone? Gone where?"

"They have been taken. Or have fled."

"Taken by whom?"

"Everyone. Anyone."

"Where is that man's brother?" Aedan indicated Two who was glaring at Lassar with an ill-concealed hatred. "The young one. The

252

poet. The one *you* took."

A raised chin. Defiance. "Taken as well."

"By whom, exactly?" Aedan asked. "Who took what was yours to take? Who reives your people?"

"In many cases, it was the Ui Neill who took. In his brother's case, it was the Dal Fiatach. My lord Baetan. He must take hostages as far north as Dun Sobairche. He is the overlord of Ulaid. It is *geis* to him not to."

Two was on his feet in an instant. "Why not one of your own to hostage? Why did you give him mine?"

"I had no more of my own to proffer. He took many things. Your brother was one of them."

Two let out a howl of rage and anguish. "How long ago? To where was he taken? Does no one dare to stop him? Does no one fight?"

From Lassar, that bitter laugh. "Look about you. Those who dared are dead."

That was when Aedan had it: the thing about Dun Sobairche that had been so perplexing him. His father had spoken of the citadel with reverence and no small amount of awe. Hearing his stories, an image of hope and strength and might had sprung up in Aedan's young mind, a great beacon of light on a high hill.

Looking about him now, a different picture came to mind. If Dun Sobairche was still a beacon, it beckoned backwards. If it was still a sentinel, it stood for nobler times long gone.

This Dun Sobairche was beaten down. The people of this Dun Sobairche lived in fear. They had been frightened and abused for so long, they had given up hope of victory, or deliverance. They had given up hope of any kind. Because, really, when you thought about it: what kind of person doesn't lock their door?

Either a person who had no fear, which was patently not the case here. Or a person who knew only fear, and had succumbed to it.

Worse, the kind who knew they possessed no lock with which to keep their enemies out.

"Listen, my lady," Aedan said. "I have three things for you. The first, I am sorry to say, will cause you pain. The second I hope will bring you joy. The third? I cannot say. Likely some of both."

Aedan placed in her hands the bag he had brought from Dun Ad, taken as booty by Stone and given back with some revulsion by Two. She did not open it or cradle it to her breast, as another might have, but held it stiffly in enraged acceptance.

"The second?" she demanded.

"South of here, on the high-king's road where it runs on the ridges over the hills, I have hidden cattle. *A lot* of cattle."

"Whose?" she demanded.

"Mainly the Dal Fiatach's."

She smiled meanly. "Good. What of these cattle?"

"Consider them ours."

"Ours? How so?"

"Well, the third thing I have to give you is my name."

"Say it."

"I am Aedan mac Gabran … "

"… mac Domangart mac Fergus Mor mac Erc," she said. "Of course you are."

She sprang to her feet. "My people!" she said. "This is our *lord*, returned home at last!"

There were shouts of incredulity from the old ones hovering around.

"Indeed!" she said. "Before we do him any obeisance, let him first prove his worth. Let him prove the rule!"

"What's that, my lady? What's that?" they cried. "What rule?"

The eyes she turned upon Aedan were glittery with challenge.

"Lordly is as lordly *does*."

# · 21 ·

# BORDERLANDS

T hey had reached a harbor. Columba surmised this because the ship began to lurch and to slow. He heard the orders to lower the sail and to man the oars, and then the ship ground its way ashore. He presumed they were still on the sea-loch Febal because they had not sailed far, the voyage steady, and the water was calm rather than boisterous, which would have been the case had they passed back out past the Tonns. They had kept to their direction, sailing south.

If the bards had spoken truly, and Columba had no reason to suspect that they had not, then he knew where they had pulled to port: the harbor of Druim Ceatt, halfway down loch Febal. Perilously close to home: as close to his old monastery of Daire as he had dared to be these last twelve years.

In fact, the last time he was here, he had been fleeing for his life out the loch the other way.

Even though he was returning in chains, his heart did a little dance. Of longing? Of dread?

He did not struggle as he was hauled to his feet and roughed over the side of the ship. Hands caught him, helped him land upright. Wet sand sucked at his boots. Then there was planking underfoot which cut across low country; marshland. It had the stench of estuary, the scents scandalously alive, as well as the seeking brush of high reeds against his face; the reeds singing as they shivered in the wind that was coming fiercely off the great loch.

Soon the ground began to rise. They ascended a low hill.

He could hear many people about. Columba's mind worked furiously: what had prompted this unscheduled royal convention? What had caused the high-king to assemble here, at the border between the Ui Neill and the province of Ulaid, out of season? This was the time of year to raid, not to negotiate. That came at the end of summer when you had goods to barter with, goods you had spent the better part of the summer collecting, mostly other people's cattle. What had frightened the high-king so?

As Columba was hauled along, voices began to rise, full of speculation and astonishment. They did not fall again behind him, but grew like a wave of wonder.

He heard his name, spoken in the old way. "Colum? Colum Cille?"

This infuriated his captors, the bards, and they closed ranks around him, cursing artfully, shutting him off from the crowd's burgeoning adulation.

But it had given him hope.

There was a creak and he was taken in hand through a small doorway of some kind, then thrown down. He landed in ankle-deep mud, and other, riper, things. It took no time for him to work out that he was encrusted in dung. He was in a pen where animals had recently been kept. The creak sounded again: the door being slammed shut behind him.

He scrambled up as well as he could with his hands still bound, then scooted backwards until he was up against the wall of the enclosure. He slammed his body against it, once, twice—would it yield to force? No.

A crowd had started to mass around the pen. Their voices rose and fell in every direction; a tight knot right behind him. They called out to him. He was startled to feel fingers pulling at his hair and tugging at his cloak. They were reaching through the slats of wattle to touch him.

At first he could not bear it, he had to try to escape, to make his way out of the enclosure immediately and find the high-king, but he pulled up short when he recognized the comfort in their touch, how they were beseeching him: "Abba! Abba! You have come home to us at last! Help me! Heal me!"

Columba was about to ask for their help when he heard a cry and realized he was not alone in the pen.

The pony they had grudgingly offered him nickered and shied. Aedan could not blame her. She did not like it, up here on the ridgeline on the edge of the Bann where the wet wind could pelt them with impunity. The day was grey and raw; the rain skidding in sideways off the screaming sea.

The wind was howling so loudly, Aedan had to strain to hear the uneasy talk of the men. The new men, the six other Lords of the Glens. Messengers had been sent out from Dun Sobairche to the six lords of Dal Riata he had not yet met, and all had obeyed the Lady's summons. There the glen lords had heard Aedan's offer, listened to his proposal, agreed that they could go on as they had ever done ... or could lift their heads in concert in pursuit of the first of what might become many common goals—the ridding themselves of Baetan, their disastrous overlord.

A thing which Aedan had wholeheartedly agreed to help them do.

They had taken him at his word: all were now ringed behind him. All eight lords and the lady, with their fully-armed retinues, had allowed themselves to be led by the new, strange lord from over the water—right there, right up in the front.

Earlier, Aedan had been able to laugh at it. He wasn't an idiot, or a chancer, much as they had hoped he was. He and his men had been shoved to the fore so as to take the brunt of the attack, the majority of the losses. The mortalities too, if it should come to that, with he the first. Earlier, he had thought this risk worthwhile. This was his end game, after all, or one very near it. But now that Baetan's forces were arrayed in the plain below, waiting with a kind of insolent disdain—they had rigged up tents, of all things, whose colorful flaps snapped in the wind; as sure a sign as any that they expected to be feasting soon—Aedan was reconsidering his hope that he could help unite the lords of the glens and bring them justice against their oppressors while he exacted his own, more personal brand of revenge.

He reconsidered his hope, but not his resolve. His family was down there with Baetan. Hopefully, Two's brother was as well. And Aedan was discovering a ruthlessness he did not know he possessed.

But the others had seen it. The others knew. Which is why they now waited behind him for his orders, without hesitation, before a much larger force.

Well, since they wanted him to lead, he would lead. Then, when it was finished and Baetan's head was in his hands, he would take over. For that was the gist of the oath they had sworn before the fire at Dun Sobairche, though the glen lords might not now remember it.

Drunken or not, it was an oath that Aedan would make them honor.


"Eogan!" Columba shouted, full of a wild hope. Because of the gag, his cry came out as an indeterminate grunt. "Is that you? Is that you? Where are you?"

The whimper on the other side of the pen abruptly ceased.

Columba threw himself forward, crawling awkwardly through the filth. "Eogan! Eogan!"

He crashed into something: the arched back of someone who had drawn in his limbs as tight as a ball. Through the rough linen on his back, vertebrae poked out like exclamations.

There was no fat on the bones. None at all.

"Oh! Oh!" Columba cried.

He reared back, unable to stop his tears.

The person was small. Too small.

It could not be Eogan.


They would honor the oath. But first, the fight: the rather large matter of making Baetan see who Aedan was.

"My lord?" said Sillan who had come alongside, his pony just as fidgety as Aedan's. His old friend was not pleased. He questioned their purpose there, could not yet see the bigger plan.

Or doubted it could be achieved.

Everyone could feel the terrible tension in the air, how the energy always spikes to an almost unbearable degree just before battle is joined. How anxious everyone is to do well, to fight with honor; to not die. And if to die, to not die badly. While many there might look for everlasting fame, Aedan had yet to meet a person who willingly sought pain.

"You know how it is, my old friend," Aedan said, offering Sillan a smile from which he had tried to erase the grimness. "Lordly is as lordly does."

The wind had picked up. It too was restless. The rain lashed harder. Raising his sword in the hopes that the others would follow but not looking back in case they did not Aedan kicked his pony down the slope.


In his despair, Columba had fallen up against the wall of the cow pen where the crowd's prying fingers had found him again. They groped, plucked, fondled. It was both repugnant and comforting at the same time. They ripped his cloak, but then some kind soul thought to inch down his gag. It dangled, caught on the stubble on his chin. When he could feel fingers at the strip of cloth around his eyes, he threw his chin downwards, pulling himself free of the blindfold; and could see.

It is as he had sensed: a round cow pen, high wattle walls, too high to see over. Cloud cover: lowering, very close to rain. People pressed up around the outside of the enclosure, peering through the slats. Dirty hands reaching for him.

There was one other captive in there with him. The one he had fallen against.

He got a good look. Gasped.

It was a boy.


Sooner than he should have liked, Aedan had cause to reconsider. His own men were fighting well, but their new allies the glen lords were not. There had been no time to train them. They had only just come together as a warband, had only just begun to think of themselves as a united Dal Riata and not traditional enemies who, a month earlier, would gladly have turned the grim edge of their weapons upon one another in the dark. They had not yet learned to see beyond the borders of their little valleys, seeing only their own people and no others.

And indeed, who could blame them? It was their own people who had held their hands through the cradle slats when they cried, who picked them up when they fell, who filled their gnawing bellies on the days when food was hard to find, forsaking their own.

Put their first weapons in their hands; then pointed them in the direction they were to use them.

All that bound them to this particular endeavor were Aedan's words, and their own oaths uttered drunkenly before the fire, under the skulking moon, when the only foe to be faced was either in memory (as easily vanquished now, as then) or in expectation.

And in those dreams of sweet things to come? Always victories.

Baetan knew this. With a cunning that was breathtaking, he was evading Aedan's blinding charge, directing his men around the flanks instead, where they began to pick off the vulnerable Dal Riata like wolves ravening the weak sheep at the edges of the fold. Both flanks were taking quick losses.

Aedan heard them cry out. He and his men doubled back, goading back the unwilling ponies with kicks. But they had to split into two forces to render any aid, one to the left, the other to the right, which Baetan had of course predicted as well.

Aedan's heart got harder, if that were possible. There was really only one way to end this.

He hunted down his foe.


Columba didn't know how he knew it, but he did. Why else had he been led here? Here, of all places?

"You are Fiachna Lurgan, aren't you?" he asked.

At the name, the tight little ball of cowering boy shook.

Columba couldn't help it. He laughed and laughed.

He laughed so hard and so bitterly, he rattled the cage.


Try as Aedan might, Baetan was eluding him, slipping around the outside every time Aedan got close. It was infuriating for Aedan—and deadly for his men. If Baetan had honor, he would meet Aedan before the companies to decide the outcome of the battle by single combat. The king that survived was the king that won. It was why you chose strong men to rule. It spared lives. It left farmers alive to bring in the harvest.

It was the price of kingship.

But Baetan wanted carnage. Baetan wanted annihilation. These were not his people, so why not? Indeed, in some quarters his tactics would be considered good war-craft. Baetan wanted to make the people of Dal Riata pay for their comeuppance, to decimate them before they had a chance to unite.

Those things first. And then he would slaughter the one who dared to try to lead them.

The sky had finally dumped its load. It was chucking down rain, turning the effluence in the pen into filthy rivers of shit. With the help of the crowd, Columba had entirely freed himself. First, he checked the door of the enclosure. But it was fastened with a stout lock and not even the efforts of the willing crowd could get it open.

He went to the boy, hunched down on his heels. The boy had not spoken. He could not speak. There was an iron bit in his mouth that curled his lips back cruelly. His hands and feet were bound with chains to a slave collar clamped around his scrawny neck, forcing him into the shape that Columba had mistakenly assumed was one of self-defense. The iron bit into his collarbone, scraping the skin raw. Little rivulets of blood trickled down his thin torso. His wrists and ankles also bled. Columba would not be able to free him without the help of a blacksmith or some tools.

"Son," he said. "Please. I will not hurt you. Take comfort, if you can. Your long captivity will soon be at an end."

He reached out to smooth back the boy's filthy clumps of hair, but the boy flinched.

Columba withdrew his hand. "I am Colum Cille of … Daire," he said. "And lately of Iona, in Dal Riata in Caledonia. Perhaps you know of me? It is you I have come home to seek. I will help you. Will you let me help you?"

The boy did nothing. He did not grunt. He did not move. He only stared at Columba out of the corners of his wide, wary eyes, as still as a hare in the fox's sight.

"Your sister sent me," Columba remembered to say at last. "Your sister, Covna."

The boy's head whipped around. He gasped, then began to pant, air bellowing in and out of his lungs.

He let out a wail, inchoate, feral. It was a sound to break the heart.

As the knotted length of rope was slipped over the wattle walls into the pen behind them, Columba took it as assent.

Suddenly there was a horn blast. And another. And another. Then the massive crass booming of swords thumped on shields to announce the appearance of another retinue onto the field of battle.

An enormous warband was cresting the hill to the west, casting the plain into shadow. Their banner cracked in the wind. Aedan startled, but even from the back of the desperate knot of men fighting, he had seen it correctly: the banner bore the sigil of a bloody hand, hacked off at the wrist, at this distance little more than a messy red splotch on a crisp white field.

It was a huge force of men. Aedan didn't know them, but the others did, because they stopped and they gaped.

A lone rider dressed in sumptuous purple galloped down the hill.

They had been hoisted up and over, the boy first, his ungainly liberation softened by the multitude of arms waiting on the other side.

The boy fought his way free of them all. He snarled like an animal as he sought Columba's side. At that moment, Columba was the least terrifying thing.

The crowd had grown protective, quiet. "This way," said one. "This way is away."

"Thank you, my friends, but no," Columba said. "Not that way."

The boy's chains rattled with sharp fear.

Columba risked his hand again. This time, Fiachna let it rest upon his shoulder—lightly though; as insubstantial as the flutter of a dove's wing.

"Please," Columba said to the boy. "Will you trust me? I will let no harm come to you. Will you let me bear you upon my back?"

His eyes never leaving Columba's, the boy's chin dipped.

Columba knelt down. The boy threw the length of his wrist-chain around Columba's neck and scrambled on.

"Take us to the high-king," Columba said.

Baetan called in his men. They scurried to him. Aedan could see the animated discussion, the heated disagreement; and then Baetan's forces withdrew en masse towards the gap in the hills to the south.

Aedan nudged his pony across the plain to meet the rider.

The messenger met him halfway. "You!" said the man, haughty and gorgeous in his formal purple robes. "Gather your wounded. Bury your dead. You are to come with us."

"On whose authority?"

"Don't be an idiot."

Aedan wasn't. He just wanted it confirmed. There was only one man in Hibernia who could make Baetan turn tail and run.

The high-king.

"Good," said Aedan. "He got my message then."

# · 22 ·
# THE CONVENTION OF DRUIM CEATT

The harbor at Druim Ceatt was so important a border outpost that two hillforts flanked it. The crowd had borne Columba and Fiachna right up the slope to the gate of the highest one. Agitated guards tried to stop them, but the growing crowd pushed through, bursting through the gate and sweeping inside. There was a grim intent about the whole procession, until the crowd saw the great lords gathered there, huddled in the high-king's grand tent around the raging fire.

The crowd let loose, venting their anger with jeers and demands: "Here is Colum! Here is our Colum Cille who has healed us! Why is he in chains?"

The lords jumped to their feet. Weapons were drawn and Columba did not know what would happen, when he saw a glorious young man striding towards them, shouting. It had been years since Columba had last seen him as a child, but the high brow, the long nose, the height and coloring and aristocratic bearing were undoubtedly his own family's: this was Aed mac Ainmerech, the son of Columba's beloved and treacherous cousin Ainmire, now high-king in his place.

Columba would have rushed to embrace his long-lost kinsman had Aed's manner not been entirely forbidding.

Instead, a boy broke free of the lords and ran to Columba. He pulled up short to stand in awe. Columba could not imagine the image he was setting: covered in cow shit, cloakless, battered, and bruised, a manacled wild boy clinging to his back; and yet the young princeling was as reverent as could be. That brow, that nose: here was another kinsman, but one Columba did not know.

The high-king bellowed. He grabbed hold of the boy—this boy who must be his son—and threw him down. "Domnall!" he cried. "Remember your place!"

"Bless you, son," said Columba to the princeling on the ground as he knelt down to let Fiachna off his back. "Thank you for welcoming me."

"Now," Columba said to the lords as he rose. "Where is he?"

"What? Who?" shouted Aed mac Ainmerech. "Where is who?"

"The lord you all here think to cower into submission. The one causing you all this trouble. Truth be told, it has the stench of the familiar about it. Ah, there he is!"

And from the lords, Aedan stepped to the fore, head cocked in amusement and smiling grimly in greeting.


Some order had been restored, but not much. The people had been herded back outside, but they continued to clamor in the courtyard. They were joined there by the band of bards, furious that their vaunted prize had managed to find his way inside the high-king's esteemed assembly when, thus far, and in opposition to all their eloquent complaints, they had not.

The crowd was restless, volatile; growing in number as word spread that Colum Cille, the infamous, beloved local holy man and exile, had come home at last.

The boy Fiachna was being held upright by guards. Columba

discerned a subtle straightening of the boy's spine; some defiance in the lift of his chin.

This emboldened Columba. "Listen," he said. "This boy, here. Your hostage, Fiachna Lurgan. Release him from these awful chains and we will talk."

Aed mac Ainmerech scoffed. "You are everything father said you were, and more. But I will not be told by you."

"You know that this boy was freed from his captivity by a god, do you not?" Columba said.

Aed mac Ainmerech spluttered. "So he claimed. And yet it was in the care of some slavers who had fished him out of the ocean to be traded like so much chattel that I found him. How so, if what you say is true?"

Columba wanted to say: so he could end up here, now, with us, just so; but he doubted the young high-king would appreciate the subtlety of it all. How divine it was to get them all here, around this fire, at the same time—and before more damage could be done. As if orchestrated by the high hands of the gods, all of them, who together sought peace for this region, so long rent by war.

"Will you not release the boy?"

"Are you joking?" Aed mac Ainmerech said. "If I do, he,"—the high-king was glaring at Aedan—"gets Ulaid. I am not stupid."

With a nod, Columba acknowledged the backhanded compliment to his friend. "Ulaid was never yours," Columba said to the high-king. "And he will take it anyway, eventually, as is his right. At least this way, it will be peacefully."

"Now you threaten me?"

"It is not threat to speak the truth. Some might even call it prophecy."

The lords gasped. Columba stifled a snort. It proved useful, sometimes, to play the saint.

"All right," Columba said. "I can see that you need a little help here." His kinsman's lack of civility was beginning to rile him. Didn't he know who Columba was? He had known it, when he was a boy. He had seen Columba at his father's side: his right-hand man, his chief counsel. None higher or more beloved.

Columba needed to proceed quickly, before he lost the brief upper hand afforded him by the adulation of the crowd. "I can see that the bonds of kinship and affection that bound your father, who was my cousin, to me, the one to the other our whole lives, have weakened to the point of incivility. As has the natural deference enjoyed between princes of the blood. So … let me be the one here to do what is right and honorable."

Columba surged forward, to add effect to his gambit. This drew everyone's eye. He also knew that the guards at the gate were whispering all that they are witnessing to the crowd outside. The bards were no doubt also taking note—the bards, whom Columba also needed on his side.

It was theatre, made grand by what was at stake.

"I will forfeit my life for the boy's," Columba declared.

Now Aed mac Ainmerech really laughed. He threw back his head and guffawed. "Ha! Hollow words! Your life was forfeit anyway! The minute you came back here!"

"Indeed?" Columba cocked his head; made a point of listening to the crowd. The people hereabouts were his—not the high-king's, not the lords', not Aedan's, not the bards'—and he needed everyone here to know it.

Aed mac Ainmerech heard the commotion, paused; considered. "Why would you do that?" he said. "Why give your life in forfeit for this boy's?"

Columba yearned to say, "Because it is the right thing to do". Or, "Because you won't". Of all of the truths he might give at that point, these were the most convenient.

But he had come too far to continue the falsehood. He owed the truth, especially to Fiachna.

They had all been led here, at a cost greater to some than to others.

At greatest cost to those he cared least to hurt.

"Because my life is forfeit for the boy's," he said.

All their dumbfounded faces stared back.

"His captivity? His sister's enslavement? They were my doing."

Without the slightest effort, the horrible memory spewed forth, released at last. They, the Ui Neill, Columba and his cousin Ainmire, had been waiting on the sidelines for years, hoping for their chance. When word of the imminent Battle of the Seven Kings had reached his cousin's court at Grianan, the Palace of the Sun, Ainmire had called up what men he could and had ridden hard to the east, for Ulaid.

There might be spoils. There might be a throne. A province for the taking! And not just any province, but Ulaid, the ancient heart of Hibernia. So, they had thundered to the field of battle, only to pull up short at the unholy and unexpected sight of seven kings and their retinues strewn on the filthy field; a feast for crows.

And they were not the only wolves to have come ravening.

The man who was high-king at the time, Dermot mac Cerball, had also come. For the same reason, and with the same aspiration—to take over the Dal nAraide and, with it, control of Ulaid. And there were his forces—there, on the ridge to the south, with the would-be boy-king, Black Hugh, perched on a little pony up at the front.

Ainmire had surveyed the landscape, the size of the high-king's warband. "We cannot win this," he had conceded.

Columba had had to agree. "No. Not today."

"A shame. Sound the horns for retreat," Ainmire had called. "We shall have to take the battle to him another day. Let us muster all our forces, and contrive to lure Dermot back onto the field—perhaps at Cul Dreimne. There, with all our men, we cannot hope but to prevail."

"Yes. That is wise counsel."

Counsel that would, God willing, put his cousin on the high-king's throne at last.

Columba had spurred his horse.

"Where are you going?" Ainmire had asked.

"To get the children."

Covna and her brother Fiachna Lurgan. They had left them on the hill that morning, alone.

"Leave them."

"Leave them? We promised to return."

"No longer."

"No longer? It is the least we can do. We can do it. We have the men to go get them."

"But not to win against Dermot."

"No! Not to win. But we can retrieve the children."

His cousin had had that look on his face that Columba would later learn to hate.

"I said, leave them," Ainmire said. "If we stay, even a moment longer, we risk losses. Men we cannot afford to lose, if we hope to take the next engagement."

"Cousin … "

"The children go with the throne."

How to respond? How to sway his increasingly power-hungry cousin? "They are not jewels, cousin," Columba had said. "They are not spoils."

"You are not naïve," Ainmire had replied. "Do not act so. The children are the throne."

"But there are none left alive to protect them! All seven kings, dead!"

"Cease this, cousin! You cannot save all the world! Will you sacrifice that man? Or that man? Your own kin, for the lives of … foreign-born children … who we are not even certain will be at risk? Dermot will not hurt them. The little prince Black Hugh will not hurt them, his own cousins. As you say, they are but children. And who would hurt a child?"

Indeed, who would?

All of them, as it had turned out.

When they had ridden away from the children earlier that

270

morning, headed towards the field of battle, full of schemes and grand plans for themselves, the children had followed them out of the tent. Columba would never forget it: Covna's blond hair blowing sideways, her forlorn figure fierce with a protective courage called up for the sake of her brother. Fiachna's little face, holding back a terror he would soon have cause to believe in.

How she had taken her brother's hand.

Here now, having heard the tale of his father's perfidy, of Columba's long shame, Aed mac Ainmerech simply scoffed. "Aye. There was a choice to be made. I cannot see but that Father made the right one."

Columba nodded. "So did your father believe. He never questioned it later. But it has never sat right with me."

"Hmm. And so you have run back here to put it right ... twelve years later?"

"Yes. That is also to my shame. Nevertheless, as you say, and as all here now know: my life is forfeit. Doubly so. For returning to this, my beloved homeland, when it was forbidden me. And also for this child's honor. So leave me in my chains. But release him from his."

It was later said that the boy was released from his chains simply because Columba had asked that it be done. That Columba was held in such esteem that no one would go against him. But Columba knew better. There were too many witnesses to the event, later to be called a miracle, who would repeat the tale, both the common people and the bards (whose tongues could not always be bought). The high-king was a man who had to value his reputation for justice, whether or not that reputation was truly earned. And so Fiachna Lurgan was grudgingly released.

Which was fine with Columba.

He did not mind being thought capable of miracle as long as his will was also done.

"Now, this is what I propose … " Columba said.

"You propose?" Aed mac Ainmerech exclaimed. "What breathtaking hubris! You sit there, in chains! Chains traded for a boy! Who are you, to propose?"

"Nothing binds my tongue. Or my mind. Nothing should be binding yours. It is clear what must be done here. About him." A nod at Aedan.

"Is it? I come here to find this man on the field of battle with Baetan."

"He is ruiri of Dal Riata," Columba said of Aedan. "It is his right to bear arms against his enemies."

"His 'overlord', you mean. Baetan is his overlord, not his enemy," Aed mac Ainmerech said as he bestowed Aedan with a withering look. "Ruiri of Dal Riata, you say? Perhaps. But only in Caledonia. Not here, not here in Dal Riata in Hibernia."

"Is that so?" Columba hazarded a guess: "Are those not the lords of Hibernian Dal Riata that I see there, standing with him? A sight to see! And so many! In all my youth, I never saw it so—these lords united".

Aed mac Ainmerech drew his sword and aimed it at Aedan. "A situation easily remedied! If we cut off the head. Then we should see them scatter again, and retreat to their corners, and tear at each other's throats much as they have ever done."

Aedan did not so much as flinch at the high-king's provocation. "If you were to try to do so," Aedan said flatly, "it was on the battlefield that you should have tried it. Instead, you have brought me here before your hearth. Here, now, let us find a way to be at peace with one another. Let us all profit from this moment of unity. Let Columba speak."

"Peace!" the high-king spat. "That's novel, when suggested by a pirate."

"It is a question of the province of Ulaid, yes?" Columba said. "You want it, but at the moment it belongs to him." A nod of acknowledgement at Aedan.

Aed mac Ainmerech laughed again, which was good. Columba

was being deliberately provoking. "Your reputation as a silver-tongued snake is rightly earned, cousin," the high-king said. "Ulaid does not belong to that man, it belongs to Baetan."

Good! Columba thought. He had riled the high-king enough to concede a point nearer the mark. Now, to drive it home.

"Hmm. If so, that is a problem. But luckily I know what to do. This is what I propose," Columba said. "The question is: what is Hibernian Dal Riata to Caledonian Dal Riata? The one half of the kingdom to the other, after all these years sundered in two?"

He turned his bound hands to the high-king. "Then, what are both Dal Riatas to you?" he asked him.

Aed mac Ainmerech's eyes narrowed, but before he could respond, Columba asked the same question of Aedan. "And to you?"

He let neither man speak. "What are you to each other?" he asked.

This caused them to contemplate their counterpart across the fire; to really look upon the face of the other. He hoped each saw what was plain to him, the immense possibilities: two powerful kings, each a strong stone citadel on the opposing shore of the sea.

And Columba the boat between them.

Or, by the way the two men were glaring at each another: the two killing edges of a sword.

In that case, he would have to be the sword's lethal point, his job today to pierce the target, to create a hole into which the blade could be slid in.

"Let us decide," Columba said to the two men. "You are men of might. Nearly peerless. Let us find agreement. An alliance. In fact, I challenge you to do it. War is easy. This is hard. So, aside from 'everything … I want everything', which is how a child would speak, what is it you desire? What must you have?"

Columba spoke his words to the high-king first, so as to prevent claims later that he had given insult to the man's higher status, which would invalidate what might be achieved here. But in truth, it was a rhetorical question, and Columba answered it himself. "You, cousin, are first of all ruiri of the Ui Neill," he said, "free and clear, with no opposition. That is not easily done. You are a strong king, and it has brought you the high-kingship of Hibernia too. But there is the question of the province of Ulaid. Always the question of Ulaid—which everyone wants, and no one has freely or clearly. You wish to be the suzerain of Ulaid too, at last, and without opposition. With the obedience of all. And all that goes with it. The tribute. The taxes. The fleet. The men. Their swords in battle."

The high-king's eyes gleamed. This was, of course, the heart of it. Why people wanted power, and why he wanted Ulaid in particular—that untapped, glorious resource, there at the island's edge.

Columba turned to Aedan, speaking for him too: "And, as ruiri of the people of this Dal Riata, here in Hibernia, you want these things too. Plus something greater, without which the other things cannot be had or enjoyed by all. Peace in Ulaid".

The high-king broke in with a brittle laugh. "Peace in Ulaid? The people of Dal Riata have been free from law and from military service for years! Years! Peace? How so? They are nothing but pirates!"

Such contempt. Such disdain. Had the young man's father been this way? Felt these feelings? Had Columba known his beloved cousin at all?

"Cousin, please!" Columba said. "Though there seems to be cause for war here, there is not. There need be no disagreement, no more cause for rancor. No more retribution based on the things of the past. We here have all the pieces we need."

Columba's encompassing hand brought in all of Aed mac Ainmerech's lords, all of Aedan's, his own self, the boy. "It is all assembled. Peace is at hand. We need but agree on where to place each piece."

He had them. He had their attention. And their hope. The tip of the blade had pricked open a hole.

"All that we here desire can come to pass," Columba said, "with you the lord here, and you the lord there, and no one to gainsay either of you, in fact the one to help the other as a second front, a friend, to help us all … "

He drove it home.

"If we rid ourselves of Baetan."

The high-king rocked back on his heels to hear it so openly proposed. He called his men around. Conferred with them. It was a heated moment in which Columba and Aedan could only share a quick questioning glance.

The high-king swept back. "Once Baetan goes," he said, "your man here may have Hibernian Dal Riata."

"He already has Hibernian Dal Riata," Columba said. "The question is the greater one: what of the province of Ulaid as a whole?"

Aedan cut in. "How does Baetan go?"

The high-king glared at Aedan out of the corner of his eye.

"By my hand," Aedan answered for him. "You want me to take him out. That is rich. Had you not intervened today, it would already be done."

"It didn't look that way to me," Aed mac Ainmerech sniped, but in Columba's direction, not yet having fully acknowledged Aedan as a peer with whom he would directly speak.

"You don't know him yet," Columba replied evenly. "I'd believe him there, if I were you."

Aed mac Ainmerech inclined his head. Said, "Does he want Hibernian Dal Riata, or not?"

"He has Hibernian Dal Riata," Columba said.

"With all my heart, I want Dal Riata," Aedan broke in. "All of it. This half, and the other. And I will also gladly rid Ulaid of that Pale Shouter. To do it, I require Dal Riata's men, its fleet, its taxes, and its tribute."

There was a gasp from the lords. Aed mac Ainmerech's cheek twitched. Columba could not help but smirk. The high-king, who had thought to ensnare Aedan, had also been trapped himself.

There was a flare of consternation in the high-king's camp,

more robust conferring. Finally, Aed mac Ainmerech said, "For this hosting against Baetan, he may have these things. But after it is done, they return to me."

But Aedan wouldn't be swayed. "After this hosting," he said, "their fleet, their taxes, and their tribute will stay with me, for I will have their men and be their lord in truth—in action as well as in oath."

"No."

"Then, no."

The high-king, clearly unused to impertinence of any kind, turned on Aedan with a righteous roar. "Who are you to demand such terms?"

Good, thought Columba even as he winced. At least he is speaking to Aedan now.

Aedan moved in close to the high-king in a manner which managed to convey both acute nonchalance and unquestionable power. When the high-king did not step back, Columba put himself between them, hoping to create a bridge between his friend and his kinsman.

"He is *ruiri* of Dal Riata, as I have said, cousin," Columba said, calling up the tone of voice he used when coaxing the fighting dogs out of the bull's pen when the scent of the badger had lured them in unawares. "The *ruiri* of both Dal Riatas. A combined Dal Riata. A thing not accomplished in over seventy years! That's no mean achievement. And, lest you forget, he treats with all the British kings. All of them. And they with him. But most ... let us say, most importantly, he is also the son-in-law of the man who is king of the Caledonii now, and the father of the man who will be king next. Or did you not know this?"

Columba paused, careful to hide how much he was coming to enjoy the high-king's growing discomfort.

Aedan, for his part, just stood there, towering. For what more could be said? The high-king was in the presence of an extraordinary person, one who had the power to change the tide, and it was high-time he knew it.

Just one more nudge. "Do you really want that kind of weapon pointed in your direction?" Columba asked.

"I am the high-king of Hibernia!"

"Yes! Yes you are! And that is the point. It is in your power to ask that that weapon be directed at somebody else. Or—better yet—to join with him to point both your weapons at an enemy you have trapped between you."

The high-king was panting heavily, but reason was taking hold. The anger was draining from his face. He broke eye contact with Aedan, looked at Columba, considering. Finally, he said to Aedan directly, "After this hosting, the men of this Dal Riata return to me".

"After this hosting," Aedan replied, "the men of this Dal Riata serve whomever has earned their fealty. That may be you. It may not. It may be me."

"How dare you … "

Aedan shrugged. "We are kings, you and I. But all men are free to choose. It is up to us to earn their fealty. "

Columba leapt in quickly. "So it is agreed," he said. "The men of Dal Riata return to Hibernia—and serve whom they will. Yes?"

After a moment, the high-king nodded. "But if it is not done, if Baetan is not dealt with, then nothing. All back to me."

"All back to Hibernia," Columba said.

"I agree to this," Aedan said. "When it is done, the service of the men of this Dal Riata returns to Hibernia. But their fleet, their taxes, and their tribute go with the other Dal Riata, with the men of Caledonia."

The high-king's cold stillness was his assent.

Aedan smiled. "They will remain with me. For I will be their lord in truth."

"If you do it."

"Watch me."

Aedan gathered the Lords of the Nine Glens around him. "You have heard the terms. What say you, my lords? My lady?"

277

"We have no love for that Ui Neill dog there."

Aedan held his tongue. He let them find their minds and speak them.

"But we love the Pale Shouter less."

Nine pairs of eyes were firm. Fiery.

"When this is done, will you be content to call me ruiri?" he asked, then chuckled. "If I live, that is."

There was more thought, but less than before.

"Aye."

"Aye."

"It is you we love the less least."


"And the boy?" Aedan asked, back at the hearth with the high-king.

"It is not ours to decide!"

Columba had shouted. He needed the guards to hear it, and for them to pass news of the proceedings through the door to the crowd, and to the bards. "The young man is free now! He is free to choose!"

Fiachna Lurgan was staring at them all, his eyes flicking back and forth between the mighty men. Finally, a voice emerged from the pallid little face, still too timid, but growing stronger. "Where is my sister? Where is Covna?" he asked.

"Your sister is with me," Aedan said. "Safe. Back in my Dal Riata."

"Then it is with you that I shall go."


"Now," Aedan said to everyone, "what of him? What of Columba? Does he live? Or does he die?"

# · 23 ·

# THE LAW OF THE INNOCENTS

Just then, a horn sounded stridently from outside. The guards frantically shouted. "Ships! Ships at the harbor! Warships coming in!"

They all rushed out to see, Aedan grabbing young Fiachna in one hand and Columba in the other, herding them both protectively before him.

"Where's Eogan?" Aedan demanded in Columba's ear.

"I don't know!" Columba said. "I don't know! I had hoped to find him here."

"Is he dead?"

"I don't know. I don't know. I fear … "

Aedan growled. "You fear at your own peril. If something has happened to him … I swear to the gods I will … He was yours to protect."

There were three ships barreling into port in full battle-mode: men out, drawn weapons murderous, ready to storm the harbor. One was Aedan's own warship, the one that had escaped out to sea after the disastrous meeting of the kings at Ros-na-Righ. Seeing it, Aedan's heart swelled with a savage pride and gratitude: his men had come back for him.

It swelled further when he saw the two other vessels, for they were from Caledonia, one a true Pictish vessel, the other the ship Aedan had sent north to the Fortress of the Bulls laden with the slaves being returned home. His brother-in-law, Drust, captained one ship; Drust's second-in-command, Uurguost, captained the other. Upon escaping the ambush at Ros-na-Righ, his men must have sailed for all they were worth to catch up with the Pictish party, to beg for help in rescuing Aedan and his men.

It was being given, fabulously and fully. The Picts and Scots threw themselves from the ships but, upon seeing Aedan and his men alive, fanned out menacingly on the docks to await his orders.

Aedan held up a hand.

The crowd, which had poured down the hillside in a panic, pulled up short in fear of the Picts.

Aedan hauled up on the slope. "My friends!" he called out. "My friends! What of him? What of this priest?"

The crowd turned.

Aedan shoved Columba unceremoniously to his knees. He grabbed Columba by his hair none too gently and yanked back, exposing his throat. He drew his dagger and held it up.

"What of this priest?" Aedan called again.

The high-king spun on his heel, confused by this turn of events. "What? What are you doing? What about them?" The Picts and the Scots.

With his dagger, Aedan waved him back. "This man was spat out in exile from this country! And he fetched up on my shore! My shore! He is my priest, to do with what I will!"

Aedan pointed his dagger at the crowd. "I will honor the people's wishes!"

Aedan pulled hard on Columba's hair until the strong, pulsing column of Columba's throat was laid fully bare. He pressed in the tip of the dagger. It drew blood.

"What say you?" Aedan cried. "What of him? His life is forfeit! Shall I take it? What say the people?"

"Colum Cille! Colum Cille! Colum Cille!"

The cry went round the crowd like a rising wave.

"He healed me!" someone cried.

"I too was healed!" testified another.

"Spare him! Spare him! Spare him!"

Their desire for his life was thunderous.

"You forgive him his debt?" Aedan cried. "You release him from his bonds? You forgive him his exile?"

"Yes! Yes! Yes! Spare him! Spare him! Spare him!"

Aedan looked pointedly at the high-king who was, in turn, taking in the impassioned crowd, the bards observing critically from a safe distance; the tense cohort of Picts and Scots on the dock ready to do battle for their own true king.

The high-king gave a quick dip of his chin.

The crowd erupted in joy. Aedan hauled Columba back to his feet and cut his bonds, whispering urgently in his ear, "Make for the ships! I will meet you there!" before shoving him into the arms of the heaving crowd where he was deliriously swallowed up.

"You're welcome," Drust said as Aedan slapped him on the back in gratitude.

"Gartnait? Domelch?"

"Safely home. Your men found us at The Fortress of the Bulls. We sped here in all haste to save you—as usual. What do you need?"

"Many things, I'm afraid. But first, let us make for Dun Sobairche before the high-king changes his mind. You're scaring the life out of him."

The swell of Loch Febal took up their ships on the outgoing tide, the twin hillforts at the harbor of the convention of the kings receding behind them.

"That was risky," Columba said to Aedan. "Too risky."

"Was it? In the tent, he might have gone through with it, killed you and bundled your body out the back door. But not where everyone could see. He could not risk their ire. Killing their beloved Colum Cille? He would never live it down."

Columba rubbed the nick on his neck. "For a minute there, I thought you might actually go through with it."

"I might yet, if we do not find Eogan."

"Aedan … "

"No! Do not say it. I do not want to hear it. I will not—I cannot—believe that he is dead until I see it for myself."


"About Fiachna and Covna," Aedan said. "You should have told me."

"I was too ashamed."

"It was no more than others have done. Less, really."

"Still—it was craven and wrong. And I cannot forgive myself for it."

Aedan laid a hand on Columba's shoulder. "Who were you to save them? There is no law to protect the innocents. Not in war."

Aedan sighed. "Not even in peace."

Aedan's kind words sparked in Columba a sudden thought, some new purpose of mind that would, in time, come to give him respite from his long shame.

"There should be," Columba said.

"There should be what?"

"There should be such a law, one to protect the innocents. A law that everyone must be made to obey. Kings. Queens. Lords. Ladies. Everyday people. You. Me. Everyone."

Columba could see it all unfolding. "And I will make it. I will make such a law. Because I tell you this: if there is evil is this world, it is in the knowing destruction of the innocent. The kind that hurts the young? That targets a young one? A vulnerable one? And hurts them? And rejoices in it? That kind is pure, pure evil. And I have had enough of it."

And it was many years later, at the Synod of Birr in the year of Our Lord 697, that The Law of Innocents, which protected women and non-combatants in war, was come to pass, promulgated by Adomnan, who was ninth abbot of Iona after Columba, Columba's own distant heir and kinsman.

It was the first law of its kind in the western world.

"We got off lucky there," Aedan said to Columba as the ships sailed swiftly eastwards to Dun Sobairche.

"Did we? I'm not so sure."

In Columba's mind was a growing certainty: that Aedan's rise to power in Hibernian Dal Riata, and the freeing of the boy, and the forgiveness of his own debt, had indeed required a sacrifice.

But that his own life had not been it.

In a wind-lashed hut on a hill on a plain, Baetan brooded.

"They think to keep me out? I will keep them out of comfort for the rest of their days."

Baetan spared a cold glance at the figures trussed in the corner, moaning.

He went closer. Bent down. Got a good look.

Made his choice.

"Bring that one to me."

*To be continued …*

# · CHRONOLOGICAL GUIDE ·

| 367-68 | *Conspiratio Barbarica*: Picts, Attacotti, Scots, Saxons and Franks overwhelm Roman outposts in Britain and Gaul |
|---|---|
| 381 | Magnus Maximus drives back the Picts and the Scots |
| 397 | General Stilicho repulses Picts, Scots and Saxons |
| 406 | A confederate force of barbarians breaches the Rhine and lays waste to Gaul and Spain, breaking contact between Rome and Britain |
| 407 | Constantine III withdraws remaining Roman legion from Britain |
| 408 | Devastating attacks by Picts, Scots and Saxons |
| 409 | Britons expel remaining Roman officials and fight for themselves |
| 410 | Rome abandons Britain |
| c. 432-61 | *Floruit* of St Patrick |
| 450s | Pictish invasions; civil war and famine in Britain |
| c. 500 | Traditional settlement of Dál Riáta |

Battle of Mount Badon

c. 521-97          *Floruit* of St Columba

c. 534-608        *Floruit* of Áedán mac nGabráin

c. 537            Battle of Camlann in which Artur and Medraut fell

538-58            Gabran mac Domangairt rules Dál Riáta

c. 540-70         *Floruit* of the British monk and writer Gildas

c. 556            Bridei, son of Maelchon, rules the Northern Picts

560-65            Diarmait mac Cerbaill rules the Southern Uí Néill from Tara

561               Battle of Cúl Dreimne

562               Council of Teilte

563               St Columba's exile to Dál Riáta

574               Battle of Arfdyredd

574               Battle of Telocho: death of Conall mac Comgall

574               Áedán mac nGabráin becomes king of the Scots of Dál Riáta

Paula de Fougerolles

# · GLOSSARY AND PRONUNCIATION GUIDE

Aed mac Ainmire: (**Aid** mac **An**-ver-a)

Aedan mac Gabran of the Cenel Gabran: (**Aid**-an mac **Gav**-rine of the **Ken**-el **Gav**-rine)

Aes Dana: (**Ace Dah**-na) A special learned caste of jurists, physicians, wrights, smiths, skilled craftsman, and later monks and clerics, that had privileges separate from kings, lords, commoners, and slaves; literally "The People of the Craft".

Ainmire mac Setna: (**An**-ver-a mac **Set**-na)

Anamchara: (**Ah**-nem **Kah**-ruh) Spiritual director; confessor. Soul Friend?

Arawn: (**Ar**-oon) Lord of the Underworld.

Ard-ri: (**Ard**-ree) The High-King; the king who ruled over the five provinces of Ireland. The highest grade of Irish kingship.

Artmuircol: (Art-**moor**-cul)

Baire: (Bah-re) A game played with sticks and a ball akin to modern Scottish shinty or Irish hurling.

Baithene: (**Bay**-then-eh)

Ballaun stone: (Bull-**lawn**) A ritual stone with cup-shapes depressions in its surface, often found at water shrines.

Belenos: (**Bel**-en-os) The Celtic sun-god, associated with the festival of May Day.

Beltane: (**Bel**-tan-a) The festival associated with the god Belenos, held 1-3 May to celebrate the arrival of summer and the return of livestock to open pastures.

Boaire: (**Bo**-ar-e) A grade of free man, the prosperous farmer, or strong farmer.

Brenhines: (**Bren**-hin-es) Queen

Brenin: (**Bren**-in) King

Bridei son of Maelchon: (**Brith**-ee son of **Mail**-kon)

Broichan: (**Broy**-ken)

Budic: (**Bu**-dic)

Cailleach Bheur: (**Kal**-ex **Ver**) A figure in Irish legend and poetry, a pre-Christian tutelary goddess of the land who celebrated sacred marriage with those who would become king.

Caim: A prayer for protection.

Caledonii: (Kal-eh-**dohne**-ee)

Cenel, Cenela: (**Ken**-el, **Ken**-el-a) Kin-group; extended family; clan. A term used particularly for the kin groups of Scottish Dal Riata.

Cenel Gabran: (**Ken**-el **Gav**-rine)

Cenel Loarn: (**Ken**-el Lorne)

Cenel Oengussa: (**Ken**-el **En**-guss-ah)

Ceo: (**Kee**-oh) Mist, shadow.

Clientship: The Irish system (céilsine, **Kel**-shin-eh) under which a lord or nobleman supplied livestock and sometimes land (the fief or rath) to a farmer in return for goods and services, including military service and labor.

Cobthach: (**Kov**-thuck)

Coeling: The descendants of Coel Hen.

Coibche: (**Kov**-x-e) The "bride-price", the price a husband paid to purchase his wife from her father.

Columba (Colum Cille): Kolumba (**Kol**-um **Kill**-eh)

Comaltae: (Kov-**al**-tie) Foster-brother.

Combrogi: Fellow-countrymen. Used by the British for other Britons.

Comthinchor: (Kom-**tin**-xor) The property brought into a marriage by both husband and wife.

Conall mac Comgall of the Cenel Loarn: (**Kon**-all mac **Kov**-gall of the **Ken**-el Lorne)

Crech Ríg: (**Crek Ree**) The inaugural cattle raid undertaken by a newly acclaimed king.

Cul Dreimne: (**Kool Drev**-enee)

Curragh: (**Kur**-agh) A round-bottomed boat covered with animal hide stretched over a wicker or wooden frame.

Cruithni: (**Kruth**-neh) The Irish term for the Picts.

The Daghdha: (**Dach**-thuh) "The Good God", or "The Mighty One of Great Knowledge." The Daghdha was king and father of the Irish gods.

Dal: (**Dahl**) An archaic name element meaning "the share of".

Dal Fiatach: (Dahl **Fee**-ah-tak)

Dal Riata: (Dahl **Ree**-a-ta)

Derbfine, or Fine: (**Derv**-ine, Fine) Kin, family group, kinsman. The kin-group or "certain" family comprising one's conjugal family of parents and siblings but also all those males who had a great-grandfather in common, up to and including second cousins. The derbfine, or fine, was the basic unit for law-enforcement and land ownership in early Irish society. With marriage, women passed into their husband's derbfine.

Dermot mac Cerball: (**Der**-mot mac **Ker**-val)

Din Eidyn: (**Din Eye**-din)

Drust son of Bridei: (**Drust** son of **Brith**-ee)

Domelch: (**Doh**-melck)

Donn: (Don) "The Dark or Brown One." The Irish God of the Dead who presided over the Land of the Dead. He was the dark, somber, aspect of the afterlife. Both benign and terrible, he created storms and shipwrecks, but also protected cattle and crops.

Dun: (Doon) A fortified dwelling or stronghold.

Dun Ad: (**Doon**-Ath)

Dunchad: (**Dun**-chad)

Dun Mor: (**Doon Mor)**

Eilean Righ: (**Ei**-leen **Ree**)

Eireann: (**Air**-in-a) The tribal grouping, to which the Dal Riata belonged, which claimed to be the original tribe of Ireland.

Eithne: (**Eth**-nee)

Enech: (**En**-ech) A person's honor (literally, their "face").

Eogan mac Gabran of the Cenel Gabran: (**Ow**en mac **Gav**-rine of the **Ken**-el **Gav**-rine)

Failend: (**Foy**-len)

Fennid: (**Fenn**-id) The champion, or warrior, of a king.

Ferann claidib: (**Fer**-ann **Kla**-div) "Sword-land"

Fiachna Lurgan: (**Fee**-ach-na **Lur**-gan)

Fidchell: (**Fith**-chel) A board-game.

Filidh: (**Fee**-lee) A poet.

Fingal: (**Fin**-gall) The unlawful killing of a king.

Forindan: (**Fore**-in-din)

Gabran mac Domangart: (**Gav**-rin mac Doh-**man**-gart)

Geis (pl. Gessa): (**Gesh, Gesha**): A prohibition or taboo, or a positive injunction or obligation, the violation of which could lead to death.

Gododdin: (Guh-**da**-thin)

Gwyr y Gogledd: (**Gweer**-y-Gogleth) The Men of the North; a British term for themselves.

Himbas Forosnai: (**Im**-bas For-**os**-na) A form of divination practiced by the druids; the "Second Sight".

Hinba: (**Een**-ba)

Iona: (Eye-**oh**-na)

Kynfarch the Old of Rheged: (**Kin**-varch the Old of **Reh**-ged)

Luan: (**Loo**-an)

Lughnasadh: (**Loon**-a-sa) The Celtic festival celebrated 1-3 August in honor of the start of the harvest and associated with the god Lugh.

Manannan mac Lir: (Ma-**nan**-nan mac **Llyr**) Celtic god of the sea.

Manau: (**Man**-ow)

Meall: (**Mull**)

Medb: (**Maeve**) The legendary queen of Connaught in Ireland, a quasi-historical figure who led her armies against the Ulstermen in the saga Táin Bó Cuailnge. Of considerable sexual prowess, Medb was also known for her ruthlessness in battle.

<u>Miathi</u>: (Mee-**ath**-ee)

<u>The Monastic Hours</u>: A system of communal prayer with set services in each daily cycle:

*Matins*: said in the middle of the night
*Lauds*: said immediately after matins
*Prime*: said at dawn
*Terce*: said at the third hour of daylight
*Sect*: said at the sixth hour of daylight
*None*: said at the ninth hour of daylight
*Vespers*: recited before the community retired to bed

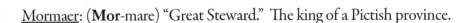

<u>Mormaer</u>: (**Mor**-mare) "Great Steward." The king of a Pictish province.

The <u>Morrighan</u>: (**Mor**-ee-thin) The Irish triple-goddess of war, comprised of the <u>Morrighan</u>, the "Phantom Queen"; <u>Badb</u> (**Bayv**), "Crow, Raven of Battle"; and <u>Nemhain</u> (**Nev**-in), "Frenzy", who spread panic amongst fighting men.

<u>Nemeton</u>: "Sacred place", often used of a sacred grove, a sanctuary for druidic ritual and assembly.

<u>Ocaire</u>: (**O**-gar-e) A grade of freeman, the less prosperous farmer, or small farmer.

<u>Oenach</u>: (**Oi**-nech) An annual assembly or fair.

<u>Ogham</u>: (**Oh**-gum) A twenty-character alphabet consisting of grooves or strokes cut at different angles to a vertical line, used especially in inscriptions, primarily those on stone.

<u>Rath</u>: A ring-fort; a circular fortified farmstead consisting of a protective earthen embankment and ditch within which sheltered one or more family homes.

Rechtaire: (**Rek**-ta-ra) A steward who rules in the absence of a king.

Regulus: The sub-ruler of a Pictish province.

Rheged: (**Reh**-ged)

Rigdomna: (Ree-**dov**-na) A prince of the royal line, eligible for the kingship.

Ri ruirech: (**Ree rur**-ech) Very-King; king of over-kings; the third rank of kings. A ri ruirech was king of a province.

Ri (pl. rig): (**Ree**) Lord; leader; the lowest grade of king. A ri ruled over only his own tuath or cenel. The Irish system of kingship can be schematized as follows, with each grade of king drawing on the tribute of those below it:


Ard-ri

ri ruirech    ri ruirech    ri ruirech    ri ruirech

ruiri ruiri ruiri ruiri  ruiri ruiri ruiri  ruiri  ruiri ruiri ruiri ruiri

ri ri ri ri ri ri ri ri ri   ri ri ri ri ri ri ri ri ri   ri ri ri ri ri ri ri ri ri
ri ri ri ri ri ri ri ri ri

Rigain: (**Ree**-gan) Lady; queen.

Ros-na-Righ: (**Ross**-na-**Ree**)

Ruiri (pl. ruirig): (**Rur**-ree) Over-King; great king; the second rank of king. A ruiri ruled over his own tuath or cenel, and at least two others as well.

Samhain: (**Sow**-an) The greatest of the four major Celtic festivals, held from 29 October to 2 November, roughly equivalent to Halloween. It marked the return of livestock from the summer pastures. The start of the Celtic year, it was the Day of the Dead, the juncture between summer and winter, when it was believed that the barrier between worlds was temporarily broken down and that the dead could walk amongst the living and the living amongst the dead.

Tanaise: (**Ta-n**aise) Heir-apparent to the kingship.

Tairbert Boitter: (**Tar**-bert **Bot**-ter)

Teilte: (**Tail**-te)

Tir Iath: (**Tye**-ree)

Tir na nOg: (**Teer**-na-nOhg) The Land of the Young. A paradisian world beyond the motal realms where there is no sickness, old age, or death.

Toiseach: (**Tee**-shuck) A leader or chieftan. A grade lower than king.

Tuath (plural Tuatha): (**Tooth**; **Tootha**) "A people"; a petty kingdom; territory; tribe. The most basic unit of governance in early Irish society, the tuath was in essence an extended family group sufficiently large enough to be ruled by a king. Standing amongst kings was assessed by the number of tuatha subordinate to one and the level of subordination. It has been estimated that at any given time between the fifth and the twelfth century there were between 80 and 150 kings in Ireland.

Ui Neill: (**Ee**-nail) The descendants of Niall Noigiallach ("Niall of the Nine Hostages").

Ulaid: (**Oo**-lah)

Urien: (**Yuh**-ri-an)

Uurguost: (**Ur**-gust)

# · HISTORICAL NOTES ·

My purpose with these notes is to let the reader know the historical bases for the narrative choices I have made in this book, as well as the sites in Scotland and Ireland I've used as locations, all of which can (and should!) be visited. The notes have been organized according to chapter, as needed. Unlike a novel of fictionalized history set, say, in the nineteenth century, very little remains for us by way of primary sources for the earliest history of what would become Scotland and Ireland. What we do have is very rarely straightforward, if not altogether incomprehensible. We can glean a general account of events in the sixth century from a handful of chronicles which began to be written in monastic settings at this time, the Annals of Ulster, the Annals of Tigernach, and the like. These annals have as their core stratum an earlier chronological accounting, now lost, known as the Chronicle of Iona, which was written on Iona about events that concerned that monastery, possibly by or at the behest of Columba—the first of its kind in the mediaeval West. (That lost chronicle is the inspiration for the title of this series.) The other primary documentary sources for this period include hagiography, law tracts, place and personal names, linguistics, and a handful of proto-histories about the sixth century, most of which were composed at a date later than and from a perspective outwith the area. I have spent time at all the historical sites used in this series so as to recreate, as accurately as possible with the aid of archaeology and available scholarship, what these places might have looked and felt like when Columba and Áedán lived. With all of these sources, I have as a rule put greater weight on those with provenance and date closest to sixth-century Scotland and Ireland. For a fuller account of the historical sources used in this series as a whole, please also see the appendices of books I and II, Exile and Prophet.

The main source for the historical personage of Columba, or Colum Cille as he was known in Irish, a prince-abbot who lived about 521 to 597 and is now regarded as a saint as well as the greatest statesman of his age, is the Life of St Columba, written in the 690s by the equally impressive Adomnán (627/28-704), the ninth abbot of Iona and Columba's direct kinsman. Adomnán based his collection of stories on an earlier work written in the 630s or 40s by Cummléne Find, the seventh abbot of Iona (from 657 to 659), who may have known Columba when a boy, making the Life a first-rate source for the period. (Cummléne's book has not survived.) Since the Life is a hagiographical text, written to promote Columba's cult and prove his sanctity through miracles he is said to have performed, rather than a straightforward biography, the writing of which was unknown at the time, care must be taken when excavating the text for historical fact, as well as to interpret those facts in such a way as to render them both intelligible and palatable to a modern audience. And yet, wonderfully, quite a lot remains in the Life that can illuminate for us what it was like when and where Columba lived as well as what kind of a person he was. Unlike many a dry, or weird, saint's Life, Columba springs from the pages of his fully formed and recognizable, full of common human flaws and foibles but also ferociously alive. We feel as if we might know him. To this end, the extensive endnotes provided by the editor and translator Richard Sharpe in his masterful translation of the Life (Admonán of Iona, Life of St Columba, London, 1995) help to elucidate what can be known about Columba and his wider world and are a delight to read.

As for Áedán mac nGabráin (Aedan in the book), who was certainly the greatest warlord of his age (living about 538 to 603), I like to think of him as "like King Arthur, but true", and his life and remarkable achievements like George R. R. Martin's world in Game of Thrones—but, again, true. Áedán appears frequently in Columba's Life as an ally, co-conspirator, and friend. Together, they were architects of a new dawn, transforming their communities into what, under their direct descendants, would come to be known as Scotland's and Ireland's "Golden Age".

It has been such fun to bring their stories to life and I hope that that passion and joy, more than anything else, comes through in these pages.

I have made all the illustrations, maps, and charts in the book. The book's front cover is a close-up of Ulster, Northern Ireland, taken from my map "Hiberniae Britannicae Insulae, Nova Descriptio" (Abraham Ortelius, Theatrum Orbis Terrarum, of c. 1573, page 6D). For the drawing of the animal-head terminals which features on the map of "The Sea of the Hebrides", I used one of the glorious silver brooches from the St Ninian's Isle Hoard, a Pictish treasure-trove dating from about 750-825 that was unearthed off St Ninian's Isle, Shetland, in 1958. The map of "Ulaid" has a simple but potent spiral triskele such as those incised on the massive uprights of Newgrange, the passage tomb built in County Meath, Ireland, in about 3200 B.C.E. The illustration underlying Part One is of a hanging-bowl escutcheon from about 675 that began life in Ireland but ended up in Miklebostad, Norway as viking loot (and is now in the Historisk Museum, Bergen). The annal excerpt underlying Part Two is the entry announcing the arrival in 500 of Fergus Mor mac Erc to what would become Scottish Dál Riata. It is from the Annals of Tigernach, an annal written in Latin and Old and Middle Irish and compiled probably at Clonmacnoise, Ireland, in the fourteenth century (now fol. 7r of MS Rawlinson B. 488, The Bodleian Library, University of Oxford). The drawing of the two clerics, the angel, and the harpist which lays under Part Three is from the cumdach (book shrine or reliquary case) of the Stowe Missal, an illuminated Mass-book in Latin from 792-803 (now Royal Irish Academy, MS D ii 3: Cat. No. 1238). This particular clerical panel dates from 1025-1052 (National Museum of Ireland, no. 1883, 614a).


Preface: Shadows
The version of the Pater Noster, the Our Father (Matthew 6:9-13), which Columba recites is from the Vulgate version of the bible, a late-fourth-century Latin translation of the bible that in the sixteenth

century became the official bible of the Catholic Church. It is the bible that would have been known to Columba and others of his day.


## Chapter 1: Crech Rig

This chapter takes places in and around the majestic hillfort of Dunadd, the capitol (*caput regionis*) of the early kings of the Scots of Dál Riata (Dun Ad in the book; Kilmartin Glen, Argyll and Bute, Scotland). The hillfort nestles in a bend of the twisty river Add to rise majestically over the vast peat moss that surrounds it. Lording over its valley, Dunadd is easily the most important of the early-mediaeval stratum of pre- and historic monuments in Kilmartin Glen, which itself has the highest concentration of such sites in the whole of the U.K. The long, wide, breathtaking valley is littered with them, attesting to the glen's importance as a sacred landscape to the earliest inhabitants of these isles and making it an outstanding and evocative place to visit today.

Southeast of the hillfort of Dunadd there is another equally prominent though less imposing hillfort at the farmstead of Dunamuck, known as Dun Mor. This is where in the book Ama now lives. It is one of over thirty hilltop sites encircling Dunadd that were also fortified and occupied in the early-mediaeval period, with the citadel of Dunadd the irrefutable center and powerbase of the local social hierarchy and the region as a whole. Dun Mor is oval in shape and measures 33 by 36 feet, with walls on average 12 feet thick. From Dun Mor's summit you can see two to three miles in every direction, including to Dunadd. (My thanks to Willow and her mother for allowing me to explore their "fairy stones".)

The Early Irish Law Tracts, the codification of the laws and norms which helped regulate early-mediaeval Irish society, the oldest texts of which date from the eighth century, state that a newly inaugurated chief or king should prove his worth, nobility, and status by undertaking a cattle-raid, known as a *crech rig*, as one of his very first acts of kingship. The cattle he successfully raided would then be distributed amongst his chief supporters as a way to build up enthusiasm, so to speak, for his new reign. This was the local expression of the fact that what bound early-mediaeval society together were relationships, as those between kings, and between lords and their people—personal bonds that had to be renegotiated each time someone new came to power.

The form of election employed by the people of Dál Riata in the early-mediaeval period was acclamation. Upon the death of a king, the *rigdomna* would assemble—that is, those men within a set degree of kinship from the previous king who were thus also eligible for kingship, literally the "king-worthy", and from their ranks a new ruler would be acclaimed. (In *Prophet*, I recreate what this ceremony might have looked like.) Once acclaimed, the new ruler would be "sanctified" by means of a series of rituals that had their origin in pre-Christian kingship and were meant to symbolize and make manifest the sacred marriage of a ruler with his land. At Dunadd, this ceremony was performed by means of a number of special features cut into the bedrock of the distinct plateau that sits just below the summit of the hillfort—a footprint, a bowl, a stone slab with carvings of a boar and an inscription in *ogham*—which are amazingly still extant. There, high-up where he could be seen by all the people, the acclaimed man would be blessed by the priests or priestesses (in Áedán mac nGabráin's case his friend Columba) while drinking the blood of an animal sacrificed for the occasion (possibly a white mare or a bull) which had been collected in the rock-cut basin. He would then place his foot into the footprint (which in Dunadd's case points towards the mountain holy to the Dál Riata, Ben Cruachan) while swearing an oath to protect everything over which he has just come to rule. These acts "wed" the king to his people and to his land, thought of and venerated as sacred and feminine.

The inauguration footprint that still exists on the plateau of Dunadd is one of a handful of such ancient, sacred sites in Argyll that correspond to those citadels we believe to have been the seats of regional kings. Two of these footprints can be found carved into a rocky outcrop overlooking the mediaeval chapel at Southend, Kintyre. While one of the footprints there is Victorian in date, the other, known as Columba's footprint, is early mediaeval, and is believed to have been used in the inauguration ceremonies of the kings of the Cenél nGabráin who held Kintyre during this period (Cendtire in the book). Upon his acclamation, Áedán mac nGabráin would have sworn his oath to his own people, the Cenél nGabráin, there. And indeed, standing in that glorious spot on a clear day, Áedán would have been able to see the Glens of Antrim across the North Channel in Ulster, the ancestral homeland of his people, the Dál Riata of Ireland (Ulaid, Hibernia in the book).

There is a similar tradition of a footprint stone at Finlaggan, on the island of Islay, where the mediaeval Lords of the Isles were later inaugurated (Ile in the book). It is there that I have had Aedan assert his rule over the Cenél Oengussa as their new overking. (Both of these secondary king-makings occur "off-camera".)

Once home again after his *crech ríg* with the cattle he had "collected", the new-king, Áedán mac nGabráin, would have held an assembly. The three extant groups of standing stones that flank the river Add below Dunadd at Dunamuck are all that remain of a series of prehistoric monuments that may also have included two stone circles and a ceremonial avenue which signposted a sacred assembly site. Dunamuck continued to be a local meeting place, including for the great Kilmichael Tryst, an important regional fair and cattle market, well into our times.

Chapter 2: Artmuircol
This chapter takes place at various locations around Ardnamurchan, that strikingly beautiful but barren peninsula that sticks out into the Sea of the Hebrides north of the Isle of Mull, considered remote to us today but at that time part of the sea-lanes that connected the islands and coastal lands of the sea-kingdom of Dál Riata. Adomnán calls the region *Artmuircol* (Life I.12, II.10 II.22) and it is the setting for a wonderful cluster of miracle stories which tell us through incidental detail much about Columba's adventures off

Iona as well as the early workings of his monastery. Indeed, the Life of Columba is the first written documentation we have about the west of Scotland.

Adomnán tells us that the Iona monks would periodically set sail in search of resources they could not find on the island, most importantly timber, Iona being almost denuded even then. Specifically he says that Columba needed oak and pine logs to repair Iona's church and magna domus, its "great house" or main building. The monks also needed their own long ship, Iona experiencing an extraordinary period of expansion under Columba and Áedán mac nGabráin's stewardship. One place from which they harvested timber was an ancient oak wood at the mouth of a river called the Sale (Life II.45), probably the river Shiel which drains Loch Shiel. While most of the temperate rain forests which used to fringe the Atlantic coast of Scotland—the mystical Forests of Caledon; the awed Roman's Caledonia, the wondrous "Wooded Heights"—have long since disappeared, Columba's oak wood is still there. (Two others are too: one runs along Loch Sunart in Ardnamurchan where Columba, Eogan and Diarmait head next; the other Loch Sween in Argyll.)

On the River Sale, Columba and his companions stopped to fish for salmon, it being *fluvius piscosus* ("fishful") and they being keen fishermen, catching there a fish *mirae magnitudinis*, "of miraculous size" (Life II.19). (Much later, Alexander MacDonald, as quoted by W. J. Watson in The History of the Celtic Place Names of Scotland (Edinburgh, 1926), p. 76, would report that "Good for net and rod, for reel and for fish, is green-hued Shiel of the big trout".) The island of *Airthrago* along whose foreshore the monks shelter during the sudden contrary wind and the location of yet another of Columba's miracles (Life II.45) is identified by Watson in Celtic Place Names, pp. 75-7, as Eilean Shona.

While in Ardnamurchan, Columba also spends time with a poor man called Colmán (Life II.21, II.22) whom he loves so well that he agrees to increase the size of the man's meager cattle herd from five to 105 through prayer (Life II.21). (Since the roots *Col-*, and *Colm-* are ridiculously common in Old Irish personal names, I have changed Colmán to "Dovey" to avoid confusion with other similarly-named characters in the series.) Colmán was the victim of repeated raids by two brothers, Ioan mac Conaill maic Domnaill and Lám Dess (Ian and Lam Dess in the book), said to belong to "the royal lineage of Cenél nGabráin"—Áedán mac nGabráin's family (Life II.22 and II.24). The patronymic mac Conaill suggests that they may have been the sons of Áedán mac nGabráin's cousin Conall, and indeed I have made them so.

In the Life, three different locations in Ardnamurchan are mentioned: Ioan sails away with Colmán's cattle from a place called *Sharp Bay*, with Columba cursing him from the waters of the foreshore (Life II.22), perhaps modern Sanna Bay; Irish sailors arrive with news of the deaths of some noteworthy Irish kings at a place called *Paradise Bay* (Life I.12), which Sharpe and others have equated with Kentra Bay (Life, n. 93, p. 275); and finally there is a place where Columba strikes a hard rock with his staff, drawing forth a copious clear spring for the baptism of the child Ligu Cenncalad (Life II.10), perhaps at modern Ardslignish above the beautiful bay of Camas nan Geall where a holy well dedicated to Columba still survives. It is at this last location that I have conflated these three events and set the majority of this chapter. For the monks who wash up on shore after the storm, see the notes to Chapter 7, below.

Chapter 3: Gartnait son of Domelch
Beltane, one of the four major cross-quarter festivals celebrated in pre-Christian Ireland and Scotland, was held over three days and nights starting on the evening of April 31st. (The other festivals were Lughnasadh, starting on July 31, Samhain on October 31, and Imbolc on January 31.) Beltane marked the ending of the "dark half of the year", the start of spring. It was the earliest that crops could be sown or herds taken to their high summer pastures, and was held in honor of the god devoted to those concerns, Belenos. People would congregate *en masse* to trade, marry, renew old alliances and make new ones, and celebrate having survived yet another winter.

Caitlín Matthews, The Celtic Tradition (Dorset, 1989), p. 90, lists the prohibitions that I have Aedan name on Beltane, against murder and theft and the like, the goal being to keep the peace when such a large number of people had gathered together under the auspices of alcohol. The lovely sentiment "for between the body's response and the knowing soul there could never be falsity" is from John O'Donohue, Anam Cara (London, 1997).

Chapter 4: Afrella
"Woe is to the one who must wait for love to come out of longing" is from "The Wife's Lament", The Exeter Book, fols 115$^a$-115$^b$, a corpus of poems in Old English dating from the tenth century and now Codex Exoniensis, Exeter Cathedral Library, MS 3501. Aedan, gazing upon the night sky above Dunadd, is contemplating the constellations of the Herdsman (or Boötes), the Northern Crown (Corona Borealis), and the Maiden (Virgo). Aedan's pledge that "It is time to come into my strength, to make manifest my desires. It is time to take the path of strength" is inspired by John Matthews, The Celtic Shaman, (Shaftesbury, U.K., 1991), pp. 39-40, 92. A man by the name of Taran "who belonged to a noble family in Pictland but who was living in exile" appears in Life II.23. I have made him the son of the under-king of the Orkneys, mentioned in Life II.42.

Chapter 5: Beltane
The various rites to celebrate Beltane—the lighting of the new fire, the cleansing of the hides of the kine between bonfires, using rowan twigs to counter mischief by the fairy folk, festooning dwellings and particularly entranceways with hawthorn, which blooms in May, to protect against evil, the sun-wise rituals, the rolling of bannocks to foretell fortunes, washing in the dew of Beltane morn—survived in Gaelic-speaking areas of Scotland into the nineteenth century. See I. F. Grant, Highland Folk Ways, (Edinburgh, 1995) p. 357.

According to the Vindolanda tablets, Coria is the local name for the old Roman fort of Coriosopitum on Hadrian's Wall, modern-day Corbridge. Caer Ligualid was the British name for modern Carlisle.

305

Based on exciting new archaeology from Trusty's Hill, (Gatehouse of Fleet, Dumfries and Galloway, Scotland), that hillfort is very likely to be the long-lost capitol of the early-mediaeval British kingdom of Rheged. (See the Galloway Picts Project, gallowaypicts.com.)

The celebrated sixth-century British poet Taliesin left a number of works in praise of his primary patrons Urien and his son Owain, overlords of Rheged. These poems, some of the earliest we have in Welsh, survive in a Middle Welsh manuscript conventionally called The Book of Taliesin (Peniarth MS 2, National Library of Wales, Aberystwyth) which dates from the first half of fourteenth century, but is based on an early-mediaeval core believed to have been composed in as early as the sixth century—one of our absolute treasures of early-mediaeval Britain. Amongst other things, Taliesin praises Urien and Owain's exploits against the Saxons who were violently settling Britain at this time, giving us an unparalleled, evocative view of life in the British Kingdoms of the Old North. In his poem "The Battle of Argoed Llwyfain", Taliesin calls Owain *"Dwyrein ffossawt"*, or "Scourge of the Eastlands", for raids the young warlord had led against the encroaching Saxons in what was in due course to become the kingdom of Northumbria.

Chapter 6: Lam Dess son of Conall

The maxims "A king must be without miserliness" and "And all men must be without jealousy" are inspired by Alan and Brinley Rees' observations on the nature of kingship in early-mediaeval Ireland, specifically the three prescriptive qualities essential to a king if his reign is to be prosperous for his people: that "he must be without jealousy, without fear, and without sluggardliness". (See Celtic Heritage (London, 1961), p. 130 where they quote the legendary Medb, Queen of Connaught, who in the Early Irish prose saga Táin Bó Cúalnge says that her ideal partner and consort must be this kind of man.) In Life II.22, Columba is said to have cursed Ioan mac Conaill mac Domnaill, "a man of evil who persecuted good men", for running off with his friend Colmán's cattle (Ian and Dovey in the book). Succumbing to Columba's "terrible words"—proof in the early-mediaeval belief in the power inherent in the spoken word, be it prayer or curse—Ioan's boat was overwhelmed by a sudden "violent squall", drowning all therein.

Chapter 7: The Battle of the Seven Kings
In the sixth century, the historical province of Ulster in present-day Northern Ireland (Ulaid in the book) was roughly divided between three main ruling groups. The Dál Riata lay east of the river Bann, in the Main and Lower Bann Valleys, and on the Antrim plateau. The Dál nAriade lay south of this in the interior lowlands between Belfast Lough and the Mournes, to Strangford Lough. The Dál Fiatach controlled the Mournes to the Upper Bann as well as the coast of County Down. (See the maps at the start of this book.) In general, overlordship of the province of Ulster fluctuated during the early part of this period between the Dál nAriade and the Dál Fiatach, with the Dál Riata out of the running altogether. All this was soon, however, to change …

Áed Dub mac Suibne was a sixth-century king of the Dál nAraide. To prevent confusion with the other characters in this series called Áed-something-or-other (as popular an element in Old Irish as Col-), I have used the anglicization of his name, Black Hugh. His fascinating life-story, thoroughly bound up in the glorious and messy geopolitics of sixth-century Ireland, and can only be condensed here. In short, there was a battle in 563 called Móin Daire Lothair, my so-called "Battle of The Seven Kings" (the Annals of Ulster say that seven kings fell there), which was a victory of the alliance of Columba's old kingroup, the Northern Uí Néill, over the Cruithin (otherwise known as the Dál nAraide) that resulted in a comprehensive and bloody turnover of power in Ulster (Annals of Ulster 563; Life I.7). Occurring after the battle of Cúl Dreimne of 561 (Life I.7), the two battles seem to be linked to Columba's subsequent exile to Scotland in 563 and to his cousin Ainmire mac Sétnai's emergence not long after as the ultimate overlord of the province of Ulster and "high-king" of Tara. For the sake of continuity and, more importantly, the characters' motivation, I have flipped these two battles in time and separated them by a matter of months.

According to the Annals of Ulster and the Annals of Tigernach, in 565 Áed Dub (Black Hugh) killed Diarmait mac Cerbaill, king of the Southern Úi Néill and "high-king" of Tara, who was his foster-father. When describing how the priest Findchán arrived in Britain with Áed Dub seeking sanctuary for Áed Dub's crimes, Adomnán calls the latter a "very bloody man and a slayer of many" (Life I.36 and n. 158). For Áed Dub's murder and blasphemous dismemberment of his foster-father Diarmait mac Cerbaill, his exile to Britain, the reversals in his kingship of the Dál nAraide, his taking of the clerical habit, and his rancorous dealings with Columba, see Life, n. 158, and the primary sources cited there.

Fiachnae Lurgan (Fiachna in the book), who died in 626, was another extremely colorful character livening up the social scene at the time. Descended from a rival branch of the Dál nAraide, Fiachnae was Áed Dub's cousin. He had a sister called Cuimne Finne (Covna in the book). For a more comprehensive breakdown of the bewildering dynastic feuds that characterized Ulster in this period, which I have had perforce to simplify, see Life, n. 158, and Gearóid mac Niocaill, Ireland before the Vikings, pp. 74-75, 87-89. See also the cast of characters I provide at the start of this book.

Chapter 8: Sea Roads

We know from the archaeological record and from documentary sources that the island of Tiree, northwest of Iona, began to be settled with monasteries during this period, and not just as dependents of the ever-growing Iona. Adomnán tells us in Life I.36 that Áed Dub (Black Hugh) retired to a monastery called *Artchain* founded by his friend Findchán on Tiree (Tir Iath in the book). Not to be outdone by his old adversary, Columba set up his own monastery on the island, dependent on Iona and to house her penitents, at a place called *Mag Luinge* (which has not yet been securely located). Baithéne went on to head this up as prior (Life I.19, I.30, II.15, II.39, III.8, and notes 107 and 182.)

Aedan's words of love to Ama, "To separate us two is to/ separate the children of one home/it is to separate body from soul … " is from Gráinne's Sleep-Song for Diarmait which dates from 1100 x 1150, ed. and trans. by Gerard Murphy Early Irish Lyrics (Oxford, 1956; reprinted 1962).

Chapter 9: Banchorr

The story now moves to Northern Ireland (whose people, landscape, and culture it has been my great pleasure to rediscover while doing research for this book.) Ireland at this time was home to a number of extraordinary monastic schools founded by that generation of monk-teachers who taught Columba. These monasteries, the "ivy league schools" of their day, worked together to make Ireland a powerhouse of learning and culture in the dark days of the sixth century and later. Banchorr is of course the monastery of Bangor, on the south shore of Belfast Lough (County Down, Northern Ireland). It was founded by Comgall (who lived about 517-601/02), a childhood friend of Columba's who, along with a handful of their other soon-to-be famous schoolmates, is an abiding presence in the Life (I.49, III.13, III.17). The patron saint of the Dál nAraide, Comgall studied with Columba, rising up with him through the ranks under the tutelage of mentors like Finnian of Clonard and Mobi of Glasnevin, who were themselves veritable titans. At Bangor (founded 555-59), Comgall trained up his own missionaries, men who became cultural innovators in their own right, including Cellach, later known as St Gall (c. 550-645, the "Apostle of the Suevi and the Alemanni") and the towering Columbanus (c. 543-615) who founded Annegray, Luxeuil, Fontaines, and Bobbio, amongst others—that generation of monk-scholars which via the vehicle of Christianity was almost wholly responsible for bringing learning back to a shattered Mediaeval West. For his part, Comgall was well known for both intellectual rigor and a particularly austere form of asceticism. The seventh-century Antiphony of Bangor refers to a "Rule" in which Comgall is called "strict, holy and constant". His student Columbanus then wrote his own, equally-severe "Regula coenobialis" and "Regula monachorum" based on this <u>Penitential</u> of his master's, now lost.

From Bangor, the party travels overland a short distance to present-day Moville at the head of Strangford Lough, staying clear of Scrabo Head where I surmise a Dál Fiatach watchtower would have stood since there they come to that kingdom's northern border.

At this point we arrive at an infamous incident from Columba's early life—his illicit copying of a book of Psalms not owned by him. (Adomnán does not mention this episode in his <u>Life</u>, perhaps out of embarrassment for his idol, but the Early Modern Irish <u>Life of Columba</u> of 1532 by Manus O'Donnell does.)

Finnian (living c. 495-c.589), another of that seminal generation of monastic founders in Ireland, had set up his great school at Moville (Movilla in the book) in about 543. He is said to have returned from Rome bearing a copy of St. Jerome's <u>Vulgate</u>, a copy of the Psalms hitherto unknown in Ireland. Columba, a student of his at the time, scandalously copied it without his permission. This Psalter is possibly the Cathach (Royal Irish Academy, Dublin, MS 12 R 33), our oldest surviving manuscript of Irish origin, dating from the sixth century and possibly written by Columba himself. Columba was unrepentant and Finnian, furious, took him to court. The case was heard before the "high-king", Dairmait mac Cerbaill (the king who was later to throw Columba out of Ireland). Dairmait issued a very famous ruling, effectively against Columba but with much wider ramifications, to whit: "*Le gach bó a lao agus le gach leabhar a leabhrán*"; "To every cow its calf and to every book its copy". This is the first case of copyright infringement and enforcement we know of in the West, and Columba is known for this exploit to this day.

<u>Chapter 10</u>: Dun Druma
After leaving Moville, Aedan, Columba and Eogan reunite with their ship to sail south to the hillfort (and later Norman Castle) of Dundrum, County Down (Dun Druma in the book, the "Fort of the Ridge"). Dundrum presides over two remarkable bays, one within the other, and is overlooked by the forbidding granite mountains

of the Mournes to the south. The hillfort would have been in the hands of the Uí Echan Coba at the time, a minor kingroup later absorbed by the Dál Fiatach. There is a souterrain (a stone-lined pit) in the field north of the present-day castle and it is here that I have imprisoned the boy Fiachna Lurgan.

If you are at Dundrum at just the right time, you can witness a remarkable natural phenomenon known as the *Tonn Rudraige*, or Rudriaghe's Wave, one of the "three magic waves of Ireland". (Ireland's two other magic waves are the *Tonn Tuaige* (Túag's Wave) which occurs at the head of the Bann estuary, County Derry, and the *Tonn Chlíodhna* (Cliodhna's Wave) at the neck of Glandore harbor, County Cork.) At certain times, especially in storms, powerful tidal surges come roaring over the sand banks and rock fissures just offshore there, emitting a tremendously loud roar almost like a scream. Since this rare phenomenon was meant to portend events of great significance, like the death of a "high-king" or some other terrible calamity, the hapless guard would naturally have credited Manannán mac Lir, his Lord of the Sea, with having saved the boy. Manannán is said to have been born on the Tonns, the prominent sand bank north of Malligan Point at the entrance to Lough Foyle. He coursed the sea in his chariot, pulled by his steed Enbarr of the Flowing Mane.

Chapter 11: Patrick's Road
In this chapter, Columba and Eogan work their way overland towards Lough Neagh, the largest lake by area in the British Isles, until they come to Coney Island off the south shore of the lough, opposite present-day Maghery County Park. Coney Island is connected to the mainland by a causeway or submerged ridge, easily seen in summer, which is known locally as St. Patrick's Road since the saint is said to have used the island as a place of retreat.

Manus O'Donnell's Life of Columba of 1532 says that Columba "understood the language of the birds of the sky", a divine attribute common to the holy. While not commonplace, waterspouts do form on Lough Neagh. Lasting five to ten minutes and of amazing ferocity, they are spawned when super cell thunderstorms touch down on the surface of the lough. The Dollaghan Brown is a large speckled trout unique to Lough Neagh; the lough also abounds in eels that go down the Bann in huge numbers to spawn in the Saragossa Sea before returning again in the spring. In Modern Irish, the Bann is called *An Bhanna* which is said to derive from *Banda*, a compound of *ban* and *dea* meaning "goddess".

Chapter 12: Island of the Blackwater
In Irish, Coney Island is called *Inis Dabhaill*, the "Island of the Blackwater", referring to its location opposite where the Blackwater River enters Lough Neagh. The interior of Coney Island has a rich archaeological history including a well in which gold treasure was found in 1567 as well as a 400-year-old yew tree which serves here as a cloutie tree (a tree upon which revenants thread strips of cloth as a kind of prayer for divine intervention, a practice still very much alive in the British Isles). The stone that Columba pulls up from the bottom of the well is a Lough Neagh pebble. Yellow and veined with red, it is a kind of chalcedony.

Chapter 13: Ros-na-Righ
The Book of Lecan (Royal Irish Academy, MS 23 P 2, dating from 1397 x 1418, and edited and translated by W. F. Skene, Chronicle of the Picts and the Scots (Edinburgh, 1867) pp. 127-29) says that "Áedán mac nGabráin, Gabran's son, yielded to him [Baetan mac Cairell] at Ros-na-Righ in Semniu". Ros-na-Righ (Rosnaree), "The Peninsula of the King", is probably Island Magee, County Antrim, with the meeting itself likely to have taken place at Brown's Bay on the far north of the peninsula. On the shore of Brown's Bay, near the high-water mark, there is a 10-12 ton erratic boulder known as The Rocking Stone. Formerly freestanding, it would rock slightly when pushed against. Now cemented to a plinth and marred by an exuberant but admittedly ugly veneer of spray paint, it nevertheless continues to exude an otherworldly, almost primeval presence on the shoreline. Aedan sends his ship around to anchor off Skernaghan

Point.

Kings in early mediaeval Ireland were subject to ritual taboos known as gessa (singular geis). These were codes of behavior inherited from a distant past designed to curtail bloodshed and violence, thus helping to ensure the peaceful functioning of society. The king of Ulidia (Ulster), for instance, had to begin any expedition from Emain Macha (Navan Fort), spend three nights there with his weapons before crossing his southern frontier, and take hostages from as far north as Dun Sobairche (Dunseverick, County Antrim). "He is not a king who does not have hostages in fetters" and "you have no house under whose roof I might make my submission" are maxims in the same vein. For the prophecy that Baetan quotes about himself, see stanzas 23-36 of Berchan's Prophecy, a Middle Irish historical poem written about 1165 × 1169 in the form of a prophecy and ascribed to an abbot Berchan (now Royal Irish Academy, MS 23 G4).

Chapter 16: Stone
These next chapters take us through the breathtaking countryside of the Nine Glens of Antrim (County Antrim, Northern Ireland), a contracted version of which formed the old core of the divided early-mediaeval kingdom of Dál Riata. Before the construction of the modern coastal road the A2, the glens were only accessible by boat.

The clearing where Aedan awakens is just below present-day Glenarm Castle (Glenarm, County Antrim), a stronghold of the Latharna people, a minor *tuath* of the Dál nAraide who were soon to be absorbed into an expanded Dál Riata. The Gobbins are a series of towering cliffs on the sea-side of Island Magee.

Chapter 17: The Beachmarket
From present-day Glenarm Castle, the captives are taken down to Glenarm harbor and then over Straidkilly Point, heading north to Glencloy via the old drove road. They ford the shallow river at Glencloy Bridge to set up the slave market on the shore of Carnlough

Bay. Once done, they head up Glencloy to overnight in the safety of Doonan Rath, close to Doonan Waterfall.

Chapter 18: The Nine Glens
Aedan's party is led north along the coastal path, raiding first the hillfort that rises straight from the shore at Loughan Mound, and then the prehistoric fort of Dunmaul. Leaving behind Glenarm and Glencloy, Aedan comes overland to Garron Point, beyond which he admires the "White Lady", or Cloghastucan, a natural limestone sea-stack 5.85 meters (19 feet) high, which looks remarkably like a primordial giantess gazing out across the water. Coming up and over the headland to Red Bay, Aedan at last enters the historic heartland of Dál Riata (comprising the glens of Glenariff, Glenballyeamon, Glenaan, Glencorp, and Glendun and, further north, Glenshesk and Glentaisie).

Chapter 19: The Tonns
Columba, meanwhile, has drifted out of the River Bann (presumably via Coleraine, County Derry) to Loch Foyle which was then considered to be a magical route into the underworld kingdom of Manannán mac Lir, since The Tonns, the prominent sand banks at the mouth of the Foyle estuary, were where that god was born. The votive offering which Columba pulls up from the water is the Broighter Hoard boat, a miniature gold boat made from shimmering sheets of gold, 18 cm (7 inches) long, complete with tiny but perfectly fashioned fittings and oars. The boat was found along with a gold torque (a neck ring), a bowl, and two chains on farmland near the town of Limavady in 1896, land that was part of the foreshore of Lough Foyle at the time the objects were fashioned. These very beautiful treasures date from the first-century B.C.E. and are considered to be the finest examples of Iron Age gold working ever found in Ireland. (The precious originals are in the National Museum of Ireland, Dublin; replicas can be seen in the Ulster Museum, Belfast.)

There Columba is picked up by a roving band of bards whom it may be helpful to think of as the "free press" of their day. In early-

Irish society, poets were part of a special learned caste called the *Aes Dana*, "The People of the Craft", a caste which also included jurists, physicians, wrights, smiths, skilled craftsman, and later monks and clerics. They were the skilled members of their society, and as such had privileges separate from the kings, lords, commoners, and slaves. Members could rise from any social class. The secret language the bards use to converse silently with one another is *ogham*, normally written, but also capable of being tapped out with the fingers and hands.

## Chapter 20: Dun Sobairche

After crossing the Antrim Plateau via the old hill-route, Aedan picks up the most important of Ireland's five ancient roads, the *Slige Midluachra*, which ran from Tara to the north coast. This was the "High-King's Road", and it ended at Dunseverick Castle, County Antrim (Dun Sobairche in the book). Dunseverick, a most imposing rock-stack hillfort almost entirely surrounded by the sea, was the capitol of Irish Dál Riata. In the hollow leading up to the hillfort is a small mound, topped by what is perhaps an inauguration stone. Inside the wonderful grounds, up on the height, are further cult objects including a holy well, hinting at the prehistoric ritual function of this amazing ancient site.

## Chapter 22: The Convention of Druim Ceatt

It is for the remarkable, very famous Convention of Druim Ceatt that Columba's return to Ireland is primarily known. Up to this point, the status of the two halves of the divided kingdom of Dál Riata, the Irish and Scottish, had been constantly and contentiously in question. Was it one kingdom, or two? To whom did the taxes, the fleet, the tribute, and the men of each half belong? To the overlord of Ulster? To Ulster's overlord, the Northern Uí Néill? Or, as had not yet happened by 575, to the king of that half of Dál Riata in Scotland? At a time when a ruler's relative power was determined by the number of kin groups over which he ruled, these were questions of the utmost importance. Indeed, the question of to whom it

315

"belongs" continues to vex Northern Ireland to this day.

The Convention of Druim Ceatt was convened in 575 (Annals of Ulster) to discuss the future status of the Dál Riata in Ireland in relation to Áed mac Ainmerech, ruler of the Northern Uí Néill and the most powerful man in the north of Ireland at that time, as well as to Áedán mac nGabráin, newly king of the Dál Riata in Scotland. Strikingly, Baetan mac Cairell, the *defacto* overlord of the province of Ulster at the time, seems to have been excluded from the party. Adomnán mentions the meeting three times, calling it a *condictum regum*, a "conference of kings" (Life I.49, I.50, and II.6; also I.10 and I.11). We think it was held on Mullagh or Daisy Hill, near Limavady, County Derry, which was at that time a harbor with two hillforts flanking, on borderland. Easily reached by river, Mullagh had commanding views over the countryside, and both Grianan of Ailech, Áed mac Ainmerech's main stronghold, and Dál Riata lay close by. As such, it would have been an ideal location for a meeting of these rival kings.

The Convention of Druim Ceatt is known for a number of major triumphs achieved there by Columba (Life, n. 88). The first concerns the freeing of a royal hostage called Scandlán mac Colmáin who was later to become king of Osraige in mid-Ireland, who was held in chains by Áed mac Ainmirech. Adomnán says that Columba comforted the young Scandlán, telling him that he would in time be free of his captivity and would go on to lead his people (Life I.11). (Later Middle Irish accounts credit Columba with freeing the boy there and then, outright.) In order to honor this act of kindness and to keep the story's narrative strands moving towards a close, I have substituted the character of Fiachna Lurgan for the royal hostage Scandlán.

Secondly, Columba is said to have performed many miracles, curing "the ailments of various invalids during the brief period when he was at Druim Ceatt to attend the meeting of the kings" (Life II.6). Some were healed by his outstretched hand, others by being sprinkled with water he had blessed, and still others by having touched the edge of his cloak. This illustrates beautifully, I think, that it is his care for the people, his decency and humanity, that Columba is best known and loved to this day.

At Druim Ceatt, Columba is also said to have protected the poets. Before the arrival of Christianity, bards had been amongst the only educated people in Ireland and were therefore revered, but by Columba's time their inflated privileges were causing them to fall foul of the people who had previously been required to feed and house them. Their retinues had grown so large in number that they effectively bankrupted anyone who was obliged to host them. Worse, when thwarted the poets would maledict, or ritually curse, their victim so badly that he or she lost their honor or, as it was known, their "face" (think social media trolling today, but perhaps somewhat worse, especially if the person trolled were a king). By 575, the poets were on the verge of losing their special status as members of the *Aes Dana*, indeed were close to being expelled from Ireland altogether. The second preface to the Amra Choluim Chille, a late-sixth or early-seventh century elegy composed by the poet Dállan Forgall on the occasion of Columba's death, our oldest surviving vernacular Irish poem, asserts that at Druim Ceatt Columba used his considerable influence "to keep the poets in Ireland". (This will be further explored in Book IV of the series, Island-Soldier.)

The convention was most noteworthy, however, for a peace treaty enacted there between those in power in the North of Ireland and in Scotland, a treaty credited wholeheartedly to Columba's personal mediation. He was perhaps the only person at that time that could converse as an equal with both the overlord of the Uí Néill, his cousin Áed mac Ainmerech, a man who also happened to be the "high-king" of Tara, and the overlord of Dál Riata, his friend and ally Áedán mac nGabráin. The convention ruled that henceforth the right to the armed forces of the Dál Riata in Ireland would go to Áed mac Ainmerech as overlord of the Northern Uí Néill. For his part, Áedán mac nGabráin would now receive the fleet, the taxes, and the tribute of the Irish Dál Riata, and thus their effective governance, in addition to those resources already coming out of what was effectively his own half of Dál Riata in Scotland.

This was a major turning point in the power politics of not just the province of Ulster but the Irish Sea region as a whole, and its importance cannot be overstated. This is our first confirmation that the Scottish Dál Riata and the Irish Dál Riata were linked, with Áedán mac nGabráin ruler of the greater kingdom. Thereafter, this combined Dál Riata was on the rise. The Dál Fiatach under Baetan mac Cairrell were sidelined, with the Uí Néill and the Dál Riata forming a powerful alliance, an extremely impressive achievement given the fragmented and combative nature of kingship and polities in the region at the time. Even more extraordinarily, the peace ushered in by Columba lasted; the descendants of these men, those who came to rule in their place, continued to uphold the agreement forged at Druim Ceatt well into the next century.

Chapter 23: Law of the Innocents
Finally we come to what is known as "The Law of Innocents", the Cáin Adomnáin, one of the first systemic attempts in the West to protect non-combatants in war (that is, women, children, clerics, clerical students, and peasants on clerical land). It was promulgated by Adomnán, Columba's kinsman and ninth abbot of Iona, at the Synod of Birr in 697 before a large, international gathering of chieftans and clerics from Ireland, Dál Riata, and Pictland. An audacious propostion to begin with, "The Law of Innocents" succeeded in large part because it had the force of Columba, Scotland's greatest and most beloved saint and statesman, behind it.

Made in the USA
Las Vegas, NV
05 August 2022

52698122R00208